They all had something to hide . . .

Dr. Becca Landau: Her career at Boston Memorial Hospital was cut short by scandal. Now, at Manhattan General, she has been accused of a terrible crime.

Dr. David Hardinger: He would do anything to keep the lovely Becca in his bed . . . except stand up to his imperious father.

Arnold Hardinger: The powerhouse head of Manhattan General, he has more than one reason to want Becca destroyed . . .

Sam Stedman: Becca's defense attorney — and her only hope — provided that Becca will trust him with her past . . . and her future.

Agatha Bates: She alone knows what really happened . . . and she's counting on her lover, Dr. Garfield Gottlieb, to help her.

Dr. Garfield Gottlieb: When Agatha comes to him, he faces the most agonizing decision a doctor ever has to make.

*MAYBE YOU SHOULD CHECK
UNDER YOUR BED... JUST ONE MORE TIME!
THE HORROR NOVELS OF*

STEPHEN R. GEORGE

WILL SCARE YOU SENSELESS!

BEASTS	(2682-X, $3.95/$4.95)
BRAIN CHILD	(2578-5, $3.95/$4.95)
DARK MIRACLE	(2788-5, $3.95/$4.95)
THE FORGOTTEN	(3415-6, $4.50/$5.50)
GRANDMA'S LITTLE DARLING	(3210-2, $3.95/$4.95)

Available wherever paperbacks are sold, or order direct from the Publisher. Send cover price plus 50¢ per copy for mailing and handling to: Zebra Books, Dept.3857, 475 Park Avenue South, New York, NY 10016. Residents of New York and Tennessee must include sales tax. DO NOT SEND CASH. For a free Zebra/Pinnacle Catalog with more than 1,500 books listed, please write to the above address.

A DOCTOR'S SECRET

Betty Ferm

ZEBRA BOOKS
KENSINGTON PUBLISHING CORP.

ZEBRA BOOKS

are published by

Kensington Publishing Corp.
475 Park Avenue South
New York, NY 10016

Copyright © 1992 by Betty Ferm

All rights reserved. No part of this book may be reproduced in any form or by any means without the prior written consent of the Publisher, excepting brief quotes used in reviews.

If you purchased this book without a cover you should be aware that this book is stolen property. It was reported as "unsold and destroyed" to the Publisher and neither the Author nor the Publisher has received any payment for this "stripped book."

First printing: August, 1992

Printed in the United States of America

ACKNOWLEDGMENTS

My thanks to all the medical personnel who gave so unstintingly of their expertise, but especially to:

Beth P. Abrams, M.D., Child, Adolescent, and Adult Psychiatrist

Scott Weiss, M.D.

Priscilla Scherer, R.N.

Ursula DeSimone, R.N.

Lauraine Somekh, R.N.

Part One

A Doctor's Secret

Prologue

The morning of the inquiry at Manhattan General that was to decide the fate of Dr. Becca Landau dawned hot and misty for June.

By eleven o'clock, the haze had been replaced by a blistering sun that hung overhead like a fuzzy red ball. It scalded the moss-lined bricks of the paths that led from the street to the hospital and punished the guards who tried to control the waiting crowds. They were there to catch a glimpse of the young resident accused of attempting to murder the daughter of South American billionaire, Jose Vargas.

Anticipating trouble, every side door of the hospital had been locked and the emergency entrance was being carefully monitored. The publicity seekers and the offbeat petitioners had gathered early. The reporters, the photographers, and the white TV vans with their roof-mounted cameras had come later.

A chauffeured black Cadillac pulled up to the curb below. At sight of the accused and her attorney, Sam Stedman, the crowd surged forward with a roar, threatening the flowering azaleas and rhododendrons anchored precariously in their huge clay pots along the way.

Dressed in an austere navy suit that made her look older than her twenty-nine years, Dr. Becca Landau carried herself with an air of authority. Outwardly she appeared sedate — a slender, patrician-looking woman with a generous mouth and high-cheekboned face capped by a volume of shoulder-length black hair. But there was nothing sedate about her eyes. The reporters who came upon her first could see in them both intelligence and integrity and something else that outraged those convinced of her guilt. A fearlessness, a defiance that refuted the ongoing proceedings and proclaimed to the world that she felt no guilt for her actions.

Prodded forward by her attorney, Becca Landau willed herself not to react to the sea of faces converging on her. Not by even a flicker of the eye would she give them the satisfaction of knowing that inwardly she was cringing. It wasn't because she found the crowd overwhelming. She had marched in crowds herself. At Amherst for student rights and at Tufts Medical School to protest the endless hours demanded of first-year interns. But the crowd she had marched in had always stood for something. Or against something. This crowd stood neither for nor against. They were a mob who relished spectacle. And they were as bloodthirsty as the Romans in Caesar's arenas who turned thumbs down when a life hung in the balance.

"Sonsofbitches," Sam Stedman muttered as he gripped her elbow. "I didn't know it would be this bad." He positioned himself in front of her. Lanky and cantankerous, his unruly hair was slicked, his gray "undertaker's suit" a concession to the court appearance that was expected of him. He held his attaché case before him like a shield and braced his lean legs in a footballer's stance. "Stay close behind me," he yelled, "and don't answer any questions." The rest of what he said was drowned by the explosion of noise that burst around them.

She blinked as a flashbulb went off in her face. The purple aftereffect distorted her vision and magnified the long-nosed camera that zoomed toward her face. A reporter from the *Times* queried her in a clipped probing voice.

"Is it true you were responsible for the death of another child when you were at Boston Memorial?"

Sam Stedman glared at him. "No comment."

"Do you think the hospital's financial crisis will affect the verdict of this inquiry?" a reporter from the *News* shouted at him.

"No comment!"

"Did you have anything to do with the death of Judge Ryker's boy?"

She stumbled forward, hugging Sam's pinstriped back. The wall of people closed in around her, cutting off what little air there was in the stifling heat. She couldn't breathe. She couldn't see. Her only guidepost was the lean gray back that inched slowly up the hospital steps. She shut her ears to the shouts and epithets flung her way, but a few of them filtered through.

"Murderess! Quack!"

She kept her head high, but she could feel the hysteria welling up in her. She wanted to laugh. She wanted to cry. A woman jabbed her in the ribs then pressed up against her. A fleeting impression came to her. Of pungent-smelling makeup. Coarse hair. A tendency toward jaundice.

The woman's smile was pleasant. "If the little girl dies, they'll send you up for thirty years."

Becca felt her legs buckle. She pictured Angelica Vargas lying in coma in the Pediatric ICU, her elfin face still, the eyes that mirrored her terror hidden by her closed lids. If Angelica died, she'd never forgive herself.

Just as she hadn't forgiven herself the last time.

The woman's face disappeared from view. The fetid smell of jostling, sweating bodies was overpowering. Panic swept her as one of the bodies wedged itself between her and Sam. She felt it pushed out of the way, and Sam's hand reached behind him, groping. She grabbed it like a lifeline. "I said stay close," he shouted as she tripped on a step. He pulled her up as they reached the landing. Seconds later the uniformed guards surrounded them and propelled them toward the haven of the carved oak doors that opened to receive them.

In the vestibule adjoining the inquiry room on the top floor, Becca paced the oak floorboards while Sam Stedman sat on one of the scooped plastic chairs the hospital had provided for them. Perspiration oozed from her like sap from a tree. God, how she longed for some fresh air. The narrow room was a sauna! Windowless and pine-paneled, it doubled as a minikitchen. Sam had helped himself to a mug of coffee from the fresh pot that perked on the two-burner stove, but she had declined. Her throat was too constricted to get anything down.

Unable to contain herself any longer, she halted in front of her attorney and dug her fingers into his shoulder urgently. "Sam, please . . . call the Pediatric ICU."

He set the mug on the floor and rose to stand beside her. "I did. Just before we left. There's been no change. Angelica's still in a coma. I gave instructions for them to reach us here immediately if there was any news."

Remorse flicked at her like a live wire. "Sam, I can't stand it," she whispered. "If she dies, it's because I—"

He laid a finger across her mouth. *"No!* Don't say it! Don't even think it! For God's sake, Becca, we're going into an inquiry in a few minutes to convince the powers that be that you had nothing to do with what happened to Angelica Vargas." He took his hand away. "Hell, I'll be up against enough in there. Don't make it any harder for me." His scowl made him look older than his thirty-eight years.

Her lips compressed. So much for comfort from her thin-skinned attorney. But she forgave him his temper. He was brilliant and she needed him. Besides, he was right. He was up against an impossible situation. From the beginning the media coverage had been brutal. Of the newspapers, perhaps the *Times* had been the kindest of all when they wrote:

> At ten p.m. on Sunday, June 21, Dr. Becca Landau was found with Angelica Vargas, daughter of billionaire Jose Vargas, in the Pediatric Intensive Care Unit at Manhattan General Hospital. Caught with her hands on the ventilator, she is suspected of dislodging the respirator sustaining the child's life. Dismissed from the Vargas case a week before, Dr. Landau, who was cited with negligence in the death of another child when she interned at Boston Memorial, could give no plausible explanation for her presence there. To date, Angelica Vargas remains in a coma.

The facts would have been damning enough, but Becca knew she wasn't being tried on the facts alone.

Considered New York's "silk stocking" hospital, Manhattan

General catered to the rich and famous from all over the world. But a hospital is only as good as its reputation, and because of the unexplained deaths of several prominent patients in the last year and a half, that reputation had become tarnished. The result was a drop in the occupied bed count, finances that had become critical, and a staff that deserted daily.

Reeling under the threat of bankruptcy, the hospital attorneys would press for a quick indictment. And given her tainted background, their job would be an easy one.

"You okay?" Embarrassed by his outburst, Sam's voice sounded gruff.

"Yes." She said it because it was what he wanted to hear. But she didn't feel okay. All morning she'd had a terrible sensation of déjà vu. She had been here before. The year had been different and the hospital had been different, but the intent had been the same. She knew what the inquiry board's opening statement would be. *"We wish to reiterate that this is an inquiry, not a trial . . ."* But it *was* a trial. A trial to determine whether she had tried to murder Angelica Vargas.

She turned away from Sam and walked to the door leading to the inquiry room. Through the glass pane at the top she could see the raised dais and the members of the panel that would sit in judgment of her. The chief of Pediatrics, the chief of Medicine, the dean of the Medical School, the vice president of Pediatric Nursing—a battery of hospital bigwigs that could turn the blood of any resident cold.

And greeting them all with a warm handshake and the charismatic smile that was identical to his son David's, was Arnold Hardinger, president and administrator of Manhattan General. Tall, with silvered hair and a barrel chest, he was powerful and unforgiving. The anticipation of her downfall was clearly written on his face. What a fool she had been not to realize from the outset that he was her enemy.

She felt Sam come up behind her and turned as he spoke.

"You know, there's one thing about you that puzzles me."

She had the feeling he was trying to distract her.

"What's that?"

"Well, you may be a lot of things, but you're not self-destructive. Knowing how vulnerable you were because of the incident at Boston Memorial, I would expect you to lay low at Manhattan General, not call attention to yourself. Instead, you take on someone of Angelica Vargas's prominence, knowing that if anything went wrong you'd be the first one blamed. Wouldn't it have been smarter to duck the case?"

"I tried."

"How hard did you try?"

She didn't speak for a long moment. "Not hard enough, I guess."

It was a lame answer, but she had no better one to give, because she didn't understand it herself. Perhaps involving herself with Angelica had been her way of doing penance for what happened in Boston. Perhaps there was a masochistic streak in her. But Sam Stedman was right. From the moment Angelica was admitted to the hospital, she had set herself up for what happened as surely as if she had taken a knife to her throat.

She remembered that the day had been filled with a series of emergencies that were a doctor's nightmare.

It had started that morning with a cardiac arrest . . .

One

"Code Red! Four East!" Kept carefully unalarming, the voice over the loudspeaker at Manhattan General signaled an arrest on the pediatric floor.

From Four West in the old building Dr. Becca Landau and her team — Kip Flanders and Wanda Alpert — raced down the ancient corridor decorated with crayoned drawings, patchwork quilts, and posters of Mickey Mouse and Donald Duck.

"It's got to be the leukemia patient in 427," Kip said. "He's hanging on by a hair. The blood I took from him this morning was so thin it looked like Kool-Aid."

Becca nodded. There was nothing sustaining the boy — soaring white count, dismal platelet and red count. The disease in its acute stages — excruciating for the patient, agonizing for the parents.

"It would be a *mitzvah* if he went," Wanda said. "A blessing."

"We don't talk like that on this team," Becca said sharply.

She knew Wanda was voicing the consensus of opinion on the floor. She also knew there were a few doctors ready to help it along. But she wasn't one of them. If her patient was going to die, he would check out on his own. Because she intended to do everything she could to save him.

For the third time that day, she damned the inefficient floor plan. Seconds counted now. But Manhattan General wasn't designed for emergencies.

Overlooking the East River at Eighty-Second Street, it had been built in 1880 as a clinic for the poor. Bolstered by Ford, Gould, and DuPont monies, through the years wings were added, facilities expanded, and staff multiplied to form a vast medical teaching and research center. But the original building she and her team were speeding through had been left intact, its plaster walls cracking, its plumbing corroded, its floors creaking underfoot. And the extension tacked on to it in 1968 hadn't helped. It had been added with great regard for matching the medieval facade, but little for practicality. The result was a pediatric floor extending between the old building, West, and the new one, East, with a long hallway separating the surgical facilities at one end and the Pediatric Intensive Care Unit at the other.

The narrow hallway was an obstacle course this morning. It was filled with abandoned babies in playpens waiting to be claimed or placed in institutions, shrieking their discontent or battering at the bars that confined them. Candy stripers wheeled linen carts to supply rooms. Aides supported ambulatory rehabilitation patients on their morning constitutional or collected long-overdue breakfast trays strewn with stale remainders that gave off unpalatable odors. And medical staff dodged each other in their haste to get to the various rooms.

Ignoring the bedlam, Becca hurried past the nurse's station that heralded the entry to the East Wing. Farther down, she could see the emergency light flashing its urgent summons above number 427.

The patient's father was being prodded from the room. "I was just talking to him a minute ago," he cried. He looked wildly about, his upturned hands pleading with the nurse who guided him toward the solarium. " 'Bring me my teddy bear, Papa,' he said. Clear as I'm telling it to you now. 'Bring me my teddy bear.' "

Becca closed her mind. When she let the anguish penetrate, it opened the door to memories that were best kept at bay, and there was no way she was going to allow that. She hurried into the room with Kip and Wanda following closely behind. The curtain was drawn around bed one, farthest from the window. The crash cart, the EKG, and the defibrillator were already in the room. Two nurses were administering CPR to the small body in the bed. One was holding an ambu-bag—a manual respirator over the child's face. The other was doing closed chest massage. The cardiac monitor had been set up at the side of the bed. It was signaling ventricular fibrillation. The child's heart was quivering, all its electrical impulses firing randomly, lacking coordination.

As the first doctor there, Becca automatically took charge. "Kip, start an I.V. Get me an amp of lidocaine. And mix a lidocaine drip."

"The emergency team's on the way," the nurse holding the ambu-bag said. She shifted position. The child's face became visible. His eyes were closed, his skimpy lashes a golden smudge against his skeletal face. The bruising produced by the leukemia was evident in the purple discolorations on his arms and legs. He wore a red felt hat with a polka dot band around it. The hat was askew now, and his small bald head peered like a bleached skull from beneath it.

Becca squelched the pity that welled in her and let the anger take over instead. Rage was always her reaction now when death came to claim one of hers. It had been that way ever since the incident at Boston Memorial that had claimed the life of her young patient and made her an object of speculation.

A rush of purpose washed over her as she pushed the lidocaine into the IV that Kip had set up. She had learned in the last two years that the only way she could ward off the accusatory voices from the past was to cheat death of its quarry.

Come on! she urged the limp little body beneath her. *Come on!*

There was no change. The fibrillation continued.

"Prep for defib!" she demanded. Kip placed the charged defibrillator paddles in her hands. Wanda's face suddenly turned pasty. "Don't you dare," Becca hissed. She wouldn't tolerate the med student fainting now. Becca positioned the paddles against the boy's torso—one to the right upper sternum below the clavicle, the other on the left side near the base of the lung. "Stand clear!" she called, then triggered the charge. The child's body convulsed skyward as massive volts of electricity shocked his heart.

The silence in the room was palpable as all eyes fixed on the monitor.

The jolted heart sputtered into activity, then faltered. The hope that had risen, died.

The emergency team arrived. Made up of two residents and an anesthesiologist, the chief pediatric resident took over. "Get me epinephrine!" he called to Kip.

"What's this kid got?" the anesthesiologist asked as he inserted an endotracheal tube and attached the ambu-bag to it, ensuring a reliable air passage.

"Leukemia," Becca said. "Blood count, rock bottom."

They worked on him for twenty-five minutes, repeating the dosage of medication and defibrillating twice more. The heart remained disorganized, irritated—quivering but refusing to beat. The nurse resumed chest massage as the leader straightened up. "This is pointless," he said.

"No!" The single word burst from her.

She could feel them all staring at her. They wanted no part of this personal vendetta of hers. She knew what they were thinking. The patient had suffered horribly for the better part of six months and her reluctance to relinquish him at this point was nothing short of cruel.

The chief resident pulled the stethoscope from about his neck. He regarded her coldly. "Look, Becca, you can do what you want. In my book this kid's had it." He signaled to the members of his team to follow, then left abruptly.

Their censure had no meaning for her, she told herself. It was predicated on the consensus that Death was inevitable here, and she knew it would reverse the moment she proved them wrong. And prove them wrong she would!

"Kip, I want a repeat on the medication," she instructed. "And a recharge on the defibrillator."

They worked for almost half an hour. She refused to think of the boy's pain-wracked body. What rode her was her refusal to be beaten. On a final try, she doubled the voltage and replaced the paddles. "Clear!" she cried. The boy's body jerked upward. The tension in the room was as keen as the smell of Lysol that pervaded it.

A jagged blip plunged across the screen. Wanda's sharply indrawn breath sliced the silence like a scalpel. The tentative blip, was followed by another . . . stronger this time. The monitor's peaks and valleys settled into a recognizable pattern.

Becca's heart began to pound with a certainty. *Not this time, you bastard!* she taunted her receding foe.

"Check for pulse and pressure," she cried.

"I'm getting a pulse," Kip Flanders said.

The faces of the others were immobilized in disbelief.

"Pressure palpable at sixty," the nurse called out.

A cheer went up in the room almost drowning out the sound of the beeper clipped to the breast pocket of her short white coat. Becca removed the beeper and pressed the button at the top. The numbers came up 4308. The summons was from Helen Walters, head nurse of the pediatric floor, and one of the few friends Becca had made in her two years at Manhattan General.

"See that this patient gets into Intensive Care immediately," she instructed Wanda Alpert. Then with Kip in tow, she headed toward the nurse's station at the entry to Four West.

Partially concealed behind a high, L-shaped counter, the nurse's station served as the communications center for the entire fourth floor. Clerks, nurses, residents, and interns filtered in and out, referring to the patient charts housed between slots in a metal cart, viewing x-rays on the board that covered the side wall, telephoning the dietician to confirm restrictive foods or the pharmacy to change a prescription, and continuously writing to keep ahead of the massive amounts of paperwork that threatened to swamp them all.

And the responsibility for keeping all of it in smooth working order rested on the broad shoulders of the head nurse, Helen Walters.

Helen Walters had been with Manhattan General for fifteen years. Raised in Brooklyn, she was proud of the nasal inflection that gave it away. She had a broad face, a flat nose, and a tenacious manner that had earned her the nickname "Bulldog" among the hierarchy she harassed steadily in her crusade to better working conditions for nurses.

"Congratulations," she said as Becca approached. "I just heard about your big save in 427. You bucking for a medal or something?"

Short and stocky, Helen's only weakness was a penchant for anything chocolate—cakes, cookies, Hershey bars. In her less compulsive moments, she talked of abstaining, but the increasing roll of fat around her middle proved it was a losing battle.

Becca grinned. "I'm glad someone in this place has a sense of humor."

Though she threatened to quit daily because of the pressure on "her girls" due to the critical nursing shortage, Helen never did. She wasn't married, and if she had any family she rarely saw them. She was always there, sometimes filling in herself when an emergency called for it and there was no one else she could get.

"I wasn't trying to be funny," she said. "The staff views it as an exercise in futility. And so do I."

Becca's grin was replaced by a scowl. "I don't care how anyone views it." She eyed the head nurse in puzzlement. It wasn't like Helen to count any life negligible. "You suffering from PMS this morning or is something else making you this bitchy?"

"It shows?"

"It does. Care to tell me about it?"

Helen nodded. She shuffled some papers on the desk and came up with a copy of an admission sheet. "For the fine work we've been doing on this floor, we've been rewarded. An eight-year-old has just been admitted. Her name is Angelica Vargas. The daughter of Jose Vargas." Her brows lifted above her horn-rimmed bifocals. "Ring a bell?"

The name sounded familiar, but Becca couldn't place it. "I'm not sure. Should it?"

"It sure should," Kip said at her shoulder. "Oil! Billions of dollars worth of it in South America. According to the press, Vargas has used the money to buy up half of the U.S. and is now trying for the other half."

It didn't surprise Becca that Kip Flanders was aware of Vargas's status. She suppressed a smile as she glanced at him. The product of a Newport and Palm Beach upbringing, even in his hospital whites he managed to look preppy.

He rolled his eyes heavenward. "That's all we need now—another celebrity kid. The newspapers haven't finished crucifying us for the Ryker boy yet. If anything was to go wrong—"

"Nothing's going to go wrong!" The head nurse's vehemence testified to the panic that rode the entire hospital. And with good reason.

The first of the unexplained deaths to afflict Manhattan General had been a well-known actress who had suddenly "crumped" after a gallbladder operation. The second was the seventeen-year-old son of Judge Ellen Abbot Ryker, who was admitted to the pediatric floor presenting with a fever and a feeling of malaise. The judge waited until she was assured that her son's condition was stable. Then she left. Shortly afterward, the boy's fever escalated and despite heroic efforts, he died within a few hours.

The judge, a widow, and well-respected in political circles, was vocal in her cries of negligence. The hospital and the Medical Examiner held an immediate inquiry. The district attorney and the State Health Department were slower to conduct their own. But the grieving judge refused to accept their verdicts of "death by natural causes." She instituted a malpractice suit and roused the media to investigate what she termed, "a hospital care system that cures by knowledge and kills by negligence."

The resulting exposés altered forever the public's image of the hospital as trusted caretaker and had a devastating effect on Manhattan General.

"I hope to God Dr. Ervin's team is handling this one," Becca murmured.

"You're taking the name of the Lord in vain," Helen said. She broke off a piece of Swiss Toblerone and popped it into her mouth. "The girl is in 401 East — your territory. Besides, the attending is specifically asking for you as resident. That's what you get for your misplaced heroics."

"What's the girl presenting with?"

Helen read from the admission sheet. "Low-grade fever. Weakness in arms and legs. General feeling of malaise."

Becca was silent for a moment. Helen knew nothing of what had transpired at Boston Memorial, and she preferred to keep it that way. But she was courting disaster if she got involved in this case. "I'd really like to duck this one, Helen."

"So would we all." She shrugged. "Look, take it up with the girl's attending. See what you can do."

"Who is the attending?" The attending was the patient's private physician and the governing hand on the case.

"Gottlieb. He admitted her himself. He's waiting for you in 401 East now. Do me a favor. When you see him, tell him I think I've got a replacement for the nurse. A good one, name of Bates. He'll understand."

Two

At precisely that moment, another emergency was being addressed. A meeting was in progress on the top floor which held the executive offices of Manhattan General. It had been called suddenly by the chairman of the board, Charles Rankin Peabody, and though only five members had been able to attend on such short notice, Arnold Hardinger knew that the meeting carried the seeds of dissension that would quickly plunge it into a name-calling shambles.

The meeting was being held in the sumptuous conference room that was part of Peabody's suite. On top of the oval conference table lit by a crystal chandelier, the limp remains of a succulent lobster salad, flaky croissants, and assorted petits fours lay forgotten on the Rosenthal china platters. The hastily eaten three-hundred-dollar lunch had been ordered from Lutèce by Peabody, who for the last three minutes had been holding forth on the need for further financial cutbacks but as usual hadn't given a single concrete suggestion as to how to implement them.

Fidgeting in his chair as Peabody droned on, the craving to smoke clutched at Hardinger as it always did when he was bored or under stress. At the moment he was feeling both. Reaching inside his jacket pocket, he withdrew a shiny black cigarette holder, slid it into his mouth, then massaged it sensually between his lips. The holder jerked upward as he clenched down, irrationally angry at the doctor who had insisted he quit smoking and at his need for a pacifier to do it. It seemed a pointed reminder that not everything could be accomplished through willpower alone, a theory he had spent his whole life refuting.

Doctors! he thought contemptuously. What the hell did they know? He had soothed them and coerced them and manipulated them at the hospital for over twenty years, and a more inflated bunch of egos he'd never come across. People treated them like gods, so after a while they began to believe it.

A shaft of sunlight glanced off the glass showcase opposite him, and he saw himself reflected there. He straightened in his chair. Only his silver hair and the slight sag beneath his chin hinted at his fifty-six years. His chest might have rounded out a bit and his waistline thickened over the years, but he was still agile enough to play two sets of tennis back to back or go three times a night with the sadistic little biochemist whose voracious appetite more than made up for her size.

He became aware that Peabody was winding down. Broad shouldered but painfully thin, with an asthmatic condition and a concave chest that his vested tweed suit couldn't minimize, the chairman waved aloft a copy of the latest *Crain's Business Report* that sported the headline, "Caught in a Tide of Red Ink, Manhattan General is Sinking Fast."

"Gentlemen," he wheezed, "the time for mulling and friendly talk is over. If drastic action isn't taken immediately, Manhattan General will go under." A poor ad-libber, Peabody always spoke from a memorized speech and tended to forget his next line, as he did now. From force of habit, he turned to Arnold Hardinger for direction, then, mindful of their changed relationship, nodded instead to Harley Minden, chief financial officer, seated across from him. "I leave it to Harley to fill you in on exactly how bad it is," he concluded.

Arnold Hardinger hid the contempt in his eyes. For twenty years, he had bolstered this aging relic whose wealth had come from his grandfather and his father and the steamship line that had been handed to him by right of birth. In his youth, because of his massive physique and tawny mane, Peabody had been likened to a lion. But he had been a lion without teeth or claws. Rendered ineffectual by indecisiveness and an inability to manage people, he had relied completely on Hardinger, whom he had personally appointed as president and administrator.

But now someone else had his ear.

Hardinger looked across at Dr. Anthony Whitcomb, the hospital's medical director and the most recent contender for his job. More than a contender, Hardinger thought grimly. He had it from a reliable source that Whitcomb would try to oust him by the end of this meeting. But forewarned was forearmed, and he had come with a couple of surprises up his own sleeve.

Harvard bred and a crowd pleaser, the forty-two-year-old Whitcomb was a formidable opponent. He had been a surgeon before he was elevated to medical director, and like all medical men, he abhorred Hardinger's business background and insisted that the administration of a hospital should be in the hands of a doctor, not the former vice president of Marketing at Eli Lilly. His eyes were on Harley Minden, who had slipped on his horn-rimmed glasses and was speaking in the dull, passionless voice that afflicted most glorified accountants.

"Gentlemen, I wish I could minimize the desperate financial straits we're in, but I can't. We're already down five million this quarter. The cost-cutting measures Arnold instituted—the layoffs and revamped purchasing procedures—have helped. But they're just the tip of the iceberg. The major problem we face is that our hospital is underutilized. Admissions fell six percent last year—that's a total of thirty-two hundred beds that weren't occupied, and if that were to continue—"

Whitcomb cut across his words with an impatient gesture. "Come on, Harley! Of course it's going to continue! Why don't we cut to the crux of this thing, instead of wasting our time with the statistics. Do you know what people are saying about this hospital? They're saying it's jinxed! That's why they're staying away in droves. And as long as Judge Ryker goes on with this vendetta of hers and wields enough influence to prompt TV shows on hospital negligence like the one Geraldo crucified us in last night, they're going to continue to stay away." He steepled the manicured fingertips of both hands and regarded them with enormous concentration. "Of course, if we hadn't relied on Arnold's assurance that he could put a stop to this . . ."

Hardinger took the holder out of his mouth. "You're out of line, Tony," he said evenly, careful not to show his fury. "I never said I could put a stop to it. I only said I could keep it in check.

Believe me, if I wasn't calling in every favor that's been owed me for the last twenty years, the publicity would be a lot worse. But it's simplistic to think you can just 'put a stop to this'. Ellen Ryker is a politically minded bitch who is using her 'grief' to kick off a crusade for hospital reform that for sure she'll use as a platform to make federal judge. And there's no way I can think of to muzzle her." He glanced at Emil Wasserstein, the legal counsel on the board who sat across from him, twiddling a pencil between his stubby fingers. "Am I right, Emil?"

By far the cleverest of the partners at Branford, Forbes and Wasserstein, Emil Wasserstein resembled a pudgy penguin in his black suit, starched white shirt, and bow tie. He spoke now in a Will Rogers "country boy" twang that always gained him points in the courtroom. "Right as rain," he said, adjusting his round spectacles. "You'd be bucking freedom of speech, freedom of the press, and more importantly, the right of a grieving mother to vindicate what she sees as the needless death of her son."

"Then what *can* we do to fight it?" Peabody asked in exasperation.

"We can do the same thing McNeil Pharmaceuticals did when the safety of Tylenol was in question," Hardinger said. "Mount a publicity campaign to show that we stand behind our product. Remind the public of the many new innovations in medicine and research we've been responsible for, pound away at our hundred years of devoted service, and assure them that the best doctors in the world are here at Manhattan General."

Whitcomb's smile was malicious. "You mean *were here*, don't you, Arnold? Because the doctors at this hospital are deserting like rats from a sinking ship. And those who haven't left are thinking of it. And if you're going to tell us that it's all because of the adverse publicity we've been getting lately, I'll tell you that's a crock. If they were asked, a lot of them would be glad to tell you that they've been dissatisfied for a long time with the way you've run things around here."

Hardinger half-rose in his seat. "That's a lie, Whitcomb!"

Whitcomb hunched forward, his voice deceptively low. "Is it? Can you deny that the staff has hated your guts ever since the DRGs were put into effect?"

Hardinger flushed. Whitcomb was going for his balls. The DRGs, better known as Diagnostic Related Groups, was the new insurance pay system for reimbursing hospitals. Under it, hospitals got a fixed fee from Medicare and the other insurance companies based on the admitting diagnosis of a patient, regardless of the length of stay.

"You know what the medical staff calls you?" Whitcomb baited him. "They call you 'Quicker 'n' Sicker Hardinger,' because if a surgical patient has complications or if a bone graft didn't take as well as it should or if a series of myeloma tests are inconclusive, you don't want to know about it. If you did, you'd have to keep the patient here past the days allotted under the DRGs and the hospital would lose money. So your orders are to send them home quicker and sicker, and if they don't recuperate there as they should, well, that's not the hospital's affair, is it?" His point made, Whitcomb leaned back in his chair.

There was an embarrassed shuffling around the table, then silence. Hardinger could feel their condemnation of him as clearly as if they had voiced it. He could barely keep the contempt from his own voice when he spoke. "Gentlemen, you can't have it both ways. You want me to salvage the hospital, but when I get down and dirty to do it, you yell foul."

"Other hospitals have managed without skimping on patient care," Whitcomb retorted.

"Other hospitals can afford to lose money. We can't!"

Peabody held up both hands in protest. The veins on their backs were a spidery network of blue that disappeared into the dry liver-spotted skin. "Gentlemen, please. We have enough problems here without your going at each other privately." He turned toward Hardinger. "Arnold, your idea of countering with our own publicity campaign is a good one. But it isn't feasible."

"Why not? Consumer marketing is the wave of the future for hospitals. Beth Israel and St. Vincent's started using the media on a small basis a couple of years ago, and Mount Sinai went whole hog last year with a splashy campaign that produced amazing results. Emergency visits went up fourteen percent in four months, and market research showed that the medical center moved from the number seven position to number one in recognition."

"At a cost of one and a half million," Harley Minden murmured dryly. "And the promise to the public of massive renovation which we need desperately and can't afford to do."

Peabody exhaled on a long sigh that ended in a wheeze. "And there you have it. Change takes dollars, and that's a commodity we're very short of."

It was then that Whitcomb made his move. Rising with studied nonchalance, he poured himself a cup of coffee from the silver urn on the carved oak sideboard behind him. Above it, oil portraits of the hospital's godfathers — Jay Gould, Henry Ford, and Alfred Irénée DuPont — beamed benevolently down on the group. "Not all change takes money," he murmured, smoothing the lapel of his charcoal Burberry suit. He was a handsome man who carried himself with the grace born of generations of breeding. It was a demeanor Hardinger envied but with his middle-class upbringing and City College education could never hope to acquire.

Whitcomb took a sip of his coffee. "For instance, a revamping of management, which I think is badly overdue, would take only some careful thought on our part. The morale of this hospital, particularly that of its medical staff, is at a very low ebb right now. If we can't afford to assuage the public any other way, let's at least try to retain the excellence of care we've always been known for. And that means holding on to our doctors. Under the circumstances, for them a change of administration would be like a shot in the arm. Now, I'm not minimizing Arnold's talents or the years of service he's put in . . ."

Hardinger rose so swiftly, he overturned his chair. It fell to the thick Karastan carpeting with a dull thud. Ignoring it, he splayed his hands on the gleaming mahogany conference table and leaned forward. "Gentlemen, what would you say if I told you that I have a donor in the offing who's willing to put up twenty million to help get the hospital on its feet again."

Whitcomb's laugh was derisive. "I'd say you were bluffing."

For a moment Hardinger thought of telling them that the money was coming from Jose Vargas, just to see the awe and respect that would cross their faces. He'd known Vargas for over fifteen years now, and it always gave him a boost when the mention of his name had that effect on people. Then he thought better of it. Jose had been called to Buenos Aires before he had a chance to make the check out. The tycoon's word was good. Still it wasn't a bird in the hand.

The chairman threw Whitcomb a reproving glance. "Arnold never bluffs."

Hardinger smiled. "Thank you, Chuck."

Whitcomb paled. It was the use of the nickname more than Peabody's remark that made him think the donation might be valid. Only Peabody's intimate friends called him that, and Hardinger wouldn't have dared use it if he was lying. Or would he?

"Would you care to share the name of this generous benefactor with us?" Whitcomb challenged.

"At the proper time, Tony." Hardinger's smile broadened in complete enjoyment. "At the proper time."

Three

Becca and Kip were halfway to Angelica Vargas's room when Wanda Alpert caught up with them. A third-year med student, Wanda was doing rotations — four-week stints of the different specialties to see which she would choose. Last month it had been cardiology. The month before, hematology. And now she was trying pediatrics to see if she would like it. Becca hoped she wouldn't. A former debating-team captain, the girl was glib but belligerent. She tended to argue, especially with Kip, and it wore Becca down.

"You know that broken leg in 408?" Kip was saying. "Well, this morning, right after rounds, I popped in to tell him that his cast was coming off tomorrow. And what do I find but that bitch of a mother of his with a notebook in her hand, taking down the names of all the nurses and doctors who even went near her kid. I could see the word *MALPRACTICE* written right across those big boobs of hers. I got out of there so fast she didn't even see me go by. And I made a note of every time I blinked around that kid."

A further symptom of the hospital's panic, Becca thought grimly. A cover-your-ass mentality that had doctors writing briefs instead of notes and nurses tiptoeing around patients as if they were treading on rice paper.

"Don't you think you're being a bit melodramatic?" Wanda's tone was sarcastic, baiting. She tossed her blond hair over one shoulder and wet her heavily lipsticked mouth.

Becca read the expression in Kip's eyes as he scowled at the girl, and the truth about them suddenly dawned on her.

As an intern, Kip was the closest thing to slave labor the hospital had devised. He was expected to perform round the clock, absorb a myriad of details, and give a creditable accounting of himself while weaving on his feet from exhaustion. If there was any energy left for sex, he took it when, where, and with whom he could find it. Kip's expression as he stared at Wanda held intimacy . . . and an aftermath of discomfort. Becca suspected that he had tumbled the med student into bed a few times and it had ended there for him.

Not so for Wanda.

It didn't make Becca like the girl any better, but she felt a softening toward her now that she recognized what the belligerence concealed. How well she knew the feeling.

She had been an intern when she'd first met David Hardinger at Boston Memorial. Ambitious, capable, and charming, he was the resident voted 'most likely to succeed.' It was common knowledge that his father was the president of Manhattan General in New York. That may have accounted for the certainty with which he carried himself, a certainty that bordered on arrogance. Yet beneath it Becca had sensed a need, a turmoil in him. It spoke to her from restless blue eyes that acknowledged the attraction between them yet held her off. Perhaps he realized that she wouldn't settle for the superficial, short-lived relationship for which he had earned a reputation, and he was wary of something deeper and more lasting.

In time, they had gone to bed just as Kip and Wanda had. But there had been no misgivings for them.

At least not then.

A sharp yearning rose in her as David's image imprinted itself on her mind. Recently the images had become so real that she could almost reach out and touch him. She forced her mind to return from where it had strayed. Dwelling on David was a hurtful pastime. It intensified her longing. And it brought back memories of the fatal incident at Boston Memorial, because David had been involved in it with her.

Annoyed with her inability to control her emotions, she quickened her pace. At Wanda's murmur, she turned to the girl. "Wanda, why don't you take an early lunch and meet us back here in, say, three-quarters of an hour." She sensed

Kip's relief as the med student nodded, then strode off.

Why was she dwelling on David so much lately? Becca wondered. Long before the crisis at Boston Memorial had brought the relationship to a head, she had conceded that there were too many differences between them for it to last. He needed to dominate; she couldn't stand being curbed. He was an egotist; she lacked self-esteem. He had the surgeon's distant approach to human misery; she had difficulty separating herself from her patients. She believed in advancing causes. He believed in advancing David Hardinger.

None of it had seemed to matter when they fell in love. All of it became crucial when they separated.

In the eight months they had been together, they had worked much of the time, argued part of the time, and made love the rest of the time. When they had broken apart — and it was a breaking, a wrenching, because their feelings were too volatile for an amicable parting — she had been hurt and disillusioned. Above all, she had been angry. The anger had been directed at herself, but she hadn't realized that until much later. She had stood accused at Boston Memorial, and, instead of helping her to clear herself, David had urged her to run.

Perhaps transferring to Manhattan General had been a wise move. Perhaps, as David insisted, it had been the only way to extricate herself from a no-win situation and salvage a faltering career. But it had been wrong for her. If David had loved her as he claimed he had, he would have understood that.

When she had left Boston two years ago, she had severed all contact with David. For her own peace of mind, she intended to keep it that way.

The sight of Gottlieb waiting for her outside Angelica Vargas's room effectively stilled her reminiscing. There was a more immediate matter at hand. If she allowed herself to be resident to a patient of Angelica Vargas's prominence, she would be placing herself in a very precarious position. To avoid it, she had to come up with a damned good excuse. But what? Her mind raced to exhaust the possibilities before she reached the attending.

"I'm glad you got here," he said warmly as she approached. "I was about to leave." He acknowledged Kip with a nod and a smile.

Gottlieb was one of the attendings Becca liked. He held a license as both a pede and a G.P., and he didn't come on to every female on the staff like some of the other attendings did. She also respected him. He was a good internist, even though the purpose of the several doctors he employed at his Fifth Avenue office was to free him so he could spend the better part of his day on the golf course.

"I didn't want to go before personally placing this case in your hands," he said.

She fidgeted in front of him like a first-year med student. She could only hope he would prove as tractable in this as he had in other things. "Dr. Gottlieb, I want you to know I'm grateful for the confidence you have in me, but would you mind if Dr. Ervin took this patient on?"

"I certainly would." He frowned. "Why? Is there some kind of trouble?"

"No. No," she assured him hastily. "It's just that my workload is so heavy now . . ." She knew it was a weak excuse, but she hadn't been able to think of anything else.

"Is that all?" He sounded relieved. "Look, Becca, I know you've got your hands full, but as far as I'm concerned, you're the best pede on the floor, and after what's happened here in the last year or so. . . . Well, I wouldn't feel comfortable unless Angelica was in your care. Keep on top of this one for me, Becca . . . please. I'll make it up to you. I promise."

Kip shifted his weight twice in the ensuing silence. It was getting embarrassing when Becca finally nodded. "I'll do my best."

Gottlieb smiled his thanks. He was about forty-five with blunted, uneven features, a perpetual tan, and sand-colored hair cropped close to his head. When he smiled like this, he looked younger, more vital. Becca suddenly remembered the hospital scuttlebutt about a different, dedicated Gottlieb of years ago, who couldn't tear himself away from his patients until his wife found out about his affair with some nurse who subsequently disappeared. Most times it hadn't seemed believable to Becca. At this moment it did.

"Did Helen Walters fill you in at all?" he asked.

"She told me what the girl was presenting with. That her name is Angelica Vargas. And that she's the daughter of Jose Vargas."

"Do you know who Jose Vargas is?"

"Of course."

Kip's mouth twitched, and she avoided his eyes.

Gottlieb fingered the stethoscope protruding from his labcoat pocket. Unlike hers, it wasn't stickered with flowers and bunnies to make it less formidable to his young patients. "I've known the Vargas family for many years," he said. "They keep one residence in Buenos Aires and a sixteen-room town house in New York. That's where Vargas's wife and mother spend most of their time. The Vargases have another doctor on tap in South America, but when they're here, I'm their family physician."

"Do you have any thoughts on what's wrong with Angelica?"

His lip curled faintly. "Probably nothing. I admitted her just to be on the safe side. Between me and you, Angelica's a spoiled brat. Moody. Fantasizes a lot. Throws tantrums. Maria, her stepmother, tends to romanticize and call them "spells." But to me they're nothing but plain old-fashioned tantrums."

He wrinkled his brow in perplexity. "It beats me why her father is so overly concerned about the girl. Maybe he feels he owes her something because he remarried so fast after he buried her mother. Whatever his reason, since her mother died four years ago, he's treated Angelica like a hothouse flower. He never lets her leave the house alone. Instead of sending her to school, he has a tutor for her. And he often takes her with him on his business trips to South America." He made a contemptuous sound. "That is, when she isn't 'ill.' When she is, all of her little foibles escalate and she's impossible to deal with." He shrugged. "There are times when I can't decide whether the girl needs a good spanking or a good therapist."

"Maybe both," Kip murmured.

"Maybe. But her father doesn't believe in either, and he runs the show in that house like he does everywhere else. Vargas isn't a bad guy, but he's so used to wielding power that I think everyone is a little afraid of him, including his young wife. He's in Buenos Aires now, not due to return before next week. But I wouldn't be surprised if he comes running back sooner when he hears Angelica is sick. And when he does, he's going to want a minute-by-minute account of what's happening to his little girl. So keep me posted on *everything*. And don't hesitate to call if you need me." He glanced at his watch. "I'll be in the hospital for the next half-hour. After that you can reach me through my office."

He started to leave, then thought better of it. "Becca, the nurse on duty was called away from the hospital on a personal emergency. Make sure Helen replaces her with someone who knows what she's doing, will you?"

"She already has. A good one, Helen said. Name of Bates."

Becca waited for him to go, but he didn't. He just stood there, eyes unblinking, still as a negative frozen in a film clip. She suddenly remembered the rumor that he'd had a breakdown years ago.

"Did Helen mention her first name?"

"No, she didn't."

He nodded, said something barely audible about "keeping in touch," then strode off.

"Well, you sure got us out of that case," Kip quipped as the attending disappeared from sight.

"There could be worse things," she said sharply. She didn't need Kip to tell her she'd put up a poor fight.

Four

Angelica Vargas's room, 401 East, was the only private room on the pediatric floor, the consensus being that it was healthier for kids to be with other kids. It was on a corner that boasted twin picture windows, one of which overlooked the round flagstone parapet that resembled a medieval turret and served as a terrace for recuperating patients. It also offered a view of Roosevelt Island to the east, the Queensboro Bridge to the south, and a panorama of New York's most majestic skyscrapers in all their towering splendor.

The room was unusually spacious, painted in pale green with matching blinds and carpeting, had calico-print drapes, extra closet space, a small refrigerator next to the deep-drawered antique dresser, and a cushioned ladder-back rocking chair in the far corner. It was always reserved for the children of VIPs.

When Becca entered with Kip at her side, a young woman was leaning over the bed, shielding Angelica from view. The young woman moved aside, and Becca drew in her breath, struck by the elfin appeal of the child who lay there.

Angelica Vargas was small for her eight years. She had shoulder-length flyaway hair of the pale platinum color usually lost in babyhood. Her skin, slightly flushed with fever, held the translucence of porcelain. It was her upturned nose, wide mouth, and huge eyes that lent her face the piquant appeal that so intrigued Becca.

What made the elfin quality so pronounced was the faraway look in her light hazel eyes. They were ringed with fatigue in her drawn faced and gazed into space with an otherworldly expression that called to mind what Gottlieb had said about her fantasizing. She held herself very still, whether from fear or illness, Becca couldn't tell. She was dressed in a pink silk nightgown smocked across the shoulders and trimmed with the finest of Brussels lace.

Becca's face began to set in the happy smile that was de rigueur for the initial meeting with a young patient. The smile never reached her lips. There was something about Angelica Vargas that drew her—a sense of despair, an air of hopelessness that made her want to reach out to protect the child.

Bewildered, she pulled her feelings up short. She reminded herself of whom Angelica was and the danger it represented. To saddle herself with this kind of emotional baggage was foolhardy. She was glad when the young woman beside the bed disrupted the tenuous bond that had begun to form.

"Nurse," she said to Becca, "I'm afraid there aren't enough extra blankets to—"

"I'm not the nurse. I'm Dr. Landau." She inclined her head toward Kip. "And this is Dr. Flanders."

The woman raised a perfectly tapered brow, then acknowledged them both with a short nod. Becca wondered if she was a sister to the child. She couldn't have been more than twenty-two. She was tall and striking with wheat-colored hair and dark eyes that tended to blink too much. There was a formality about her, an imperiousness that was accentuated by the thrust of her full lips, lips that Becca got the impression didn't smile much. She wore a long-sleeved black dress that made her appear older. A heavy gold rope chain hung about her neck. Suspended from it was a large crucifix that nestled in the vee between her breasts.

"And I am Maria Vargas. Mrs. *Jose* Vargas."

Becca understood Kip's start of surprise. From Gottlieb's words, she had expected Maria Vargas to be young . . . but not this young. Her Latin heritage was evident in her olive complexion and her large expressive eyes.

Looking about, Becca hid her distaste. Maria Vargas had turned the room into a shrine. Icons of the Holy Mother stood on the dresser and the nightstands. Pictures of Jesus rested against the mirror and the window. There were even black rosary beads draped over the bedrail. Unless she missed her guess, this woman was a fanatic.

Outwardly calm, Maria Vargas betrayed her agitation by flipping the gold cross between her red-tipped fingers. "I do not understand," she said. "Your nurse has disappeared without any explanation, and I have seen no replacement for her yet. If Señor Vargas was here, this would not be tolerated for a second." She spoke in the stilted English of the foreign born who have been meticulously taught the language.

Becca took offense at her tone. It had the ring of a mistress addressing a servant. Was it because Becca was a woman doctor and the Latin mentality fed on the myth of the macho male? Or was this a characteristic of the boundlessly wealthy of her country? Whatever the reason, Becca intended to make it clear to this overbearing child bride that she expected to be accorded respect for the title "Doctor." She had earned it.

"But it is of no consequence," Maria Vargas continued. "I have ordered a private nurse who should be here any minute." She turned toward her stepdaughter and the haughtiness dropped from her like a molting skin. To Becca's surprise, the woman seemed unsure, placating. She blinked rapidly. "Neither Dr. Gottlieb nor I think there is much wrong with Angelica, but Señor Vargas . . ." She passed her tongue over her dark lipsticked mouth, and Becca suddenly remembered what Gottlieb had said about her being intimidated by her husband. "He would never forgive me if I did not take every precaution . . ."

Becca nodded, then leaned over the bed and touched the child's hand. "Hello, Angelica."

Not by a sign or a word did the child acknowledge her presence.

Becca straightened. "I'm sorry, Mrs. Vargas, but you won't be allowed a private nurse for Angelica."

"What do you mean?" There was an unmistakable challenge in her eyes.

There were so few competent pediatric nurses available for private duty that after a few near mishaps that heightened the charged atmosphere prevailing since the death of the Ryker boy, the hospital had decided against permitting them at all. Becca wasn't about to tell her that, but neither did she want to enter into a contest of wills with her.

"It's a hospital rule, Mrs. Vargas. But you can take that up with Dr. Gottlieb when you speak with him."

"I will do more than that. I will take it up with Arnold Hardinger himself. I presume you know the president of this hospital?"

She would hardly use the word *know* to characterize her relationship with Arnold Hardinger, Becca thought. She had been introduced to him briefly when he'd come up to be with David during the inquiries at Boston Memorial. She had sensed his withdrawal when they met, but she couldn't be sure of what it meant. When she'd talked of it with David afterward, he'd pointed out that at the time tempers had been short and feelings exaggerated, and that the impression she had received was a distorted one.

Since she'd transferred to Manhattan General, she'd seen Arnold Hardinger many times. His resemblance to his son had struck her afresh in each instance. They were both tall, broad-shouldered men with piercing blue eyes and high foreheads. But unlike David, who was still in the process of forming, Arnold Hardinger was a force whose word was absolute and whose edicts brooked no questioning.

In the few times she'd seen Hardinger close up, he had never shown by word or gesture that he had met her, and Becca was happy to keep it that way. For all they had to do with each other, Arnold Hardinger might as well have lived on another planet. Or so she had believed until Helen Walters had raised a doubt in her mind. "Hardinger's secretary is always asking questions about you," she'd said. "You know any reason why?" Becca had chalked it up to Helen's imagination.

"In case you are not aware of it," Maria Vargas was saying, "Arnold Hardinger is a close friend of ours. I am sure that if I asked him, Arnold would be amenable to making an exception in this instance."

He might be amenable, but if he made that exception, he'd have to tangle with Helen Walters, and Becca didn't envy him that. The head nurse had no love for Arnold Hardinger, and she had threatened to quit more than once at what she considered his infringement of her authority.

Becca inclined her head. "That's your privilege, of course." She turned to her patient again.

Angelica lay motionless in the bed with that fixed stare that Becca began to find unnerving. Was it deliberate? A way of removing herself from surroundings that were too painful? From a father who was too demanding? How well Becca could empathize with that. She could never conform to what her father expected of her, and when the sense of failure became too overwhelming, she would run from herself . . . from him. She would hide in a wooded copse on the acreage surrounding their white-pillared Colonial in Wellesley. And she would ignore the frantic shouts of the searchers who called her name.

It was more overt than the method Angelica was using, but the goal had been the same. Again she felt a thaw inside her, a melting toward this girl. Was it rooted in an unhappy childhood that was common to them both?

She leafed through the chart clipped to the bedrail and noted the admitting diagnosis: "Fever of unknown origin."

Angelica's pressure was listed at ninety over sixty, her pulse at ninety-five, and her fever at 100F—none of it warranting any concern at this point.

Smiling, she leaned over the bed once more. "Good morning, Angelica."

She gave no answer, but her head flipped fretfully back and forth on the pillow. *"Donde esta mi abuela?"*

Becca's eyes darted toward Maria Vargas.

"She wants to know where her grandmother is."

"Your husband's mother?"

She nodded.

"Is she close to her grandmother?"

"Yes."

From the inflection in her voice, Becca gathered that Maria Vargas was at odds with her mother-in-law.

Becca reached to smooth Angelica's silken hair. The child flinched, but Becca wouldn't be put off. "Angelica, look at me." She waited for Angelica's large hazel eyes to focus on her. "In case you didn't hear me say it, I'm Dr. Landau."

The focus sharpened. "A lady doctor?" It was no more than a whisper.

Becca nodded. "A lady doctor. Do you like that?"

The spark of interest died. "Makes no difference." The voice was clearer, the enunciation advanced for an eight-year-old.

Becca noted the warmth of the skin beneath her touch. It was undoubtedly generated by the fever. "How are you feeling, Angelica?"

"Fine." Her glance flicked toward her stepmother who hugged the bed like an anxious centurion. *"Mi abuela,"* she murmured.

"I told you before, she will be here later." Maria Vargas spoke softly, careful to take the sting from her reproof. *"Querida,* if you felt so fine you wouldn't be in the hospital. Now, you know that if your papa was here he would insist that you tell the doctor everything she wants to know."

"I'm tired, Tía" the child said.

Becca had to strain to hear her again.

"Tía . . ." Kip murmured. "Doesn't that mean "aunt" in Spanish?"

Maria Vargas nodded. "I am her stepmother. I am also her aunt." She hesitated. "Her mother was my older sister." Her face closed as if she was sorry she'd revealed even that much. An odd look crossed her features as she glanced down at Angelica. Becca realized that if pressed to describe it she would have to call it fear. But that didn't make sense. What would the woman have to fear from her small stepdaughter?

Maria Vargas suddenly spun the crucifix into motion again. " 'I'm tired . . . I'm tired,' " she repeated testily. "That is all she has been saying for a whole week. She will not tell me what is wrong. She just lies in bed staring at the ceiling as if she has departed from this world. *Dios mio!"* She genuflected in foreboding. "Señor Vargas, he gives to the hospitals, but he has a fear of them. He will not be happy that Angelica is here." She rubbed the knuckles of one hand with the other. "I am sure he will blame me when he hears that Angelica has been put into the hospital for no apparent reason." She hesitated, then leaned closer to Becca. Her voice dropped a notch and there was desperation in it. "Is it not possible for you to get her well before he returns? I would be *very* appreciative."

The blood rushed to Becca's face. Her expression was one of incredulity as she stared into Maria Vargas's eyes. She hadn't misunderstood it. She was being offered a bribe to rush Angelica out of the hospital, no matter what her findings. She tried to excuse the woman's actions because of her youth and foreignness, but it wouldn't jell. Becca straightened up, her outrage evident in the set of her shoulders.

"Mrs. Vargas—"

Kip made a noise that was somewhere between a cough and a bark. Becca encountered his glance, and it checked her. How many times had she cautioned him against allowing the patient's anxiety-ridden family to rile him?

She made an effort at control. "Mrs. Vargas, I will do my best for your stepdaughter," she said coldly. "But whatever the time requirement is to get her healthy again, it will be allotted. Is that understood?"

Maria Vargas opened her mouth to retort, then closed it when a nurse entered the room and walked toward the bed. She must have been new to the floor because Becca had never seen her before. She looked to be about forty but had the springy step of a much younger woman. She was tall and lean with short ash-colored hair, a snub nose, and the glow of a sunburn high on her cheeks. Her face was worn but attractive in a natural, outdoorsy sort of way. But there was a stubborn jut to her chin that led Becca to believe she could be argumentative. Becca hoped not. She had taken enough guff for one morning, and the next person who crossed her was in for a bad time.

The nurse nodded to her then leafed through the patient chart Becca had clipped to the bedrail. Bates, Helen had said her name was. She seemed to know what she was about, yet there was a hesitancy to her movements that made Becca leery.

"Oh, nurse . . ." Maria Vargas lifted a hand in summons. "I'd like to talk to you."

As if sensing Becca's need, the nurse deliberately moved toward the window, took a stance, and waited for the young woman to come to her.

Grateful for the respite, even if a short one, Becca turned to her patient who had once again retreated into her private world. "All right, Angelica," she said with more confidence then she felt. "Let's get back to what you were telling me." Becca lifted the chart from the bedrail and took out her pen. She noted with satisfaction that Angelica was following her every move. "You were saying you feel tired. What else?"

"Nothing else." The elfin face was sullen.

It was then that Becca noticed the doll. It was propped in a chair near the dresser and was partially hidden by Maria Vargas's jacket. The doll was at least three feet tall. What made it so startling was that it was such an exact miniature of the child in the bed that it almost looked human. The doll was richly dressed in blue satin with a black lace mantilla flowing from two tortoiseshell combs firmly anchored beneath the blond hair. Draped across the face and hiding one lifelike eye was a gauze bandage that was knotted crudely at the top of the head.

In her years as a pediatrician, Becca had often used toys or dolls to get through to an unresponsive child. Perhaps the ploy would work here.

She reached to stroke the lace of the mantilla. "Is this beautiful doll yours?" She waited a long moment before Angelica nodded. "What's her name?"

"Gabriella."

"That's a lovely name. And who gave her to you?"

"My grandmother. She had it made special for me in Buenos Aires." The pride in the small voice was touching.

Becca's fingers traced the line of the bandage. "Has Gabriella been hurt?"

There was no answer.

"You must love her very much."

She shrugged her delicate shoulders, her face impassive. "Not too much."

"Oh? And why is that?"

"Because she's going to die soon."

A chill went through Becca, not because of what Angelica had said but because of the way she had said it. Death was treated more matter-of-factly by children than by adults, but still there was always some emotion displayed—guilt, sadness, fear of pain or the unknown, uncertainty, anger. The words Angelica had uttered had been devoid of any emotion and rendered in the most unfeeling voice she'd ever heard from a child.

She could sense that Angelica was waiting for her response. Instinct told her that if she challenged the doll's impending death, she would lose any chance of building a rapport with this child. "I'm sorry to hear that," she said quietly.

For the first time, Angelica looked her full in the face. Becca realized she was being measured—by what standards she would never know.

"You were saying you feel tired," Becca repeated, deciding to test the waters. "What else?"

"Sometimes I have headaches."

Becca was surprised at the relief she felt. She had not been found wanting. "Anything else?"

"My arms and legs . . ."

Becca stopped writing. "What about them?"

"I . . . I don't know. It's hard to move them."

Becca laid the chart aside. She held up her hands. "Here," she said to Angelica, "Squeeze. Harder. Now push against them." Becca noted that there was little strength in the small hands and what there was appeared to be unequal. She drew down the blanket and repeated the pushing exercise with Angelica's feet. Again the weakness was evident and there was more strength on the right side than the left.

She pulled the blanket back up to cover her. Despite both Gottlieb and Maria Vargas trying to make light of the child's physical condition, Becca felt there was something very wrong here. It was intuitive, but right now that's all she had to go on. She reviewed the symptoms. Low-grade fever. Weakness of the arms and legs. General feeling of malaise. They could be indicative of a host of diseases — spinal cord tumor, anemia, or muscular dystrophy. Then there was leukemia and probably a few she hadn't thought of yet.

"Well, what have you found?"

Maria Vargas was back to hovering over her shoulder while the nurse obligingly pulled extra blankets from the overhead compartment of one of the closets.

"Nothing we don't already know." She ignored the young woman's "I told you so" look and walked the few feet to where the intern stood. She lowered her voice. "Kip, I'm going to need you to draw blood on her. Do a favor and pick up the alcohol swabs, syringes, and tubes. And don't get lost out there." Kip's stomach was a barometer of his behavior. He had a tendency to get very social in the hallways. Especially around feeding time.

He grinned. "I'll only be a sec."

She turned to Maria Vargas as he slipped out the door. "Tell me, Mrs. Vargas, is your stepdaughter on any medication?"

"Vitamins. Nothing more."

"Is she allergic to any food or medication?"

"Not that I know of." She stepped aside to make room for the nurse who folded the blankets then laid them at the foot of the bed.

"Has she been ill recently?"

"Angelica is rarely 'ill.' But sometimes she behaves as if she is." She hesitated, trying to phrase it delicately. "She has these spells, you see . . ."

The nurse's head snapped up. Fortunately, Becca caught her expression before Maria Vargas did. There was compassion for the child in it and a contempt for the stepmother that Becca felt sure would spill over. She was having enough problems with Maria Vargas now. The last thing she needed was for an overemotional nurse to rile the woman further. She spoke hastily. "That'll be all, Nurse . . . ?"

"Bates," she supplied. "Agatha Bates." She straightened up and withdrew, but only as far as the antique dresser, which, to Becca's annoyance, was well within earshot. She had been right about that stubborn chin.

She went on with her questioning. "When did these 'spells' begin?"

Maria Vargas hesitated. "Right after her mother died. About four years ago."

Becca paused to write it on the chart. "Has Angelica had any colds or earaches lately?"

Maria Vargas cocked her head. "Now that you mention it, she did have a cold."

"When was that?"

"About two weeks ago. Does that mean anything?"

"Not necessarily."

The door opened and Kip came in carrying a covered tray.

"What is that for?" Maria Vargas questioned.

"We have to do some tests on Angelica. A few will require our drawing blood." She turned to Angelica, who was once more staring into space. "Dr. Flanders is very practiced at it, Angelica. It won't hurt more than a bee sting's worth, I promise."

"There will be no need for that," Maria Vargas said sharply. "Dr. Gottlieb already drew blood when we were in his office this morning, something I know Señor Vargas would be unhappy about. He doesn't believe in the body being invaded. Especially with this terrible AIDS disease going around."

"That may be, but hospital procedure requires that we draw blood again now."

Taking her words as a go-ahead, Kip bent over the bed, alcohol swab in one hand, hypodermic in the other. With a back-handed slap, Maria Vargas dashed the syringe from his fingers and sent it flying against the side wall. The cap fell off, contaminating the needle, and the syringe fell to the floor. "Angelica is not a pincushion." Her voice was tinged with hysteria. "Her father would never permit this."

Becca's protest was drowned by the piercing shriek that issued from Angelica's mouth. It was followed by another more terrible than the first. The girl's body was rigid, her face reddened, the pupils of her hazel eyes dilated to twice their normal size. There was nothing weak about her hands now. They were clenched into fists, the knuckles showing bare where the skin was stretched to capacity over the small bones.

Riveted, Becca could only stare. Angelica Vargas was terrified. But of what? The prick of the needle? The sight of her own blood? Her stepmother's violence?

"Angelica, please . . ." Maria Vargas bent to her stepdaughter, murmuring soothing words that had no effect. The shrieks went on. Leaning over the child, Kip's face mirrored the helpless bewilderment they all felt. All but Agatha Bates. The nurse moved to close the door as if the earsplitting screams bouncing off the walls of the room was a normal occurrence.

Maria Vargas clutched her gold crucifix in a punishing grip. *"Por favor,"* she moaned. *"Dios mio. Por favor . . ."*

Her face worked. She suddenly looked very young and vulnerable. She held out a pleading hand to Becca: "Can't you give her something? Sedate her in some way?"

"No!" The word escaped Agatha Bates's lips before she could prevent it.

Becca stared at her in disbelief.

"Sorry," the nurse murmured.

The screams escalated a notch. Maria Vargas clapped her hands over her ears. "Please . . ."

Becca raised her voice to make herself heard. "Mrs. Vargas, I could sedate Angelica. But I prefer not to."

Agatha Bates smiled her approval. Becca tried to control her temper. The nurse was out of line. It wasn't for her to approve or disapprove a doctor's decision. Becca rarely sedated any of her young patients unless it was absolutely necessary. It depressed the nervous system and sometimes led to a paradoxical reaction which furthered the agitation. Instead, she tried to calm them, cut through their hysteria. But usually she had a clue as to what had triggered the episode.

She sensed rather than saw Agatha Bates come up behind her. "Tell the intern to take the tray out of the room," the nurse whispered.

Becca stiffened. The advice was sound. That it had been tendered was outrageous. There was nothing she hated more than a smart-ass nurse.

She touched the intern's shoulder. "Kip, Wanda is probably on her way back. Why don't you take the tray and break for lunch now."

He looked at her as if she were as crazed as the bedlam going on about him. Then her meaning penetrated and he nodded eagerly, grateful to be offered an out.

The door closed behind him with a dull thud. It took less than a second for Angelica to react. Her hands unclenched, then turned upward, revealing palms crisscrossed with red marks where her nails had dug. Her screams lessened in intensity, became cries, then whimpers, then trailed off into blessed silence. Exhaustion made the skin of her face look paper-thin. Her body went limp, her eyes fluttered shut.

Becca's gaze sought the nurse's, anticipating the triumph she would see there. But Agatha Bates was no longer where she had been. Instead, she was bent over Angelica Vargas, murmuring what sounded like endearments and blotting at the tears that rolled unchecked from beneath the child's closed lids.

Becca felt as if she'd just jogged in a twenty-mile race and lost. She was completely drained. She came to the only decision she had made in the last half-hour that satisfied her. She was going to give Agatha Bates her orders, then go on a well-deserved break.

Five

Arnold Hardinger's office suite was divided into three rooms: an outer reception room done in shades of wine and beige, his own office that overlooked the East River, and a smaller, windowless office adjacent to it that belonged to Esther Pemberton, his assistant of twenty-five years.

Fortunately, there was no one waiting for him when he returned from the conference Peabody had called. The receptionist behind the desk looked up when he approached. They were forever changing, he thought. This one was a twenty-four-year-old blonde with large breasts, a perpetually startled expression, and a sawed-off brain. She had been there just four months and he knew only her first name—Debra.

"Any calls, Debra?"

She nodded and read off a bunch of messages from the pink slips she clutched in her hand. Two were from attending physicians who were thinking of severing their connection with the hospital. One was from an executor of the Ford Foundation who would require the foreplay usually reserved for a reluctant virgin before he parted with a dollar. And the rest were unimportant.

"Oh," she ended, "your son David phoned, sir. When I told him you weren't in, he talked with Miss Pemberton instead."

"Is Pemby in?"

"No, sir." Though full-bodied and melodic on the phone, her voice never rose above a whisper when she spoke to him.

"Where is she?"

"She had to go to one of the rooms on the fourth floor, sir."

"What for?"

She looked vague. "The stepmother of one of the patients came up here asking for you, sir. Something about getting a private nurse for her daughter. She must have been someone important because Miss Pemberton went right back down with her and told me to tell you she would explain it to you later."

"Did you catch the name of the woman?"

"No, sir."

He scowled. The girl irritated him. "Don't call me sir," he lashed out. "And tell Pemby I want to see her as soon as she comes in." He didn't wait for her whispered, "Yes, sir, uh, Mr. Hardinger," before he turned on his heel, went into his office, and slammed the door.

Done in dark woods against beige linen wallpaper, his office was a model of authentic English styling and a constant reminder of his wife, Laura, who had decorated it. Once photographed for *Architectural Digest,* and called "charming" by all who viewed it, to him it was a great space waster and the most uncomfortable office he'd ever worked in.

An oversized desk sat atop a blue Bohkara rug in the middle of the spacious room. Behind it was a bulky cherry wood armoire that Laura had proudly assured him was at least one hundred-fifty years old. She had mirrored the inside and had it converted into a bar with sconces made of old gaslights that lit when the doors were opened. In front of the desk were two gold-colored wing chairs that were Laura's idea of pull-up seating. They were of a size and weight that made that feat impossible. Near the windows were a round mini conference table and four Chippendale chairs. They looked untouched because they'd never been used. The only thing he liked in the room was the blue tweed couch he'd picked for himself, when the one that had been ordered failed to arrive.

He had granted Laura permission to do his office when her tiresome quest for identity had led her, among other things, to decorating. And even after he'd undermined her newest bent by having a well-known decorator inform her that her efforts were "bourgeois and amateurish," he had allowed the room to remain. It was something to which he could point in defense when Laura accused him of sabotaging every effort she'd ever made to establish some career of her own. He felt no guilt at destroying Laura's confidence in her abilities. Identity-seeking had never been part of the silent bargain he'd made with her when they had married.

He had been attracted to Laura when he met her . . . or rather to the idea of her. She was a willowy blonde with impeccable credentials to help him in his climb upward: pure WASP, raised in Darien, a Skidmore graduate, reticent in behavior — all the things he associated with "a proper lady."

And she had done her part, he thought. Before the adverse publicity had savaged Manhattan General, the parties she had hostessed for him were filled with the who's who of business and society. Invitations had been snapped up by senators, congress members, heads of foundations, presidents of companies. Unlike him, Laura handled them with a natural ease that had won her kudos and always merited them a spread in the Sunday *Times* society pages. But partnering him was a full-time job, and he had never intended for her to do anything else.

Marrying Laura had been a trade-off, he thought, because what he couldn't foresee was that in bed, "proper" would translate into "dull." Laura had been a virgin when he married her, but that didn't excuse her shrinking from him as if he were a monster. Maybe he had a tendency to be rough when he made love to her, but that was his way. He was used to taking what he wanted how he wanted it, and he wasn't about to make any changes to suit her. Why couldn't she see that a little pain mixed with the pleasure only heightened the act? Her constant yakking about understanding and patience was a bore. It wasn't guidance he sought but a woman with her legs spread in enjoyment, not the resignation of a lip-biting plaster saint.

If through the years he came less and less to her bed, she had only herself to blame, he thought. He suspected she knew of the affairs he'd had, but she chose not to discuss it. Finally dissuaded from any career moves, she filled in the time with the charities and innocuous causes that he approved of because they kept her mingling in the right circles. If she went about it like a robot, that wasn't his concern. Nor was her self-contempt at the life she led, in her words, "a lot of effort yielding little of consequence."

He had never looked to Laura to yield anything of consequence. The only worthwhile thing she had ever produced was their son David, and it had always seemed a miracle to him that anything living had been able to thrive in that passionless body of hers.

A warmth filled him as he glanced at the photo on his desk of David and himself, arms entwined, faces smiling with carefree affection. It had been taken aboard Vargas's yacht, *The Pandora*, on an impromptu fishing trip to the Bahamas when David was twelve. The trust between them had been absolute then and for a long time to come. David had allowed himself to be guided and molded by him, never questioning toward what end. There hadn't been any need to coerce David into medicine. He'd expressed the desire to become a doctor after the first time he was given a tour of Manhattan General when he was seven. He'd confided later that he saw the hospital as an empire with his father its king.

He never dreamed he was being groomed to succeed that king.

Hardinger skirted his desk now and sat down heavily in the oversized black leather chair with the curved walnut armrests. To the right of it was his "wall of fame"—a photo of himself and Jose Vargas at a White House benefit for retarded children, two honorary doctorates from prestigious universities, and several citations for his contribution of time and effort to foster various breakthroughs in radiation treatment and infertility studies. It was a heritage of achievement and respectability. One he had never received from his bricklayer-turned-contractor father. One he had intended for David to follow when he came of age. But the best laid plans . . .

He had made only one mistake with David, but it had been a costly one. He had always kept in mind that his son hadn't had his tough upbringing. Like his mother, whose coloring he had inherited, David was malleable, easily swayed. He remembered when at thirteen David's interest had turned to research. The boy had suddenly seen himself as another Pasteur or Ehrlich, giving of himself to humanity in an effort to better the world. Hardinger hadn't said a word to dissuade him. But neither had he shown him through the magnificent research facilities available at Manhattan General.

Choosing carefully, he had taken David to see a young researcher of genetic tissue, living on a small grant in a crumbling house in New Paltz, surrounded by cages of rodents, which he knew David was squeamish about. The house had smelled of rat droppings and mildew and poverty and failure. Hardinger had purposely lingered all afternoon until he was certain that David's disillusionment had effectively eroded this newfound ambition. By the time they left, David was back on track, and the subject of research was never brought up again.

From then on, he'd followed his instinct to keep his son at his side until his plans were a *fait accompli*. But he had gone against that instinct when he had allowed David to talk him into taking his surgical residency at Boston Memorial.

David had argued convincingly. He had stressed the down side of nepotism for both his father and himself. He had talked of the need to "flex his wings," to be given the chance to be "his own man." Certain that he could reel David back in after his two-year residency was up and fearing a rift between them if he stayed obstinate, Hardinger had given in. He had lived to regret it.

He could peg to the day when David had begun to pull away from him. When the closeness between them had started to disintegrate. When the trust had turned to wariness and the conversations between them became fencing matches with neither of them coming out a winner. It started from the moment that David became involved with Becca Landau at Boston Memorial, and it caused a rift between himself and David for which he would never forgive her.

The ease between them disappeared, and despite constant urging, David rarely came home. Instead of acquiescing as he always had, he now weighed every piece of advice carefully. Misunderstandings and disagreements became rampant. It was as if they no longer spoke the same language. In a matter of months, David went from being positive to suddenly being "unsure" of his plans to come to Manhattan General after his two-year residency. In every conversation, Becca's name was on his lips, and to his father's alarm, he spoke of her as if she might have a permanent place in his life.

Thoroughly aroused, Hardinger had the young intern investigated. What he learned about her appalled him. Daughter to the eminent plastic surgeon, Dr. Joshua Landau, Becca Landau was a maverick . . . a cause follower. She had marched for black rights and women's rights and been arrested in a riot. She was a throwback to the book-burning, change-the-world firebrands that had taken over City College just before he got there, made themselves legend, then later blended into society and were never heard from again. Granted there was enough excitement about a woman like that to generate a hell of a love affair. But beyond that . . . unthinkable! A marriage like that could ruin all his plans for David.

He was debating whether to go up to Boston Memorial and have it out with David or to ignore the affair and hope it would burn itself out, when Fate intervened to make David beholden to him in a way neither of them could have predicted.

In the wake of an appendectomy, a child under Becca and David's care had suddenly soured and died, and Boston Memorial had been slapped with a malpractice suit. When the questioning began, working behind the scenes and using all his ingenuity, Hardinger had managed to extricate David. But in the endless inquiries that followed, Becca Landau's behavior had come under scrutiny, and a citation of negligence was entered against her record. It effectively stymied the young intern's career, and Hardinger learned to his delight that it had caused a falling out between her and David as well.

In the months that followed, despite overtures on his part, he scarcely heard from David. Then one rainy evening in September, he was sitting in the library of his town house reading the *Wall Street Journal* when he received a phone call from him.

"Dad. Is that you?"

Hardinger's hand tightened on the phone. "David?"

"Yes."

There was an awkward silence.

"Is something wrong, son?"

"No . . . Yes. I have to talk to you. Could you meet with me tomorrow if I flew down?"

"Of course. Come to the house at —"

"No," he said tersely. "I'd rather we met at the hospital."

Hardinger didn't know which was more hurtful, David's words or his tone. He wanted to ask why the need for the impersonal surroundings. Did David require a buffer to talk to him now? The question hovered on his lips, but he never asked it. Always upbeat and filled with a vibrancy that gave people a lift when they talked with him, David's voice sounded so beaten and subdued now that he thought it wise to simply agree.

"Anything you'd like," he'd replied. "Would two in my office be good?"

"That'll be fine." The phone clicked off.

Before his son arrived at his office the following day, Hardinger fortified himself by smoking two Marlboro Hundreds and downing a jigger of Chivas Regal on the rocks. He was glad that he had when he saw David.

Usually fastidious, there was a carelessness about David's dress—the tie slung low about his neck, the button missing from his tweed jacket, the pleated slacks in need of pressing—small things, but they spoke of his distraction and pain more eloquently than words.

At his father's expression, he held up a hand in warning. "Don't say it! I know damn well what I look like!"

As he came forward, Hardinger inspected him more closely. Worn long, his wavy blond hair was in need of cutting. He had lost weight, and his clothes hung scarecrowlike on his lean body. There were circles under the blue eyes so like Hardinger's own, and his face was haggard.

"David . . ." he murmured, at a loss.

Plopping down in one of the wing chairs, David waved his father's attempt at solicitousness aside. His manner was cool and businesslike, but his voice shook. "I want to talk to you about Becca Landau."

Hardinger hid his surprise. Since the onset of the affair, his son had never talked openly to him about the girl. "All right," he said evenly.

David ran a hand through his straggly blond hair. Normally glib, it was obvious that he was having difficulty in putting words together. To give him time, Hardinger swiveled around in his chair and opened the doors to the armoire that doubled as a bar. He poured two scotches and handed one to his son.

David took a long gulp, set the glass on the desk, and nodded his thanks. His voice was a shade steadier when he spoke. "Dad, we've never really talked about what happened at Boston Memorial."

Hardinger shrugged. "Spilt milk. Why bring it up now?"

"Because I feel guilty about it. Something you wouldn't understand."

"No recriminations, David . . . please! Just remember that nothing that happened was your fault."

"I keep telling myself that."

"Then why rehash it?"

David set his glass on the desk with a force indicative of the violence contained in him. "Because, dammit, I walked away clean, and Becca . . . well, I feel responsible for her."

"David, I've told you. There's no reason—"

David rose swiftly, threw his hands in the air, and began to pace. His body held the tension of a taut wire. "I know . . . I know what you've told me. But you weren't there for the aftermath, and you can't see what it's done to Becca." He cut his father's next words off, and his voice held a savagery that made it tremble. "For chrissake, it's enough that you tell me what to do. Don't tell me what to feel." He took a few deep breaths, calmed somewhat, and let the expression on his face offer an apology.

He sat down in the chair again. His lean fingers massaged its carved mahogany arms with jerky random movements. His face took on a brooding expression. "I've talked Becca into transferring out of Boston Memorial. Her career there is finished, and the speculation about her just doesn't end. There's no point in her staying." He said that last as if he was trying to convince himself more than his father. "At first she didn't want to go. She said it would look as if she were running away. Then when she finally agreed, it turned out to be not as simple as I thought. In the last two months, she's been refused by six hospitals. And with the record she's got now, I'm afraid she's going to be refused by the next six."

"And . . . ?" he encouraged when David paused. He was aware of his hypocrisy in prompting an answer. He couldn't care less if Becca Landau never worked another day in her life.

"I don't want that to happen to her. It'll break her. She's a fine pediatrician. One of the best."

He smiled. "You wouldn't happen to be prejudiced?"

"No, I'm not. It has nothing to do with what I feel for her personally. I've worked with her. And she's good." David rubbed the arms of the chair until the burnished wood shone from the moisture of his hands.

Hardinger came around his desk, perched on its edge, and sipped the scotch. "David, why have you come to me?"

He fidgeted in his seat and spoke reluctantly. "Because I thought you might have enough influence with one of these hospitals to persuade them to overlook her record." He waited. When his father didn't answer, he gestured morosely. "Look, it was a lousy idea. I shouldn't have come." He rose from the chair.

Hardinger's lack of response wasn't due to disinterest. His mind was working at breakneck speed. It was possible that he had just been given the means to retrieve his hold over David's future.

"Sit down!" he ordered as David made a move to leave. He took a sip of scotch while he waited for David to comply. "I've got a proposition for you. You want Becca Landau to transfer out of Boston Memorial and be accepted by a reputable hospital. I can't answer for what influence I have elsewhere, but I can guarantee that if she submits an application to Manhattan General, she'll get in."

A look of hope crossed David's face. "You would do that for her?"

"No, David. Not for her. I spoke of a proposition. That usually involves a give-and-take, an exchange. Now, I've stated what it is that I'm willing to offer. Whether it becomes a done deal depends on what you're willing to give in return."

David looked bewildered. "What is it you want?"

"You. Your promise that you'll come to Manhattan General when your residency is up."

Up until now, Hardinger hadn't known whether or not David planned to return to Manhattan General. By his reaction it became obvious that he never intended to. Becca Landau had done her work well.

David held himself very still. "Your terms are steep."

"So is what you're asking. I'm putting myself out on a limb by vouching for an intern with Landau's record." He shrugged. "It's up to you. If you want to put that conscience of yours to rest, then put your money where your mouth is." His eyes narrowed speculatively. "Do we have a deal?"

There was a long pause, then David exhaled on a sigh. "We do." He stood up. "I'll trust you to put me in a slot we can both live with."

Hardinger held out his hand. He smiled as David clasped it. He had his son back. He couldn't believe how simple it had been. He knew there were drawbacks to the arrangement. David had agreed to enter Manhattan General. But there was nothing stopping him from leaving shortly thereafter. Yet somehow, he didn't doubt that once David was at Manhattan General, he would stay. David may have been blessed with his mother's looks, but through the years it had become evident that he'd inherited his father's ambition. Given a taste of power, he would crave more, and Hardinger intended to whet his son's appetite to the fullest.

"One thing, Dad. I don't want Becca to know about this."

Hardinger held back a laugh. No way would he ever tell Becca Landau anything that might make David heroic in her eyes. He was relying on time, distance, and his own ingenuity to finish this star-crossed affair. The girl was a menace, an unwanted element. But from now on she would be on his turf, where he had a reputation for eliminating unwanted elements. Under no circumstance would he allow her to be here when David returned to Manhattan General.

"You can count on me, son," he'd said.

Hardinger rose from his chair now. He recalled the warmth that he'd felt when they'd walked arm in arm to the door, a semblance of trust between them once again. That had been almost two years ago. In that time as he'd hoped, David's infatuation for Becca Landau seemed to have died from lack of sustenance.

Surprisingly, it was Becca who had fostered the break. After arriving at Manhattan General, she had refused to answer David's letters and phone calls. At first he had become frantic, blaming his father for trying to put a wedge between them. When he had realized it was strictly Becca's doing, he had initially made excuses for it, then grudgingly accepted it, then finally put it behind him. In the last six months, he had seemed much his old self, and Hardinger had it on good authority that as in the past, his son's bed was empty of a female only on rare occasions.

The only thing he hadn't been able to work out yet was how to get rid of Becca Landau. Unfortunately, the girl had turned out to be one of the best pedes on the floor, loyal to the hospital and well-respected. With the crisis that Judge Ryker's crusade had precipitated, retaining doctors had become a priority, and unless he could find a way for Becca Landau to give him just cause, he couldn't summarily remove her. But he wasn't going to allow that to dampen his elation. He'd find a way. He always did.

Six

At two o'clock that afternoon, Becca headed for Helen Walters's office. She was determined to deal with the problem of Agatha Bates. Coping with the personalities in the Vargas case was difficult enough as it was. To keep a nurse who overstepped her authority and had the control of a two-year-old would be putting herself through unnecessary stress.

In the past few hours she had changed the burn dressings on a child-abuse victim and checked to see that the low dose of Atavan she had given the cardiac arrest patient had taken effect. Then she had called Gottlieb, described what had happened in Angelica's room, and asked him to get permission from the girl's stepmother to have blood drawn. Finally, she had tackled the anorexic in 492 West, who at eighty pounds resembled a concentration camp victim and refused to eat no matter what coercion was used. In the end, it had taken Kip, Wanda, and herself to subdue the kicking, clawing thirteen-year-old, who kept screaming, "Lemmee go, muthahfuckahs," with all the power in her young lungs. They had clapped her into restraints and instituted force-feeding.

And in between it all, Angelica Vargas had never left her thoughts.

She had no clue yet as to what was physically wrong with the girl. But it was obvious there was an emotional problem there, too. Gottlieb had referred to her irrational behavior as "tantrums." Maria Vargas had called them "spells." Becca had her own theory: hysteria. Based on some underlying fear or trauma, whether real or imagined, she couldn't tell.

There were questions that had been raised in her mind. Angelica's erratic behavior had started at the time of her mother's death. How had her mother died? And what had Angelica's reaction been at the time? Becca remembered the doll staring with its unbandaged hazel eye, an inanimate duplicate of Angelica. Did the child identify with her clone? Was it her own demise Angelica was foretelling when she tolled the death knell for her doll in that passive, uncaring voice?

The questions went round and round in her head, relieved only when she concentrated on the other aspect of the case that was bothering her — her personal involvement with the child. Given the circumstances of her own background, a beleaguered Manhattan General, and the prominence of Angelica's family, it went beyond imprudence. But she couldn't seem to help herself. Why did she feel so linked to the girl? Was it some kind of dormant maternal instinct that was rearing its head? After all, she *was* getting up there, reaching an age where she might unconsciously be longing for "the patter of little feet" . . . or so her mother kept telling her.

A faint smile curved her lips. What satisfaction her mother and father would get if they knew such a thing had even crossed her mind. Her mother, because like most mothers, no matter her pride in what her daughter had accomplished, she wanted to see her married. Her father, because it would justify his contempt for the specialty she had chosen. "Pediatricians are either gays or love-starved women bent on sublimating their desire to nurture," he had jabbed at her in that "father knows best" tone that always got to her — as if the specialty he had chosen, plastic surgery, was the loftiest profession of all.

The battle between them had been going on for as long as she could remember. When she was little, she had thought it was her fault, because she couldn't conform to what he insisted was "proper behavior." But as she grew older and began to understand more, she changed her mind.

The only son of a lab technician and a governess who had fled from Hungary just before Hitler's invasion, Joshua Landau's goal had been to become a pillar of Boston society. His first step was to marry the daughter of the local alderman, a soft-spoken, impeccably dressed woman who could vie with Emily Post on

59

the proper placement of the wine glass on the table. Although Becca loved her dearly, she could never remember her mother raising her voice or contradicting her father about a single thing he said.

When Becca was born, Joshua Landau had fully expected her to be created in her mother's image. He came to a rude awakening when Becca was six and he was called to school because she had flattened the local bully who had picked on a boy half his size. Who the bully was had made no difference to Becca. That he was a senator's son made all the difference to her father.

From that moment on, Joshua Landau took an active role in raising his only child. Becca remembered her childhood and adolescence as a series of failures. What she thought of as "peer" dressing, he saw as flamboyance. The boys she dated were never from good enough families. And the causes she championed were a threat to his very being. It was a struggle for identity that she somehow survived, but not without its leaving her with a scarred sense of self-worth and a belligerence that didn't always serve her well.

She forced all thoughts of her father aside now as she reached the nurse's station. Thinking of him never failed to rile her, and she would do better in her dealings with the head nurse if she was calm. Helen Walters was known to be hard on the nurses she supervised, but let anyone else attack them and she would rise in their defense like a tigress with her cubs.

The head nurse was in her office with the door closed. It opened just as Becca lifted her hand to knock.

Framed in the doorway, Helen's warm smile made her flat-nosed face seem almost pretty. "Dr. Landau. You must have read my mind."

The formal greeting surprised Becca. She and Helen had been on a first-name basis for over a year now — ever since Helen had kept a successful twelve-hour vigil over one of Becca's patients, a sickle cell anemia baby in the PICU that Becca had been sure wouldn't pull through the night.

Helen stepped across the threshold, and Becca saw the reason for the formality. The head nurse wasn't alone. The woman who followed her out looked to be in her early thirties. She was dressed in what Becca thought of as "interview clothes," a gray business suit, prissy white blouse, and gold-rimmed cameo pin at the collar. Her straight skirt hung from very lean hips.

"Dr. Landau, I'd like you to meet Dr. Carolyn Stedman, our new psychiatric consultant for the floor."

"Welcome aboard." Becca held out her hand and Carolyn Stedman shook it firmly.

She belonged in something more casual, Becca thought. And surely more colorful. She was full-breasted, with the kind of tall, rangy body that would show off best in a plaid shirt and jeans. It was a look Becca admired but had given up on. Her waist was too thin and her hips too rounded to carry it off.

"I was just telling Dr. Stedman about our problem," Helen Walters said.

Becca looked blank.

"The anorexic in 492 West," Helen said meaningfully.

"Oh. Of course."

Carolyn Stedman smiled. "Sounds like a handful."

She had a volume of wavy chestnut hair that threatened to escape from the two gold clips pinned to the top of her head. Her face was striking. High cheekbones, warm skin, and gray eyes with the kind of understanding in their depths that invited confidence.

Becca smiled back. "Well, I don't know what you call a handful. Yesterday she kicked a nurse in the stomach for taking away the Ex-Lax she somehow managed to smuggle into the hospital. And this morning she belted another one for finding the silverware she had taped to her ribs to make her appear heavier when she weighed in." The psychiatrist chuckled. "Seriously, when can I get a consult? The nurses are screaming for her to be removed to a psych ward and I can't do it without your okay."

She nodded thoughtfully. "Well, I'm taking today to meet the people I'll be working with and to get settled in my office downstairs. What about tomorrow morning at ten?"

"Done. I'll call to remind you."

Helen Walters's face held a satisfied smile. "It would be a real boost for my nurses if you could get that settled. The girl is a repeat performer, and some of my staff put in for a vacation when they heard she was on her way back in." She looked from one woman to the other. "You know, you two have something in common."

"How's that?" Becca asked.

"You're both alumni of Boston Memorial."

Carolyn Stedman raised brows that were a horizontal slash above her eyes. "Really? When did you leave there?"

"June of eighty-nine." Becca's glance was wary. Had the psychiatrist heard of her up there?

She gave no indication of it. "It must have been right before I arrived. I still go up there from time to time. I'm a consultant for their outpatient clinic. Someday, over a cup of coffee, we'll have to talk about mutual acquaintances. I'll bet we have quite a few."

Was David one of them? Becca wondered. She had no intention of asking. The quicker they got off the subject of Boston Memorial, the safer she would feel. She hesitated. "Dr. Stedman . . ."

"Call me Carolyn — please."

Becca nodded. "I know it's an imposition. Especially on your first day. But if you could possibly talk for a few minutes to a patient of mine . . ."

"Well, you understand, I couldn't tell much in a few minutes . . ."

"No. No. Of course not. I just wanted an overall impression, a trained eye — " She broke off, feeling foolish.

Carolyn Stedman placed a hand on her arm. It was oddly comforting. "What's your patient's name?"

"Angelica Vargas. She's in 401 East."

She nodded. "I can't promise, but I'll try. Right now, I have a slew of people to meet and a bunch of unpacked cartons waiting for me in my office. I hate first days, don't you?" Her grin was engaging. "Well, as the saying goes, don't put off for tomorrow . . ." She slipped her leather envelope purse beneath her arm, and with a wave of her hand and a murmured, "See you soon," she strode down the hall, her patent leather pumps clicking with every step.

Becca watched her disappear in the direction of the elevators before she turned to Helen Walters. "Helen, we've got some serious talking to do."

The head nurse glanced at her face then pushed her door open. "Come into my parlor."

Helen's "parlor" was an oversized closet crammed with two filing cabinets, one atop the other, a desk, and two battered wooden chairs. The office hadn't been part of the original floorplan. It had been created by taking a piece of the conference room the nurses used for writing up their reports and another piece from the supply room next door. Its nine-foot-high ceiling and inadequate fluorescent lighting gave it the look of an inverted vault which Helen asserted made her feel as if she had been entombed before her time. The drab beige walls were enlivened with crayoned drawings made for her by her "children," the steady stream of frightened, sickly, maimed, despairing youngsters who landed on the fourth floor and became her charges for whatever time they were there.

She sat down behind her desk and pushed a box of chocolate-covered cherries toward Becca.

Becca shook her head. "Not on an empty stomach."

"You've come to talk about Aggie Bates, haven't you?"

Becca was startled. "She was in here?"

"Nope. That isn't Aggie's style. I just took an educated guess." She reached for a cherry. "Now suppose you tell me about it."

Becca related what had taken place in 401 East that morning. She tried to stick to the facts and tell it unemotionally, but she knew that the anger she still felt crept into the monologue.

When she was finished, Helen nodded. She lifted a letter opener from the desk and balanced it between the index finger of both hands. "Becca, do you want me to talk to you honestly? Or do you want me to hand you the subservient bullshit that nurses are forced to give out with when they deal with doctors?"

Becca's eyes narrowed at her tone. "Are you trying to tell me that I was out of line in that room, not Agatha Bates?"

"Truth?"

Becca nodded.

"I think you were both out of line. Aggie overstepped, but your reaction didn't fit the crime." Her point made, she lightened up. "Look, Becca, I'll admit we've got a lot of balloon heads among our nurses. Especially among the more recent ones. But some of the older ones are damned good."

"Like Agatha Bates."

"Like Agatha Bates. Did you know she was a head nurse at Manhattan General?" She nodded at Becca's start of surprise. "Of course that was before the educational requirements became so stringent that she couldn't qualify. I've known Aggie a long time. She's a rare one. A nurse who can smell when a kid is sick. But this is her first time on the floor after being away for ten years, so if she's not in perfect sync . . ."

She turned her hands palm up in a pleading gesture. "Becca, I need your help here. For whatever her reasons, Aggie's having a rough time getting back in harness. Right now what she needs is support, not condemnation. If I take her off the Vargas case . . ." Her shrug finished the sentence for her.

Becca sighed. "You want me to keep working with her."

"For a little while. Then if you still don't make it together, I'll pull her off."

"Fair enough."

Becca stood up. Talking of Agatha Bates had brought Maria Vargas to mind again. She wondered whether Gottlieb had reached her yet. After discussing the diagnosis possibilities with him, she and Gottlieb had decided that aside from the routine urinalysis with micro to look for bacteria, they would order a spinal tap to check for a spinal cord tumor or Guillain-Barré Syndrome. But most importantly, they needed a CBC, a complete blood count, which would either rule in or eliminate the possibility of leukemia or anemia. And for that they needed Maria Vargas's permission. Her face tightened as she dwelt on the obstinacy of the woman.

Helen read her expression correctly. "Case got you strung out?"

She nodded. "The case in general. The stepmama in particular." She was relieved to be able to talk about it. "The woman treats the child as if she'll break and talks to me as if I was one of her servants. I could ignore both if she'd stop blocking my efforts to help Angelica. And she keeps hanging this sword over my head—Arnold Hardinger," she supplied in answer to Helen's unspoken question. "Seems he's a close friend of the

Vargases."

At the mention of Hardinger's name, Helen reacted as if stung. "Don't even say that bastard's name around me." She bolted from her chair, grabbed a paper from the top of her desk, came around it, and shoved the paper beneath Becca's nose. "You know what this is?"

Startled, Becca shook her head.

"The newest order from Herr Hardinger. To make up for all the unfilled beds on the other floors, he's decreed that if there's a patient overflow in Pediatrics, which there always is, we're to put the kids into the solariums and playrooms. You know how treacherous that is?" She ticked her fears off on her fingers. "No suction apparatus if a kid starts to choke. No call bell — we have to give the kid a hand one that we can't hear half the time. No oxygen available quickly." She shook her head in disgust. "And what do we do to give the kids some recreation? Wheel them out onto the parapet? There are spaces between that stone railing that a small kid could fit through. We'd have to watch them like hawks."

She threw up her hands in disgust, put an arm about Becca's shoulder, then walked her to the door. "Ah, hell! What can you expect from a former V.P. of marketing? Hardinger doesn't think patient care. He thinks bottom line."

Becca thought back to the night David had given her a detailed account of what his father did. She had been impressed. Up to then she hadn't realized the vast responsibility entailed in running a hospital.

She tried to give that over to the head nurse now. "Look Helen, I'm not trying to defend Hardinger. But he does have to cope with the larger picture here. We have a financial crisis at Manhattan General, and it isn't just the pediatric floor he has to be concerned with. It's the whole hospital."

"Then let him take care of it," Helen lashed out. "Every floor in the old wing has water pipes bursting in the ceilings and plaster falling on patients' heads. And because he's cut back on cleaning services, there's dirt all over the place and the garbage stinks from being left too long in stairwells." She wrinkled her nose as if she was smelling it now. "In my book, Hardinger is a self-centered hypocrite. The only thing that bastard knows how to do is take care of his own."

"Meaning what?"

"Meaning we've got a wage freeze on, but old Bottom-Line has managed to thaw it out long enough to get his son in here as assistant chief of Surgery. The news just came down the pipeline. And I've got to tell you, the job comes with pretty big bucks."

A sudden movement of Becca's caused the nurse to glance at her. She frowned and instinctively cupped Becca's elbow to support her. "Are you okay? You look as if you're going to keel over."

"Not enough fuel in the furnace. I didn't get a chance to eat." It was scarcely more than a whisper.

Becca's heart was palpitating as if in arrhythmia. David coming here? It couldn't be! She felt as if the narrow room was closing in on her. She was conscious of Helen's shrewd eyes on her. She wanted to run and hide. Away from Helen. Away from herself. She had taken such pains to create a cocooned world where everything but her work had been kept at bay. It had given her an illusion of safety, and she had wrapped that illusion about her like a protective cloak. Now the past was encroaching on the present and the cloak lay in shreds about her. She felt naked, vulnerable.

With some hastily murmured words to Helen, she opened the door and fled the room.

Seven

Between the broom closet and the kitchen was "The Wreck Room," a former storage room the staff had converted for emergency purposes. One wall was lined with shelves holding bottles of medicinals, a first-aid kit, a stack of blankets, a rusted hot plate, a coil for making hot water, two flowered mugs, and packets of Sanka and herbal Red Zinger tea.

On the lumpy cot wedged crosswise beneath the high awning window, Becca lay curled under a blanket in the fetal position. The agitation she felt had chilled her body and made her hands clammy. She thought of making herself a hot drink, but chances were she'd never be able to keep it down. Her stomach felt as if someone had blown a hole in it.

Why was David coming here? It was something he had sworn he would never do. She remembered so clearly the night they had talked about it. It was on a weekend in January and it was storming outside, and they had stolen two precious hours from the hospital and raced to his apartment a convenient two blocks away. They arrived dripping and breathless, and David took forever to turn the key in the lock, but none of it seemed to matter in the wake of the urgency that had set up this clamoring need to be together after a week of forced abstinence.

They didn't bother with the lights. They murmured and touched and frantically clutched at clothing, inching toward the huge bed in the corner of the oversized studio where David bent her backward and pressed her down into the enveloping softness, covering her lips and her body with his. His hands roamed her breasts and her hips while his whispered words attacked her reticence, the "seventh veil" he insisted she shed in their lovemaking, goading her with unspeakable erotic suggestions, using his talented surgeon's fingers and his glib tongue to breach the barrier of her inhibitions until she gave herself up to him completely.

At the end of an hour, the striped sheets and down comforter were crumpled and damp, and gave off that musky odor of perspiration and satiation that Becca knew she would forever associate with the ultimate in contentment. She attempted to extricate her head from where it lay pillowed by his chest, then realized that strands of her hair were caught under his shoulder.

"I'm sore," she murmured.

Still inside her, the laughing rumble in his chest acknowledged his compliance as he rolled to release her. "Take two aspirins and call me in the morning," he quipped, then feinted in mock fear as she threatened him with a clenched fist.

"Sorry if I overdid," he said.

"Liar!"

He had the grace to grin.

It always surprised her that though he was incredibly attractive to women, David couldn't get enough reassurance. He was pleased as a teenager at her admission of soreness because it gave evidence of his staying power. A prowess half the female staff at Boston Memorial could attest to, Becca thought ruefully. But that was before she had come into his life.

She had been confused about love until she met David. Aside from a few awkward attempts in adolescence, there had been one short-term passionate affair in college and one long-term passionate affair in med school that for the sake of justifying her active gonads she had called love. But in actuality, they had been extended one-night stands, with no real desire on her part to get to know either one of the men beyond the confines of the bed. With David the involvement had been total. Especially at the beginning. They couldn't get enough of being together, relishing common thoughts, making less of those that weren't, sometimes impacting so greatly one on the other that it was as if they were joined by a physical bond as well as an emotional one.

Digging his heels into the mattress for leverage now, David

scooted backward on the bed, then propped himself against the black lacquer headboard in the shape of a half-moon. Hoisting her up by the elbows, he cradled her in his arms. Her bare legs entwined with his, and he idly stroked her breasts while they talked of his future, both of them knowing they would make love again and luxuriating in the knowledge that they had another hour in which to do it.

"But why wouldn't you seek a career at Manhattan General?" she had asked. "With your father so all-powerful there, wouldn't it be the logical thing to do?"

His features darkened, and she was sorry she had probed it. "You don't understand," he said.

Resentment pricked her like a burr.

"What's wrong?"

"You use those words too often with me."

His fingers stilled. "What's that supposed to mean?"

"You make me feel like my brain doesn't measure up to yours."

His face creased in annoyance. "Christ, Becca. I love you. But you're so oversensitive to everything I say and do that you make it damned hard for me to be around you."

She was silent but not remorseful. She wasn't being oversensitive. David's constant reference to her "not understanding," whether it was a medical concept or a financial deal or a surgical technique she couldn't grasp, had become a subtle form of contempt that struck at the roots of her confidence. She wanted to call him on it, force the issue and make him admit it, but she felt too vulnerable to instigate a confrontation that might cause a rift between them. She was so in love with him and so afraid it wouldn't last. Yet she was in the right. She had to stand up for herself, say something more.

His hand had ceased its stroking. It hovered over her breast like a tease. She was conscious that her desire for him was awakening. She opened her mouth to defend her position, but no words came out. She felt the familiar yearning start low in the pit of her stomach. Her body involuntarily arched upward. He made no move to touch her. She knew it was deliberate. He was waiting for her to acknowledge that he was right. Hating herself, she backed down.

"Tell me what it is I don't understand," she said.

He disentangled himself from her. The loss of him was a wrench. He rose from the bed and padded across the plush carpeting to the mirrored bar.

The apartment was an oversized studio in a doormanned high-rise building. Done in low-slung leather couches and expensive art deco furniture that she suspected his father had footed the bill for, it had a decorator's impersonal touch. David switched on a cubed wall sconce, mixed himself a double martini, then turned to face her.

He was six feet one with broad shoulders, lean hips, and the sleek musculature that came of working out unfailingly every morning at the hospital rehab center. He had a high forehead, intense blue eyes, and a straight nose that had been broken in childhood and had healed with a small scar across the bridge. His blond hair was wavy. Worn low at the nape of his neck it was still moist from the downpour outside.

He worried his lower lip with his thumb, a habit he had when agitated. His face was set in the unhappy brooding lines it always took on when he spoke of his father. "You have to understand, Becca. Until the day I came to Boston Memorial, I was like a bird who'd had its wings clipped, and I didn't even know it. I parroted what my father said and thought and did. I made his concerns my concerns and let his ambitions shape my future. He chose my curriculum. He chose my clothes. He even chose my women." His mouth twisted. "Subtly, of course, but his guiding hand was always there." He took a long gulp of his drink.

It had been something Becca could identify with. Her household had also been male dominated. But either her father had lacked the stature of an Arnold Hardinger or she had been more of a maverick than David, because there had never been any question of Joshua Landau bending her to his will.

"You could have told him no," she said.

His short laugh held no mirth. "You don't tell my father no. The man is a steamroller. That's why he's gotten where he is." He held his glass up to the light and contemplated the facets in it. "You know, you'd think that kind of thing would turn people off, make them run from him. But it doesn't. Look at my mother. I watched him squash her until she was nonexistent, and still she stayed with him. Not because she was afraid of him, but because he gave off a sense of omnipotence, of being bigger than life." His voice lowered and his shoulders sagged. He looked diminished, as if in the telling he had become less in his own eyes. "It's a matter of identity, you see. If you don't have one of your own, you figure that if you stay close enough, some of his will rub off on you. But it doesn't work that way, does it?"

There was an ache inside her that grew to intolerable proportions. His hurt had become her hurt. She couldn't stand his humility or his acceptance of what should never have been accepted. "Don't talk like that!" she said fiercely. "You *do* have an identity of your own!"

"Up here with you, I do."

He set the fragile-stemmed goblet on the bar and crossed to the bed. She pulled him down beside her and put her cheek next to his. She could feel the vein beating furiously in his temple.

"Don't ever leave me," he whispered.

"Fat chance."

"Swear it to me."

"I swear I'll never leave you."

He held her tight to him for a long moment, then he raised his head and kissed her lightly. She breathed a sigh of relief. There was no trace of the storm that had shaken him a moment ago. His expression was calm, his shoulders had straightened, and he was once more the splendid young god she had fallen in love with.

"Look," he said. "Let's not talk about it anymore. I cut away from him, and I'm going to stay away from him until I feel so secure about myself that it won't matter anymore if I'm around him."

She had wanted to ask him how he would know when that was, but his blue eyes had hooded over with that telling misty film that always preceded his reaching for her. The thinking had blurred and become fuzzy before it ground to a complete halt as she opened her arms to him in willing compliance.

Why couldn't it have stayed the way it was? she agonized, recalling the fierceness of the lovemaking that had followed.

The impassioned regret faded under the harsh light of reality. There was no chance that it could have continued the way it was. They were world's apart on so many issues. Still, they might have risen above their differences if David could have agreed to disagree. But David would never have been content with that. He didn't want a relationship. He wanted ownership—of her mind as well as her body. And God help her, the attraction to him had been so great that she had given it to him . . . until that fatal incident at Boston Memorial which had scarred her reputation but shocked her into an awareness of how much of herself she had relinquished to David.

She hadn't wanted to transfer from the hospital afterward, but she was weary and she was down, and she needed David to understand and support her. Instead, he had talked of "tilting at windmills," and "positive career moves," and it had been easier to acquiesce than to do battle. It was only later that she realized that giving in to David had become a pattern with her. In retrospect, she saw the full extent of her betrayal of herself and found it intolerable to live with.

Feeling steadier now, she kicked the blanket from her legs and reached for the sandals she had tucked on a shelf nearby. She buckled them on and slid from the cot.

David had been an obsession with her, an addiction. And there were only two ways to cope with an addiction. One either weaned oneself from it or one went cold turkey. She had chosen the latter. She wasn't particularly proud of the way she had handled their parting, but she hadn't been capable of more at the time. There had been no confrontations with David. No discussions or even subtle hints. When she arrived at Manhattan General, she had simply cut him off, tearing up his letters and refusing to answer his phone calls. She had counted on his pride to do the rest.

Her mouth felt dry. She crossed to the water cooler in the corner and poured a cold drink into a paper cup. What she hadn't counted on was her own hurt when it worked and the painful yearnings jogged by memories too vivid to be shut out. As an antidote she had engaged in two affairs after she transferred to Manhattan General. They had been early on and short-lived. She had unconsciously sought facsimiles who looked like David or talked like David or laughed like David, and the results had been disastrous. Her dedication to her work was a boon, but when she returned to her apartment at night, the empty bed mocked her with its sanitary smell and unrumpled feel, and the erotic dreams, from which she woke restless and unfulfilled, hollowed her eyes and left her irritable. Her decision to exile herself from David slowly eroded until the strength to remain steadfast stemmed from nothing more than the geographical separation between them.

A separation that would no longer exist.

But why was she so fearful? She wasn't the same wide-eyed intern who had fallen under the spell of the star resident. She drank the cold water in a single gulp, crushed the cup between her fingers, and tossed it into the basket nearby.

In the two years she'd been at Manhattan General, she had regained her confidence and achieved a sense of self of which she was proud. Whether she failed or excelled, the decisions that brought her to it were her own. Whatever David's reason for coming here, whatever their reaction to each other, she promised herself that she was going to keep that sense of self intact.

For her own salvation, she had to.

Eight

From the Rehabilitation Center on the lower level where he had just finished supervising the treatment of a stroke patient, Dr. Garfield Nathan Gottlieb took the elevator back to the pediatric floor of the hospital. He had wrestled with himself for over an hour before giving in to the compulsion to revisit Angelica Vargas. He needed her stepmother's permission to draw blood on the girl, but chances were he could have gotten that by phone. What was pulling him back to 401 East was the need to find out if Angelica's nurse could possibly be Aggie Bates. He didn't hold out much hope. He had been looking for Aggie for such a long time. It was inconceivable that she would turn up here where they'd first met with no warning, no word to him. It was probably a blind alley like all the others had been. Still . . .

The elevator door clanged open on the fourth floor, and he stepped out into the noisy bustling melee that had once been his entire world. It was hard to believe that there was a time when his work had been the most satisfying thing he could conceive of. When he'd first come to Manhattan General, he had lived through his patients. There were never enough hours in the day. He was at the hospital from six a.m. until midnight, and could have stayed on longer because he loved what he was doing—and because it gave him a way to avoid his wife.

His marriage to Vicky had been a mistake. He had come from poor folk in the Bronx, she from poorer folk in Virginia where he had gone to med school. The only thing they had in common was a craving for money. He couldn't remember anymore why he'd married her. Maybe it was because Virginia was a far cry from New York and he was lonely. Maybe it was because Vicky didn't put out when every other Southern belle he met did. Maybe being a Jew, he was proud to have snared the prettiest *shiksa* in town. In the end, the reason didn't matter much. Three years and two children later, it was over.

He had asked Vicky for a divorce when he started as a resident at Manhattan General. She had laughed at him. She had told him that she had never loved him. She had married him for his potential, and now that he was about to realize it, she had no intention of letting him go. He was the goose that was going to lay the golden egg for her, and if and when he could settle a fat sum on her, she would be only too happy to give him a divorce.

From then on he'd embroiled himself in his work. His dedication had brought him the highest praise. It had also brought him Agatha Bates. Aggie was trim and blond with a talent for nursing unequaled by anyone there. He hadn't sought her out because she attracted him above all other women. He'd gone after her because he was horny. He'd worked with her on a few cases before she became head nurse. She had a great body, and there was no marriage band on her finger to complicate things. She could have been nameless and faceless for all he cared. She was there to serve a purpose, just as the others had been since he stopped bedding down with Vicky the year before.

In retrospect, he wondered why it had taken him so long to realize that he loved her. Perhaps it was because she'd been so insistent at first that the relationship be platonic.

"I don't do drugs" she'd said. "And I don't break up married homes. Especially those with kids in them. If once in a while you want to split a hamburger and fries—"

"While some other guy laps up the gravy?"

"That's none of your business."

He'd accepted her terms, sure that sooner or later she would break down. When she finally did, the guilt she felt manifested itself in the limited meetings she would allow. They saw each other no more than twice a week and only on weekdays. She was adamant about the weekend belonging to the families. His to his wife and kids, hers to her sick mother in Connecticut.

He loved Aggie's body. He loved her mind. Most of all, he loved her honesty. Aggie had a no-nonsense mouth that had more than once impaled him on the horns of truth and left him there squirming.

"I'm not really dedicated," he'd explained to her one evening over a cup of coffee at Freddie's, a beat-up restaurant and bar. "The only patients I give to so unstintingly are the ones with checking accounts that have never heard the word *overdrawn*. I'm not giving out of the kindness of my heart. I'm building a cushy client roster for when I leave here."

"Bullshit," she'd said in her blunt way. "That may be the end result of what you're doing, but it's not the reason you're doing it. I've watched you. You work the way you do because you empathize so deeply with your patients that you can't do any less. If all you were after was the money, you wouldn't sit up all night with a dying derelict or put in the extra hours you do at the cancer research lab. But instead of being proud of it as you should be, you act as if it's a failing on your part. The only time you seem pleased with yourself is when you're scoring points toward that almighty buck you worship. What do you expect to buy with it in the end?"

"My freedom."

"At what cost? If money becomes your God in this business, you won't be the same kind of doctor," she'd warned. "You'll find yourself making decisions for the good of your pocketbook, not your patients. And you won't like yourself for it."

How well she had known him, he thought. Better than he had known himself.

"Hi, Dr. Gottlieb."

The voice jarred him from his reverie. He realized that he was standing in the doorway of 401 East. The orderly talking to him from inside was emptying the trash from the wastebaskets into a green plastic bag. Gottlieb looked past him and hid his disappointment. Aside from Angelica who was sleeping, there was no one else in the room.

He crossed the threshold and spoke softly. "Hello, Julio. Is the nurse around?"

He shrugged. "I ain't seen 'er." He was dark haired and swarthy with a toothy white smile and a pencil-thin mustache.

"What about Mrs. Vargas?"

"The kid's mother?"

He nodded.

"I heard her talkin' on the phone. She said she was goin' down for a cup of coffee. Anything I can do for ya, Doc?"

Gottlieb shook his head.

Julio hauled the plastic bag to his shoulder, flipped a hand in farewell, and ambled toward the door with a rocking gait.

Gottlieb hurried to the bed and lifted the chart from the rail. He caught his breath. There in the upper right-hand corner, in the round scrawl that he would know anywhere, was the signature "Agatha Bates."

He turned and walked to the window. His legs felt shaky beneath him. For years he thought he had seen her around every corner and with every child who called "Nurse" in that needy voice she could never resist. But this was no phantom. Aggie was here. She was actually here!

He looked out at the capricious sun, suddenly overpowered by massive gray clouds that threatened to overflow. The East River had turned choppy and white-crested, the churning waves in sync with what he was feeling.

Why had Aggie left him? With no word. No warning. Nothing to ease the appalling emptiness of the long years that followed. She had loved him. He had never questioned that. They had spent ten perfect months together as attuned in mind as in body, doing all the silly meaningless things that people in love did. Laughing at nonsense, teasing, buying unusable gifts for each other, making passionate love until all hours, then getting up bleary-eyed, showering, then making love again. For a brief moment in time, Aggie's bare, thrift-store furnished apartment had become their haven against the world, stopping the clock, blocking out the realities that didn't seem insurmountable when they were together.

Or so he had thought.

Had he been astute enough, he would have questioned her sudden bouts of brooding and the tears he saw in her eyes at odd moments. Instead he had chalked them up to the emotion-charged state she was in, unwilling to let the slightest shadow mar the happiness that had eluded him for so long.

He turned from the window, overcome by the thought that he would actually be seeing her soon. He glanced at Angelica and saw that she was no longer sleeping. Her eyes were open, and she was gazing at him with that wary impenetrable stare that always made him feel as if he'd barged into a room marked "No Admittance."

Looking at her now made him rethink his "better safe than sorry" reason for putting her in Manhattan General. The light hazel eyes seemed sunken in her head. The grooves beneath them were a purplish gray. Her face appeared pasty, and there was a slackness to the bilateral facial muscles that he didn't like.

He walked the few steps to the bed. "How are you feeling, Angelica?"

"Not good."

His brows shot skyward. Her answer alarmed him. He had asked the question out of rote, fully expecting her to give her usual response of "fine." The girl was a lot of things, but she wasn't a complainer.

Her small fingers picked with little strength at the loops of the thermal blanket covering her. She spoke in a hoarse whisper. "Am I going to die?"

A chill ran up his spine. She had asked it as if she were questioning the time of day. Her expression had been resigned—almost hopeful. "Of course not!"

"Then what's wrong with me?"

"I don't know yet. Try not to let it worry you. I've ordered a series of tests that should give us some answers. But you have to help, too."

She looked at him suspiciously. "How do I have to help?"

"We need blood from you to do part of that testing. Now I understand you kicked up quite a fuss this afternoon when Dr. Flanders tried to get it. We can't have that happen again."

Her breathing quickened and a flush stained her pale cheeks. "Could the lady doctor do it?"

"Dr. Landau?"

She nodded.

"I don't see why not."

"Then I won't kick up a fuss."

He felt himself softening toward the girl. It was the most civil conversation he'd had with Angelica Vargas since the night her mother had died, and it emboldened him to reach out a hand to her in comfort. Her reaction was immediate. She shrank back into herself, and he could feel the hostility coming at him in waves. Why did the girl hate him so?

A step behind him alerted him even before he heard the voice.

"Hello, Gar."

He turned. She was leaning against the frame of the doorway as if she needed support. Her pale hair was sprinkled with silver and her face had lines in it he didn't remember, but the essence of her was there. The straightforward glance, the air of competence, the inner honesty by which he had judged every woman since her and had found them wanting.

"How are you, Aggie?"

"Fine."

The conversation was inane and the setting was even more so. He'd had fantasies about meeting her again. Always in some private place where only the two of them existed. There, he'd demanded to know why she'd left him so abruptly. Why she'd halted his life as surely as if one of them had died. But he had no desire to do that now. Her reason for leaving didn't seem important anymore. What was important was whether she still felt the way she had toward him. He had a sudden irrational desire to make love to her. Here. Now. In one of the hospital beds with half the staff looking on, if necessary. He wanted to take her in his arms and sweep away the last ten years as if they'd never existed. He wanted to see those level gray eyes of hers get that blind look when he put his hands on her and she reached out to him unseeingly.

"You haven't changed," he said.

"You have."

Her eyes were relentless as they traveled slowly upward from his moccasined Bally shoes to the brown Perry Ellis suit he wore beneath his lab coat. They stopped for a second at the diamond ring on his pinky finger, continued past the blue custom-made shirt to the razor-cut perfection of his sandy hair, and came to rest on the outdoor tan of his face.

"Nurse . . ." Angelica's head thrashed restlessly against the pillow. "I'd like some water."

"Yes, lovey. I'm coming."

He put a hand on her arm as she neared the bed. "Aggie, we have to talk."

"Not now."

The way she said it prompted him to glance at her ring finger. With relief, he saw it was bare. "When then?"

"Friday. Quarter to seven. At Freddie's."

Her voice shook, and he realized that what he had mistaken for disinterest was instead a mighty effort to deny her feelings. Elation filled him. He wanted to tell her that there was no need, that he still loved her. But the look in her eyes fended him off. She glanced pointedly at his hand and he released her.

She moved to fill Angelica's cup just as Maria Vargas swept into the room, her makeup freshened, the subtle scent of "Joy" trailing behind her.

Her face brightened at sight of him. "Oh, Dr. Gottlieb. You are just the one I wanted to see. I have spoken earlier with Arnold Hardinger's assistant and apprised her of the changes that must be put into effect to satisfy what Jose would tolerate in the matter of Angelica's care. She assures me that she will take it up with Arnold immediately."

He put an arm about her shoulder. "Why don't we go into the solarium where we can discuss all this privately. There are some things I want to talk to you about also."

The last thing he saw before he stepped into the hallway was the contempt in Aggie's eyes. He couldn't tell whether it was directed at him or at Maria Vargas.

Nine

The news of Angelica Vargas's admission to the hospital hit Arnold Hardinger like a splash of ice water.

"Christ!" He rose from behind his desk, opened the armoire, and poured himself a Jack Daniels.

He regarded Esther Pemberton with a bleak stare. She was a juiceless woman in her late forties with tight gray curls and a raillike body clothed in a lackluster print dress. "What's wrong with her?"

"They don't know yet. She's presenting with fever and some weakness in her limbs."

He drank the liquor in a single gulp, secure that Pemby knew all there was to know about it. He trusted Pemby more than he did his wife Laura. He had hired her over twenty years ago, and he'd never been sorry for it.

He'd known for a long time that Pemby was in love with him and that somewhere in that prudish spinster mind of hers she had hopes of consummating it. He found it ludicrous. But that didn't stop him from fostering it. Nothing overt. An occasional lunch, the privilege of calling him Arnold in private, a single rose on her birthday — crumbs to keep an old maid happy. Because he needed Esther Pemberton. She functioned as his eyes and ears at Manhattan General. With the craftiness that was her greatest asset, she had enlisted a network of informants that were able to peer into every corner of the hospital. It was she who had informed him of Anthony Whitcomb's planned treachery at the conference that morning.

"Did Gottlieb admit her?" he asked.

She nodded. "I spoke with him earlier. He's not sure Angelica should have been hospitalized, but with Jose Vargas in South America, he's taking no chances."

"He'd be smart not to."

He knew through Vargas that last year Gottlieb had been handed a plum. He had been named medical consultant to the tristate conglomerate of corporations owned by Vargas. All personnel attached to those corporations were now referred to Gottlieb's office for checkups footed by the conglomerate. Aside from the generous consulting fee Gottlieb collected, Hardinger had to believe that the revenue from the medical exams made up for more than half of Gottlieb's high six-figure income.

"Was Maria Vargas with her?"

"Yes. She was pretty riled when I spoke with her. She wants Angelica to be allowed a private nurse."

"Did you tell her it's against hospital policy?"

"I did. But she insists you'll waive the restrictions.

Imperious bitch! Hardinger thought. And what a waste of good womanflesh. He had envied Jose when the man had married his wife's younger sister. The girl was more than half Vargas's age, beautiful as well as sensual, if he read those sultry eyes correctly, and obviously in love with him. But he hadn't envied his friend for long. Within months of the wedding, Maria had changed into a religious, psalm-singing zealot, and from the look of frustration on Vargas's face, the marriage bed had suffered for it.

"Did she mention when Vargas is coming back?"

"He expects to return in time for your party on Saturday night."

"Do you have everything arranged for the party?"

"Everything." She hesitated. "You're worried about getting that check, aren't you, Arnold?"

"You're damned right I am!"

She flinched at the epithet. "There's something else you should know. Becca Landau is resident on the case."

His face blotched with color. "Not for long, she isn't."

She shifted her weight in the wing chair and crossed her spindly legs. "It's not as simple as that. Angelica seems to trust her.

She insists she wants only 'Dr. Becca' to attend her. And her behavior has been so erratic that nobody wants to thwart her. She won't eat. She throws tantrums . . ." She shrugged her bony shoulders.

The girl was a weirdo, Hardinger thought. She'd been acting peculiar ever since her mother died. The last time he and Laura had come to the Vargas town house, Angelica had hidden in her room. She had refused to come out to greet them no matter how hard her father had coaxed. It puzzled Hardinger that Vargas, who was intolerant of even the smallest slight, would cater to this kind of behavior in his own daughter.

"I'd better get down there." he said. He crossed to the door, then halted. "Debra told me that David spoke to you earlier. What did he want?"

"Only to tell you that he's managed to clean everything up a day sooner. He'll be coming in on a Pan Am shuttle late this afternoon and will join you and Mrs. Hardinger tonight for dinner if you're available."

His face softened. "It'll be good to see him."

Thank God for one good piece of news, he thought. He would wait until Jose returned. If Angelica was still at the hospital, it would be a simple matter to convince him that a change of doctors would be in the child's best interest. In the meantime . . .

"Pemby, I want you to keep as close a watch on Becca Landau as you can. I want to know everything she does on this case, and if you think she's stepping out of line in any way, let me know immediately."

He strode from the office. With David arriving this afternoon, Becca Landau posed a double threat to him. But not for long, he consoled himself. Not for long.

One way or another, he was going to oust her.

Ten

"Another second and it will be over," Becca reassured Angelica as she watched the blood slowly siphon into the third vial. She eyed her charge covertly, remembering the hysteria the last try had triggered.

Angelica lay flat on the bed, her face turned away, her left arm held steady by Agatha Bates. Her hands were balled into fists, her body was rigid, her forehead creased into tight furrows.

On top of her lace-edged nightgown was a green circlet of thread which had a small square card attached to it that hung down to her chest. Becca had seen the circlet before. It was called a scapular and was symbolic of a part of St. Benedict's habit. There was a prayer written on the card, and superstition had it that if someone was wearing it when they died, they would go to heaven instead of purgatory. Becca couldn't answer for what the scapular would provide in the next world, but in this one it had a tendency to tangle with her stethoscope during an examination and was a royal pain in the butt.

More of the stepmother's handiwork, Becca thought in annoyance. For the sake of expediency, she had banished Maria Vargas to the waiting room for the length of the procedure. She had gone meekly. Becca suspected it was because she dreaded a recurrence of what had happened earlier.

"There!" Becca slid the hypodermic out and capped the vial while Agatha Bates applied a gauze pad to the puncture.

Becca had worked with the nurse for a good part of the afternoon, and she had to concede that Helen Walters had been right about one thing: Agatha Bates had a way with children. But the nurse's hesitation of movement was still there, and she tended to repeat orders as if willing them to sink into her memory. It made Becca nervous, but in deference to Helen, she would reserve judgment.

Angelica made a sound deep in her throat. "I'm sorry I had to hurt you," Becca said.

The child didn't answer. Becca tapped her cheek sharply. "Angelica!"

The hazel eyes opened slowly. They looked dazed, unfocused. "Wasn't afraid," she murmured.

Agatha Bates uncurled the small fingers and smiled at her. "You just didn't like the look of the needle. Right?"

There was no response. Her face was ashen, her expression was turned inward. Becca had the feeling that she had gone back to another time, another place.

"So many of them," she murmured, tossing her head on the pillow.

Agatha Bates looked at her in puzzlement, but Becca signaled for her not to interrupt as the child continued.

Her voice was distant, almost singsong. "Papa said the needles would make her better. But they didn't. I was scared they would hurt her, but Papa, he said she didn't feel the hurt. And then he told me she wouldn't ever feel hurt again."

Becca exchanged a startled glance with the nurse. She knew instinctively that Angelica was talking about her mother.

"He said . . . he said God had reached down to take her. He said that . . . that she couldn't be saved. They put her in a box. A cold, cold box." She strained forward unseeingly and clutched Becca's arms in a weak grip. Desperation replaced the emptiness in her eyes. "I tried to stop it," she whispered. "I tried."

A memory suddenly surfaced for Becca. She was six years old and her best friend had bicycled into a truck and been killed. Her father hadn't let her go to the funeral. "She'll get over it faster if she doesn't see her put in the ground," she'd overheard him say. The image those words had invoked had been worse than the reality ever could have been.

Grasping the delicate shoulders, Becca lowered Angelica to the bed, then perched on the edge of it. She could feel the child's pain as if it were her own.

"Angelica, listen to me. I deal with sick people all the time. And I try to make them better. But sometimes medicine and hope and prayer . . . well, they're just not enough. I have to face that." She took the small hands into her own. "And so do you."

The hands lay limply in hers. There was no sign that she had heard.

A rattling noise from the doorway broke the child's trance. Becca rose from the bed as an aide crossed the threshold pushing a wheelchair in front of her. Becca had never seen her before. She was short and stout with straight black hair and a sunny disposition. She smiled at the patient, then glanced at Becca's nametag. "Doctor, I have an order here to take Angelica Vargas down for a chest x-ray."

Becca nodded, aware of the panic flaring in Angelica's eyes. "It's just a minor test," she explained to her. She watched the child tense and braced herself for another screaming session. It didn't come.

"Will . . . will you go with me, Dr. Landau?"

The docility surprised her. The quaver in the voice nearly undid her. She couldn't remember anyone who had the ability to tug at her emotions the way this child did. But she had to put a halt to this madness. "No, I can't." She said it more abruptly than she had intended. "But you'll be fine. It won't hurt. I promise."

Angelica cringed as the aide positioned the wheelchair close to the bed. Becca felt her resolve begin to crumble.

Agatha Bates stepped closer to the bed. "I'll take her down if you like."

Relief flooded Becca. "Is that okay with you?" she asked her patient.

Angelica nodded.

"Do you want me to clear this with Helen Walters?" she asked the nurse as she helped the aide shift Angelica's slight body to the wheelchair. Becca's thoughts about Agatha Bates were undergoing a rapid reassessment.

"If you want to. But this shouldn't take long." Her mouth tilted at the corners. "Besides, it won't hurt me to skip lunch if I have to catch up." She slapped one slender hip. "There's too much padding on these anyway."

She turned the wheelchair toward the door, but Becca stopped her. "Miss Bates, about this morning . . ." She cleared her throat, not knowing how to phase it without coming across like a pompous ass. "I — I'm afraid we got off to a bad start."

"It was my fault. I shouldn't have offered the advice. At least not the way I did."

"It was on target."

Her smile crinkled the corners of her eyes and made her whole face look younger. "Call me Aggie," she said. Still smiling, she patted the top of Angelica's silken head with worn fingers. "Come on, lovey. Let's you and me take a ride."

Becca lingered for a moment to dispose of the syringe and to collect the precious blood samples. She wasn't taking any chances on their loss. She was going to personally see to it that they reached the lab posthaste.

With the tray balanced carefully between her hands, she turned, took two steps toward the door, and almost collided with the elderly woman who barged through it. The blood samples rattled precariously, and Becca had a hard time biting back the epithet that came to her tongue. She set the tray on a chest of drawers and turned to face her.

The woman was in her seventies. She was short with wide hips and stubby legs, and walked with the help of a cane. She was swarthy but unwrinkled. Her kinky hair was almost white. It was drawn back into a tight bun that strained the flat, broad features. She reminded Becca of a mestizo Indian she had treated the year before. She was expensively dressed in black, but the clothes appeared misplaced on her stooped, boxlike figure and gave her the appearance of an overdressed peasant.

Ignoring Becca, she looked past her to the empty bed, then stiffened. "What have you done with my granddaughter?" she demanded in a heavily accented voice. The fear in it was evident.

"Don't be frightened," Becca said gently. "I'm Dr. Landau, and Angelica is fine. She's just been taken down for testing, but it shouldn't be too long. In the meantime, you can sit in the waiting room if you like. I believe your daughter-in-law is there."

The woman's contemptuous snort spoke for itself. "If Maria is there, then I wait here." She put a hand on Becca's sleeve. It was gnarled with corded veins bulging the skin. "Tell me, what is wrong with Angelica that she must suddenly be stolen from her house with no word of warning to me? If my son was home . . ."

"Mrs. Vargas, we don't know exactly what's wrong with your granddaughter. That's why we're doing these tests. But we should have some answers in a few days, and I'm sure you'll be informed of the results."

She leaned heavily on her cane. "I'm glad you are sure. I am not. When my son is here he tells me everything that is going on. When I must deal with that *puta* he married, I learn nothing. Will you keep me informed, doctor?"

Becca hesitated. The Vargases seemed an unpalatable lot with their volatile moods and twisted family relationships. She wasn't about to single any one of them out for preferential treatment only to get caught in the crossfire between them. But there was no reason she couldn't be courteous. "If you call me, I'll be happy to tell you what I know," she said.

"Gracias."

Becca leaned against the dresser. "Mrs. Vargas, if you have a minute, I would appreciate your giving me some information."

"Information?" She regarded Becca with the shrewdness of a streetwise peddler. "You wish to talk about my son? To request a favor, perhaps?" A rapt expression crossed her face. "Everyone wishes to talk about my son. Jose, he is like the sun in the sky. All things revolve around him. He is a great man, and he is bound for an even greater destiny. I have known it since he is a little boy. In time, he will become a part of history. And his son after him will do the same."

Taken aback, Becca wondered if she was looking at senility or delusions or both. "It isn't your son I wanted to know about Mrs. Vargas. It's Angelica's mother."

She looked surprised. She fingered the rows of crystal beads at her throat with knotted brown fingers. "You wish to know about Celmira?" Her expression clearly questioned why anyone would bother to ask about her former daughter-in-law.

Becca nodded.

"What is it you wish to know?"

"For one thing, how long was Celmira ill?"

From the dispassion in the old woman's eyes, she could have been talking of a stranger. "Celmira was sick almost from the day Jose married her. She managed to bear Angelica, but she couldn't take care of her. It was I who fed the child and comforted her in the night when she cried. And it was I who coaxed her to take her first steps. My granddaughter is dearer to me than my own life."

"What was Celmira's illness?"

She tapped her left breast. "Heart."

"Is that what she died of? A heart attack?"

"Yes."

"Did she die at the hospital?"

"No. At home."

"In South America?"

She held up a hand in protest. "Doctor, forgive me, but I am weary." She limped toward the rocking chair and heaved her bulk into it. "I will be in touch," she said. She closed her eyes.

Peasant or grande dame, the Vargas women knew how to dismiss, Becca thought in frustration. She had only touched on the questions she wanted to ask. Was the grandmother really as tired as she seemed? Or had she deliberately cut the conversation off for reasons of her own? Glancing at the rocker squeaking softly as the old woman moved slowly to and fro, Becca knew she would get no answers here.

She picked up the tray of blood samples, left the room, and hurried down the corridor to the bank of elevators marked "M." She had almost reached them when her eye was drawn to an alcove just outside the linen supply room, where a couple was embracing. The man wearing the white lab coat had his back to her, but the woman was clearly visible. She took in the long limbs, the thick chestnut hair, and the drab interview suit and recognized Carolyn Stedman. Becca felt amusement and a stab of envy. Obviously the psychiatrist was finding the time that day to do other things besides unpack.

Becca turned and pressed the elevator button. A sixth sense caused her to look back. There was something familiar about the man Carolyn was kissing. The broad shoulders. The way he held himself. The curling blond hair too long at the nape of the neck . . .

The shock hit her even as the couple broke apart and David became aware of her. She saw his sudden start and the red that suffused his face. She watched him mouth her name and invol-

89

untarily reach out a hand to her. Her legs felt as if lead weights were anchored to them. She prayed that the elevator would come so she didn't have to acknowledge him because the pain knifing through her made talk impossible. But the damned elevator didn't come, and she stood there immobile with the tray clutched in her hands like a life preserver while he closed the distance between them.

"Hello, Becca." There was a catch in his voice. It was low and deep as she remembered, and it cocooned her in an intimacy that made all but the two of them recede from her awareness.

"Hi." The word was a croak. Her whole body was trembling. His nearness was having a terrible effect on her.

He looked older, she thought. And thinner. There were lines around his mouth that hadn't been there before, and she saw that some of the blond hair was flecked with gray. She felt him reading her face with an intensity that sought every nuance in it. She kept her eyes from his. She was afraid of what he would read in them.

Carolyn Stedman crossed to his side and the intimacy between them dissolved.

Grateful for the reprieve, Becca cleared her throat. "Congratulations, David. I heard about your appointment as assistant chief of Surgery here. When did you get in from Boston?"

"An hour ago." He hesitated. "I was hoping I would see you."

She laughed lightly. "Well, now you have." She couldn't believe the performance she was giving. Obviously it was possible to retain one's balance while the world spun out of control. She turned to the psychiatrist. "David and I are old friends," she said.

"So I see."

Was that pity in her voice?

Becca felt David's touch. She drew back so abruptly that the vials of blood on the tray were threatened for a second time.

He steadied them for her. "How can I . . . Where can I get in touch with you?"

Deliberately misunderstanding, she smiled brightly. "I'll be here at the hospital. All day. Every day."

The elevator door slid open at her side. She backed into it gratefully. She even managed a small salute with the fingers of one hand. The smile was still on her face when the door clanged shut in front of her.

Eleven

At ten o'clock the following morning, Becca stood outside Carolyn Stedman's office on the main floor of Manhattan General. She hoped the psychiatrist wasn't in. She hadn't called to confirm the appointment as she'd promised and only her pride had prevented her from canceling it outright. She was, after all, a professional, and she would not allow her personal feelings to impinge on her work. Besides, she had no doubt that Carolyn Stedman would know why she canceled, and she wasn't about to give her that satisfaction.

She had lain awake most of the night, tossing and kneading her feather pillow into grooves, trying to sort out her emotions. Her reaction to seeing David and Carolyn embracing had made a mockery of the promise she had given herself when she had learned that David was coming to Manhattan General, namely that whatever her reaction to him, she was going to maintain control, keep her sense of self intact. What a crock! She had based her fortitude on the assumption that her attraction to David had diminished over the last two years, but yesterday's encounter had made a farce of that assumption.

She had known by the warmth of their embrace that David and Carolyn Stedman had been intimate. It had come as a shock. Not that there hadn't been women in David's life before her. Even during her time with him she had been aware of the blatant invitations extended to him. David's charisma drew women to him like a beacon. But those that followed it were usually disappointed. Because until her, David's pattern had been hit-and-run, and only those eager to have their egos massaged for a short time with no debt incurred on either side escaped with their feelings unscathed.

Carolyn Stedman didn't strike her as that type. She was bright and serious, and if Becca had judged correctly, was given to lasting, meaningful relationships. In short, Carolyn Stedman had probably been her replacement.

She should be glad, Becca told herself. Despite her attraction to David, her reasons for ending their relationship were valid, and his affair with the psychiatrist would act as a deterrent to any thoughts she might have of starting it up again.

Bracing herself, she knocked on the door.

"Come in."

When she entered, Carolyn Stedman was seated behind her desk, folding a letter into an envelope. The small office looked as if it had been occupied for a year rather than a day. Impressionistic Renoir and Corot prints vied with ponderous black-framed credentials for space on the freshly painted walls. And a half-opened file cabinet in the corner ran from floor to ceiling and bulged with neatly tabbed folders.

It went beyond organization, Becca thought. There was none of the scattering of objects on her desk that spoke of a hasty settling in. There was a prissiness in the exact placement of her crystal clock and her glass paperweight and her silver letter opener. She had been wrong about the warmth that flowed from this woman. There was almost a dehumanization here in favor of order.

Her eye was caught by the Lucite-encased photo on the walnut credenza behind her. It was of the psychiatrist on a sailboat laughingly entwined with a tousle-haired yachtsman who bore a resemblance to her.

"My brother Sam," she informed Becca, noting where her glance was straying. "The resemblance is only surface. We're very different. He's impossible and I'm near-impossible." She smiled.

Becca didn't return the smile.

The psychiatrist wore a pink silk blouse that lent a glow to her coloring. A long strand of pearls encircled her neck and dipped below the desk. She sealed the envelope and used it to wave Becca toward a chair. "Make yourself comfortable."

Becca perched stiffly on the edge of her seat. "Doctor—"

Her gray eyes swung toward Becca as she licked a stamp and affixed it to the envelope. "Doctor? Yesterday afternoon it was Carolyn. I'm sorry to see that we've regressed."

Becca felt as if she was being played with. She deliberately glanced at her watch. "Doctor, I don't mean to be rude, but I'm short of time. If you don't mind, I'd like to skip the small talk and deal directly with the anorexic."

Carolyn Stedman tangled a glossy-tipped finger in the strand of pearls and regarded Becca steadily. "But I do mind," she said softly. "I'd like to talk about David Hardinger first."

Becca rose swiftly, her outrage evident in the stiffness of her spine. "What is between you and David Hardinger is your business, not mine. I see no necessity—"

"You're wrong. There's every necessity. You see, if we can't get past this, we can't be friends. And I'd like to think it was friendship you were offering outside Helen Walters's office yesterday." She indicated the chair again, and after a moment, Becca reluctantly sank back into it.

Carolyn spoke with no preamble, and there was little emotion in her voice. "David and I went to bed once. It was so bad we couldn't even bring it to completion. I was just coming off a messy divorce, and David was carrying a torch you could spot a mile away. I didn't know for whom until I saw the way he looked at you yesterday afternoon."

"You're jumping to conclusions."

She shook her head. "I don't think so. Anyway, we were both grown up enough to rise above the failure—" her lips twitched "—no pun intended. We conceded that what we really wanted from each other was a sympathetic ear, and when time permitted, which wasn't very often, that's what we gave to each other."

She was lying, Becca thought. And it wasn't even a clever lie. She had expected more from Carolyn Stedman. "Pardon me for doubting you, doctor, but I've never known David to settle for friendship with any woman."

She laughed outright. "I will admit it wasn't characteristic of him, but then I don't think he thought of me as a woman after that. I was sort of a neuter gender. There were others like Lila who were much more suited to—damn!" she muttered, stopping short.

"Lila? Lila Brodin?"

The psychiatrist didn't answer, but Becca could see the acknowledgment in her eyes. So Lila had finally made it to David's bed. There was a lot to be said for persistence, Becca thought cynically. The little nurse had been one of the more tenacious hangers-on all through Becca's relationship with David. If anyone deserved him, she did.

"Look, Becca, I don't know what's between you and David, and I don't care to know. All I'm trying to say is that there's nothing between me and David that should prevent you from calling me friend."

Becca was silent. She didn't like or trust the woman, and she wasn't going to be gracious to her. "Dr. Stedman, would you mind if we got onto another subject?"

She sighed. "All right. Let's get on to one that's important to us both."

"The anorexic?"

She shook her head. "We'll get to that."

"You like to run things, don't you?" Becca said.

"So my brother tells me."

Becca glanced at the photo. "The admiral?"

"That's his hobby. Sam's a lawyer. And a damned good one." She leaned forward in her chair, causing it to creak loudly beneath her. "I stopped in to see Angelica Vargas at eleven last night. The nurse who was with her—Bates, she said her name was—told me she was presenting with fever and a weakness of the limbs, and gave me a rundown of the tests you and the attending have ordered. Would you hazard a guess yet as to what's wrong with her?"

She shook her head. "I don't have a clue. I suspect that whatever she has is either being caused by or complicated by some underlying emotional problem. But that's not my area of expertise."

"No," she said quietly, "it's mine. And I think you've got a valid reason for concern." She reached into her bottom drawer, withdrew a can of air freshener, and sprayed the contents into the air in a circular motion. "I hate the smell of hospitals, don't you?" A woodsy scent of pine permeated the office as she set the can on the desk. "When I got to Angelica's room she was sleeping—if you can call it that. She was dozing in fits and starts, obviously in the throes of a nightmare that was scaring the hell out of her. The nurse, Bates, told me that she's done that at various times of the day and evening."

Becca frowned. Aggie Bates's shift ended at seven. What was she doing there so late at night?

"If recurrent nightmares are her pattern," the psychiatrist continued, "it would account for those heavy circles under her eyes." She pursed her lips pensively. "She woke up while I was there. I asked her what the nightmare was about, but she shrugged the question off. She doesn't trust easily. It was only when I told her I was your friend that she began to open up a little. She refused to speak of herself but talked instead about her doll, Gabriella, who is obviously her alter ego."

Becca nodded grimly. "Did she tell you of the doll's impending death?"

"She did—in a matter-of-fact tone that would put a mortician to shame. I also spoke to the stepmother when she came into the room. Some piece of work, that one. I couldn't believe it when I saw her add a statuette of the Virgin Mary to that shrine she's created around the child. I think she was having trouble understanding exactly what it is I do, because she kept fingering that cross of hers and looking at me as if I were some kind of witch doctor."

"Did she tell you that she is Angelica's aunt as well as her stepmother?"

"No, she didn't." She removed a pair of half-lens spectacles from a red leather case and slipped them over her nose. "She was very close-mouthed, but I did learn from her that Angelica has suddenly become very generous. It seems that for the past three months the child has been giving away her belongings. To the servants, to her tutor. . . . Why doesn't the kid go to school like other kids do?" she muttered as if to herself. She regarded Becca over her spectacles like an owl. "I don't like to make hasty judgments, but there are things here that I think might be of immediate concern. I'd like your permission to keep on seeing Angelica Vargas."

Becca hesitated. She was thinking that she should get Gottlieb's okay first. She was also thinking that the psychiatrist had a right to know what she was getting herself into. "Dr. Stedman, you're new here, and you may not yet be aware of the repercussions at the hospital because of the celebrity deaths that have occurred here over the last few years."

"I'm aware."

"Are you also aware that Angelica's father is a very prominent man? And that if anything was to happen to Angelica, anyone connected with this case would be in jeopardy."

"Of what? A malpractice suit? In my line of work I live with that threat all the time. But what about you? With your history, if anything was to happen to Angelica, the repercussions for you would be far greater than for me."

Becca had wondered whether Carolyn Stedman knew about the incident she had been involved in at Boston Memorial. She didn't have to wonder anymore. But how had she found out? Had David told her about it? Or had she learned of it through the hospital grapevine up in Boston?

"Don't worry about me," she said. "I can take care of myself."

The psychiatrist's glance said clearly that she thought Becca's bravado was misplaced. But she didn't belabor the point. She slid her spectacles off and massaged the bridge of her nose. "Look, Becca, Angelica Vargas is in need of help. Perhaps more than either of us realize. Again, I'm asking your permission to pursue it further."

"You have it." Becca felt she should thank her, but she couldn't bring herself to do it. "Naturally you'll keep me informed," she said.

The psychiatrist arched her brow at the formality of the words. "Naturally." There was a hint of sarcasm in her tone.

Twelve

The magnificent black onyx clock over the main-floor reception desk was a gift from Alfred Irénée du Pont to commemorate the hospital's fiftieth birthday. Its slender gold hands stretched to twelve-thirty as Becca rushed past it in a last-ditch effort to stay Dr. Gottlieb before he left the hospital. She finally caught up with him in the room adjacent to the reception area that had been reserved for admitting patients when Manhattan General had first opened its doors in 1880. Now obsolete, it was used as a catchall space that held packages waiting to be sorted, extra chairs, office supplies, and the paraphernalia of the attending physicians who came and went at random.

Outside, the midday sun was high in the sky. The mild breeze rippling the leaves of the tree silhouetted against the leaded window on the far wall promised a perfect day on the fairway, and Gottlieb's impatience to be gone was evident in his greeting. "Make it short, Becca. I've got one foot out the door."

"I tried to get to you earlier."

"When? You weren't there at rounds."

"The Ferrari baby was hemorrhaging. She's stable now."

"I left a message for you to be in Angelica's room at ten."

"I was in a meeting."

His smile was a flash of white in his tanned face. "Two ships that pass, right?" He shrugged out of his lab coat and hung it on a wall hook beneath his nameplate. "Did you get word yet on any of Angelica's tests?"

She shook her head. "I'm pushing the lab, but you know how they are. Short of staff. Short of patience. Short of everything but excuses." She jammed her hands into the pockets of her white coat. "Dr. Gottlieb, I know you're in a hurry, but I need a bit of your time."

Caught by her seriousness, his face tinged with apprehension. "Has there been a change in Angelica's condition since I saw her?"

"No. But it is Angelica I want to talk to you about."

He sighed and ran both hands across his thick cropped hair. "Okay. Fire away."

"Yes. Well, contrary to the impression you gave me, I think there is a physical basis for Angelica Vargas's symptoms."

He nodded. "You're right. I didn't think so when I first admitted her. I'm inclined to agree with you now. But that isn't something we have to speculate about, is it? We'll know more when the lab reports are in." He pulled the stethoscope from about his neck then reached across to a small table that held his leather bag. He unsnapped it. "If that's all . . ."

She put a hand on his forearm to forestall his movements. She felt the muscle leap beneath her fingers. "Dr. Gottlieb, I think there's something else that should be addressed here. In my opinion, Angelica Vargas has a severe emotional problem."

"Are you referring to the tantrum she threw yesterday?"

"I'm not basing it on that alone." The testy look on his face deterred her for a second, then the words came out in a rush. "I . . . I have reason to believe that Angelica feels her own death is imminent. She has recurrent nightmares that terrify her and a history of erratic behavior that seems to have started with the death of her mother four years ago. I suspect she may have witnessed that death, but I can't be sure."

"I wouldn't know anything about that." He pulled his arm out from under her fingers and snapped the bag shut. "Look, Becca, I appreciate your concern, but there's nothing you're telling me that's new and that I didn't try to forewarn you about yesterday. If what you're getting at is my permission to have a psychiatric workup done on Angelica Vargas, the answer is no. Her father would never permit it."

Anger flared in her, hot and unreasoning. It was fired by a mix of Angelica's helplessness and this man's deliberate obtuseness. How dare he concentrate on getting in nine holes before sundown in the face of her patient's obvious need. "What do you mean, 'her father would never permit it'?" she said. *"You're* her doctor, not Jose Vargas. Have you ever even discussed the necessity of it with him?"

The moment the words were out, she was appalled by them. She had accused Agatha Bates of overstepping. What she had just done was ten times worse.

Gottlieb's tan mottled to a dull red. His face closed against her as he strove for calm. "Maybe you were right in asking not to handle this case," he said evenly. "Maybe you're not up to it. Certainly if the Vargas girl wasn't so adamant about having you as her doctor, I'd have you removed right now."

How ironic, Becca thought. If she pressed it, she could have the out she had so desperately sought when she had been handed this case. But that was before she had met Angelica Vargas. "I'm sorry," she said. "I don't know what's gotten into me."

He nodded, mollified by her apology but wary still. "Look Becca, you're a damned good pede, but you're young and you're making the mistake of allowing yourself to get caught up in problems that are beyond your jurisdiction. I'm guiding this case, and I tell you that what you're suggesting is uncalled for here. Let's pinpoint Angelica's illness, treat for it, and get her out of the hospital as soon as possible. That's *all* that's required here. Is that clear?"

"Yes."

"Good. You'll keep me informed?"

"Of course."

But not about everything, she thought. Not about everything.

If Becca had any misgivings about allowing Carolyn Stedman to continue her visits in the face of Gottlieb's opposition, they were shattered at four that afternoon when she received Helen Walters's urgent message to get to the Vargas room — *stat!*

Even before she entered 401 East, she could hear Angelica's terrified cries. Inside, the scene that met her eyes could have been taken from a de Sade setting.

Angelica Vargas was thrashing about in bed. Her eyes were tightly closed, her head was whipping from side to side like a piston. Her nightgown had slipped off her shoulder, and there were a series of gouges and red crescentlike marks marring the clavicle area. Her face was flushed, her throat corded and rigid. Piercing shrieks emanated from her mouth with an intensity that lost nothing in their repetition.

On the floor, the doll Gabriella lay with her legs sprawled to a side, her one exposed eye staring skyward. Lying in a heap atop her tiered satin skirts was the white thermal blanket that had slipped from the bed. It had overturned the water pitcher on the nightstand in its descent, and one edge was slowly soaking up the puddle of water that had formed beneath it.

With one knee crooked on the mattress for leverage, Agatha Bates balanced above the child, shaking her shoulders and calling her name, while an aide on the other side of the bed held Angelica's legs in an effort to keep the small body from catapulting off the mattress.

"She's having another nightmare," Agatha Bates informed Becca through set teeth. "But this time I can't pull her out of it."

"Let her go," Becca said.

"But . . ."

"Let her go!"

The nurse and the aide reluctantly stepped aside. Freed from restraint, the child arched upright just as Becca eased down beside her. She put her arms about the small trembling body and held it tight. Angelica's skin was slick with perspiration, and where her cheek rested against Becca's, it was wet with tears. Becca's arms began to ache as Angelica battled against the constraint with surprising strength.

"Mamá!" The word was wrenched from the child in a voice raw with pain and longing.

Becca saw the compassion in Agatha Bates's face and knew it was written on her own. Crushed against Angelica, she felt as if she were in a sauna, but as the heat of her body reached the child, the shrieks slowly died to whimpers and the thrashing dwindled to a restless twitch.

Becca eased her patient back onto the pillow. The hazel eyes fluttered open. They were dull with exhaustion, the dark hollows under them pointing up the delicate structure of the cheekbones beneath. She blinked in confusion. "Dr. Becca?"

"Yes, Angelica. I'm here. You've had a nightmare. And it scared you."

She looked away. "Wasn't scared."

Becca took the small pointed chin in her hand and forced it toward her. "Angelica, do you trust me?"

"Yes."

"Then listen to what I say. It's okay to be scared. Really it is. I get scared all the time."

"You do?"

"Uh-huh. But I try to be brave about it."

"How?"

"By facing up to what's scaring me and trying to do something about it."

"Don't know what's scaring me." Becca had to strain to hear the words.

"That nightmare is scaring you. Maybe if you tell me about it, we can figure out why."

"Even if it don't make sense?"

"Even so."

Angelica fingered the blanket that Aggie Bates had replaced and glanced self-consciously toward the aide. Becca nodded to the girl. "Thanks for your help. We won't be needing you any more." Becca turned back to Angelica as the aide took her leave. "Is it okay if Miss Bates stays?"

She nodded solemnly. "Oh, yes. Aggie and me, we're friends."

Over her head, Becca and the nurse exchanged smiles.

Becca pulled a wooden spindle chair close to the bed and sat down. "Okay. I'm listening."

Even as she said it, Becca wondered if she hadn't taken too much on herself. She wasn't a psychiatrist, and a revelation of this sort could cause trauma. But she had to try something.

Angelica's fingers worried a strand of the blanket that had shredded at the hemline. "I always have the same dream," she murmured. She closed her eyes, and Becca knew she was reliving it. "It's . . . it's so real." Her chest rose and fell in agitation.

"There's sand on the floor. And its hot . . . very hot." Her hand crept to her neck. "My throat, it's so dry. I must get water or I will die," she croaked. "I . . . try to get out of bed, but I hurt all over. I can't move. And then . . . then I see the water." Her voice trailed off.

"Where is it?" Becca prompted.

"It's . . ." A furrow creased her brow. "It's on . . . on top of the ladder. In a bottle. Gabriella is trying to reach it for me."

"Gabriella is there with you?"

"Yes. Gabriella has been there all the time."

Angelica's voice suddenly changed. It deepened and grew sterner. Her face became wizened, older. Becca watched in shock as the metamorphosis took place. It was as if someone else had entered her body. The young mouth turned down to form lines on either side of it. " 'Gabriella,' I tell her. 'You must bring the water to me.' "

The face relaxed and the voice went back to its singsong chant. "But Gabriella isn't . . . she isn't big enough. She can't climb the ladder. She . . . she starts to cry." Her chest heaved again and her breathing quickened. "And then . . . and then . . ."

"Don't be frightened," Becca soothed. "You're perfectly safe." She waited until the child quieted. "And then?" she prompted.

Her hand clutched Becca's. "And then a shadow creeps up on the sand. I am so happy. I know I'll be saved now."

Again the metamorphosis took place, but this time there was a pleading set to the aged mouth. " 'Help me!' I tell the shadow. 'I must have the water in the bottle.' "

The child's face relaxed into normal lines again. Her breathing accelerated then became shallow. "But the shadow only laughs and drags Gabriella away from the ladder . . . across the sand."

Angelica's eyes opened. They were fixed and so fearful that Aggie Bates reacted with an involuntary sound. Becca cautioned her to be silent as Angelica continued.

"I'm alone. My throat . . . it hurts more and more. I can't swallow. I try to scream . . ." The words were coming in choppy gasps; the thrashing had begun again. Her back arched upward from the bed.

Becca laid a reassuring hand on her arm. "What then?" she asked after a second's silence.

The voice began again, fainter now. "My head hurts. I can't move. And then . . . then I begin to bleed. I bleed from my nose . . . from my mouth . . . from my fingers . . ." She covered her eyes with both hands and flung herself back on the pillows. "I don't want to die," she shrieked "I don't want to die!"

Becca clutched the fragile shoulders. "Listen to me, Angelica. You are not going to die! Do you hear me?"

The shrieking stopped abruptly. Her spine gradually untensed. Her eyes caught and held Becca's for a long moment. They slowly filled with trust. "I'm so tired," she whispered.

"Then go to sleep."

"I'll dream if I sleep."

"You won't know that until you try, will you? Remember what we said about being brave?"

She nodded then curled on her side. Passing a hand over the flyaway hair, Aggie Bates pulled up the covers and tucked them around the child, then dimmed the light above her. She walked to where Becca had positioned herself near the window.

Becca spoke in a low voice. "Aggie, what are those red marks on her shoulder?"

"They're self-inflicted. When she's in the throes of that nightmare, she pulls and tears at her skin as if she wants to destroy herself. Those marks were made when she dug her nails in."

"See that you cut her nails when she wakes up."

"Will do." She bent to retrieve Gabriella from her unladylike sprawl on the floor. She smoothed the doll's skirts, then squinted up at Becca in perplexity. "What do you make of all that gobbledegook she was spouting? Seems to me you'd need an interpreter to make heads or tails of it."

Becca smiled. "You're right, Aggie. But it just so happens I've got one on tap."

Thirteen

Convinced that Angelica's nightmares were the key to her erratic behavior, Becca was fired by the need for an immediate explanation. But her search for Carolyn Stedman proved fruitless. Her office door was locked, and though the psychiatrist had left word at the Bureau of Records in the adjacent office that she would return within two hours, she never did.

With unreasoning certainty, Becca came to the conclusion that despite Carolyn Stedman's elaborate denial, the psychiatrist was with David. Unable to admit to simple jealousy, Becca blamed her anger on the childish way Carolyn had sought to dupe her. It would take a much less sophisticated mind than Becca's to believe that tale of a one-night sexual encounter gone awry and the platonic friendship that had followed.

So draining was her refusal to deal with her feelings that despite the surprising lack of emergencies to disrupt the routine caseload of the ensuing day, she found herself exhausted by the time she left the hospital at eight that evening.

The clear sky in the gathering dusk gave promise of a balmy June day to follow, but a light drizzle began to fall as Becca reached the brick pathway that wound from the hospital to the street. Caught without an umbrella and wearing only a blue challis blouse, print skirt, and worn leather sandals, Becca ran the few blocks to her apartment building. By the time she reached it, she was out of breath and sticky damp, her black hair an unruly swirling mass that refused to conform to the shoulder-length pageboy in which it had been cut.

Generous in its perks to doctors, Manhattan General had

provided a two-bedroom apartment for her on Eighty-Fifth Street and York Avenue, for which she paid a mere four hundred and eighty dollars. On the open market, Becca knew it would go for at least triple that, because this part of the city was a desirable one. Some of the more disgruntled medical staff that occupied the ten-story building had nicknamed it "The Coop" because of its small rooms, lack of adornment, and boxlike structure. But for Becca, whose life revolved so much around the hospital, the accommodations were adequate and nearby, and she could ask for no more than that.

It wasn't until the elevator reached her floor that Becca realized she had forgotten to stop off at Chum Lee's Takeout for the spareribs she had looked forward to all day. Damning the rain that had frazzled her memory, she took out her keys and walked down the gray carpeted hallway to the last apartment in the long row. She stopped suddenly as it came into sight.

Arms hugging his drawn-up knees, David was jackknifed into a corner on the floor near her apartment, waiting for her. He was dressed in khaki linen slacks with an open-necked white shirt and brown docksiders on his bare feet. His face was resting on his arms with a drowsy expression on it that told her he had been there for a while. At his side was a shiny white shopping bag.

Her first reaction was elation. So he hadn't been with Carolyn Stedman after all! It was quickly tempered by caution as he uncoiled and rose to face her. Denying her feelings for David amidst the distractions of a busy hospital was one thing. But a one-on-one in a dimly lit hallway with her apartment a hairsbreadth away was quite another.

She stood before him damp and frumpy, keys dangling from limp fingers. The shock of seeing him there had left her feeling defenseless. She made an effort to rally.

"How did you find out where I live?" she demanded.

His smile relegated the question to unimportance. "Your hair is longer," he said. "And you've lost weight."

Spoken casually, the comments seemed idle but the gaze that roamed her body wasn't. Wherever it touched, she felt a warmth on her flesh that left her wanting. She took a step back as he reached out a hand to her. He let it drop to his side.

He held up the white bag. "A peace offering," he said. "Spareribs, fried rice, and fortune cookies.

"I've had my dinner."

"Then join me in mine."

"David—"

"Don't shut me out, Becca . . . please." His voice held the little-boy entreaty she had found so endearing when she had first met him.

She was conscious of the sudden weakening of her legs. She looked at his hands clutching the bag. She had always loved his hands. They embodied so much that was good in David. They were beautiful hands with long tapered fingers that wielded a scalpel with the intuitive sensitivity of a divining rod. And they could rouse her to a mindless pitch. She was torn by ambivalence. She dreaded for him to touch her and ached with the longing for it. But it was wasted emotion. Nothing had really changed between them.

Finish it, she told herself. *Now. For good. While you still have the strength.*

She started to tell him to go, then bit the words back as the blowsy rehab therapist across the hall came out of her apartment. Single and seeking, she had more than once offered to arrange a date for Becca and had resented it when Becca had rebuffed her for lack of interest. She smiled at Becca now as she locked her door. "Second thoughts?" she asked, her eyes fixed meaningfully on David.

Taking advantage of Becca's outraged silence, David took the keys from her nerveless fingers and opened her door. Recovering herself, Becca mumbled something cutting to the therapist, then followed him inside and switched on the light.

He set the white bag on a chair and looked around. His eyes brightened with amusement.

Nowhere was the difference between them more apparent than in their decorating taste. Professionally done, David's apartments were always as perfectly turned out as he was—sleek, muted, no sentimental carryovers to intrude on the all-important sense of the present. In contrast, Becca reveled in cushy camelback sofas, calico prints, antique armoires, and shelves . . . row upon row of pine shelves to hold her things—

books, some of them so old the bindings were held on with rubberbands, and cherished doodads she had saved from babyhood on, including a shredded Raggedy Ann doll with shoe-button eyes that David always claimed glared at him as if he were an intruder.

"Did I ever tell you that you have the instincts of a pack rat?" he teased.

There was warmth and relief in his voice, and she knew that the familiar clutter of the room was reassuring him that they could pick up where they had left off.

"Habits die hard," she said coldly, annoyed with herself that she had allowed him to take the decision of whether to be admitted out of her hands. How quickly she reverted to pattern when she was with him, she thought bitterly.

He picked up the white shopping bag. "If you show me where the kitchen is, we can warm up this food and . . ."

Her face contorted with anger. How dare he intrude upon her life with no warning and plunge her back into the "push me-pull you" tug of war she had run from in such despair two years ago. He had no right! She smashed at the bag with a fist and watched it tumble to the oak parquet floor. "To hell with the food!"

The violence confounded her even more than it did him. At a loss, he moved to take her into his arms. She reacted as if he'd struck her. "Why did you have to come to New York?" she demanded in an impassioned voice.

"I came because of you."

"You wasted your time."

"Why? Is there someone else?" His expression was strained. A thin purple vein pulsed at his left temple as he rubbed his lower lip.

"Yes."

He studied her face. "You're lying."

She didn't deny it. "You swore you would never come to Manhattan General. Never place yourself under your father's domination again. Was it a lie? Or do you make vows the way you change clothes—to suit your needs at the time?"

Stung by her words, he grabbed her shoulders and pressed her back against the table. She could feel the edge bite into her spine. "No, it wasn't a lie. I told you I wouldn't come to Manhattan General unless I felt secure enough about myself that it wouldn't matter if I was around him."

"And do you?"

"I don't know. But I have to find out. Being near him, yet having the strength to keep separate from him — maybe that's a rite of passage I have to put myself through before I can be certain I'm my own man."

"Some rite of passage! Assistant Chief of Surgery is hardly trial by fire!"

He shook her hard. "Stop it, Becca! That was my father's choice, not mine. And where do you come off accusing me of lying?" His voice mimicked hers. " 'I swear I'll never leave you, David'!" His grip tightened. "Remember, Becca. Remember how many times you told me that up in Boston? What was it all about, Becca? Where is your fine sense of integrity now?"

"You're hurting me."

He released her shoulders but didn't step back from her. His expression was raw with pain. She had known of her own longing. Now she saw the depth of his. "How could you cut me off that way, Becca? With no warning. No discussion. One day we're everything to each other. The next you don't exist. I don't understand. You're not a coward. I watched you take the worst kind of punishment at Boston Memorial and stand up to the lot of them with enough spunk to defeat an army."

"I couldn't leave you any other way, David." Her voice was low.

"Why not? Why couldn't you confront me? Tell me what was wrong? Have it out?" He closed his eyes, the memory of anguish too close to the surface.

Always when she'd thought of the way she'd left David, there had been a sense of shame. But it had been eased by the certainty that he would be quickly consoled by the slew of standbys waiting to take her place. Now she saw that it hadn't been that way for him.

"Christ, Becca," he muttered. "Have you any idea what you did to me?"

She tried to twist away from him, but he wouldn't let her. He pulled her close suddenly and punished her mouth with a hurtful kiss. She almost fell when he released her.

"I'm sorry, David." The words came from trembling lips. The familiar feel of his body against hers had set her to shaking.

He smoothed her hair absentmindedly. She understood his need to touch because it reflected her own. "Sorry isn't enough." His voice was rough. "Give me some explanation, Becca. Help me understand."

"I tried to. So many times, I tried. But you wouldn't listen."

"I'm listening now." He fisted his hand and let his knuckles caress her cheek. "Why did you run from me, Becca?"

"I ran because when I was with you there was no me. You wanted to guide my life, shape my thoughts. . . . My God, David, you even tried to assure me that I like the same foods you do. It would have been bad enough if we agreed on most things, but we don't."

"You're talking about my convincing you to leave Boston Memorial after the hearings."

"I'm talking about that and other things. I'm talking of intolerance and coercion and possession. And I'm also trying to be fair. Because more than anything I'd like to put the blame on you for what happened between us and I can't. You see, the act of domination takes two, and I was a very willing participant. I *let* you do it."

He spoke slowly. "You're telling me that I do to you what my father does to me. Or at least tries to do."

"Yes. And my running from you . . . well, maybe the independence I gained in the two years away from you was my rite of passage. I like what I've become, David, and I have no intention of letting you back into my life to bollux it up again." She ignored the hurt in his eyes. "I'm not proud of the way I left you, David, but at the time, I couldn't do any better. I was scared that if I confronted you I would stay."

His gaze locked with hers. "Because you loved me?"

She didn't answer.

His eyes darkened to cobalt. She saw his intent and put up her hands to stop him from reaching for her. "No! It's no good David. Nothing's changed."

"You're wrong. Everything's changed. Because I know now what it is to be without you." He pushed her protesting hands out of the way. His fingers threaded through her hair, and he cupped her head in his palms, bringing her face nearer to his. She could smell the musky odors of Polo aftershave and Yardley soap that had always been uniquely his. "Give us another chance, Becca," he said huskily. "I'll do better. I promise."

He kissed her this time with infinite tenderness, his lips moving on hers, his tongue probing her mouth. She tried to summon up all the reasons why she shouldn't let this happen, but in the light of what he was making her feel, the past was receding and the future becoming a hazy unknown. Only the now was real, and she hurt with need for him.

"Where's the bedroom?" he whispered urgently.

They made love the way famished people eat — frenzied and in huge gulps, gorging themselves until their initial need was sated. Then they made love again, this time slowly, savoring the feel and smell and taste of each other's bodies after so long a time. She had forgotten so much, Becca thought. She had forgotten how he knew to rub his fingers up and down her spine, massaging the base of her neck until all the tension ebbed from her and she could give of herself unstintingly. And she had forgotten the way he used words to encourage her and to tell her of the joy she was giving him, until the barrier of her innate shyness crumbled along with her inhibitions.

Curled into each other in the queen-size canopy bed, they slept afterwards, for how long, Becca didn't know. She was awakened by a clenching of her stomach, followed by an audible rumbling.

David grunted. His hand slid downward between their bodies and came to rest on her navel. "How far apart are the pains?" he croaked sleepily.

"Don't be funny. I'm starving."

"You lied about that too."

"Mmm. Do you think that Chinese food is still edible?" she asked wistfully.

He chuckled, then unwound himself from her and pulled on the trousers he'd flung toward the foot of the bed. He tugged at her hand. "Let's go see."

They ate at the small white table in the kitchen. She had put on an oversized T-shirt but left her feet bare. They were stretched out to rest on David's while he ate his spareribs, licking his fingers with relish when they became too sticky with sauce.

"That's obscene," she said, using her napkin with exaggerated daintiness.

"Uh-huh." He licked his fingers again. "What are you doing Saturday night?"

"Are you asking me out on a date?"

He nodded, his eyes warm on hers. "I have a craving. I want to take you to Côte Basque. I want to wine you and dine you and enjoy all the things with you that we didn't do in Boston because there was never any time." His happiness was apparent in his smile. "I want a new beginning for us, Becca."

A lump gathered in her throat. "It's a date," she said. She wanted to tell him what it meant to her to feel loved and cared for again, and that more than anything she wanted a new beginning for them also, but she felt too overwhelmed to say it, and all that came out was a rather formal, "Thank you for asking."

He grinned. "You may take that thank you back. There's a catch to the date. I promised to show up at a party first, and I want you with me."

"A jeans and T-shirt party?"

"A black dress and pearls party."

"I hate those things."

"I know. But it'll only be for an hour. And I want to show you off." He reached across the table and slid his hand up her arm. "Say yes," he murmured.

She smiled at him. "Yes."

They ate for a few minutes in companionable silence then he shifted his feet and cracked a fortune cookie. He held it up to the light. " 'When you play with fire, expect to get burned,' " he read. "Now *there's* a profound statement!" He let the paper flutter to the table. "Speaking of getting burned," he said, "I understand that Angelica Vargas is your patient. Under the circumstances, do you think that's a good idea?"

She hesitated. "No, I don't." For some reason, she didn't want to discuss it with David.

"Then why?"

"I don't know why! Leave it alone, David. It's just something I have to do, okay?"

Startled at her vehemence, he stared at her.

Impulsively, she stretched her hand across the table. "I'm sorry." He covered her hand with his. The questions were there in his eyes. She was grateful he didn't ask them. "Who told you that Angelica was my patient? Carolyn Stedman?"

"Carolyn? No." His surprise seemed genuine. "My father told it to me. I was hoping I'd find you there when I went to Angelica's room."

"You went to visit Angelica?"

"Of course I did. Why do you look so surprised? Our families have known each other for years."

She looked at David as if he was a winning lottery ticket. She had never thought of him as a source of information, but why not? "David, tell me about the Vargas family. Tell me about his first wife, Celmira. What was she like?

He shrugged. "A nice-looking woman. Nothing to compare with Maria. But then Vargas never married Celmira for her looks. Or so my father tells me."

"Why did he marry her?"

"For position. Vargas didn't marry until he was in his mid-thirties. By then he had parlayed a small ship chandler's business his father left him into a conglomerate of holdings that included a shipbuilding enterprise, an oil well, and a good chunk of South American real estate. But Vargas came from peasant stock. His mother is part Indian and it always rankled. He wanted to refine the bloodline."

"Sounds like he was choosing a horse," Becca murmured.

"Is there any difference? Ouch!" He grinned and withdrew his toe as she stomped on it under the table. "Anyway, Vargas chose Celmira Estevez, the older daughter in a family with a lot of lineage but very little money."

"How long were they married?"

"Ten years. I met Celmira twice during that time. Once when they were just married and once a year before she died. She looked so awful the second time I could hardly recognize her. She was bedridden and had turned into a hating, complaining invalid who didn't have a good word to say about anyone but Angelica. She adored that kid even though she hadn't been able to take care of her from birth." He shook his head. "I didn't know who I felt sorrier for . . . her or Jose. I wasn't surprised when he married Maria so fast after she died."

"Maria must have been a good deal younger than her sister."

"Twenty years. She was only a kid when Jose married Celmira. When her father and mother were killed in a car crash, she was sent to Switzerland to be educated. She was seventeen when she came back to live with Jose and her sister. And she was a beauty." He caught Becca's glance and laughed. "Not my type. But a beauty!"

"What did Celmira Vargas die of?"

"According to my father, it was a myocardial infarction. The heart just gave out." He stretched then stood up to help her as she rose to clear the dishes.

"What about Angelica?" she asked. "Did your father happen to mention whether Angelica was with her mother at the time it happened? I realize that he wouldn't have too many details about what happened in South America, but it's just possible . . ."

He shook his head. "My father never mentioned whether Angelica was with her when she died, but I don't understand what you mean about South America. I distinctly remember my father telling me that she died in the town house here in New York."

She turned off the faucets abruptly. "David, would you happen to know who her attending was at the time?"

She knew the answer even before she heard the words.

"Gottlieb, of course. He's been the Vargas physician for years." He came up behind her and nuzzled the skin at the base of her neck.

If that were so, she thought, then why had Gottlieb denied any knowledge of her death?

She drew in her breath as David's hands came round to cradle her breasts. "David, the dishes . . ."

He turned her in his arms. "To hell with the dishes," he whispered.

Fourteen

"It's amazing that Angelica remembers every detail of her dream so well," Carolyn Stedman said, contemplatively tapping the butt end of a pencil on her desk. "But then terror can carve images into the mind with unbelievable clarity."

Becca nodded impatiently. She was in Carolyn Stedman's office, seated across the desk from her at nine the following morning. "But what does the dream *mean?*" she prodded. "Angelica talks of being very hot and seeing sand on the floor and being deprived of water. Does that suggest a desert?"

"I doubt it. But I'm less interested in the surroundings right now than I am in the characters who people her dream. Angelica tells us that she herself is in the dream. She also says that her doll Gabriella is there. Now we know that in real life Angelica identifies Gabriella with herself . . ."

"Are you saying that in the dream Gabriella actually represents Angelica?"

"I'm suggesting that it's a possibility."

"If that's so, then it would follow that Angelica represents someone else." Excited, Becca leaned forward in her chair. "Remember I told you that when Angelica related the dream to me, she spoke in her own voice. But when she quoted word for word what had been said in it her whole personality changed. She spoke in a deeper, more somber voice, her face seemed to age . . ."

"As if she were slipping into someone else's shoes."

"Exactly. And that character is older, sterner . . ."

"And bedridden."

Becca slapped the desk in triumph. "Her mother!"

"Maybe. But don't get hung up on it. That's only one interpretation. There may be others. Besides, even if we've got those two pieces of the puzzle right, we haven't got a clue as to the third." She rose and stretched. "My kingdom for a window in this place. I feel so claustrophobic in here, I can hardly function."

"What third?" Becca asked.

"The shadow, of course. That's the most important one. According to what you told me, Angelica—or whoever she represents in the dream—knows she'll be saved when the shadow appears before her. 'Help me!' she begs, but the shadow only laughs at her."

"And leaves her alone to die."

Becca remembered the afternoon she had drawn blood from Angelica. The desperation in the child's voice when she had spoken of her mother had stayed with her for hours afterward.

Papa told me she wouldn't ever feel hurt again. He said God had reached down to take her because she couldn't be saved. They put her in a box . . . a cold, cold box . . .

She had sought to comfort Angelica then. She had explained that if death was inevitable it had to be accepted.

But what if it hadn't been inevitable?

"Dr. Stedman, do you think its possible—"

"What I think is that you're jumping to conclusions." Her voice held a warning. "We may very well be dealing with a child's vivid imagination here, nothing more." Her tone softened. "Look, you're already embroiled in a case that leaves you vulnerable to all kinds of ramifications if anything were to go wrong. Don't make it any worse for yourself than it is. Let me give this more thought—work a little longer with the child. At this point we don't even know for sure if Angelica was with her mother when she died."

The psychiatrist was right, of course, but Becca couldn't help resenting the efficient way in which she had been checked.

"You don't mince words, do you, Dr. Stedman?"

Her smile revealed even white teeth. "According to my brother, it's my greatest failing. Sam believes that a wise woman soft-peddles her aggressiveness."

Becca watched her repin her wavy chestnut hair where it had escaped from the amber combs that held it. Carolyn Stedman was really a striking woman, she thought. Much too attractive to be a "friend" to a man like David. After making love with him through half the night, Becca wished she could feel secure enough to rule her out as a rival. But she couldn't.

"Did I tell you that I stopped in to see Angelica early this morning?" the psychiatrist said. "It was while the nurse was trying to coax her to eat some breakfast." She frowned. "Seems a good sort, that Bates, but a nervous Nellie. Anyway, Angelica wouldn't touch the food. She says nothing tastes right anymore. Does that have any meaning?"

"It could. But without the test results from the lab, I can't draw any conclusions. And they're dragging their heels. What do you mean about Bates being a nervous Nellie?"

"Well, when I was there I noticed the marks on Angelica's shoulder and asked Bates about it. Instead of answering, she clapped her hands over her mouth with as stricken a look on her face as if she'd robbed the crown jewels. 'My God,' she said, 'I forgot to cut her nails.' I felt so bad for the poor woman that I found myself assuring her that no terrible damage had been done. Does she have a hard time remembering other things?"

"Some." There had been more than some. But that was none of the psychiatrist's business. "Aggie Bates is a competent nurse. And I've never seen kids trust anyone the way they do her."

Even as she praised her, Becca wondered if there might be more to Aggie's forgetfulness than the lack of confidence Helen Walters had spoken about. After all, what did she really know about the workings of Aggie's mind.

At seven-thirty that evening, Gottlieb was thinking much the same thing as he perched on a barstool at Freddie's. He had nursed two Jack Daniels in the hour he'd been there, staring at the faded photos on the green walls in the flickering light given off by the glass sconces. He knew them by heart. Freddie with Richard Nixon. Freddie with Sammy Davis Jr., Freddie with Mayor Lindsey. With Carol Channing. He had memorized them in an effort to distract himself from the thought that Aggie might have changed her mind about coming.

How strange, he thought, that this seedy establishment, housed in a tenement building that should have been condemned years before, should have been the scene of so much between them. The only thing to recommend it was that no one he knew went there.

He suddenly recalled the afternoon early on in their relationship when he'd discovered that his patient, a friend he'd known all his life, had been diagnosed with inoperable cancer. It had devastated him. He'd met with Aggie that night at Freddie's, blindly looking for the breast to suckle and the shoulder to cry on. But when he was seated across from her he found himself so bottled with misery, he couldn't get the words out.

With infinite patience, she'd coaxed them from him and when he was finished with the telling, he'd seen the enormity of his pain mirrored in her face. She'd reached across the table and grasped his wrists, her eyes intent on the sheen that misted his eyes. "A man isn't weak if he cries," she'd said.

"I never cry."

"Maybe on the outside you don't."

As far as he could remember, no woman had offered him comfort since his mother had died in an accident when he was ten. It had touched him deeply and unnerved him. He'd pulled away from her and walked out of the bar, unwilling for her to see the extent of his vulnerability. But she hadn't allowed it. She'd caught up with him just outside. They were almost of a height. Regardless of the passersby, she had taken him in her arms and held him until gradually the knot inside him had eased.

He recognized her footstep now before he heard her voice. He looked up.

"I'm sorry I'm late," she said.

She had held well, he thought. She still had the same lean body of ten years ago. Maybe a little more poke to the belly, a bit of extra flab on the backside . . . no longer "the classiest ass in town." There were new lines in her face, too, and her wheat-colored hair was tipped with silver. He had the feeling that she didn't smile much anymore.

"No problem." He gestured toward his drink. "What would

you like to have?"

"A Dewars on the rocks."

He ordered her drink as she seated herself next to him. He felt his palms begin to sweat. For days now he'd existed in limbo, waiting for this moment to be alone with her. He wanted her to tell him that she still loved him. He wanted to know why she had left him so abruptly. He wanted to know everything she'd done in the last ten years without him. But for some reason, the intimacy he'd felt between them in Angelica's room wasn't there now.

"How's your mother?" he asked, needing to break the ice with something. Too late he remembered she never liked to talk about her mother.

There was an odd stillness in the way she held herself. "She died a month ago," she said finally.

"I'm sorry." She looked tired, he thought. Bone tired. "Tough day?"

She shrugged. "They're all tough now."

She stepped aside for the thin mustached waiter who placed their drinks onto a plastic tray and led them to a booth.

She sat opposite him across the scarred wooden table. She wore a pale yellow shift that sallowed her skin. He had long ago conceded that her taste in clothes was a couturiere's nightmare, but it had never mattered to him.

"I think what bothers me most are the new work shifts," she was saying. "When I was head nurse, my staff worked seven and a half hours, five days a week, and put in lots of overtime besides. Now a lot of the nurses are working twelve-hour shifts for three days a week. It takes getting used to."

"I know. I've got cases where the nurse meets my patient for the first time on Monday then disappears until Friday. By then the patient has been discharged. It makes for a lack of consistency in patient care."

"It also makes for a lot of errors."

He took a swig of his bourbon. "Aggie, why didn't you go in as a head nurse?"

Her smile was rueful. "Believe it or not, I didn't have the credentials. In the nineteen seventies I got promoted to head nurse on the basis of practical experience. Today that doesn't wash anymore. You need a BSN, which I never got. Besides, I . . . I didn't want the responsibility."

"Is that why you're doubling up on your shifts and spending enough time with the Vargas girl to call it private duty? I wouldn't say that's not taking on responsibility, would you?"

She shrugged. "I've been asked to help out. The girl's stepmother wants Angelica to have a private nurse, but there's a hospital rule against it, so Helen Walters asked if I could spend as much time with Angelica as possible. It's a way of keeping the stepmother quiet and I . . . well, Angelica seems to like me."

"And Angelica always gets what she likes."

"The child is hurting, Gar."

"Yes, she's hurting. She's also a manipulative, self-serving little monster who has blackmailed everyone around her into giving in to all her desires by using her mother's death to make them feel guilty."

She splayed her hands on the table and half-rose in her seat. "I won't listen to this!"

The outrage in her voice brought him up short. What was he doing?

"Aggie, I love you," he said abruptly.

She sank back into her seat, a defeated look on her face. "Don't say that."

"Why not?"

"Because I came here to tell you I wouldn't be meeting with you like this again. Whatever was between us—"

"I want you to marry me, Aggie."

"Don't!"

The pain in her face confused him. Why was she reacting this way? He knew she still cared for him, as he for her. Other things had changed between them but not that.

The waiter brought them a ten-item menu then left. He could see that she welcomed the respite. He didn't. "Aggie, if it's because of Vicky, I think you should know we've been separated for years now. I live at the Claymore here in the city. I had no reason to file for a divorce before, but—"

"Gar, I can't marry you."

Anger began to override the confusion. "Because you don't love me?"

She didn't answer.

"Why, Aggie?" he demanded.

She spoke low. "Because you've changed so much I don't know you anymore." Her eyes went over him in distaste. "Those clothes and that tan . . ."

He shook his head. "Window dressing. I haven't changed as much as you think. But there were circumstances . . ." His dark eyes pleaded with her to understand. "After you left, I . . . I came apart. I tried to forget you were gone by burying myself in my work, but that only made it worse. I couldn't sleep. I dropped weight. One day I woke up and I couldn't function at all. I was a cripple, Aggie. An emotional cripple."

He took a sip of his bourbon. "I went to see Thorsen, the hospital shrink. He lined it up for me. I needed to get on Elavil and I needed to take an interest in something besides my work, otherwise I was going to crack up for good." He toyed with a fork. "Golf and antidepressants. They became my crutches."

"And that fancy suite of offices on Park Avenue. Is that a crutch too?"

"It's not a crime to have fancy offices, Aggie."

"It is when the only way you can pay the rent is by doing routine checkups for Vargas's corporate employees."

He flinched. "Who told you that?"

"I overheard Kip Flanders telling it to Helen Walters. My God, Gar. Checkups!"

"You don't understand. There are reasons . . ."

"They can't be good enough to warrant that." Her eyes filled with sorrow. "What happened to you, Gar? You were the most talented resident the hospital ever had. And you felt so deeply for your patients that half the time I had to drag you out of that hospital." Her gaze turned contemptuous. "Now you wear custom-made suits and have so little compassion that you can accuse a sick little girl of being a culprit instead of a victim."

The waiter came to the table with a pad and pencil and a bored expression. "Are you ready to order now?"

She pushed her drink to one side and stood up. "No. I've had enough." She ignored the waiter's raised brows and pulled the strap of her tan leather purse across her shoulders. "I'll see you at the hospital, Gar."

She turned and left, and he didn't try to stop her. He leaned forward on his elbows and put his head in his hands. He felt hollowed out, empty. He had found her, but it had done him no good. She was still eluding him, and he didn't know why. Oh, the reasons she had given had been valid enough. But he knew Aggie. Her disillusionment wasn't sufficient to merit her withdrawal. The old Aggie would have lambasted him, shown him the error of his ways, made him promise to change, then taken him into her arms.

Why hadn't she done that?

He sat there brooding about it until he'd downed the next bourbon and the one he ordered after that. When he finally arose, he was weaving, but he'd come to some conclusions. Aggie loved him. With everything else she'd said she had never denied that. There had to be something else going on with her. Something she hadn't told him about. Something crucial enough to keep her from him. And he wasn't going to rest until he found out what it was.

Fifteen

Beneath the oversized Waterford chandelier that lit the huge living room of his Fifth Avenue town house, Arnold Hardinger was basking in the heady glow of success. The turnout for the party had gone beyond his expectations. From behind the tall Sèvres urn where he halted to survey the scene, he could randomly pick out Senator Aaron Clagman, Congressman Warner Otis, Ledhaven from the Ford Foundation, Almato from Cuomo's headquarters, the society editor from the *Times*, and a host of other notables clustered in groups along the ivory faux marble walls. The scene was reminiscent of the seventies when he was riding high.

His eye caught that of Chuck Peabody's, and he took in the smug expression on the hospital chairman's face. Under pressure Hardinger had been forced to divulge to the doddering figurehead that it was Jose Vargas who was behind the proffered twenty million dollar donation. He had sworn the chairman to secrecy, but he wondered now if Peabody had leaked the information. It would certainly explain the turnout.

He stepped from behind the urn to greet Sinclair from Banker's Trust, then moved on to the bar and ordered a brandy. From across the room, he saw Laura pointing him out to the editor of *Medical Tribune*. She smiled at him and he smiled back. She was the consummate actress, his Laura. Always able to measure up for appearance's sake. They hadn't talked in days. Not since she'd found out about the little biochemist.

He swirled his brandy in the goblet. Surprisingly, she'd brought the affair out in the open this time. It had amused the hell out of him. When Laura got mad she always sounded as if she had a broom up her ass. "This humiliation will not be borne!" she'd said. He'd almost laughed in her face. It would be borne all right. She'd swallow it like she had all his other indiscretions. What other choice did she have? She was too much of a weakling to make it on her own. She'd tried it once five years ago and had come running back in less than a month with her tail between her legs.

He made a mental note to have Pemby pick up something for her at Tiffany's. It would speed the process. Given a sop to her ego, she'd go through the motions of "forgiving him" and continue bravely on as before. Laura was as much a martyr as she was a masochist.

"Great party, Arnold!" Reenie Whitcomb said at his elbow. She was a thin freckle-faced woman with generations of breeding behind her who looked as if she would be more at home straddling the race horses she bred at her Kentucky stables than clinging to her husband's arm at this gala.

"Thanks, Reenie."

At her side, Anthony Whitcomb viewed the turnout with a sardonic smile. It was no secret that he thought Hardinger's parties in bad taste. "Thinly disguised fund-raisers," he'd called them. Hardinger had invited the medical director only at Peabody's insistence. "Got to make a show of force, Arnold," the chairman had said. "Hold our heads high in the face of all this blasted publicity that Ryker woman is drumming up."

"More lambs for the fleecing?" Whitcomb said, nodding toward the crowd. Though black tie was optional, the medical director had arrived in a custom-tailored tux and paisley cummerbund that set off his broad shoulders and lean hips. "Wouldn't that twenty million make the need superfluous or are you hedging your bets in case Vargas doesn't come through?"

Damn Peabody and his loose mouth! The chairman's revelation had put him in the position of being a pompous blowhard if Vargas reneged. But why was he borrowing trouble before it was realized? He had been in touch with Vargas in Buenos Aires to assure him that everything possible was being done for Angelica. Jose was due back at any minute now, and there had been no indication in their talks that the magnate was displeased in any way. With luck that check would be in his hands within a few days, and he could get the first good night's sleep he'd had in months.

He stared at Whitcomb's flat midsection and unconsciously sucked in his gut. "I won't need to hedge my bets," he said.

From a passing hors d'oeuvre tray, Whitcomb speared a stuffed mushroom cap with practiced ease. "That's what I like in a man," he murmured to his wife. "Confidence."

Embarrassed at the sarcasm, Reenie Whitcomb put a placating hand on her host's arm. "Tony tells me that your son has been named assistant chief of Surgery at the hospital. You must be very proud."

"I am."

"Will we get a chance to meet him tonight?"

"I'm expecting him very soon."

He glanced at his watch and hid his annoyance. David was late. On this night of all nights. He tried to curb his impatience. He reminded himself that David was still unmindful of the role he was being groomed for at Manhattan General. Until now all his son's battles had been fought in the operating room. But his climb at the hospital would depend more on politicking then medical knowhow. Networking! That was the name of the game. And what better time for him to start than tonight with the hospital's top hierarchy and staunchest supporters under one roof.

And there was yet another reason for David to be here. Laura had invited Charles Peabody's only granddaughter for the express purpose of meeting David. Nancy Peabody had all the credentials needed to make him a proper wife. She was malleable, attractive, soft-spoken, a Wellesley graduate, and in line to inherit a good chunk of her grandfather's steamship company.

"I believe your wife is trying to tell you something," Reenie Whitcomb said.

He looked toward Laura, then followed her eye signals to the marble tiled entryway. Triumph shot through him like a bromide. Reflected in the mirrored walls and the buzz that swept the room was Jose Vargas in black tux and ruffled white shirt. He smiled casually as he accepted the homage his presence always elicited. Next to him, looking more like his daughter than his wife, stood Maria Vargas in a clinging backless gown, her long blond hair twisted into a shining coil low on her neck. Not as schooled as Laura in hiding her emotions, she wore a sullen expression on her beautiful face that gave Hardinger the impression that they'd been quarreling.

Aware that Laura was threading her way toward the foyer, Hardinger started to do the same.

"Lucky bastard!" Whitcomb flung at his retreating back.

Unable to resist, Hardinger turned and regarded the medical director with undisguised contempt. "Not luck, Tony. Talent. Something you wouldn't know anything about."

Twenty minutes later Becca stood in the entry to the resplendent town house feeling underdressed and overawed. "You," she said scathingly to David, "are a devious man."

He handed her jacket to the butler who greeted him with familiarity. "I said black dress and pearls, didn't I?"

She snorted delicately. "The understatement of the year."

She remembered that large parties had always been an area of dissension between them. Unlike herself, David was comfortable with the barrage of introductions to strange people that they entailed.

A kaleidoscope of Oriental rugs, richly burnished antiques, and high carved ceilings impressed itself on her mind before he guided her forward. "One hour, Becca. That's all I ask."

"You'll owe me," she said.

He looked lean and elegant in his cuffed black suit. His blue eyes traced the curves of her figure in the silk shift, and his lips mimicked a leer. "I know just the coin I'll pay in." He reached out to tuck a stray wisp of her hair into place. "We won't stay long, I promise. Just give me enough time to wade through the introductions my parents have lined up."

"For you, not for me. What makes you think they would even want me here?"

"They'll want you because I want you."

A warm sense of belonging suffused her. She hadn't realized how sorely she'd missed that feeling in the last two years. She leaned close to him, needing to touch. He clasped her hand in his and laced their fingers together. She could feel his sudden tension when he tightened his grip. She glanced up and followed his gaze.

Silvered hair contrasting vividly with the ruddy glow on his face, Arnold Hardinger was making his way toward them through the back-slapping, joke-quipping crowd. Completely at ease, he paused now and then to parry some snide remark with a rejoinder that left bellows of laughter in his wake. The man should have been a politician, she thought.

He was all smiles as he reached them. He put an arm about his son's shoulders, and his deep voice boomed in her ear. "David, glad you could make it. Any later and you'd have missed the surprise I have in store for you. And Dr. Landau, isn't it? I'm so pleased that David brought you. I was just telling my assistant, Pemby, that I wanted to personally thank you for the care you've given to Angelica Vargas. The girl can't stop singing your praises."

"Thank you," she said.

She saw David relax and knew that despite his reassurances, he had been worried about his father's acceptance of her. She remembered her impression of Arnold Hardinger when they'd first met in Boston at the time of the inquiry. David had called it a distorted one. At the time she hadn't been sure. Flattered at her host's congeniality now, she was inclined to admit she'd made a mistake.

Until she looked up and met Hardinger's eyes.

A coldness enveloped her. She hadn't been mistaken in Boston. The animosity was there, cloaked in the trappings of cordiality, but as obvious to her as the rhinestone studs on his starched white shirt. What she couldn't figure out was why.

A blond-haired woman in a beaded blue gown appeared at their side. She was in her early fifties but smooth-skinned and slender as a girl. She kissed David's cheek as he reached out to hug her. "I'd almost given you up," she said.

He broke from her and slid an arm around Becca's waist. "Mother, this is Dr. . . . this is Becca Landau."

If the upper half of David's face resembled his father's, the aquiline nose, generous mouth, and pointed chin were clearly his mother's. She regarded Becca thoughtfully now and extended a delicate pink-tipped hand. Becca shook it. "I'm pleased to meet you," she said.

"What's the surprise you were talking about?" David asked his father.

"Lahgerhorn. He's here."

David's eyes widened. "Karl Lahgerhorn?" At his father's nod, he turned excitedly to Becca. "Becca, you remember me speaking about Lahgerhorn. He's the Norwegian cardiologist responsible for the breakthrough on the new laser technique in bypass surgery. I'm going to attend a seminar in Boston in a couple of weeks to hear him lecture on it."

"How would you like a preview of that lecture?" his father asked.

"Now?"

"Why not?" He regarded Becca coolly. "That is, if Dr. Landau wouldn't mind spending a few moments with your mother."

How effectively he'd excluded her, Becca thought. Actually, she did mind. She had little in common with David's mother, and Lahgerhorn's findings promised to be interesting. She waited for David to say something, to ask what she preferred, but he didn't. Color stained her cheeks. If she protested she would sound ungracious.

David's fingers slid along her side drawing intimate, sensuous circles. Was that a promise of things to come? she fumed. A reward for her understanding? A consolation prize for his allowing her to be treated as his appendage?

Oblivious to her turmoil, he let his hand drop and gave his full attention to his father. "How did you ever get Lahgerhorn to come here?"

"By pressing the right buttons," the pied piper said as he led his son away. "Influence, David. That's where it's at. But you'll learn that soon enough." They disappeared into the crowd.

Beside her, Laura Hardinger spoke in a soft, breathy voice. "There's someone here who wants very much to meet with you."

"Who?"

"You'll see." She linked her arm companionably with Becca's and guided her forward.

There was something familiar about Laura Hardinger,

Becca thought, then realized how much the woman reminded her of her own mother. Their marriages were structured so similarly that the two women could have been interchangeable. Like her mother, Laura Hardinger was the sidekick, the enabler, her identity so bound up with her husband's that it was a wonder she could still call her name her own.

When she had interned at Boston Memorial, it had galled Becca that though she and her father had quarrelled on almost every issue, David had agreed with Joshua Landau on many things. Having met his parents now, she could understand why. David was a product of this type of marriage and though he had sworn to change his thinking for her sake, was he strong enough to do it? Certainly his allowing his father to exclude her from the conversation with Lahgerhorn just now was no indication of it.

She became aware that Laura Hardinger was leading her across the floor toward the window in the far corner of the room. In front of the massive grand piano that blocked it, she could see Maria Vargas talking intimately with a stocky older man at her side. Even from this distance Becca could see the gold crucifix that dented the silk of her dress. Becca's lips compressed. This was carrying politeness too far. She'd had enough of Angelica's stepmother at the hospital. She had no desire to talk with her here.

She was about to voice her annoyance when the man with Maria turned slightly and his face — so like Angelica's grandmother — came into view. With a shock, Becca realized that she was staring at Jose Vargas. Fed on the larger-than-life publicity that had preceded him, she hadn't known what to expect. But certainly not this unimpressive man before her.

She was less than a few yards from him when she felt the full impact of his presence. He stood no more than five feet ten, but he appeared much taller. It had to do with the surety with which he carried himself and the authoritative look in the black eyes that contrasted so sharply with his thick white hair and olive skin. Though his features were similar to his mother's, what had seemed crafty and coarse in the old woman was refined to a subtle arrogance in the son. It added to the quiet power he exuded.

Maria Vargas whispered something to him, and he turned fully about. As Becca came abreast of him, he didn't wait for an introduction. He took her hand in his, made her a courtly bow, and lifted her fingers to his lips.

"Dr. Landau. I am very pleased to meet you." Though formal in the way he strung his words, his voice was soft-spoken with scarcely a trace of an accent.

She tugged her hand from his self-consciously. "Thank you."

Laura Hardinger beamed at them. "Well, now that you two have met, if you don't mind . . ." She gestured at the crowd, begged their understanding with a glance, then flitted away.

"I must say I'm surprised to see you, Mr. Vargas," Becca said. "When I spoke to Angelica this morning, she didn't tell me you were coming back so soon."

"That's because she didn't know. I rushed my business in Buenos Aires to get here as soon as I could. The thought of Angelica in a hospital . . ." He shuddered. "But let us talk of more pleasant things. I have just come from Angelica and listened to my daughter speak of nothing but your kindness to her. I wish to thank you. She also spoke of the trust you inspired in her. For that I wish to commend you. It is a feat of no little accomplishment. Angelica does not trust easily."

"Mr. Vargas, I did for Angelica what I would do for any of my patients and I'll continue to do so."

"Again, my appreciation, but there will be no further need."

She looked at him blankly. "I don't understand."

He shrugged. "There is little to understand. Since her mother's death, my daughter has been sheltered a great deal. And with good reason. As you must realize by now, Angelica does not do well outside her own element." He nodded toward his wife. "Maria has told me of her increasing depression and the unpardonable furor she has caused at the hospital, and I have come to the conclusion that it would be best for Angelica to be taken home."

"You can't do that!" She hadn't realized that her voice had risen until she saw people near them turning to look.

"I beg your pardon." There was more shock than anger in his response.

Becca turned to the woman at his side. "Mrs. Vargas, surely

you have told your husband—"

"Dr. Landau," Vargas interrupted coldly. "Unless Angelica's condition can be exorcised by the church, I suggest you address your remarks to me." There was a mixture of pain and contempt in his eyes as he regarded his wife.

The man could be cruel, Becca thought, as Maria Vargas flinched. She lowered her voice. There was an element of pleading in it when she said, "Mr. Vargas, your daughter is ill. She belongs in a hospital."

"I will agree with the first but quarrel with the second. Dr. Gottlieb and I have spoken of Angelica's condition. The fever she had when she entered the hospital is gone. And there are no findings of particular note in the blood or urine tests that came in late this afternoon from the laboratory."

"But the results of the spinal tap aren't in. And the weakness in the arms and legs hasn't abated." She realized that she was overreacting. The man had a right to remove his child if he wanted to. But she couldn't stop herself. Her commitment to Angelica was too strong. The only way that little girl was going to get the emotional help she needed was through herself and Carolyn Stedman. "If you would only wait," she pleaded.

"Wait? For what? The hospital is contaminated with filthy diseases that can be transmitted through the very air my daughter breathes." He shuddered. "Angelica will be better attended in her own home."

Becca remembered what his wife had said about his being afraid of hospitals. Did he really fear them to such an extent that he would put his daughter's well-being in jeopardy? Or was it something else he feared—like the accessibility to Angelica that he had been so careful to bar until now?

She had to give it another try. "Please understand, Mr. Vargas—"

"What is it that Jose must understand?"

Hardinger's hearty voice echoed behind her. Becca exhaled on a sigh of relief. She might be at odds with the head of Manhattan General, but she respected his powers of persuasion. Hardinger would undoubtedly succeed where she had failed.

She raised her hands in a helpless gesture. "Mr. Vargas has just told me that he's taking Angelica out of the hospital."

His surprise was erased before it surfaced. He spoke to her, but his eyes were on Jose Vargas. "That is his prerogative, Dr. Landau."

"But—"

"No buts." His voice held a warning note. "Please remember that Manhattan General is not a prison, doctor. The patients are free to come and go as they choose." His eyes narrowed at her combative stance. "Dr. Landau, I'm sure you'd like to hear what Karl Lahgerhorn has to say on the latest techniques in by-pass surgery. You'll find him with David just beyond the hors d'oeuvre table."

Rage filled her, so blinding that it distorted her vision. She was being dismissed as summarily as if she were a child. And there wasn't a damned thing she could do about it.

Jose Vargas inclined his head. "It's been a pleasure," he said. There was no animosity in his voice.

With an aborted nod, she turned sharply and left.

She jostled her way through the maze of people. She stopped when she reached the hors d'oeuvre table. Breathing heavily, she tried to calm herself before she reached David. It took her a minute to realize that she didn't want to join David. What she really wanted was out!

She made it to the foyer in record time. "My jacket, please," she said to the butler.

He had just brought it to her when David came charging through the crowd. His hair was disheveled, the sleeve of his suit pushed off a shoulder. He caught her arm and stared at her set lips. "Becca, what's happened? Where are you going?"

"Home."

She waited for him to say something about polite behavior or cutting short his interview with Lahgerhorn or the duty he owed his parents. She knew that if he did, she would end the relationship then and there.

He held up the jacket for her. "I'll take you," he said.

"Your father is a monster," she hurled at him, sweeping her hair from her face as she tried to twist from his arms. She had kicked off her silk pumps in a fury when they had entered her living room a few minutes earlier, and she could feel the worn spots in the rag rug beneath her feet.

His hands looped around her waist. "Becca, be reasonable. What did you expect my father to say when Vargas insisted on taking his daughter out of the hospital?"

"Let go of me!"

"No. Don't you see that legally Vargas was within his rights?"

"I'm not talking legally. I'm talking morally. Your father could have put up a fight. At least shown his displeasure."

"And incurred Vargas's?"

"Yes! Just as I did."

His sensitive fingers massaged her back in long soothing strokes. "The stakes are different, Becca. I'm breaking a confidence when I tell you this, but it might help you understand. Jose Vargas is about to donate twenty million dollars to Manhattan General. Without it, the hospital will go under. And so will my father's job."

She was silent, absorbing it, weighing it. She understood it now, but she still couldn't condone it. It was the kind of command-decision thinking that generals did when they sent soldiers on suicide missions. But she wasn't a general. She was a doctor. When she finally spoke, her words were carefully spaced. "You're telling me that the end justifies the means, aren't you?"

"It isn't like that."

"It's exactly like that! Your father didn't blink an eye. To him sacrificing the welfare of a child is a small price to pay to get that twenty million. And you go along with it."

His arms tightened about her. "I never said I go along with it."

"You don't have to. It's as plain as the Lahgerhorns he dangles under your nose. He leads and you follow. And where you go, I'm not welcome." She felt as if her anger was choking her. She wanted to lash out at him, humiliate him as she had been humiliated. And she knew just how to do it. "You're so alike you know. Two fingers on one hand. I should have seen it before. You even have a similar look about you. High foreheads, piercing eyes, predatory manner. Hawks, the both of you. The same desire for power, the same need to dominate—"

"Stop it. You hear me? Stop it!" His hands moved spasmodically along her shoulders, her spine, her buttocks. His voice sounded hoarse. "Don't do it, Becca. Don't punish me for something he did!"

He felt her begin to quiet. "I'm sorry about Lahgerhorn. I got carried away when I heard he was there. It wasn't until I was with him that I realized you might have preferred to be with us. I went looking for you, but you'd already headed for the foyer. It won't happen again. I swear it!"

She shook her head when she saw his intent, but he pulled her closer. His mouth brushed hers. Then he caught her to him and kissed her deeply.

"Doesn't solve anything . . ." she murmured against his lips.

"Nothing to solve. I love you."

His hands were moving, cupping her breasts, feathering her nipples. Becca fought her response to him. There was more to be said, a better understanding to be sought . . . She was drowning in sensation. She reached out to him blindly, relinquishing control.

"I won't let him come between us," she heard him mutter. It sounded more like a prayer than a statement.

Sixteen

When Becca reached the hospital at ten the following day, she felt like a retread of her former self. There had been desperation in the way David had made love to her last night, making her promise over and over that she wouldn't allow anything to come between them. But if he were insatiable she had been a willing partner. She had wanted to lose herself in sensation, forget her disillusionment . . . force the happenings of the evening from her mind. And she had succeeded—to a point.

She had fallen asleep immediately after David left, only to jar herself awake an hour later. Fused with images of the child's death at Boston Memorial, she had been wracked by distorted dreams of Angelica being sucked into a huge vortex. She was filled with a sense of failure toward the girl. She knew that it had no basis in logic. She had done everything she could to help Angelica. It wasn't her fault that it was being taken out of her hands now. Still, the guilt and the images had lingered and with them an overwhelming premonition of disaster that had chilled her despite the muggy June heat. Worn out, she had finally fallen into a druglike sleep at the first sliver of dawn.

When she arrived at the hospital five hours later, the slower weekend pace had given way to the usual Monday morning bustle. Chafing at her lateness, she raced up the stairs to the fourth floor then made a beeline for the nurse's station where she almost collided with Helen Walters who was rounding the corner at a marathon pace.

The head nurse put out a hand to steady herself then looked at Becca in disbelief. "Where the helluv—" Discretion took over. Her friendship with Becca warranted the familiarity. Her position didn't. "Where've you been? I've been calling since eight."

A band tightened around Becca's head. "Why? What's happened?"

"You'd better get to 401 East. The Vargas girl has taken a turn for the worse." Her expression was grim. "God spare us from the rich and famous! Another casualty on this floor and—"

Becca missed the last few words because she was racing down the hallway at breakneck speed. She skidded to a stop at the entrance to the private room. Her glance flew to the bed as she crossed the threshold. She could see the doll Gabriella propped high on the pillows, but her view of Angelica was obscured by Gottlieb. The attending was bent over the child watching Aggie Bates check the vital capacity of the lungs.

"You see how the numbers are going down, Aggie," he was saying, his sandy head close to the nurse's curly one. "Remind you of anything? Like maybe that Elliot kid we took care of in '79?"

"I think you're right, Gar."

Becca was surprised at their intimacy. She hadn't even been aware that Aggie had met the attending before this case.

"The loss of muscle tone," Gottlieb murmured. "The brackish taste in the mouth . . . it all fits together."

What fit together? Becca wondered uneasily. What was happening here? "Dr. Gottlieb?"

Aggie's head whipped up. She opened her mouth to say something, but Gottlieb spoke first. "Ah, Becca . . . I've been trying to reach you all morning." To Becca's relief, he sounded more preoccupied than annoyed.

"Dr. Becca?" The voice from the bed was a weak croak.

Gottlieb patted the child's hand. "Yes. It's your Dr. Becca." He smiled. "Now remember what I told you. Don't do anything without calling for a nurse first, and try to get as much sleep as you can. I'll be back later on to see you."

He straightened and turned to Becca. His smile dissolved into worry lines, and he spoke in a low voice. "Don't be long. I'll be waiting in the hall to talk with you."

She nodded and hurried to the bed. Shock slowed her footsteps. Angelica seemed to have diminished overnight. Her baby-fine hair lay in lank blond strands about her face. Her eyes looked sunken, hollowed by the deep purple grooves that contrasted sharply with her pasty skin. Agitation made her breathing choppy, and the smell of fear was all about her.

Becca had a sudden terrifying feeling that she was going to lose this child just as she had the other. In a moment of panic, she reached toward her. She wanted to clasp the small body to her own, lend her the strength to combat whatever was happening to her, reassure her that it would be all right, that they would fight this thing together.

The sound of Aggie clearing her throat brought her to her senses. Her arms dropped to her sides. She was appalled at herself. What was the matter with her? Where was her control? Her perspective? Shaken, she ran a knuckle down Angelica's cheek, noting the clamminess beneath her hand. "How are you feeling, Angelica?"

"Fine."

"No, you're not. Tell me the truth."

Her fingers crept to Becca's lab coat. She tugged at it until Becca covered the fingers with her own. "Dr. Becca . . ." The words were almost garbled, the eyes frantic. "Don't let him . . . don't let him do it!"

Becca glanced at Aggie for an explanation. What had Gottlieb said to frighten the child so? Aggie's shrug indicated her bewilderment. For a moment Becca wondered if Angelica's concern about her illness was producing signs of paranoia. Carolyn Stedman hadn't said anything about it, but then she hadn't spoken to the psychiatrist in two days. "Let who do what, Angelica?"

"Papa," she said. "He came last night. He told me I couldn't stay here anymore. Please don't let him take me home. I'll be good. I'll eat more and I . . . I'll make myself sleep. You'll see. Just don't let him take me . . ." The words trailed off, her strength depleted.

My God, Becca thought. Angelica wasn't worried about her illness. She doubted the child was even aware that her condition had worsened. Her concern was that she would be returned to

136

her home. But why? What was it she feared in that house? Or whom?

"Angelica, Dr. Gottlieb is waiting outside for me. Why don't I talk to him and see what I can do. Okay?"

She nodded and closed her eyes. "Please," she whispered.

When Becca crossed the threshold, Gottlieb was leaning against the outer doorframe, tapping his foot impatiently. His tanned face was alive with a vitality that made him look ten years younger. Even his clothes had altered from the usual double-breasted suit to an open-necked shirt and linen slacks. Becca wondered what had caused the change.

The attending wasted no time in preliminaries. "Angelica has Guillain-Barré Syndrome."

Becca nodded thoughtfully. "When did the results of the spinal tap come in?"

"Early this morning. It was the elevation of protein in the spinal fluid that tipped me off. Afterward, I had Gladstone check her out. He's the best neurologist in the hospital, and he concurs with my findings.

"Did he give an opinion as to how severe it was?"

"He said that from all indications it looks like it's a mild case. I was part of the team that administered the swine flu immunization in 1976, and the adverse reaction to it was Guillain-Barré. I saw a lot of it then, and I tend to agree that it's mild. But you never know. Are you familiar with the syndrome, Becca?"

She shrugged. "I haven't worked directly with Guillain-Barré, but I've seen a few cases. I know that it attacks the peripheral nervous system. If I remember correctly, it starts with a weakness of the extremities followed by difficulty in swallowing and a loss of taste."

"And often progresses to paralysis of the respiratory system," Gottlieb supplied. "If that happens, Angelica will be put on a respirator."

Becca spoke slowly. "Some of the patients I knew who had it recovered. Some didn't."

He nodded. "It can be fatal. It can also disable." He put a hand on her shoulder. The familiarity surprised her. "Look, Becca, I know we've had our differences on how to handle this case. But our goal has always been the same. To get Angelica on her feet and out of here. Guillain-Barré is tricky. It has to be monitored carefully to protect against respiratory failure and cardiovascular complications. I'll be here when I can, but I need to be able to count on you when I can't. Do we have a problem here?"

"None that I know of."

"Good. The only medication I'm going to prescribe is twenty milligrams of prednisone. I see no reason to put her in the ICU or on a respirator, since Gladstone agrees with me that her breathing hasn't been affected yet. It would serve no purpose except to frighten her and from the looks of her she's scared half to death already."

"That's because she's afraid of being taken home."

"No chance of that now." His tone hardened. "Vargas will have to live with it whether he likes it or not."

For the second time Becca caught a glimpse of the dedicated doctor whose accomplishments at the hospital ten years ago were still being talked about. The man was an enigma, she thought. He had denied any knowledge of Celmira Vargas's death, even though he had been the physician of record at the time. He had refused to back her in the matter of psychiatric help for Angelica because he feared Vargas's displeasure. Yet he spoke now as if he would take on the magnate bare-fisted if he were challenged about keeping Angelica in the hospital.

She had the feeling that Gottlieb was a man straddling a fence. He was torn between what he wanted to do and what was prudent for him to do. It was fine as long as he could maintain his balance, but if pushed to make a choice, she wondered which way he would jump.

Though admirable, the stand Gottlieb had taken was needless. Faced with the seriousness of his daughter's illness, Jose Vargas did not press for her to leave the hospital. Instead, he coerced Arnold Hardinger into bending the rules and allowing his daughter a private nurse. Aware of what the repercussions would be on the pediatric floor, Hardinger attached a requisite to it. The nurse was to be carefully supervised by the hospital staff.

The concession did nothing to placate Helen Walters.

"That bastard's got the integrity of a two-bit whore," she ranted to Becca. "We don't have the staff to monitor a private nurse every minute, yet if that nurse screws up, it's our ass that will be on the line."

Becca might have been less apt to agree with her if she had respected the private nurse Vargas had hired, but she didn't.

Margaret Quinlan was fifty-two. She was of Irish and Spanish extraction but still retained the manner of speaking acquired in a girlhood spent in County Cork. She treated Angelica as if she were three instead of eight, phrasing her sentences as if the two of them were inseparable entities — "Let's be havin' our breakfast like a good little girl so we can take our nap afterward?"

A self-serving snob by dint of her affiliation with Vargas, she considered herself to be a cut above the hospital nurses and resented their "interference." "I'll not be talked down to by a bunch of biddies who make one dollar to my three and don't have half my know-how," she informed Helen Walters.

"Half her know-how!" Helen had scoffed to Becca afterward. "That one wouldn't know a catheter from an I.V.! But I have to give her credit. She's got Vargas believing that she's indispensable to Angelica, when she never even talks to that kid. All she does is sit in front of the TV watching the soaps." She snorted. "Would it surprise you to hear that her favorite is 'General Hospital'? Come to think of it, that's probably where she gets all her 'know-how.'"

Aside from Quinlan's pompous personality, there was another negative element to consider: the private nurse's presence threatened the exposure of Carolyn Stedman's visits. Because Quinlan was working double shifts, there was no way to hide those sessions from her, and it was difficult to tell whether she was perceptive enough to realize that they were being scheduled without Gottlieb's approval. Becca would have suggested that the psychiatrist suspend her sessions with Angelica for the time being, but the need seemed greater than ever.

In the week that followed the diagnosis, a parade of visitors came to see Angelica. Her tutor, Walter Heilbrun, paid his respects. Jose Vargas came twice a day. Esther Pemberton dropped by to nose around and, not surprisingly, became Margaret Quinlan's most willing listener. Arnold Hardinger came frequently, and David visited intermittently.

On his evening visit, Vargas always brought his mother with him. Faced with her granddaughter's obvious decline due to a disease she couldn't understand, let alone pronounce, the old woman's depression manifested itself in constant, almost incoherent, babbling. It was hard on the nerves and further convinced Becca that the grandmother was bordering on senility.

Maria Vargas came alone and only once. She scarcely spoke to Angelica. She rearranged the icons and statuette of the Virgin Mary and demanded to know from Becca where the scapular was.

"I'm sorry," Becca told her, "but it interfered with procedures so much that we had to remove it. You'll find it in the top drawer of the dresser."

When Becca came back into the room five minutes later, Angelica was wearing the scapular, and Maria Vargas was gone. Becca assumed that she had left the hospital, until she saw her through the picture window. She was standing on the gray flagstone parapet, alongside a few recuperating patients and their nurses. She was leaning against the cement column railing, knee bent, one patent pump wedged into a space between two of the columns. Usually expressionless, her youthful face held a look of determination that aged and hardened her. Even as Becca wondered at it, Maria Vargas looked toward the room and became aware of Becca at the window. She turned and left abruptly. Becca hadn't seen her since.

There was no significant change in Angelica's physical condition during that time, but emotionally she showed signs of deterioration. Her dependency on Becca grew to the point where she clung like a burr each time the resident had to leave the room. She retreated more often into the sanctuary of her private fantasy world. She scarcely slept. When she did, the dreaded nightmare recurred, and she woke in screaming terror. She spoke in monosyllables except when Becca or Aggie were there and visibly shrank when the private nurse reached to touch her.

It was late on Friday when Becca found out why.

That afternoon the city had been deluged by a downpour so fierce that the windows in 401 East had become opaque sheets of rain. Becca had just finished checking on the diminishing mobility in Angelica's legs. Margaret Quinlan had offered to assist her, but Angelica's aversion to the nurse had made that impossible.

By the time Becca was ready to leave, Angelica's eyes had closed. Hoping the child would get the sleep she so desperately needed and trying to avoid the difficult leave-taking, Becca opted not to disturb her by saying goodbye.

She was edging toward the door when Margaret Quinlan caught up with her. A notorious talebearer, the private nurse spent a good deal of her spare time gathering gossip. From the look on her face, Becca had a feeling she was about to be offered a juicy tidbit.

"It's no wonder that poor baby doesn't trust me," the nurse whispered, "with her rememberin' me with her mother and all."

Arrested in motion, Becca could only stare at her. "You knew Angelica's mother?"

"I was her nurse up to the day she died, God rest her soul."

Angelica stirred, and Becca motioned for the nurse to step outside. Becca positioned herself across the hall so that she could keep Angelica in sight.

"Miss Quinlan . . ."

"Call me Margaret."

"Margaret, it would help me a great deal with Angelica to hear about her mother. Now, I know she died of a heart attack . . ."

Her smile was supercilious. "That's what the report says."

"Are you suggesting it isn't true?"

The nurse spoke cautiously. "I'm not sayin' I don't believe it. It's just that with the goin's-on in that household and all . . ." She leaned closer and warmed to her tale. "I mean, the wife so sick half the time she couldn't lift her head off the pillow and that younger sister of hers eggin' him on with those great big eyes of hers, heatin' his bed more than likely, and lookin' to take her sister's place before she was cold in her grave. And what with the old lady watchin' it all, not carin' who got her son as long as they birthed a boy to carry on the name—

Well, it makes a body wonder, it does."

What was innuendo and what was fact? Becca wondered. Aloud, she said, "Celmira Vargas had a heart condition of long standing. There would be no reason to think she died of anything else."

She gave Becca an arch look. "No reason, you say. And if I was to tell you that the day after she died Señor Jose fired every one of the help who had been there when it happened . . ." She nodded with satisfaction at Becca's start. "That would put a bee in your bonnet, wouldn't it?"

"What about you? Were you fired also?"

"No, because I wasn't there when his wife died. The Lord must've been lookin' out for me when he made it happen on my day off. But he sure wasn't lookin' out for Fiona — the relief nurse," she explained. "Fiona Andrews her name was. She had a temper to match that red hair of hers, she did. Threw a fit when he fired her. Not that he didn't give her proper severance like he gave them all, but she had a sick baby in Jersey City and she needed the money bad. They all did. Garcia, the cook, she got a job at the Kessler house a few doors down, but the others . . ." She shrugged.

"And what about you?"

"I was lucky. He kept me on for a few months after that."

"Why? I would think that with Mrs. Vargas dead . . ."

She jerked her head toward the private room. "Angelica, that's why. That poor baby was beside herself. Only four years old, she was. After her mama died, she stopped talkin'. She wouldn't hardly eat. And if she fell asleep, she woke up screamin'. No one could get near her, not even her grandma, and they were always closer than two peas."

"Was Angelica with her when she died?"

She waited impatiently as the nurse screwed up her face in thought. The answer was key in validating her interpretation of Angelica's nightmare.

"I think so, but I ain't sure. I wasn't about to ask questions, you know. I mean, bein' what happened to the others and all. But the next day when Angelica had to pass her mother's bedroom — that's where it happened — she screamed and carried on like she wasn't fit to live in this world. After that the poor baby took to her own room, cryin' and huddlin' in a corner, holdin' onto that doll of hers for dear life. She was scared to be alone, but she didn't want anyone with her either. I stayed in a small den near her with the door open so she could call if she wanted me."

"And did she call?"

"No, she didn't." She leaned even closer, her ample bosom almost touching Becca. She was shaped like a pear beneath her uniform, narrow of shoulder, broad in the beam. "Do you know that Aggie Bates has a thing goin' with the attendin', Gottlieb?"

Becca took a step backward. The woman was a fount of information, but not all of it was palatable. "No, I don't," she said coolly. "I'll be leaving the hospital soon. I'll be home all evening if you should need me."

She glanced at her watch as she walked down the hall. It was ten after six. If she were to make dinner for David tonight, she had to get moving. But first she was going to relay what she had just learned to Carolyn Stedman.

Seventeen

"Are you out of your mind?" David shouted. He disentangled himself from her arms, rolled from the queen-sized bed, and pulled on his jeans.

Sprawled amid the crumpled, stained sheets that had been the scene of their unrestrained lovemaking for the last hour, Becca wanted to kick herself as she watched him bolt from the room. She had made a mistake. She had told David of her suspicions regarding the death of Angelica's mother.

Perhaps she wouldn't have if she had been able to locate Carolyn Stedman after she left Angelica's room. But the psychiatrist was nowhere to be found. It wasn't until she was ready to leave the hospital that she had learned of her whereabouts. An agitated Aggie Bates had silently handed her a note.

Becca:
Tried to raise you on your beeper, but you weren't answering. Important that I talk to you about Angelica before I leave at six for the clinic in Boston.

Back in the morning—
Carolyn Stedman—

Becca had spoken sharply to the nurse. "When was this given to you, Aggie?"

"At four-thirty." She cleared her throat with an effort. "I'm sorry. I forgot." There were deep crevices on either side of her mouth, and her eyes held a defeated look.

There were too many mistakes lately, Becca thought. Too

much forgetting. She watched the nurse worry a button on her uniform until it hung by a thread "Are you all right, Aggie?"

"I'm fine. A little tired, is all." There was so much remorse in her white face, Becca hadn't the heart to say anything more.

She had gone home in a state of bottled elation, wondering if Carolyn's note might have had anything to do with what Margaret Quinlan had revealed to her. Though Margaret hadn't confirmed it, she was certain that Angelica had been in the room when her mother died. And that would lend credence to the interpretation of the dream and the suspicion that Celmira Vargas hadn't died a natural death. The more she thought of it, the more sure she became that Vargas's behavior bore that suspicion out. Why else would he have fired all the help that had been there at the time his wife died?

The question swirled round and round in her mind as she prepared the dinner. She had always loved to cook, but tonight she had outdone herself—coq au vin, Caesar salad, and brandied pears, each of them a favorite of David's. When he arrived at eight, he brought white roses and a fifth of Moët and Chandon with him. "I'd say you missed your calling," he teased, spearing a chicken wing, "but you're too good a doctor for that." He hadn't taken his eyes from her while he ate. Time and again he'd reached out to touch her fingers across the table. And later . . .

It had been good. So good. They'd made love slowly, savoring the leisure time that was still a precious commodity to them. They'd allowed the craving to build at its own pace, hands and bodies touching, stroking, ferreting out all the sensitive places they'd memorized over the years. They'd made the ascent whispering short out-of-context words that shouldn't have made sense yet somehow did. And when they'd reached the peak they'd drawn the exhilaration out as long as they could, then lingered in each others arms until the sweat on their bodies had dried and chilled.

She slid a hand across the rumpled sheet now to the empty place beside her and felt the loss keenly. Dammit! Why couldn't she have kept her big mouth shut! She pulled her robe out of the closet and went to find him.

He was staring out the window of the living room, watching

the storm abate. His hands were clasped behind him. The discipline of his daily workouts at the Nautilus room showed in the firm-toned muscles of his torso. She knew from the tensing of his shoulders that he was aware of her presence.

"David . . . I'm sorry."

He turned abruptly. "Not for what you're doing. Only that you told me. Right?" His tone was clipped, his blond hair in disarray.

The anger in his lean face sparked her own. "Wrong! I was apologizing because I ruined the evening. I don't have to answer to you for anything else." She pivoted on bare feet.

He caught her before she'd gone half a dozen steps. He wrapped his arms about her and pulled her tightly against him. He cradled her back against his chest and spoke in a taut voice. "It isn't me you have to answer to. It's yourself. Maybe you've forgotten the horror of those inquiries at Boston Memorial, but I haven't. Think carefully about what you're doing, Becca. It's taken you two years to build your career back to where it is now. If you go on probing this Vargas thing, you're putting that career on the line again."

She turned swiftly in his arms. "Don't you think I realize that?"

"No. Because if you did, you'd never think of going as far as you have. My God, Becca. Have you given a second's thought to what my father's reaction would be if he ever found out what you're doing?"

"That's your only concern, isn't it? Your father!"

"No, it isn't my only concern. But I do empathize with the man. Vargas still hasn't given him that twenty million, and in view of Angelica's illness, he can't press for it without looking unfeeling. He's caught in a bind, and when he gets like that, he can be vicious. He'll strike out at anybody that gets in his way. And I don't want that anybody to be you. As is, he doesn't approve—" He bit the words back.

"Go on. Finish it. You're father doesn't approve of your seeing me. Isn't that what you were going to say?"

He didn't answer. Did he think that not acknowledging it would make it less true, she thought scornfully. She tried to break free, but he wouldn't let her. She was hurt by his silence.

He should be telling her it didn't matter. He should be making light of it, such as, "He doesn't approve of women who've got more looks than money." Instead, he wasn't saying anything. And that made her feel as if the inadequacy was in her. It was the way her father had always punished her when she didn't measure up.

Her laugh was brittle. "You're behind the times, David. I could have told you after the party that your father thinks of me as Lizzie Borden."

"It isn't like that," he murmured, rubbing at his lower lip with a knuckle. "My father feels that where you go, trouble follows."

"And you, what do you feel?"

"You know what I feel."

"I want to hear it."

His arms tightened fiercely. "I love you. I want to spend the rest of my life with you. But I can't condone what you're doing. For God's sake, Becca, don't give my father the ammunition to destroy you, because in the end it will destroy us."

"You're being melodramatic."

"No, I'm not. As resident to Angelica Vargas, you're in a vulnerable enough position. For you to compound it by suggesting that her mother was murdered is madness."

"I don't think it's madness. I think that a little girl has been made to pay for an injustice that should be brought to light. Don't you care about the truth, David?"

"The only thing I care about is you. The official report on Celmira Vargas says she died of a heart attack. Let it go at that." He nuzzled her ear and pressed her close to him. "Promise me you will."

Anger warred with her body's response. The weapon he used to win his battles demeaned her, but she couldn't bring herself to tell him that. "I promise I'll think about it," she said.

He wasn't happy with it, but he accepted it. He probably wouldn't have if he had known that before she left the hospital she had asked Helen Walters to help locate Fiona Andrews, the relief nurse who had been with Celmira Vargas when she died.

Carolyn Stedman seemed distracted the following morning

as she listened to Becca's accounting of what Margaret Quinlan had told her. To Becca's annoyance, she fidgeted in the oversized chair behind her desk. She toyed endlessly with a letter opener. And at least twice she repositioned the amber combs that held her mane of chestnut hair.

"There's still no proof that the child was in the room with her mother," she said when Becca had finished.

Seated across from her, Becca hid her disappointment. She had been so sure that the psychiatrist would share her elation. "Then you don't agree with the conclusions I've come to?"

"I didn't say that."

"Then what *are* you saying?" She gritted her teeth as the psychiatrist reached toward her hair again. "Dr. Stedman, please."

She blinked as if suddenly emerging from darkness. "I'm sorry. I'm distracted and I guess I'm showing it."

"Yes, you are."

She clasped her hands on the desk. "That note I sent you. There's something I have to tell you. I . . . I won't be able to see Angelica anymore."

Becca grew very still. Without Carolyn Stedman's expertise where would she turn? "Why? Is it the pressure of the work?"

It couldn't have come at a worse time, Becca thought. She tried to rationalize away her disappointment. The reality was that Carolyn Stedman owed her nothing. She had put herself out on a limb for Angelica in the last few weeks with little to gain but a wrap over the knuckles. It was surprising that she had lasted this long.

The psychiatrist's mouth twisted. "No. It's not the pressure of the work." She ripped a sugar packet across the top with such force that the contents spilled across the desk. "Dammit," she muttered, "why don't they stock sugar cubes like they used to?" She splayed her hands flat on the burled wood surface. "I was called into Hardinger's office yesterday and told by him to stop the sessions with Angelica."

The sudden movement of Becca's arm spilled the coffee onto her lab coat. "How did he find out about them?"

"My guess? A triple play. From Quinlan to Pemberton to Hardinger. I suppose I should be grateful. He seemed more nervous than angry about it and made it clear that he didn't want word of these sessions getting back to Vargas."

"Did you tell him that I had given you permission for them?"

"I saw no reason for that. He assumed I'd done it on my own, and I let it stand that way." Amusement crinkled her eyes. "After all, I *am* new here and hospital procedures differ from state to state. It's conceivable that it would take me a while to learn the ropes."

Becca let her breath out slowly. "Thanks."

She waved the appreciation aside. "For what? We may both be off the hook for the moment, but it still leaves us with the problem of Angelica."

Becca looked at her in disbelief. "You still want to be a part of this?"

"As much as I can be without seeing her. I don't believe in shirking responsibility."

Nor in deserting a friend, Becca thought. And that's what this woman had been offering from the first day they'd met. Friendship. It was in that moment that Becca knew that Carolyn Stedman had spoken the truth about her relationship with David. The lady was made of too-fine stuff to be underhanded.

The psychiatrist took off her shell-rimmed glasses and laid them carefully on the desk. "Becca, I don't disagree that there may be something odd about Celmira Vargas's death. But right now I'm concerned with prevention, not cause."

"Meaning what?"

"Meaning that in my opinion, Angelica Vargas is suicidal." She ignored Becca's sudden start. "I didn't complete my workup on her, but the evidence seems irrefutable. The depression, the insomnia, the recurrent thoughts of death, the apathy, the guilt, the lack of appetite — they're all part of the pattern."

"But some of those are symptomatic of her illness too."

"Agreed. But I spoke to her tutor, a tall drink of water named Heilbrun, Walter Heilbrun. Have you met him?"

"Briefly."

"Did you know that Angelica was an avid reader with a collection of books and poetry that go way beyond her years? When her bouts of depression made it impossible to read, she had Heilbrun do it aloud for her. I suppose it was the one escape left to her in that house she couldn't escape from. Heilbrun tells me she's saved every book she's ever read. She cherishes that collection so much that she wouldn't even allow the maid to dust her bookcases for fear the girl would harm something."

"I don't understand the point you're making."

She held up a pink-tipped hand that clearly asked for patience. "In the last few months, Angelica has been offering those books to Heilbrun, to the maids, to the cook, even to the delivery boy. The giving away of precious possessions is a strong sign of suicidal contemplation."

Becca nodded slowly. "That may explain what happened this morning. I stopped off at her room right after grand rounds." She paused, suddenly overcome. "God, she looked awful." She took a sip of her coffee and cleared her throat. "She cried. Lately she's been too apathetic to do even that. Afterward, she clung to me and told me that Gabriella didn't have much time left. She was worried that no one would miss the doll after she died."

"What did you tell her?"

"Not much. That idiot Quinlan began to make those fatuous noises I can't stand." She mimicked the nurse's high-pitched brogue. " 'It's no wonder we're not sleepin' when we have such terrible thoughts in our head.' I told Angelica I would talk with her later and got out before I impaled that woman on an I.V."

"You realize, of course, that you're about the only one Angelica trusts. Any rift in your relationship at this point could be disastrous. But the support you're giving her is only a finger in the dike. The child needs treatment. It doesn't matter whether from me or from any other qualified psychiatrist."

Becca shook her head. "There's no way that's going to happen with her father running the show. The best we can hope for is that Angelica makes a move that reveals her intentions so obviously that he's forced to take action."

The psychiatrist balanced a silver letter opener between her fingers and regarded it gravely. "It may be too late then."

Carolyn's warning came close to being prophetic. Four days later Becca and Kip Flanders had just finished stabilizing a burned three-year-old when a beeper call came in from Aggie

Bates. Becca was wanted immediately in 401 East.

Leaving Kip to supervise the application of the Silvadine dressing, Becca sped down the corridor to Angelica's room. She tried to control her rising panic. Carolyn's revelation had increased her concern about Angelica Vargas. It had also changed her focus. The reasons Angelica had come to the point of suicide had been put on hold. The immediate need was to block it. And Becca was determined to do that. She was not going to lose this one!

In the last few days she had spent as much time as possible with Angelica. She would have liked to have enlisted Gottlieb's aid, but she knew that was out of the question. Instead she confided in Helen Walters and Aggie Bates. And she attempted to put the fear of God into Margaret Quinlan.

"Angelica must be watched, Miss Quinlan. At all times. Don't leave any sharp instruments or medication around. If you have to take a break, call a nurse to replace you. If Angelica gets agitated or excessively depressed, let me know. There'll be no excuses if you slip up here. I'm counting on you to monitor her every move. Do you understand?"

The nurse had faced her, tight-lipped. "I'm after bein' a nurse for more than twenty years, doctor. A good enough one to be hired by Señor Vargas himself. There's no one here has to be tellin' me my duty." Her bosom had heaved with the vigor of her resentment.

Let her resent, Becca thought now as she reached 401 East. Just let her do her job.

She stepped through the doorway and confronted a grim looking Aggie Bates. Becca's eyes flew to the empty bed. She broke out in a sweat. *"Where is she?"*

"Quinlan took her to Gladstone in Neurology."

Relief made her testy. "Is that what you called me in here to tell me?"

"No." She pulled Angelica's doll from the dresser and held it up by a satin-clad arm. Gabriella dangled downward, the bandage across her eye slipping. Her legs were askew, her blond hair caught in the twisted lace of the black mantilla.

"I thought you should see this," she said. She turned the doll upside down. The tiered satin skirts tumbled over the doll's head. Aggie caught at the white petticoat that remained, then smoothed it to reveal the zippered pocket sewn into it below the waist.

She moved closer to Becca. "Take out what's in it," she directed.

Becca unzipped the pocket then shook the doll until six pills fell into her hand. "My God," she whispered. "She's been hoarding."

Aggie nodded. "Prednisone. It couldn't kill her."

"But she didn't know that."

They stared at each other, appalled by the revelation.

A step at the threshold alerted them both. Margaret Quinlan stood in the doorway, twisting a coral ring on her plump finger.

"I came back for the doll," she said. "The little devil's been throwin' a fit down there. Says she won't let them touch her unless the doll is with her." Insensitive to the silence in the room her eyes went to the dresser, then the bed, and finally fixed on Gabriella in Aggie's hands. "Oh, there it is!"

All of Becca's fury converged on the private nurse before her. She grabbed the doll from Aggie before Quinlan could reach it. "Aggie, would you mind stepping outside. I have something I want to say to Miss Quinlan."

Finally sensing something, Quinlan went on the defensive as soon as Aggie left. "Look here, doctor, if you're goin' to be reamin' me out for leavin' her downstairs, I want you to know there's plenty that's watchin' her there. Now, if you'll be givin' me that doll . . ."

Becca's voice was deceptively quiet. "Miss Quinlan, do you know what these are?" She opened her hand to reveal the pills.

The nurse squinted at them. "They look like the pills I've been givin' to Angelica."

"They are. And do you know where I found them?"

She shook her head cautiously.

"In the pocket of the doll's petticoat." She held the zippered pocket up to her, then shook the doll in her face.

The nurse took a step backward. Her full cheeks splotched with red. "Now, hold on here, Dr. Landau. If you're accusin' me of not given' Angelica her pills—"

"I'm accusing you of not watching her take them. And after I warned you . . ."

Quinlan put her hands on her hips. Her jaw jutted forward belligerently. "Dr. Landau, I've been watchin' this child round the clock since you spoke to me. But there's no way a body can pay attention every single second of the day and night."

"There is if that body doesn't watch TV all day long and isn't diverted by every bit of rumor and gossip that floats around this hospital like so much garbage."

The nurse drew herself up as if she were being pulled by strings. "I don't have to listen to this. You're forgettin' that I don't work for the hospital. I work for Señor Vargas."

"And what do you think Señor Vargas will say when he finds out you've allowed his daughter to hoard pills."

A knowing smile flitted across her lips. "My guess is he'll be sayin' nothin'." She wrenched the doll from Becca's hands and stalked from the room.

Eighteen

At five o'clock that afternoon Hardinger reached across his desk to hang up the phone. He had trouble finding its cradle because his hands were shaking so badly. He had just finished speaking with Jose Vargas. Rage filled his whole being—all of it directed at Becca Landau. If he'd had her in front of him now, he would surely have killed her!

But that was a pipe dream. He had to control his temper. Use his brain instead. The girl was a menace. If he were to secure that twenty million after what had just happened, he had to make moves, put a leash on her.

He rose from behind his desk and began to pace, long, swift strides broken too soon by the confines of his office. Vargas's voice had come across quietly, insidiously, more threatening to him than if the South American had used open violence. His tone had been almost quizzical on the phone just now.

"A man who isn't responsible for the actions of his staff can't call himself a leader. And a hospital that has no leader is a poor investment. Wouldn't you say so, Arnold?"

Unheeding of where his footsteps were taking him now, Hardinger stubbed his toe on the low credenza at the far end of the room. He didn't feel the pain, only the frustration of events slipping beyond his control. His lips drew back in a snarl. He had the primitive urge to bodily throw the girl out of the hospital. But he couldn't do that. Hell, he couldn't even remove her from the case!

"Since Dr. Landau is the cause of the trouble, why don't I just replace her?" he'd suggested to Vargas.

"I'd rather not do that. It would upset Angelica."

Hardinger cursed under his breath. The need to vent suddenly overstepped the bounds of caution. He picked up the porcelain buddha that had been Laura's last find and threw it with all his might against the wall. He watched in satisfaction as its fat blue belly smashed into bits and pieces that rained onto the mahogany surface of the credenza.

He heard his office door fly open and knew by the scent of her girlishly cloying perfume that Esther Pemberton had stepped inside.

He turned to face her frightened stare. "Two things," he said. "See that this mess is cleaned up. Then go down to the fourth floor and bring Becca Landau back with you."

Becca braced herself as Esther Pemberton knocked on Hardinger's office door, ushered her inside, then left. She could only assume that he'd found out she'd given permission for the psychiatric sessions without proper authority. But thanks to Aggie's finding the pills, she was in a better position to defend her actions now.

Hardinger's office surprised her. She had pictured it sleek, modern, and impersonal—a counterpart of David's apartment. Instead, it held the charm of burnished woods, Oriental rugs, even the unexpected warmth of antiques.

Unsmiling, Hardinger was a forbidding figure behind his carved mahogany desk. Shoulders hunched forward, he clenched a black cigarette holder between his teeth that clicked ominously as he shifted it from side to side. He made no pretense at friendliness. "Sit down." He gestured toward a gold-colored wing chair opposite him.

Resentment rose in Becca. She had never knowingly done anything to harm this man. She wasn't going to let him intimidate her. She seated herself in the wing chair and crossed her legs. The silence lengthened. He was studying her, making her feel ill at ease.

"You sent for me, Mr. Hardinger?"

His silver hair lay sleek against his temples. His face was cleansed of expression. He took the cigarette holder from his mouth and spoke carefully. "Jose Vargas just called me. Margaret Quinlan phoned her resignation in to him a few minutes ago. The reason she gave was harassment. *Your* harassment of her." He didn't look at her. He wiped the holder clean with a handkerchief he took from his breast pocket.

Relief flooded her. This would be easier to handle than his accusing her of bringing in a psychiatrist without authority. "It isn't true. I've never harassed a nurse in my life."

"Then why would she say such a thing?"

"Because Margaret Quinlan is an incompetent who's trying to cover up her own deficiencies by accusing others."

"That isn't what Jose Vargas believes. Quinlan has worked for him on and off for eight years. He's never had a reason to question her competency."

"Then he wasn't looking close enough!"

He ignored her outburst. She got the feeling he was pleased at her sudden lack of control. He still hadn't looked at her. What kind of cat and mouse game was this?

He nudged a crystal paperweight on his desk. "Margaret Quinlan claims that you have an unprofessional attachment to your patient. That your overprotectiveness and your demands of her as a nurse were unreasonable."

"Not under the circumstances."

"By circumstances you mean Angelica's illness?"

"Not exactly." She hesitated. She had seen this man's heartlessness at the party, his willingness to sacrifice Angelica's welfare for his own ends. Where before there had been only suppositions regarding Angelica's precarious situation, however, now there was proof. And that changed everything. She plunged ahead. "Mr. Hardinger, in my opinion Angelica is not only suffering from Guillain-Barré Syndrome, she is emotionally ill as well."

His eyes were more steel than blue when he finally raised them to meet hers. "What do you mean by emotionally ill?"

"I believe that Angelica Vargas is contemplating suicide. The reason I came down so hard on Margaret Quinlan this morning . . ."

The peculiar noise he made halted her. He leaned forward across his desk, his gray pinstriped jacket puckering open across his barrel chest. His tone was strangely soft for so big a man. "I didn't hear that, Dr. Landau. Not a single word of it."

Desperation edged her voice. "Mr. Hardinger, you must listen to me. Margaret Quinlan has been allowing Angelica to hoard . . ."

He slammed his hand on the desk for silence. He stood up. The rage was evident in his florid face and the strained cords in his neck. "What kind of fool are you, doctor? It isn't enough that you show no gratitude for being permitted to work at Manhattan General for the last two years. Now you try to sabotage the hospital by circulating rumors that Angelica Vargas is contemplating suicide. You must know what the climate is at Manhattan General since the Ryker boy's death. Which is it you're trying to destroy, Dr. Landau? The hospital or yourself?"

Becca was taken aback by his venom. "Neither. If you'd only hear me out—"

His hand sliced the air. "I've heard enough. You were a mistake, Dr. Landau. I never should have taken you on when David came to me."

Becca sat frozen in place. "What does David have to do with this?"

"David has everything to do with this. He came to me two years ago. He felt guilty because he had been exonerated at Boston Memorial while you bore the brunt of it. He convinced me that the hospital had been too harsh with you." He laughed shortly. "In my opinion they weren't harsh enough."

"Are you telling me that the only reason you accepted me at Manhattan General was because David pleaded with you on my behalf?"

"That and his promise to follow you here after he finished his residency."

Becca slumped back in the wing chair. She felt as if all the blood had drained from her. So much for her precious "sense of self." She should have known that the leopard hadn't changed its spots. David had made a bargain. A bargain of which she was a part, yet had no say in. A bargain that had put him in league with the devil. But then perhaps that was where he belonged.

"Why else would I have taken you on?" There was open contempt in his voice now. "What other self-respecting hospital would have accepted you with your record? But you won't be allowed to drag this hospital through the mud the way you did Boston Memorial. If you continue to talk up this ridiculous theory of suicide, I will see to it that your license is revoked and that you never practice medicine again." He reached to press a buzzer beneath his desk. "I advise you not to take what I've said lightly, Dr. Landau. I can do what I say."

Esther Pemberton appeared in the doorway as if on cue. "Miss Pemberton, show Dr. Landau out," he said. He swiveled in his chair and turned his back on both of them.

"I'm sorry my father told you about it," David said.

Becca stared at him in disbelief. There was a rueful half-smile on his face. The little boy caught with his hand in the cookie jar. He wasn't sorry for what he'd done. Only that he'd been found out. And now he had to find a way to smooth it over. Just another upset that needed taking care of, like the relatives of his patients who came to him for consolation after the surgery went awry. He had never understood what they expected of him either. "What do they want me to say?" he'd asked her time and again. "That it was my fault? It wasn't. Why don't they leave it alone? It's over. Done. Past tense."

Is that how he regarded this? Past tense? Something that didn't matter anymore?

"Is that all you have to say?"

"No. I think you couldn't have chosen a poorer place to discuss this."

It was the only thing she agreed with him about so far. The hospital cafeteria with its long lines, rattling trays, and white tiled walls was no place for this confrontation. Privacy was at a premium here. The tables were set too close to one another, and it was heading into the dinner hour.

He glanced at his watch. It was gold and wafer-thin, a Patek-Phillipe given to him by his father on his twentieth birthday. "I have to be back in the O.R. in fifteen minutes." His face was stiff, controlled.

She had a terrible urge to laugh. She had expected him to be contrite. Instead, he was angry.

He picked up his coffee cup then set it down with a clatter. "Becca, I'm not going to apologize for what I did. You had already been turned down by six hospitals when I approached my father. Chances are you would have been refused by all the others. Your career was going down the tubes. I saw what I had to do and I did it!"

"Without consulting me."

"You would never have agreed to it if I told you."

"But that was my *right!*" She lowered her voice as the two nurses at the next table stared at them curiously. "Don't you understand how you undermined me as a person when you interceded for me with your father?"

He didn't answer.

"David, if I can't make my own decisions, then there is no me. There's only a reflection of you." Her voice was almost pleading now.

"Even if those decisions are in your worst interest?"

Why had she never noticed that the planes of his face paralleled his father's to a T? "Are you talking about what happened at Boston Memorial?"

"I'm talking about what happened then. And I'm talking about what's happening now. I'm talking about you and Angelica Vargas and an obsession that's got you so caught up that you can't see you're standing on the brink of disaster. You fling words like *suicide* and *murder* around with little proof and less thought as to what the repercussions will be. I've warned you of what my father is like when he gets riled. But you're so busy making your own decisions that you don't want to listen. What'll you do when he revokes your license, Becca? Peddle papers at a newsstand?"

"I'm not as scared of your father as you are." She saw him flinch and was glad.

"I don't see any point to this, Becca."

"Neither do I. Maybe . . . maybe you shouldn't come by tonight."

He stood up. "I didn't intend to after this. I think we both need a cooling-off time, don't you?" He turned and left.

Nineteen

Plush and pretentious, the waiting room at Stedman and Grant was a glass-and-marble advertisement for the nineties. Seated within it the next morning, Becca felt like a fool. She had allowed Carolyn Stedman to talk her into this over cocktails yesterday evening.

"Becca, Arnold Hardinger has threatened to revoke your medical license. He's trying to intimidate you, and I don't think he has the right to do that. Talk to my brother Sam. It won't cost you a thing. He's a busy lawyer, but he'll see you if I ask him to."

Unstrung by the threats from Hardinger and devastated by the scene with David afterward, she had agreed. But that had been only after three martinis and a morose helping of self-pity with which Carolyn had little patience. "You knew there might be repercussions in what you were doing. Stop crying in your cocktail and handle it."

Becca had allowed Carolyn to think that it was Hardinger's threat alone that was causing her maudlin state. But it was more than that. She had missed David terribly last night. Her earlier anger toward him had cooled and been replaced by rationalizations that made his behavior more acceptable to her.

David may have overstepped himself in going to his father behind her back, but his goal had been to help her. And he had bartered his freedom to do it. Something that couldn't have been easy for him. Besides, it had taken place two years ago, and a lot had happened to change both of them since then.

They had just found one another again. The relationship was so fragile at this point. If she allowed old wounds and distrust to take their toll, it would never be given the chance it deserved.

A voice above her interrupted her thinking. "If you'll follow me, please..."

The carefully manicured secretary went with the surroundings. In the sober light of morning, Becca had regretted allowing Carolyn to make this appointment with her brother, but she was too embarrassed to cancel. The only thing she could do now was cut it short.

The secretary led her through a set of double doors into a wide corridor that held streamlined gray desks outside private offices on either side of it. Becca got the impression of maximum activity with minimum confusion. Telephones rang, computers hummed, messengers scurried, but all of it seemed muted and well-organized. The secretary halted at an oak door midway down the corridor, knocked briefly, and ushered her in.

Becca felt as if she'd been catapulted into another world. There should have been a sign on Sam Stedman's desk that read, "Organization stops here!" Not that anyone would have seen the sign. It would probably have been buried beneath the profusion of books, folders, and papers that swamped the surface like a mound of litter.

Sam Stedman sat at his desk, half-turned toward the window behind him, the phone to his ear. He wore no jacket. His lank brown hair fell forward on his forehead, his blue and white striped shirt was open at the collar, and his green tie hung like a noose below it. He scowled into the phone. "A quarter of a million, Casey. No less." His voice was strident, and he punctured the air with his index finger for emphasis. "And if Monahan doesn't like it, he can—"

At the sound of the closing door, he swiveled round in his high-backed leather chair and glanced up. His dark eyes ran swiftly over her. Pressed for time, Becca hadn't bothered to change before she'd taxied over. She wore a green tailored blouse and slacks beneath her lab coat. Her bunny-stickered stethoscope had worked itself loose and dangled from one of the pockets. Conscious of his keen appraisal, she made a furtive move to tuck it back in.

He lowered his voice, said a few more words into the phone, then hung up. He ran a hand through his unruly hair and came around the desk. She saw that his tan cord trousers were held up by wide yellow suspenders. The profusion of colors he wore jarred her. The man had to be color blind, she thought as he stopped a few feet from her. He was very tall, wore heavy black-rimmed glasses, and looked older than the "couple of years shy of forty" Carolyn had said he was.

"You must be . . . uh . . ." He frowned.

God! He couldn't even remember her name. He obviously wanted her there even less than she wanted to be there. She was so sorry she'd come. He had none of Carolyn's graciousness. "Dr. Landau," she supplied. "Becca Landau." She covered her resentment with belligerence. "Your sister thinks I need some legal advice."

"So she told me." He swept his hand toward his overcrowded desk. "I suggested one of my associates, but she insisted . . ."

That did it! Wasted time. Wasted effort. She was just as busy as he was! "Mr. Stedman, why don't we do this some other day." She edged toward the door, but he caught her hand. She was surprised at the strength of his fingers.

"No. Wait!" He smiled at her, and his resemblance to the young yachtsman in Carolyn's photo became more apparent. "This is senseless. You're here and I'm here." He pulled her toward the burgundy leather couch against the beige wall. A signed Chagall print in purple hues hung above it. He seated her at one end and took the other. "Now tell me about it," he said.

She went over all of it — the incident at Boston Memorial, her belief that Angelica was contemplating suicide, her suspicions about the death of Celmira Vargas, and a replay of the scene in Hardinger's office yesterday. She saw no reason to mention her relationship with David or her inexplicable attachment to Angelica. When she was finished he reiterated some of her statements to clarify his thinking.

"You say that Hardinger has threatened to revoke your medical license."

"Yes."

"Because he claims your theory that Angelica is trying to

commit suicide is unfounded."

"Yes. But don't you see? Hardinger doesn't want to know the truth because then he'd have the responsibility of telling her father, and he can't afford to rile Jose Vargas because of that twenty million dollars in the offing."

He waved her explanation aside. "His reasons aren't important." He slumped back against the leather couch and slid an arm across its brass-studded top. "He's right, you know. About your theory of suicide being unsubstantiated."

"But Carolyn came to the same conclusion."

"That may be. But it's still supposition."

"What about the pills Angelica hoarded?"

"That's not proof. There could be any number of reasons that the child put the pills in the doll's pocket. *If* she put them there. There have been a lot of people coming and going in that room. Have you questioned Angelica about it?"

"I didn't get a chance to."

He shrugged. He stood up and went to his desk. He groped beneath a sheaf of papers and found a crumpled pack of Carlton Menthols and a soot-filled ashtray. He returned to the couch and plopped down into the waiting groove. He set the ashtray on a table and pulled a cigarette from the pack. Unaware of her look of distaste, he lit up.

He inhaled deeply and let the smoke filter out through pursed lips. "Look, doctor. You may not like what I'm going to say, but I'm going to say it anyway. I know Arnold Hardinger. I represented a hospital patient in a malpractice suit two years ago and lost, because Hardinger was instrumental in squashing it. I won't go into the whys and wherefores, but I can tell you this: the man wields a lot of power; he can be devious; and he's a formidable enemy to have."

"You're telling me to back off."

"No." He flicked the ash from his cigarette toward the ashtray on the table. He missed. The ashes fell to the rug. "I'm telling you that with your record at Boston Memorial you're an easy target to snipe at. And Hardinger knows that. Now, if you had some solid proof . . ."

The smoke-filled air, the attorney's "only the facts, ma'am" reasoning, and her own stupidity at allowing herself to be subjected to this shredded the last of Becca's reserves. She jumped to her feet. Her hands swatted the air wildly. "Proof! That's all anyone asks for. Proof! The only way all of you will have your proof is if Angelica commits suicide. And what do I do then? Stand beside her grave and reap satisfaction because I was right all along?"

Unfazed by her vehemence, he rose from the couch. "Look, I wasn't trying to tell you what to do. You're a big girl. You'll make your own decision about that. I was only trying to inform you of what you're up against."

"Would you mind putting that out?" she said.

He followed to where she was pointing, an expression of surprise on his face. "Oh. Sorry." He stubbed the cigarette into the ashtray. For the first time he looked at her as if she were a person, not an unwarranted disruption. The perception seemed to startle him, then make him uncomfortable. "Uh, Dr. Landau, if I've said anything to offend . . ." She got the odd feeling he was trying to placate her. His face flushed. "I mean, in law circles I'm known for my ability, not my bedside manner."

She had no doubt of that.

He pulled awkwardly at a yellow suspender. "What I'm trying to say is that whatever decision you come to, if you should need my help, I'll be here."

"Thanks for your time," she said.

When she left, she found she wasn't as angry as she'd been when she first met him. He was an oddly behaved man, but like his sister, there was something about him that inspired confidence.

It was one o'clock by the time she reached the hospital. Coming off the elevator onto the fourth floor she ran into a woebegone Kip Flanders, munching on the last of a blueberry muffin. In the last few weeks the intern's pessimism had reached depressing proportions, and Becca had little patience with him.

"What now, Kip? Lost your best friend?"

"No, but you might be losing yours."

"Kip, I am in no mood for guessing games."

"Angelica Vargas. She crumped right after you left this morning. We measured her vital capacity. It had gone down. She wasn't moving enough air. We took blood gases, and, based on the results, Gottlieb decided to tube her."

Becca paled. "Did they do a trach?"

"No. They put her on a respirator in the PICU." He shook his dark head gloomily. "I've got bad vibes on this one, Becca."

"Keep your vibes to yourself!" She moved off. "If anyone wants me, I'll be in the ICU."

"Becca, there's something you should—"

"Later, Kip. Okay?"

She sped around the corner to the Pediatric Intensive Care Unit, hit the wall switch to open the double doors, and peered inside. The white-tiled PICU was a long room with a central nurse's station in its midst. It held six beds in small glassed-in cubicles all lined up against the wall to her left. Surrounding the beds were life-support machines of every sort banded together by a jungle of crisscrossing wires. Opposite them was a row of chest-high cabinets that held all the medicine and supplies. The only bright spot in the otherwise sterile-looking room belonged to the green crash cart wedged into the back corner near the window.

Of the four beds that were occupied, Angelica was in the one nearest the door. Becca could see the hookup to the respirator and half of the cardiac monitor. Other than that, her view was obscured by Gottlieb and Aggie Bates who were bent over Angelica with their backs to the entry.

Aggie straightened up. At the sight of Becca her gray eyes widened. She shook her head and made an imperceptible motion toward the hallway. Puzzled, Becca stepped farther into the room. What was Aggie trying to tell her?

Alerted by the nurse's contortions, Gottlieb turned toward the door. His face grew cold as a cadaver's flesh. "Would you please leave?" he said to Becca.

A foreboding filled her. "Can I see Angelica for a moment first?"

A movement from the bed told her Angelica had heard.

"No. Outside please. Now!"

Becca stepped into the corridor. A second later, he joined

her. His face was grim beneath the uneven pallor of his fading tan.

"How is Angelica?" she asked.

"Stable. But it's no longer any concern of yours. You're off the case, doctor."

She had known it was coming, but it was still a blow. "When did Hardinger decide this?"

"The order didn't come from Hardinger. It came directly from Jose Vargas. He wants you nowhere near Angelica."

"Why?"

His glance was stony. "Because he learned about her sessions with Dr. Stedman."

She understood Gottlieb's anger now. But she refused to kowtow to him. If he had been a more responsible doctor, she wouldn't have had to be devious. "And why is that such a terrible thing, doctor? Is her father afraid we'll find out something we're not supposed to know?"

"You overstep yourself," he said angrily. He made a move to return to the PICU, then halted. He ran a hand across his close-cropped hair. For just a moment his anger abated and the Gottlieb of old surfaced. "For God's sake, Becca. After I warned you of how Vargas felt about it, how could you arrange for Angelica to see a psychiatrist?"

She couldn't keep the contempt from her voice. "For Angelica's sake, Dr. Gottlieb. After you saw how great her need was, how could you not?"

She walked away a second before Aggie Bates came out of the PICU.

The nurse stared at her receding back. "How did she take it, Gar?"

"Not well." He shook his head regretfully. "I had to do it, Aggie."

"I know."

His smile thanked her for her understanding. There was no animosity in her eyes, and he meant to keep it that way. She had finally consented to see him outside the hospital as he knew she would. He wanted nothing to mar the progress he was making. Sooner or later she would be his again. He was sure of it.

* * *

The following week was the hardest Becca had ever spent in her life. At least twenty times a day she passed the Intensive Care Unit and had to wrench herself away from the door. She tortured herself by imagining Angelica's terror—lying in a room filled with eerie hums and beeps, unable to speak, her mouth and throat sore from the chafing of the respirator and the feeding tube, allowed visitors for only a few minutes at designated times—and deprived of the one person she trusted.

She went about her work by rote, but there was an emptiness at the core of her. She had never analyzed her relationship with Angelica. If pressed to describe it she would have said that she was the giver, Angelica the receiver. But asked now, she might have reversed that order.

She knew that David's absence was compounding the emptiness. She hadn't seen him since he'd stalked out of the cafeteria. She'd tried to call him from the hospital the following day, but she hadn't been able to reach him. When she'd arrived home that evening, there had been a message from him on the answering machine. "I'll be in Boston for close to a week attending Lahgerhorn's lecture. Take care."

She had stared at the machine dismally. She needed "I love you," not "Take care." She knew that when David found out she had been dismissed from the case he would say that it was in her best interest. Even so, would he realize what a void it had left? How badly she was hurting? How much she needed comforting? How much she needed him?

The week would have been intolerable if not for Carolyn's steady bolstering and the news about Angelica that Aggie Bates imparted to her daily. Normally only a trained ICU nurse would have been used to care for Angelica, but because the removal of Becca had been so traumatic to the child, the hospital had made an exception and allowed Aggie to tend her so long as there was another PICU nurse in the room at the time.

Aware that prying eyes might take note of their lengthening tête-à-têtes, Aggie had taken to stopping off at Becca's apartment for a few minutes every evening on her way home. As the week wore on, Becca began to feel a kinship with this woman who had the courage to stand by her convictions. Gradually the few minutes lengthened to coffee and pie and by the end of the week had progressed to a light meal.

"I don't care how much money Vargas has," Aggie ranted to her on Thursday night. "The man is an asshole. The only thing that kid had going for her was you. I don't know what's going to happen to her now. Her condition hasn't worsened, but a blind man could see she's given up. I've done everything I can to reach her. I've brought her doll to her. I've tried to read to her. I even tried yelling at her today. She doesn't respond no matter what I do."

"Aggie, can she move her hands?"

"A little."

"All right. I want you to do something for me."

The following day, Aggie waited until the other nurse in the PICU busied herself with the patient at the far end of the room. Then she leaned over Angelica. The child lay with her eyes closed as if in a stupor.

"Angelica," she whispered, "I want you to know that I visit with Dr. Becca every night. She's very worried about you. Now, I know you can't talk with that tube in you, but if you want to write her a note, I'll see that she gets it."

Angelica's eyes opened with an effort.

"Blink twice if the answer is yes. I've got a pad and pencil with me."

The blinks came rapidly, the dulled eyes suddenly lit with a spark of hope. With Aggie's help, the laboriously scrawled notes followed. They were all the same. *"Please come."*

Staring at the third one on Sunday night, Becca could stand it no longer. She threw an old lab coat over the sleeveless pink cotton shift she was wearing, left her apartment, and walked the few blocks to the hospital in stockingless sandals. She didn't question what the consequences would be. She only knew that she had to see Angelica, if only for a moment.

The city had sweltered in the nineties that day, and the sultry heat had scarcely abated for the night. The air was a heavy wet blanket that made breathing a punishment. By the time she reached Manhattan General, her shift was stuck to her in patches, and rivulets of perspiration were running down her sides.

The cool air of the hospital came at her in a welcoming blast.

"Evenin', Dr. Landau," the guard at the elevators said. "You forget somethin'?"

"Nope. Just checking on a patient of mine."

"All work . . ." he said, grinning.

"You're so right." She smiled back.

It was ten o'clock. And it was the weekend. Tomorrow morning the stream of admittances would begin again. But tonight the pediatric floor held a peaceful quiet. Aggie was working until eleven. In another hour she would be gone. But perhaps somewhere during that hour, the other PICU nurse would leave the room and Aggie could smuggle her in to see Angelica. Just for a minute. Long enough to reassure the child that she hadn't been deserted. Long enough to convince her that her condition wasn't fatal, that she was going to pull out of this just fine.

She went by the supply room then passed the kitchen. A stocky young intern stood in front of it. "Hello, Dr. Landau," he said. He had short red hair and looked familiar. She nodded and moved on. The electronic double doors to the PICU were closed. Becca used her fist to hit the four-inch metal button on the wall. The doors slid open with a slight whir that was lost in the noises surrounding it. Becca blinked against the harsh white light overhead. She peered inside.

Aggie was nowhere in sight, but she spotted the other PICU nurse bending over a bed in the farthest glassed-in cubicle from the door. Becca shivered as if a freezing wind had passed over her. She was suddenly remembering the strange premonition she'd had just before the little girl at Boston Memorial had soured. She had that same feeling now.

Hugging the wall, she took a step inside. Angelica lay as Aggie had described her — eyes closed, body limp, hands lying open at her sides, face turned away. Again that sixth sense told her something was wrong. But what? Her eyes sought the jumble of wires and tubes that connected Angelica to the cardiac monitor, the respirator, and the feeding apparatus. Everything looked to be in place, but she was a distance of four feet from the bed, and her view was angled.

She took a few steps toward the bed. Panic exploded in her.

She rushed to Angelica's side. She saw it all simultaneously: the blue tinge to the skin, the stillness of the chest, the adhesive that had been worked loose from her cheeks. The feeding tube was still in place, but the respirator had been pulled out. Oh God, she thought. For how long? And why hadn't the alarm gone off?

She grabbed the tube in palsied hands. If she could reinsert it quickly enough . . .

She felt rather than saw someone come into the room. "My God, Becca," Aggie said over her shoulder, "what are you doing here?"

Part Two
The Trial

Twenty

The inquiry room on the plush top floor of the hospital was catty-cornered to Charles Peabody's office and adjacent to the executive dining room. It was actually an obsolete lecture hall maintained to brief staff on current techniques, but for prestige purposes was also loaned out for health care conferences and the like.

Despite Arnold Hardinger's frantic efforts to contain it, the news of what had happened to Angelica had been leaked the day after it happened. By the time the inquiry took place a week later, Becca had already been "tried and fried" by the media thanks to Judge Ellen Ryker's ongoing crusade against Manhattan General. Citing Becca's tainted record at Boston Memorial, the judge was using this latest example of "inferior staffing" to bolster her accusation of hospital negligence, and the public response was evidenced by the crowds surrounding the hospital.

A four-member panel sat on the dais in judgment of Becca. Libby Gruber, chief of Pediatrics, Anton Forlay, dean of the Medical School, Esther Bancroft, vice president of Pediatric Nursing, and Webster Bartlett, chief of medicine, who was to chair the inquiry.

It was Bartlett who had decreed that in keeping with past procedure, the media would not to be allowed at the hearings, but that in a break with tradition, both Becca and the hospital would be permitted to have attorneys represent them.

"Thank God for that," Becca whispered now as Sam led her to the long oak table that had been placed just below the dais. "I don't know what I'd do if you weren't here." The heel of her patent pump caught on the leg of a chair. "Damn!" she muttered, swaying.

Sam gripped her elbow to steady her. He could feel the tension in her as she straightened up. Her strides were hampered by the narrow skirt of the black linen suit he had insisted she wear. Its starkness was relieved only by the ruffled white blouse beneath it and the gold cameo pin on the jacket lapel. He had wanted her to look more mature than her twenty-nine years, more believable. Instead he had succeeded in making her appear colorless and haggard.

He eased her into her seat and pushed the chair in behind her. "Don't be so grateful. Bartlett's giving ice in winter."

"I don't understand."

"Then let me explain. Webster Bartlett is Arnold Hardinger's boy. Hardinger got him his job." He gestured toward the doorway where Jose and Maria Vargas were just entering. "That's why Vargas and his wife have been allowed to sit in on the hearings — an unheard-of precedent. And having representation won't benefit you as much as it will them." He yanked a thumb toward the twin table on their left that held Emil Wasserstein, the leading hospital attorney in the country.

"Why not? Won't it work the same way it does in a courtroom?"

"In some things, yes. I'll have a list of all the participants at the inquiry, and I'll be told the night before who's to testify the following day. I'll have the right to cross-examine the opposition's witnesses and to object to anything slanderous — for whatever good it will do me. Unless it's so blatant he can't help himself, Bartlett will rule against me."

But he couldn't give an opening statement or summation, Sam thought, both of which he always scored points on. And he couldn't request a gag order from a judge to sequester the panel because his client was being crucified by the media.

"The major thing," he said, "is that if this were a court of law, I'd have the right to keep you from testifying, and here I can't do that." Scowling, he mopped at his brow with a crumpled handkerchief. "Damn pressure cooker," he muttered.

A remnant of a bygone era, the room had walnut block walls,

tapestry print drapes, and huge leaded windows that made it impossible to air-condition well.

"Why would you want to keep me from testifying?"

Sam busied himself with the papers in his attaché case. It had been a mistake to raise that subject now. "I'll tell you when we meet at your place later."

"But what if I'm called today?"

"You won't be." He cut off her attempt to speak. "I think Davey is trying to get your attention."

"His name is David," she said coldly.

She turned slightly. She saw Arnold Hardinger first. His eyes were inscrutable as they encountered hers. He brushed a piece of lint from the lapel of his Savile Row suit then looked through her. His face broke into a smile as he tendered a hearty greeting to an associate. He exuded confidence—the boxer sure of the win even before the match began. In contrast, David sat next to him, agitatedly running a finger along his lower lip. She caught his eye. He gave her a smile of encouragement. It faded as he realized his father was watching the interplay.

"Has he called you?" Sam Stedman asked.

"That's none of your business."

"I've told you before. Everything about you is my business now."

Anger danced along her nerve endings as she glared at Stedman. She needed the man. She was grateful to him. But he irritated the hell out of her. And he had no right to pry into her private life. Her mind reverted to the session that had taken place in her living room last Tuesday evening.

Sam and Carolyn had been there. Aggie Bates was due to arrive any minute. The attorney had been toying with the porcelain knob on the six-foot pine armoire that housed her TV and stereo equipment. He was in shirt-sleeves and suspenders again. This time the suspenders were fire-engine red. Becca remembered wondering whether he really had no color sense or whether he deliberately chose to be outlandish.

"I think it would be wise if you didn't see the Hardinger boy for the duration of the hearings," he had said bluntly.

"Who told you about David?" she had retorted.

"I did," Carolyn said. She was seated on the couch in a cotton print dress, balancing a cup of coffee on her knee. "I'm sorry, Becca, but this is no time to keep secrets. Sam is your attorney, and I think he may be right."

"David would never hurt me."

Carolyn had set the coffee cup down on the antique trunk in front of the couch. "A few weeks ago I might have said the same thing. But I've spoken with him recently. David has changed since he's come to Manhattan General. I think he's not sure anymore of where his loyalties lie."

"You're wrong about him. But then it really doesn't matter anymore. David and I had an argument a few days before . . . before Angelica went into coma. He left for Boston and I haven't heard from him since."

Sam Stedman had stopped toying with the knob. He gave her a look she couldn't interpret. "You will," he said dryly.

He'd been right, as usual. That night David had turned up on her doorstep at midnight carrying a navy Valpak. Usually vain about his looks, she'd never seen him this disheveled. He wore stained jeans, an oversized T-shirt, and a crumpled bush jacket. There were shadows under his eyes, and his face was drawn and anxious. But there was no sign of the friction that had been between them at their last meeting.

He had thrown the Valpak on the floor and taken her into his arms as soon as she closed the door. He had run his hands along her back and shoulders over the robe she wore, and the differences between them had evaporated along with her tension. She needed him so badly now.

"I came the minute I heard," he said. He held her as if he couldn't bear to let her go. The stubble of his beard abraded her cheek as he rubbed his face against hers. "My God, Becca, what have you gotten yourself into?"

She helped him pull off his jacket, then drew him to the couch. She told him everything that had happened, not sparing herself in the telling. "The worst thing," she concluded, "is that I'm being treated like a leper at the hospital. I've been taken out of the clinical area and shunted off to Pathology on the lower level. It's like working in a dungeon. And I deal with tissues, not people. The hospital gave out to the press that I was temporarily taken off clinical duty, 'to relieve me of stress at a very stressful time.' It's bullshit." She shook her head in despair. "I miss my work so terribly, David. I feel as if I've deserted my patients."

"I can understand that. But you've got to be grateful it isn't worse. You didn't just bend the rules, Becca. You broke them in two. I don't understand how you could even think of going to see Angelica after—"

She waved her hands to ward off his words. "I know, I know. But I couldn't stand not seeing her anymore, David. I know it was stupid to seek her out after I'd been taken off the case, but I tell myself now that if I hadn't, she wouldn't be alive today."

"If you can call that being alive."

"She has a chance, David."

"A slim one. And even if she does pull out of the coma, if oxygen was denied to the brain for long enough . . . But I don't have to tell you." He rubbed his thumb across his lower lip. "Becca how do you think that respirator was dislodged?"

"I think Angelica did it herself."

He made a derisive sound in his throat. "Hell, are you still on that kick? Give it up, Becca. The girl couldn't have done it. You told me yourself that she was paralyzed with Guillain-Barré."

"Not completely."

"Can you prove that?"

"I . . . I don't know."

He took her hands in his and turned them over. He drew a diagonal line across her palm with his finger. "Becca, my father's going to try to prove you pulled that respirator."

She stiffened. "When did you talk to your father?"

"He was waiting at the airport for me. He wanted to make sure I didn't go anywhere near you. He's afraid the publicity will rub off on me." He stood up and rammed his fists into the pockets of his jeans. His lean face took on a brooding look. "Christ, it already has. The minute it hit the papers in Boston, they raked up all the speculation again on that death at Boston Memorial. They named you. They named me. 'Where there are repeated fires,' they said, 'there's got to be an arsonist.' I got out of the hotel as fast as I could. If the reporters ever found out I was up there . . . I couldn't take it again, Becca. The questions and the insinuations . . ." His voice trailed off.

She spoke slowly, her hands still open on her lap where he'd abandoned them. "My attorney feels the same way your father does." She didn't tell him it was because Sam didn't trust him. She hesitated. "Maybe it would be wise for you not to see me until after the hearing."

She waited for him to deny it, to argue with her. She waited for him to tell her that his father and her attorney could both take a flying leap. That he would see her whenever he damn pleased!

But he did none of those things. He came to sit beside her once more. He cupped her shoulders, and his eyes probed hers. She was struck by their blueness and the relief in them. His voice sounded stronger. "You wouldn't be angry?"

"No, I wouldn't be angry." She spoke in a monotone.

He glanced at her face. "But you'd be hurt. You'd feel as if I turned from you when you needed me most."

With an exclamation, she pulled away and stood up. "David, what do you want me to say? That I want you now? That I need you now? Of course I do. But I can't tell you what to do. What you decide has to come from you — from what you feel."

Stay with me, David, she pleaded silently. *I can't go it alone now.*

His hands balled into fists. "You want to know what I feel? I feel torn up. I want to stand with you and support you more than anything else in the world. But if I link myself to you now, the publicity could cost me my career." He stood up and went to her. He held her tightly. "Listen to me, darling. What's important here is that we both come out of this whole so we can go on from where we left off." He stroked her hair away from her face. "We'd only be apart a short while. And when all this dies . . ." He bent to kiss her. "There'll never be anyone else for me, Becca. I love you."

Bartlett's voice brought her back to the present.

"Before we begin the proceedings, I wish to offer up a silent prayer for Angelica Vargas's swift recovery." Becca followed his lead and bowed her head, then straightened up a few seconds later as he began the familiar litany. "I wish to stress that this is not a trial but an inquiry . . ."

His speech paralleled so closely the one that had been made at Boston Memorial that her mind did a fadeout. She tuned in again when she heard him say, "Will Melissa

Anheim please come forward."

Becca leaned toward Sam Stedman. "Who is . . . ?"

He frowned. "I told you yesterday. That's the nurse who was in the PICU when you got to it that Sunday night."

Melissa Anheim was a slender four feet nine with snapping dark eyes and short gray-white hair. She took her place on the stand, a blue leather armchair that had been set up on the dais at an angle that could be viewed by both the panel and the other participants.

Emil Wasserstein rose to approach her. His gait was surprisingly light for his short bulk. "Would you state your name and occupation, please." His smile was disarming. "Just for the record," he said amicably. In his muted plaid suit, bow tie, and sideswept brown hair, he gave off a "country boy" sincerity that belied his reputation as one of the keenest brains in the business.

"My name is Melissa Ellen Anheim. I'm a registered nurse, trained for intensive care duty." She blinked rapidly, her back ramrod stiff in the chair.

"Specifically pediatric intensive care duty. Right?"

"Yes. I work in the PICU. Recently on the three to eleven shift."

"And were you working that same shift last Sunday night?"

"Yes, I was. Along with Agatha Bates."

"Is that usual? To have two of you working the PICU?"

"Well, it depends on how many patients we have in the unit. The PICU holds six beds, and we generally like to keep a ratio of one nurse to two patients. That night we had four patients." She ticked them off on her fingers. "A seven-year-old burn victim, a four-year-old with congenital heart disease, the infant with AIDS . . ."

From the corner of her eye, Becca saw Jose Vargas's face blanch at the thought of his daughter lying almost side by side with an AIDS victim. It gave her a perverse feeling of satisfaction. Anyone who ever worked in a hospital could have told him that illness was a great leveler of class distinction.

"And, of course," Melissa Anheim finished, "there was Angelica Vargas with Guillain-Barré."

"Miss Anheim," he made an apologetic gesture, "we're not all doctors here and just so we get a clear picture, would you describe where Angelica was located in the PICU and in layman's terms what form the Guillain-Barré had taken."

"Well, Angelica was in the bed closest to the door. She couldn't move her body or her limbs. She couldn't breathe without the help of a respirator. She couldn't talk because of the plastic airway and endotracheal tube that ran through her mouth and was hooked up to that respirator. She also had a feeding tube threaded through her nose—"

"Excuse me, Miss Anheim. If I'm not mistaken, that life-sustaining respirator had an alarm on it so that if it were somehow dislodged, it would give off a warning signal."

"That's correct."

"Yet that alarm didn't go off when the respirator was dislodged."

"No, it didn't."

"And do you have any explanation for that?"

"No, I don't."

He nodded. "Miss Anheim, would you tell us in your own words what happened in that PICU at approximately ten o'clock last Sunday evening."

"Well . . ." She fidgeted in her chair and ran her hands along the sides of her white uniform. "I was alone in the PICU because Aggie had stepped out for a moment to go to the bathroom."

The attorney held up a hand again. "Excuse me, Miss Anheim. There is no bathroom in the unit?"

"There is, but it's small and it's always piled with extra supplies because there isn't enough room for all the stuff we have. Most of us use the one in the hall, you see."

He nodded and she went on. "Well, right after Aggie went out, I was checking on Willie, that's the boy with congenital heart disease, when I noticed that his EKG monitor wasn't working correctly. Willie had been squirming a lot, and when I bent over him I saw that two of the leads to the monitor had loosened and that was what was causing the problem. I was trying to re-attach them when—"

"Excuse me again, Miss Anheim, but where was the congenital heart patient located?"

"In bed number six. The one farthest from the door."

"So that while you were bent over working on this child, you could see nothing else that was transpiring."

"No, I couldn't."

"You couldn't see that Dr. Landau had entered the room?"

"No."

"Nor that Agatha Bates had returned from the bathroom."

"No. I didn't know that until I heard Aggie speak."

"And when you did hear her speak, what did you hear Agatha Bates say?"

The nurse's hand fluttered to her throat in agitation. Her small breasts rose and fell rapidly. "She said, 'My God, Becca, what are you doing?'"

Twenty-one

Becca's gasp was lost in the buzz that swept the room. The nurse's statement was a lie! She tried to catch her attorney's attention, but he had already uncoiled his long legs from the chair next to her and was approaching the stand. The buzz died to a hum. The witness sat up straighter as Sam Stedman towered over her, his face grim. Becca couldn't help wondering if his irascible personality would draw an adverse reaction from the panel.

"Miss Anheim," he began, "do you have a hearing problem?"

Her pixie face turned hostile. "I wear a hearing aid, if that's what you mean."

"And were you wearing that hearing aid on the Sunday night being referred to?"

"Yes, I was."

"Tell me, Miss Anheim, were the double doors to the PICU open or closed after Nurse Bates left the room?"

"They were closed. They're always closed unless someone is entering or leaving."

"And when those doors do open, they do so electronically, isn't that so?"

"Yes. There's a four-inch metal button on the wall outside the PICU that you can hit with an elbow or an arm if you're carrying something or taking care of a patient at the time."

"And when these doors open, do they make a noise?"

"Yes. It's a whirring kind of sound."

"Aptly described."

Sam Stedman's court appearance contrasted sharply with

the discordant impression he usually made on Becca. She almost wished it didn't. Next to the casual portrait the affable Wasserstein portrayed, he came across stiff and proper with his carefully brushed hair, dark suit, and black-rimmed glasses.

"So that even if you couldn't see that Becca Landau had entered the room, you could certainly hear it," he continued.

"Well . . . not exactly."

"Oh? And why not?"

"Well, bed six is the farthest cubicle from the door, and there was all this noise from the different machines. I mean, we've got ventilators and cardiac monitors and hypothermia blankets—"

"So what you're telling us, Miss Anheim, is that you couldn't hear the sound of the door opening."

"What I'm telling you is at that precise moment it's possible I didn't."

"And that therefore someone else besides Dr. Landau might have slipped into that room."

"That's very unlikely. We're talking of no more than two minutes at most."

"But it *is* possible?"

She looked uncomfortable. "I suppose so."

Sam straightened up and faced the dais. "And what you're asking this panel to believe is that though you couldn't hear the sound of the door opening, you could clearly hear Agatha Bates say, 'My God Becca, what are you doing?' " She opened her mouth to answer, but he cut across her words. "When in fact what Nurse Bates actually said was, 'My God, Becca, what are you doing *here?*' The addition of one word, Miss Anheim, but it makes all the difference, doesn't it?"

Obviously flustered, the nurse turned up her hands in appeal. They were small and white, the nails unpainted and cut very short. "Well, it's possible that's what she said, of course, but—"

"That will be all, Miss Anheim. Thank you."

He stepped from the dais and walked toward Becca. She watched him approach with shining eyes. In that moment she forgave him everything. His tactlessness, his cantankerous behavior, his outlandish color sense. Carolyn had been right when she called him brilliant. Becca wanted to tell him so, but she had a feeling he wouldn't appreciate it.

Emil Wasserstein rose from his chair a second before Sam Stedman returned to his. His face was all sympathy as he addressed the witness from where he stood. "Are you all right, Miss Anheim?" His concern suggested that Stedman had done everything but beat the poor woman. She nodded, and he looked relieved.

"Miss Anheim, what kind of hearing loss do you have?"

"A minor one in my left ear. Without the hearing aid I have difficulty from time to time in distinguishing between sounds."

"You mean you can't hear the difference between one monitor and another."

"Exactly."

"But you have no difficulty in hearing words."

Sam Stedman leaped to his feet. "Objection! Mr. Wasserstein is leading the witness."

Webster Bartlett's eyes flicked toward Arnold Hardinger. "I will allow the question," he said.

"No," Melissa Anheim confirmed, "I have no trouble hearing words."

Again the buzz sounded in the room. Bartlett held up a hand for quiet. "I call a ten-minute recess," he said.

In the vestibule, Becca slumped forward in the scooped out plastic chair against the wall, an untouched mug of coffee in her hands. Her head was bent low, her sweep of dark hair fell forward to shield her face. She had used this time to inquire about Angelica's condition. The answer: no change.

She raised her face to Sam. His lean frame was braced against the stove, his feet crossed at the ankles. He was drinking his coffee and watching her, obviously displeased about something.

He set his coffee mug on the counter with a bang. "If you're going to mope, do it on your own time, will you?" His scowl was fierce.

"Why are you so angry?"

He took off his glasses and used a napkin to clean them. "Do you know what a stacked deck is?"

She nodded. "It's to arrange the cards in order to cheat."

"Well, that's the kind of deal we're playing out in that inquiry room." He held up the glasses, squinted at the lenses for missed specks, then put them on. "And when you walk back in there looking like you do now, you're going to give them an added edge, because they're going to know that you're psyched out. It's called 'tipping your hand,' and it's something I never allow a client to do."

She spoke low. "Look, you don't have to go through with this. You can bow out anytime. I can always get another lawyer."

He looked at her incredulously. "Are you suggesting I quit?"

"Well, I realize you took this on because of Carolyn . . ."

"Is that what you think? That my sister could talk me into doing something I didn't want to do?" His gaze was speculative. "You don't know me very well, do you?"

Her eyes sparked with anger. She straightened until her spine was rigid. "I don't know you at *all!*" The man was impossible, she thought.

"There!" he said. "That's the way I want you to look." He took the mug of coffee from her hands and set it on the sink. He grabbed her arm. "Come on. Let's get back inside before you lose it!"

Agatha Bates's appearance on the witness stand resembled that of a fledgling performer with stage fright. Her hands clutching a sweat-drenched tissue in her lap, she sat in the chair white-faced and immobile.

"Miss Bates, would you tell us exactly what you saw in the Pediatric Intensive Care Unit when you returned from the bathroom that Sunday night?" Emil Wasserstein prompted.

Aggie swallowed, but no word came from her lips.

"Take your time, Miss Bates."

Wasserstein could afford to be generous, Becca thought. *Say something, Aggie,* she silently urged her friend. They had rehearsed her answers over and over in the apartment last night with Sam playing devil's advocate, throwing every possible question at her their opponents could ask.

"You were walking back . . ." Wasserstein prompted.

Aggie moistened her lips. "No. I—I was running." Her voice was pitched two octaves higher than usual.

"You were running because you were concerned with what was happening in the PICU?"

"Yes . . . *no!*"

"When you got back to the PICU, what did you see?" Wasserstein repeated.

"I saw Dr. Landau bending over Angelica Vargas."

"And did you say anything to her?"

"Yes. I said, 'Becca, what are you doing here?' "

"You're sure that's what you said?"

"Yes, I am."

"Why were you so surprised to see Dr. Landau?"

"Because she had been dismissed from Angelica Vargas's case a week before that."

"So she had no business being there."

"No, she didn't."

"And when you came closer to Angelica's bed, what did you see?"

"I saw that the respirator had been dislodged from Angelica's mouth and that she was cyanotic—her skin was turning blue. That meant she wasn't getting enough oxygen to the blood."

"And did Dr. Landau have her hands on that respirator when you came in?"

"Yes. She was trying to reinsert—"

Wasserstein's gentle voice turned sharp. "That's an assumption, Miss Bates. She could, in fact, have just finished pulling that tube out. Isn't that so?"

Sam's strident, *"Objection!"* rang out before she could answer.

"I withdraw the question," Wasserstein said. "Continue please, Miss Bates."

Outrage gave Aggie's speech the strength it had lacked. "As I was saying," she repeated indignantly, "Dr. Landau was trying to reinsert the respirator, but she wasn't having much luck. It's a tricky thing to do at best, and the trauma of the tube being pulled from the lungs and the trachea had caused laryngospasms, which was making it even more impossible. Dr. Landau did the only thing she could do at that point. She called a Code, and when they didn't respond fast enough, she performed a tracheotomy that probably saved the child's life. Unfortunately, Angelica went into coma."

"Then in your opinion we shouldn't be slandering Dr. Landau, we should be lauding her as a heroine."

"Yes."

"Even though she may have precipitated the incident for the express purpose of being regarded that way."

Sam Stedman moved with the speed of a bullet. "Objection!" For the first time he saw the direction the prosecution would take and a chill went through him.

Again Webster Bartlett glanced toward Hardinger before ruling. "Sustained!" he said.

Wasserstein opened his jacket to reveal a pot belly cinched tightly by a belt that barely made it around his girth. He smiled at the nurse in the chair. "Miss Bates, I hate to go over ground I've already covered, but indulge me." He leaned closer to her. "Miss Bates . . ."

Aggie wasn't listening. The door to the inquiry room had just opened, and Gottlieb was making his way to his seat. Her mouth tightened imperceptibly as she watched him take his place beside a pink-suited Maria Vargas who held out her hand and greeted him warmly. It was obvious that he had allied himself with the opposition. He turned his attention to the witness chair. She saw his eyes darken with pain as she deliberately averted her face from his.

"Miss Bates . . ."

She blinked. "I'm sorry."

The attorney nodded. "Miss Bates, when you ran into the PICU and saw that the respirator was detached, were you surprised that the alarm on it wasn't sounding off?"

"I . . . No, I wasn't." The tissue in her hands was in shreds.

"Would you explain that to us, please?"

She hesitated, then cleared her throat. "When a patient is on a respirator, their lungs have to be cleaned out every two hours. To do that the respirator has to be disconnected from the trach tube and the alarm has to be turned off. Otherwise it would keep going off. I had finished cleaning out Angelica's lungs just before I left the room. I had turned the alarm off, but it wasn't until a few minutes afterward that I realized

I had forgotten to turn it on again."

"And so you were rushing back to correct it."

"Yes."

"Very understandable. Tell me, Miss Bates, do you make many mistakes?"

Her face flushed a dull red. She lowered her head. "Some."

"Speak up Miss Bates. We can't hear you?"

"I said, 'Some.' "

"As serious as this one?"

"Objection," Sam called.

Ignoring it, Wasserstein crowded the chair. "As serious perhaps as not remembering the exact words you said to Dr. Landau when you came running into that PICU? Or in stating that she was reinserting a respirator when she had in fact just finished pulling one out? That serious, Miss Bates?"

"Objection!" Sam thundered.

Wasserstein tossed up his hands and backed off. His face was as innocent as a cherub's. "Your witness, Mr. Stedman."

"No questions."

"Thank you, Miss Bates. You may step down."

They ate at Becca's apartment that evening. For the last four nights it had been used as a strategizing center that included Aggie and Carolyn.

The lukewarm Chinese food in its cardboard containers had been demolished down to a few grains of rice and a limp eggroll when Sam Stedman dropped his bombshell.

"You're going to testify tomorrow, Becca." He ignored her sudden start. "And you're not even going to hint at the word *suicide*." He pointed his chopsticks at her for emphasis. "Is that clear?"

Carolyn Stedman's exclamation rent the silence. "Sam, you're off your rocker. It's the only defense she has."

"That may be. But they'll bury her if she uses it."

"But there's proof," Aggie Bates said in bewilderment. "What about the pills Angelica was hoarding?"

"And her insistence that her doll's death is imminent?" Becca challenged in a voice roughened by anger. "It's obvious to anyone who's willing to see it that her doll is her alter ego. And then there's Carolyn's conclusion that Angelica is suicidal. Or don't you feel that your sister who's a trained psychiatrist can give a qualified opinion?"

Sam scowled at her. "If you're out to fight me, I'm not having any. I get enough of that in the courtroom. If I tell you to do something, there's a reason behind it. You're supposed to trust me, remember?"

High-handed bastard! she thought, glaring at him. His long frame was caved into her ladder-back chair. Except to shed his jacket, he hadn't bothered to change before coming to her apartment. Quit of the inquiry room, he had reverted to type. His trousers were marked by deep creases, his white shirt was soiled at the cuffs, his brown thatch of hair tumbled onto his forehead, and his sprawled legs took up half her dining area. Despite her personal animosity toward this man, she had never before questioned whether she had made the right choice in an attorney. She did now.

"You'd better explain yourself, Sam," Carolyn said.

"I'd be glad to. Everything you've mentioned that points to suicide would be torn to shreds by Wasserstein. There isn't enough substantial proof for any of it to stand up. Added to that, Angelica Vargas has Guillain-Barré, and it would be a hell of a feat to prove she could even move let alone accomplish such an act."

"What would it take to make it plausible?" Becca asked.

He shrugged. "A history of suicidal attempts or a motive . . . a reason why this child would try to take her life. And don't tell me about the possibility of her mother having met with foul play. Without anything to back it up, it's just more supposition."

"It's still the best defense you've got," Carolyn said stubbornly. "I've seen you go into courtrooms with less." She eyed him shrewdly. "Is there some other reason you won't try to prove suicide, Sam? Something you're not telling us about?"

He hesitated, then turned a brooding gaze on Becca. "Look, it's like this. Coming on top of the other two celebrity deaths, the publicity on this thing will kill the hospital. The only hope they have is to whitewash Manhattan General completely of negligence and hopefully salvage that offer of twenty million from Vargas. To accomplish that they need a scapegoat. In this case, Becca. But to pin an attempted murder rap on Becca, they need to come up with a motive—some driving reason for her to commit such an act."

"They'll have a heck of a time finding one," Aggie said fiercely. "Becca is as dedicated a doctor as any I've ever seen. Why, her whole life is bound up in her patients."

"Exactly. And unless I miss my guess, that's going to be the basis of Wasserstein's prosecution. He's going to try to prove that Becca's dedication stems from a twisted need to appear heroic."

"I don't understand," Becca said.

"I think I do." Carolyn was frowning. "I think what Sam is talking about is Wasserstein accusing you of having a savior complex. It usually goes along with overdedication and can be seen a lot where life-and-death situations are prevalent—like hospitals and police stations. I think we all crave a certain amount of it. I mean, who doesn't want to be regarded with admiration? But in some people it goes out of whack. What it leads to then is the deliberate setting up of circumstances, no matter how destructive, to give that person the ego charge they must have."

"Like that nurse down in Texas," Aggie said, "the one who injected dozens of babies just so she could try to save them and make herself look good."

Carolyn nodded, but her attention was focused on Becca. "Are you all right?"

Becca avoided Carolyn's eyes and patted her stomach tremulously. "I love Chinese food, but it doesn't always love me."

It was a lie. She felt nauseous, but it had nothing to do with the food. She hadn't realized until now to what depths the opposition would sink. Her mind raced over her past, wondering what Wasserstein could use to bolster such a contention. If she could anticipate his thinking, there might be some way she could defend herself.

"If only Angelica would pull out of the coma," Aggie murmured."

"We're all hoping that," Sam said, "but we have to be realistic. We have to plan Becca's defense without taking that into consideration. With the flimsy proof we've got, if Becca tells that panel that Angelica was suicidal, Wasserstein will accuse her of trumping up yet another situation to make herself appear heroic."

"Then what defense does she go with?" Carolyn asked in exasperation.

"I think what we've got to go with is that someone else came into that PICU after Aggie left and dislodged that respirator before Becca came on the scene. I already laid the groundwork for that when I questioned Melissa Anheim."

Becca looked dubious. "You're talking about less than two minutes. How are you going to prove a thing like that?"

"I don't have to prove it. I only have to create enough of a doubt in their minds for them to exonerate you." He gripped the edge of the formica table and jackknifed his long frame into an upright position. "I'm sorry," he said. "But right now, that's the best we've got."

Twenty-two

The following morning was a scorcher. By the time Becca was called by Webster Bartlett, the temperature in the inquiry room had climbed to eighty-six degrees, and the leaded windows were steamy with condensation. The crackle of makeshift fans disturbed the quiet, and the drone of the overtaxed air-conditioner was a constant. Both attorneys had long since discarded their suit jackets, and Becca, her nerves on edge, sweltered in a dark cotton dress.

Sam Stedman had coached her for half the night, then tried to calm her on the way there. "We've gone over everything they could possibly ask you. Just answer the questions the way we rehearsed them and you'll be all right."

She took the witness chair now and waited for Bartlett to approach. The view from the dais was unnerving. There were more enemies out there than friends, she thought.

Beyond Sam Stedman who doodled idly at the long oak table less than twelve feet from her, she caught a glimpse of Gottlieb, his brooding glance on Aggie who sat two rows in front of him. Not far from him sat Jose Vargas, stiff and uncompromising in a tan cord suit. His leonine head was bent toward Maria Vargas who appeared cool and self-possessed in a sleeveless green dress, a jade crucifix dangling from a beaded chain about her neck. Two rows behind them she saw Arnold Hardinger talking intimately with a colleague and next to him sat David.

Suddenly conscious of her gaze, he raised his eyes to hers. She read into them all the warmth and steadfastness she wanted to see there.

He had called last night at ten. His voice had been thick with concern. "My father told me you're going to testify tomorrow."

"That's right."

He'd picked up on her tone immediately. "You're not alone there, are you?"

"No. My attorney is with me."

"I wish I could be there instead."

She was silent. He made it sound as if it were out of his control . . . as if someone else was responsible for his actions.

"Becca, I feel so helpless . . . so ineffectual . . ."

"David, I have to get back. They're waiting for me."

"Yes. Of course. Becca . . . no matter what happens on that witness stand, just remember that I love you."

He'd clicked off then, but she'd held to the phone a moment longer. Her feelings about him were so mixed. But she didn't want to probe them now. She was too vulnerable. She needed an anchor, something to hold to. And flawed as he was, David was all she had.

Certainly her family hadn't come through for her. Her mother had called five days ago. There were the usual tears and bewilderment at the predicament Becca had gotten herself into, followed by the self-reproach at being unable to help and the self-pity at the effect the devastating publicity was having on her social life. "Your father says to tell you he'll call as soon as he gets a minute," she'd said, then in tentative tones had offered to come to New York for a few days "to stand by your side." She was unable to hide her relief when Becca had declined.

It was so much like what had happened at the time of the Boston Memorial scandal that it shouldn't have hurt. But it did.

"Good morning," Emil Wasserstein said to her now. His smile was as open and kindly as that of a benevolent uncle. "How do you feel?"

"Fine." Her fingers balled tightly around the curved arms of the chair.

"Would you tell us a little about yourself, Dr. Landau. Where you went to college and to med school. Where you interned?"

He's going to start slow, Sam had told her. *Try to lull you into a false sense of security.*

"I went to Boston University, then Tufts Medical School, then

I interned at Boston Memorial."

"From where you transferred to Manhattan General two years ago."

"That's correct."

"A transfer that was forced upon you by an incident you were involved in at Boston Memorial."

"It was not *forced* upon me. I transferred voluntarily to Manhattan General."

He ran his hand along the silver watchchain that hung between the pockets of his plaid vest. "Would you describe that incident to us please?"

Becca nodded. Her heart was pounding, but thanks to Sam Stedman she could have recited the words backwards. "I was doing a surgical rotation in Pediatrics and was part of a team in which Dr. David Hardinger was senior resident. The incident took place on a Saturday night in January. A four-year-old patient was given into our care after undergoing a routine appendectomy. Her vital signs were good, and she seemed stable. Dr. Hardinger, who had been on duty for over twenty hours, left to get some sleep. We had a full load of patients that night, and his instruction to me was that if anything unusual were to happen to any of them, I was to reach him immediately."

"When you say, 'Dr. Hardinger left,' do you mean he went to an on-call room at the hospital?"

"No. Dr. Hardinger lived a block from the hospital and was allowed to go to his apartment when he was on call."

Wasserstein nodded and she continued. "At about ten o'clock that evening, I was called to the room of the appendectomy patient by the nurse. The patient—"

Wasserstein grimaced. "Excuse me, Dr. Landau. Would you mind calling the patient by name. This anonymity you are giving her sounds so . . . inhumane. Especially for a four-year-old. You do remember her name, don't you?

Her lips tightened. "Yes, I do."

He'll probably try to make you look callous, Sam had said. *Don't let it throw you.*

"As I was saying," she continued, "the patient, Gloria Ames, was running a fever of a hundred and seemed restless. I prescribed aspirin and told the nurse to watch her. An hour later the nurse called me again. Gloria's fever had escalated to a hundred and one, and she had become even more restless. I phoned Dr. Hardinger immediately. On both his telephone number and his beeper number. When he didn't answer, I called both numbers again. There was still no answer. When the fever continued to escalate, I stayed at Gloria's bedside and worked with the nurse to get it down. We couldn't do it. Within twenty minutes it had climbed to a hundred and four; the child was thrashing in the bed, and her vital signs had become unstable. I tried Dr. Hardinger again and again, but I couldn't reach him. I was still trying when the patient . . . Gloria, went into arrest."

"And what did you do then?"

"I called a Code and the nurse and I began CPR. Then a medical student wheeled in the crash cart and another intern arrived at the scene. We . . . we tried everything." She faltered as the horror of it came back to her. She swallowed convulsively, and her eyes sought Sam's.

When you feel yourself slipping, look at me, he had instructed. He nodded to her encouragingly now. It steadied her, and she went on.

"We used an ambu-bag—a manual respirator. We did external heart massage. We tried a mix of lidocaine, bicarb, and calcium in the I.V. and repeated it at calculated intervals. No matter what we did, the monitors stayed flat. We worked on her for over an hour, but it was no use." Becca shuddered as she relived the moment. Her voice was an empty hollow. "I was so sure I could save her."

"And what a feather in your cap if you had!" Wasserstein gestured eloquently toward the panel. "Think of it, a mere intern just out of med school, pulling off a coup like that! Tell us, Dr. Landau, did you feel yourself capable of taking charge of a cardiopulmonary arrest?"

"I had already been present at two, but it wasn't a matter of whether I felt capable or not. I had no choice. As the only doctor there, I had to take it on until someone senior to me arrived."

"Someone like Dr. Hardinger, you mean? If you had reached Dr. Hardinger and he had come to the hospital, he would have been given the chance to save that child instead of you. Isn't that right?"

195

"Yes. Dr. Hardinger was my senior."

"Tell me, Dr. Landau, when you phoned Dr. Hardinger, did you do it from the patient's room?"

"No. There was only one occupied bed in the room and the child's family had seen no reason to have the phone hooked up."

"Then I assume that you made those calls to Dr. Hardinger from the nurse's station on the floor."

"No, I didn't. Gloria Ames's room was at the end of the floor, the one furthest away from the nurse's station. But there was a telephone booth right outside the room and that's where I made the calls from. It was a matter of expediency, you see."

"No, I don't see. If you had made the first call from the nurse's station, you could have asked the head nurse to keep on trying Dr. Hardinger while you took care of your patient, isn't that true?"

"I suppose so. But it didn't occur to me. I was pretty tired at the time, and I may not have been thinking straight."

"I disagree. I think you were thinking very straight. Tell me, Dr. Landau, did anyone in that hallway see you make those phone calls to Dr. Hardinger?"

"I don't believe so. There wasn't anyone who came forward afterward to say they did."

"Then if you had never made these phone calls, no one would ever have known. Would they?"

"Objection!" Sam Stedman cried.

"I withdraw the question." He consulted several notes he clutched between his pudgy fingers. "I believe that Gloria Ames's father, who is a radio announcer, instituted a malpractice suit that the hospital finally settled. Isn't that so, Dr. Landau?"

"Yes, it is."

"I also believe that after lengthy inquiries, Boston Memorial saw fit to cite you for negligence and poor judgment." He looked at each member of the panel, smiling ruefully and shaking his head in wonder. *"Negligence and poor judgment!* A slap on the wrist — a mere spanking. Such a small price to pay compared to the one Gloria Ames paid, wouldn't you say, Dr. Landau?"

"Objection!" Sam Stedman was on his feet in a fighting stance.

"Sustained." Bartlett mopped at the perspiration beading his upper lip. His face was almost as wilted as his starched white collar. "I call a ten-minute recess, after which the questioning of Dr. Landau will resume."

"He's making me out to be a monster," Becca railed within the confines of the tunnellike vestibule.

"He's trying," Sam Stedman agreed. "But that's his job. Yours is to answer his questions and to keep your head. So far you're doing great."

"I don't feel like I'm doing great." She lifted her hair with both hands and held it away from her neck. The vestibule was a furnace. "What's he going to attack with next?"

He shrugged. "He's bled the Boston Memorial thing to death. My guess is he'll update quickly to the night Angelica went into coma."

She looked away. "I'm scared, Sam." The words came from her mouth unbidden. The admission embarrassed her. She wasn't used to showing him her vulnerability.

"Understandable," he said. "Everyone's scared on a witness stand. Even those who have nothing to be scared about."

She was amazed at his compassion. So far he had shown her very little of it.

He turned her to face him. "Look, you've told me everything that happened that Sunday evening, right?" She nodded. "Then there should be no surprises. Tell you what. You do as well as you've been doing up to now and I'll bring along a bag of leechee nuts tonight. Deal?"

She laughed. "You must have heard me tell Aggie I loved them."

"Never mind where I get my information."

When she entered the inquiry room five minutes later, it was with a lighter heart.

"Dr. Landau, why did you try to see Angelica Vargas after you'd been dismissed from the case?" In deference to the heat, Wasserstein had removed the vest but not the bow tie that seemed to be his trademark. It was bright blue and hugged his fleshy neck like a chin strap.

"In the few weeks I'd known Angelica, a trust had grown between us. I wanted her to understand that I hadn't deserted her."

"Very commendable. Do you get this attached to all your young patients?"

"No, I don't."

"Did you get this attached to Gloria Ames when you were at Boston Memorial?"

"No, I did not."

"Dr. Landau, would you please describe to the panel what happened after you entered Manhattan General at approximately ten o'clock last Sunday night."

She nodded. "I took the elevator up the PICU on the fourth floor—"

"Did you see or speak to anyone on the way?"

"I spoke to the security guard. The one at the elevators on the main floor."

"Go on, please."

"When I reached the unit, I pressed the button to open the doors. I could see only one nurse there at the far end of the room. Angelica was in the bed nearest the doors. I felt something was wrong with her from the moment I entered, but I couldn't figure out what it was. Then I stepped closer to the bed and saw that Angelica was cyanotic and that the respirator had been pulled out. I tried to reinsert it, but I couldn't. I remember wondering why the alarm hadn't gone off. Then I heard Agatha Bates speak to me."

"And what did she say?"

"She said, 'My God, Becca, what are you doing here?' "

Becca waited for him to challenge her on the wording, but he didn't.

"And what did you do then?"

"When I couldn't reinsert the respirator, I called a Code to signal an arrest. In the PICU, it's done by pressing the button on the side wall."

"And did anyone respond to your call?"

"They did, but not quickly enough."

"In *your* opinion, Dr. Landau."

"Yes. In my opinion." Her voice was tart. "I had to make a judgment call. Angelica Vargas was turning blue. I knew we were dealing in seconds. Maybe even less. If she couldn't get air into her lungs right away she was going to die. I did the only thing I could do under the circumstances. I performed a tracheotomy."

Wasserstein tipped an imaginary hat to her. "Bravo, Dr. Landau! How heroic of you! And what an ego boost. Just like the one you got when you were handling the cardiac arrest of Gloria Ames."

"Objection!" Sam Stedman stated.

"I withdraw the statement," Wasserstein conceded, knowing he'd made his point. "Dr. Landau, a tracheotomy is a surgical procedure, I believe."

"Yes."

"And did you feel qualified to do this procedure?"

"I performed a tracheotomy when I was doing a surgical rotation at Boston Memorial."

"I ask you again, Dr. Landau. Would you be considered qualified to perform this procedure?"

"No. I would not be."

"And so you took a gamble. One that again gave you the opportunity to shine in the eyes of your colleagues. Just as your inability to reach Dr. Hardinger at Boston Memorial had. But I suggest to you, Dr. Landau, that the opportunities in both these cases were not created by chance but deliberately engineered by you."

"Objection!" Sam Stedman cried.

Webster Bartlett's eyes flicked toward Hardinger. "I'll allow it," he said.

Wasserstein took a step closer to her. Becca could feel herself shrink as the man's bulk blocked her view of the panel. "Dr. Landau, did you go to the PICU unit last Sunday evening and deliberately pull that respirator from Angelica Vargas?"

"No, I did not."

"Then who did?"

"I don't know. Someone could have come into that PICU just before I did."

From the corner of her eye, she saw Sam Stedman nod in approval. *It's almost over,* she thought. *Thank God, it's almost over.*

Wasserstein opened his mouth to say something, but a commotion at the far end of the room brought his words to a halt. Esther Pemberton had pushed open the door. She had in tow a short man in a white lab coat whom Becca couldn't see clearly. He remained standing at the door while the secretary made her way to Arnold Hardinger's side. After a quick whispered conversation between the two, Hardinger rose and signaled to Wasserstein.

The attorney begged the panel's indulgence, then met with Hardinger in the center of the room to confer. The conference over, Hardinger once again took his seat and Wasserstein came forward to address the panel.

"Ladies and gentlemen," he inclined his head toward his opponent, "and Mr. Stedman. I would like to offer my apologies for the delay. Because of unexpected knowledge that has just come to my attention, I feel it would be in the best interest of this inquiry to interrupt my questioning of Dr. Landau and call to the stand a witness who was not previously scheduled."

Sam Stedman was on his feet immediately. "I strongly object. Not only is it out of order, but it would not allow for preparation to cross-examine." He watched the panel whisper among themselves and almost laughed aloud at the farce. Their decision was a foregone conclusion.

Within seconds Webster Bartlett straightened up and addressed the room at large. "In the interest of justice, the panel has decided to waive protocol. Mr. Stedman, you will be given the option to recall the witness for cross-examination at any time in the proceedings." He cleared his throat. "Dr. Landau, please step down. Mr. Wasserstein, you may call your witness."

"I call Dr. Peter Alton," Wasserstein said.

Sam Stedman's mouth was a thin line. *"Who is he?"* he demanded of Becca as she slid into her seat beside him.

"I don't know," she whispered tensely.

The stocky figure in the white lab coat left the shadowy confines of the door and began to make his way to the stand. The overhead lights glinted on his short red hair, his ruddy face and the spattering of freckles that dotted his prominent forehead.

Becca closed her eyes as a sick feeling came over her. "Oh, my God," she said. "I forgot about him."

Twenty-three

Wasserstein ran a finger beneath his collar and adjusted his bow tie. His face was shiny, his smile almost beatific. "Dr. Alton, you are an intern at Manhattan General?"

"Yes. A first-year intern." He spoke slowly and kept his eyes on his hands. "Right now I'm doing a rotation in Pediatrics."

"So you know Dr. Landau."

"Well . . . mostly by sight." He glanced covertly at the panel of his superiors, his awe of them obvious. I met her for the first time on grand rounds about two weeks ago."

Reminded now of where she had first seen him, Becca also remembered her impression of him. Adequate but plodding—one of the many doctors who would suffice but never shine.

"As I understand it, you also saw her on the pediatric floor last Sunday evening."

"Yes, I did." He wet his lips and worried the lapel of his lab coat.

Becca could identify with his fear, but she was too traumatized to sympathize with it. She was painfully aware of Sam sitting next to her yet withdrawn from her. He was like a fighter in a championship bout suddenly unable to do more than shadow box. And she was the cause of it.

"Would you tell us about that, Dr. Alton?" Wasserstein prompted.

"Well, I had just taken a break at about ten o'clock that night, and I was waiting for my girlfriend. She's a med student doing a stint in Hematology, and we usually meet for a few minutes at ten to have a cup of coffee and," his florid face grew redder, ". . . and to talk."

"And this takes place on the fourth floor."

"Yes. In the small kitchen up there. It's just past the supply room."

"And from the doorway of this kitchen, do you have a view of the PICU?"

"Yes. A full view."

"Would you please tell us what you saw last Sunday evening?"

His brow creased. The freckles on his forehead ran together like inkblots. "Well, that night my girlfriend was late, so I poured myself a cup of coffee and stood in the doorway, waiting for her. At about ten o'clock, I saw a nurse leave the PICU and walk up the hallway. A moment later, Dr. Landau came off the elevators and went past me."

"Did you say hello to her?"

"Yes, I did."

"And did she acknowledge your greeting?"

He thought a moment. "She nodded to me, but I got the feeling she didn't remember who I was." He looked at Becca apologetically.

"Tell us what happened then."

"I saw Dr. Landau go into the PICU, and a minute or two later I saw the nurse who had left come running back there."

Becca knew what was coming. She was helpless to prevent it. Why hadn't she remembered the incident? Given it over to Sam. At least there would have been a fighting chance then. She felt very much alone. As if the whole world had dissolved around her. Sam's anger was so palpable, it was a living thing between them. She had failed him. She had failed herself, and worst of all, she had failed that little girl who lay in the PICU clinging to life by a thread.

Wasserstein's pause stressed the importance of his next question. "Dr. Alton, think carefully. Between the time the nurse, Agatha Bates, first left the PICU, and the time Dr. Landau entered it, was there anyone else who came into that intensive care unit?"

"No. There was no one."

"You are positive of that."

"Yes, I am."

"Thank you, doctor. Yours to cross-examine, Mr. Stedman?"

Sam shook his head. "No questions." He doodled on the yellow pad in front of him with great intensity.

The attorney nodded. "You may step down, Dr. Alton. I recall Dr. Becca Landau to the stand."

Becca rose on wobbly feet. She could no longer think. She could only feel. The confidence she had exhibited earlier had deserted her along with Sam's belief in her. Wasserstein gestured toward the witness chair with exaggerated politeness. She kept her glance from the panel as she sat down. She could feel their condemnation of her as if they'd voiced it.

A triumphant smile played about Wasserstein's mouth. "Dr. Landau, I ask you again. Did you pull that respirator from Angelica Vargas in the PICU last Sunday evening?"

He was standing so close, she could smell the pungent aftershave lotion he used. No longer the affable country boy, he was closing in for the kill. She made no move, but inwardly she felt herself retreating, cringing. She was cornered, and she was panicked. She wanted to run and hide, the way she had as a child.

When you feel yourself slipping . . . Sam had said. She glanced at him. His head was still down over that damned yellow pad. Another emotion began to surface in her. Anger. She was no longer a child. The years had given her the ability to rationalize, to put things in perspective. The sole crime of which she was guilty was trying to save Angelica. Maybe she had forgotten about seeing the intern on the pediatric floor that night. But the only reason it was so crucial was that her entire defense was predicated on a lie. And she wasn't going to let it go on any longer. If she was slated to go under, then let it be with the truth on her lips.

"Dr. Landau . . ." Wasserstein pressured.

"No!"

He looked blank. "No what?"

"No, I did not pull that respirator."

"Who else could have?"

"Angelica Vargas."

A shocked silence blanketed the room. Wasserstein's words cut through it. "Dr. Landau, are you saying . . . ?"

"I'm saying that Angelica Vargas tried to kill herself."

* * *

Her impressions afterward were as fleeting as the patterns in a kaleidoscope. She remembered the buzz in the inquiry room. The look of disbelief on Jose Vargas's face. The lack of emotion in Sam Stedman's. She remembered seeing Maria Vargas cross herself, and she recalled Arnold Hardinger's fury. Only David's expression held sympathy for her.

After Bartlett had announced an end to the proceedings, she had gone back to the confines of the pathology lab. For once she was grateful to be shielded from humanity. She didn't want to see or speak to anyone. She wanted to lose herself in her work. But even that was denied her. Her brain was so scrambled that nothing registered. Within two hours she left the hospital disguised and sneaking past the reporters who thronged the back exit like buzzards waiting to pounce.

The phone was ringing when she opened the door to her apartment.

"Have you seen the *Post?*" David demanded when she picked up.

She closed her eyes at the sound of his voice. She needed him so badly now. "Yes, I have." The newspaper had just hit the stand at her corner when she passed it on the way home. Tied and bundled, the headlines had screamed at her. "DR. BECCA'S ALIBI: ANGELICA SUICIDAL!"

"Bastards!" he muttered. "How do they get their information so fast?"

She didn't answer.

His voice gentled. "Are you okay?"

"I need to see you."

"I know, darling. I feel the same way. But it's impossible right now." He hesitated. "Becca, Wasserstein just called to tell me I'll be testifying tomorrow. He feels there is no gain on either side if our relationship is revealed. He's going to try to suppress it. I promised him I'd do nothing in the meantime to upset the applecart. If I come to see you — You understand, don't you?"

"Oh, yes. I understand. From your point of view I understand it very well."

"Becca . . ."

"Look, David, I'm tired and I'm down and at the moment I don't give a damn about your point of view."

There was a hurt silence.

"I'm sorry, David."

Why was she apologizing? She had nothing to apologize for.

"We'll talk later." His voice was low.

"Yes."

She hung up. She was grateful for the feeling of numbness that took over then. It persisted until Aggie and Carolyn Stedman showed up at six carrying two oversized pizzas in sagging cardboard boxes. She wasn't surprised that Sam wasn't with them.

Carolyn didn't seem bothered by her brother's absence. "Sam has a temper," she said, "but he comes around eventually." She took a slice of the sausage pizza from its carton on the livingroom table and sat down cross-legged on the hassock. "It's a pity my former sister-in-law didn't understand that. She was too easily intimidated to hold him."

Becca had wondered how Sam could afford to spend so much time away from his family until Carolyn had told her, "Sam's family consists of me and an eight-year-old son who lives with his mother in California. I'm afraid neither Sam nor I have been too successful at choosing the right people to live with. Maybe it's something in our genes."

Becca was silent now. The last thing she wanted to hear about was her attorney's past marital problems. She suspected that if she did, her sympathies would be with his wife.

"I'm glad you told them about the suicide attempt," Aggie said fiercely. "I wish I could have been there when you did." Still in her uniform she was slumped into a corner of the couch, the strain of a double shift evident in the sagging lines of her face.

"And the truth shall set ye free," Carolyn quoted softly.

"Like hell," Becca murmured. "Aggie, is there any change in Angelica? Anything at all?"

"I would have told you if there were."

Becca nodded. She had known that, but she had needed to ask. The bell rang. "I'll get it," she said. She uncurled herself from her chair and went to the door.

Sam Stedman stood outside, tall and rangy in a pair of faded jeans, a bright green T-shirt that made his skin look bilious, and

205

worn sneakers. "I walked from my apartment," he said.

She didn't know where he lived, but she got the impression that it was far. It had rained earlier, and his sneakers were splattered with mud. His hair was damp, and the side part in it was gone. Some of it stood up in tufts; some had given way and fallen forward onto his forehead. He hadn't worn his glasses, and he was peering at her like a myopic owl. There was no sign of anger in his face.

"I'm sorry I blew it," she said.

He shrugged. "Spilt milk. You did what you had to do." He scowled. "You going to invite me in? Or do we conduct our business here on the doorstep?" He pushed past her without waiting for an answer.

Impossible man, she thought, elated that he was there.

"Well, well," Carolyn said as he crossed the foyer. "The spy who came in from the heat."

He scooped up a piece of pizza, sat down on the couch, and boosted his long legs onto the trunk that served as a cocktail table. "There'll be no kibitzing from the bleachers," he said.

He finished stuffing the pizza into his mouth, then picked a piece of crust from his lap. "Okay. Let's get down to it. Right or wrong, the specter of suicide has been raised at the inquiry. We can't change that."

"So what do we do?" Becca asked.

"We try to prove it."

"You said we couldn't do that," Carolyn pointed out.

"I said we couldn't do that with what we have."

"I'm confused," Aggie said.

"Let me explain. Right now there are three things that point to Angelica's try at suicide — the pills she was hoarding, the dying doll she identifies with, and Carolyn's conclusions. Believe me, Wasserstein will rip all three apart."

"So what do we do?" Becca asked.

"We use them as a stall for time. And we try to get more. What we're missing is motive or a past suicide attempt or both. Becca and Carolyn believe that Angelica tried to kill herself because she saw her mother murdered. If we can prove there was a murder and that Angelica witnessed it —"

"We can't do that without Angelica," Becca said.

"Sure we can. I cut my teeth on criminal law. A murder is like a jigsaw puzzle. When you get enough pieces that fit, the whole picture comes clear. Margaret Quinlan gave you some of those pieces. Find out who can give you the rest."

"There was a relief nurse at the Vargas house on the day it happened," Becca said, "name of Fiona Andrews. But she was fired the next day along with the servants, and she disappeared. I've asked Helen Walters to help locate her, but so far . . . nothing."

"Ask her again," Sam said. "Start using your brain. Try to locate the others who were fired. They're one of your best bets because they've got no love for the Vargases. I'll try to free up one of my investigators to help."

Carolyn untangled her legs from the hassock. "If we establish that Angelica witnessed a murder, that will give us motive. But how do we go about proving a past suicide attempt?"

"Gottlieb might help there," Becca mused. "Except that he's so firmly entrenched with Vargas he's useless to us."

"That may not be so," Aggie murmured.

Becca looked at her sharply. She remembered what Margaret Quinlan had said about Aggie and the attending. "Got any ideas, Aggie?"

She looked thoughtful. "Maybe."

"What about Walter Heilbrun?" Carolyn asked. "Angelica's tutor. I got the impression when I talked with him that he'd been with her a long time. He may have witnessed a suicide attempt."

"Good thinking," Sam said. "Get on it as soon as you can." His thick brows met in a V above the bridge of his nose. "There's another problem we've got. Angelica has Guillain-Barré, a disease that paralyzes its victims. Wasserstein will try to prove that Angelica couldn't move enough to pull that respirator. We've got to prove otherwise."

Aggie made a triumphant noise. "But we can do that!" She looked more animated than she had all evening. "Don't you remember, Becca? The notes Angelica sent you. They prove she could move her hands."

Sam looked puzzled. "What notes?"

"Of course!" Becca swiveled toward Sam. "Angelica wrote me a series of notes during that week, asking me to come to see her."

"Do you have the notes?"

Her face fell. "Damn! I threw them out."

"I have one," Aggie said. "Angelica wasn't happy with it and insisted on doing another. I threw it into the top drawer of a cabinet in the PICU."

"Wonderful!" Sam's exuberance embraced them all. "Get hold of it as soon as you can. It's an important piece of evidence." He crammed another piece of pizza into his mouth then glanced at his watch. "I've got to get back to the office."

"At this time of the night?" Carolyn questioned.

He shrugged. "My desk looks like a cyclone hit it. I've got to make some order out of it." He glanced at Becca. "Walk me to the door, will you?"

It was said casually, but Becca knew he had something to tell her. He waited until they were in the small foyer, out of sight of the others.

"Davey's due to testify tomorrow," he said.

"I know."

Fair enough, she thought in the ensuing silence. She hadn't cried foul at the belittling nickname and he hadn't asked her how she knew about it.

She slid her hand onto the brass doorknob. She didn't look at him. "David and I don't want it known that we . . ." She cleared her throat, wondering why she was having such a difficult time putting this into words. He was a grown man, for God's sake. "What I'm getting at is that Wasserstein's going to try to keep our relationship from surfacing at the inquiry."

"So will I. I don't see anything to be gained right now by revealing it. But understand that if at any point it comes to telling it or throwing you to the wolves, I'm not going to hold back."

"I understand."

"I hope so." A strand of her hair had fallen forward across her lips. He lifted a hand to push it back into place, then thought better of it. The hand dropped to his side. "I'll be in touch," he said.

Twenty-four

He should have been an actor, Becca thought as she watched David take the stand the following day. He sat back in the chair and rested an arm along the top of the brass-studded frame. He nodded to each panelist as if they were seated at the same dinner table. He smiled at Wasserstein with that ingenuous "I have nothing to hide" smile that had drawn her to him when they'd first met. Only when he rubbed his thumb across his lower lip did she become aware of the tension beneath the surface calm.

Next to her Sam Stedman sat with his head lowered, drawing bold concentric circles on a yellow pad. They'd had a particularly hard time this morning getting through the media that bottlenecked the entrance to the hospital, and his anger was reflected in the ferocity of his doodling.

"Dr. Hardinger," Wasserstein began, "you are at present assistant chief of Surgery at Manhattan General Hospital. Isn't that so?" The weather had cooled to a bearable seventy-eight, and the attorney's herringbone suit and gray bow tie reflected the change.

"That is correct."

"And before that, what hospital were you at?"

"I was at Boston Memorial."

"And did you take your surgical residency there?"

"Yes, I did."

Becca watched him glance around the inquiry room. At Vargas. At Gottlieb. At his father. At everyone but her. She tried to rise above the empty feeling it gave her when he passed her by. Was it Wasserstein's idea for him to ignore her or his own, she wondered?

"Dr. Hardinger," Wasserstein continued, "at the time of that residency, did you head up a team with Dr. Landau as intern?"

"Yes. She was doing a surgical rotation then."

"And it was during that rotation, specifically two years ago on the night of January 26th, that a four-year-old patient of yours, Gloria Ames, went into cardiac arrest and died."

"Yes."

"Would you tell us about that night, please."

"Well, I had assisted at an appendectomy on Gloria Ames late that afternoon."

"Excuse me, Dr. Hardinger, but was there anything odd or different about that operation, anything to cause you worry?"

"No. It was a routine appendectomy. The operation was successful, and when the patient left the recovery room, she seemed stable. I waited around for another two hours to make sure everything was all right, then I decided to get some sleep. I left Dr. Landau in charge and told her to get in touch with me right away if anything went wrong with Gloria Ames or any of the other patients. Then I went to my apartment a block away and went to sleep."

"I assume you slept in your bedroom. I mean, this wasn't a studio apartment or something like that."

"No, it wasn't. I slept in the bedroom."

"And where was the telephone?"

"On the nightstand next to the bed."

"And your beeper?"

"Same place."

"And were your telephone and beeper in working order?"

He shrugged. "As far as I knew, they were."

"Tell us what happened then, please."

"Well a little after eleven o'clock, I got a call from the head nurse on the pediatric floor. She told me that Gloria Ames was in cardiac arrest and that I'd better get over there fast."

Wasserstein waved a blue-backed legal document at the panel. "I have here a deposition from said head nurse, Anna Moffit, corroborating that statement." He handed it up to Webster Bartlett then turned back to the witness. "Go on, please. What did you do then?"

"I threw on my clothes and rushed to the hospital. But I was too late. Gloria Ames was already dead."

"Doctor, do you think that if you had been there from the onset that you could have saved her?"

"Objection!" Sam Stedman called. "Counselor is calling for a conclusion."

"I withdraw the question," Wasserstein said. "Dr. Hardinger, did you get any other phone or beeper calls from the time you left the hospital until the head nurse called you?"

"No, I didn't."

"You had left Dr. Landau in charge of your patients with instructions to call you if anything went wrong. When you heard that Gloria Ames had arrested, weren't you surprised that she hadn't called you?"

"Yes, I was. But Dr. Landau explained afterward that she had tried to do so."

"Tried over and over. And failed."

"Yes."

"Can you explain why she failed?"

"No, I cannot."

"In the light of Dr. Landau's failure, can you explain why the head nurse, Anna Moffitt, had no trouble reaching you on the phone the very first time she tried?"

"No. I cannot."

It was Anna Moffitt's testimony that had damned her at the Boston inquiry, Becca remembered. She had twisted her mind inside out trying to figure out why the head nurse would lie, then after talking with her later had come to the conclusion that she hadn't. Becca had toyed with the idea that she'd been calling the wrong numbers all along but discarded it when she remembered that she had checked the numbers more than once. There was simply no explaining what had happened that evening.

"Thank you, doctor," Wasserstein concluded. "Your witness, Mr. Stedman."

Sam Stedman approached the stand. He was in his court mode again—hair and undertaker's suit both in place, white shirt and dull tie testifying to his "sincerity." "Dr. Hardinger, let's go back again to the night Gloria Ames died at Boston Memorial hospital. You have stated that you left the hospital at nine that evening. How long had you been on duty before that?"

"Twenty hours."

Sam nodded sympathetically. "A long time to be confined and under such tension. If you're like I am you must have wanted to unwind, stop in for a beer, maybe talk with friends for a while . . . certainly not go straight home."

David looked at him with cold blue eyes. "I don't mean to downgrade your work, Mr. Stedman, but I don't think you can compare it to a surgeon's. The only thing I wanted to do after twenty hours in that O.R. is sleep. Besides, I was on call, and I don't take that lightly."

Embarrassed, Sam shook his head in apology. "I'm sorry. I didn't understand. That had to be an exhausting stretch for someone who holds life and death in their hands on that table as you do. When your head hit that pillow you must have fallen asleep like a dead man."

"I did."

"Too tired to even hear the ring of a telephone, I'll bet."

David started to say something, then hesitated.

Becca could see his mind working. If he admitted to the possibility of not hearing the phone, he gave her an out, but he cast a slur on his own image.

"I don't think so," he said finally. "I heard the telephone when Anna Moffitt called."

"Ah, but that was two hours later. Any sleep expert will tell you there are varying depths of sleep. Isn't it possible that the level of your sleep at the time Dr. Landau called you was so deep as to render you unconscious to the ring of the beeper and the phone, while two hours later, with your exhaustion somewhat lessened, you were able to respond to sound in a more normal fashion?"

"Objection!" Wasserstein cried. "Calls for a conclusion."

"Sustained," Bartlett said promptly.

Sam Stedman looked unperturbed. He unbuttoned his jacket and hooked a thumb onto his suspender. "Dr. Hardinger, do you consider yourself a good judge of character?"

"Yes, I do."

"I'm glad to hear that. During the time that Dr. Landau was on your surgical team, would you say you got to know her fairly well?

In her seat, Becca tensed. What was Sam leading up to?

David spoke cautiously. "I had the highest respect for Dr. Landau professionally, if that's what you mean."

"That's exactly what I mean. Would you say that Dr. Landau was a caring physician?"

"Very much so. She was also precise in her work and conservative in her thinking. In my opinion she would have made an excellent surgeon."

"Did you tell her that?"

"I did."

"And what was her reply?"

"She said that she was a caretaker, not a cutter, and that even though she knew it was in the cause of healing, she couldn't stand to slice into people."

Sam Stedman couldn't resist a satisfied glance at the panel. "On the strength of that, I ask you now, Dr. Hardinger, if in your professional judgment Dr. Landau could have been capable of deliberately endangering the life of either Gloria Ames or Angelica Vargas purely for her own glorification?"

There was a split second in which David could have said no before Emil Wasserstein's "Objection!" resounded in the room. It was an answer that might not have meant all that much to the panel but which Becca would have given a great deal to hear. But David never gave it and Sam Stedman didn't seem to expect it. He cut across Wasserstein's protest even as it left his mouth.

"Question withdrawn," he said. "Thank you, Dr. Hardinger. You may step down."

The session in her apartment that evening ended early. Aggie couldn't come because of a dental appointment, and Becca made it plain that she didn't care to rehash David's testimony. She saw nothing to be gained from it, and hearing it again would only depress her further. Though she agreed with Sam that they had scored more points today than they had lost, she knew it had been because of Sam's astuteness not David's generosity. Her lover hadn't sacrificed himself one iota to benefit her.

Carolyn seemed down also. She sat at the table munching on a potato chip, then brushed her hands together to rid them of the salty residue it had left. "I don't have very good news," she said. "I called Walter Heilbrun, Angelica's tutor. Not only wouldn't he discuss a past suicide attempt, he flatly refused to corroborate what he'd told me before. He said if I tried to use the information in any way, he'd say I lied."

"There's a man who knows which side his bread is buttered on," Sam muttered.

"Oh, I can match that," Becca said. "I called Margaret Quinlan today, hoping to get the names of some of the former Vargas employees."

"Did she hang up on you?" Carolyn asked.

"Not at all. She was very agreeable. Told me she couldn't remember a single one, but that if she did she'd be sure to get in touch. I should have given it up for the day, but I'm a glutton for punishment. I decided to try one more possibility. Angelica's grandmother. The old lady is a bit looney, but she and I had developed a kind of rapport when I was on the case. She claimed that her son and his wife didn't keep her properly informed about Angelica, so from time to time she called me to check on her granddaughter and I made myself available to her. I figured she might have kept in touch with a former employee or could at least give me a name."

"Good thinking," Sam agreed. "What did she say?"

"I wouldn't know. I never got through to her. A man with a Spanish accent answered the phone. Probably the butler. He refused to talk to me unless I gave him my name. I should have lied, but I couldn't bring myself to do it. When I told him it was Dr. Landau, he politely informed me that Señora Vargas was not in."

Sam looked thoughtful. "The grandmother is a good bet. From what you told me she and Angelica were inseparable. She probably knows where a lot of the skeletons are buried. Why don't you try reaching her another way? Maybe writing to her."

"I already did. But I have a feeling my letter will be intercepted. I don't think Vargas is taking a chance on my contacting any of his family."

"You're probably right, but it's worth a try." He stretched his hands in front of them, clasped them, then pushed them outward and cracked his knuckles. Becca shuddered at the sound. "I have one good piece of news to report," he said. "Aggie called to tell me she found the note Angelica wrote to you exactly where she had left it in the PICU. She dropped it off at my office in case we should need it."

Carolyn stood up and reached for her straw shoulder bag. "I've got to go." She pursed her lips. "I suppose one hit out of three isn't bad."

"Try two out of four," Sam said. He pulled his jacket from the chair back. "You're forgetting about Davey's testimony today."

How she wished that she could, Becca thought as she walked them to the door.

When the telephone woke her before seven the next morning, she could have cheerfully killed. Insomnia had claimed her the first part of the night, then fitful and dream-filled sleep took the second half. She had finally succumbed from exhaustion at five in the morning, and the last hour and a half had been more precious than all the rest. She groped for the phone and knocked a half-eaten raisin cookie off the night table on the way.

"Becca, wake up! It's David."

She lifted her head from the pillow and pushed the hair back from her face. She wet her lips. "What's wrong?"

"Nothing is wrong. In fact, everything is very right."

Wide awake now, she filled with anger. "Is that what you woke me up to tell me? *Really, David!*" All the resentment she had stored up against him in the last few days was embodied in those two words.

"Listen to me, darling. Angelica pulled out of the coma at two o'clock this morning. My father just called to tell me about it."

For a moment she couldn't talk. What does one say when one has prayed very hard and the wish has been granted? "Thank God," she murmured. "How is she?" Her voice was hoarse and there were tears on her cheeks.

"According to my father, she's in good shape. Her vital signs are stable, and so far she's showing no residual deficits."

"What about the Guillain-Barré?"

"Gladstone is trying to do a neurological workup on her now."

"Can she communicate in any way?"

"Don't know yet. Her father is with her, and he's being very protective. I'm sorry I had to wake you, but I wanted you to hear it from me first." His voice became husky, intimate. "Becca . . . Becca . . . God, how I miss you! I can't even think straight without you. I'm hoping as much as you are that Angelica clears you and puts an end to this damn business. We need to get back to the way we were."

Was that possible, Becca wondered? So much had happened between them in the last week. Could it ever be the way it was?

"I love you," he whispered. "I think about you all the time."

"I think about you, too."

She was glad he hung up then. She didn't want to elaborate on what those thoughts were.

Twenty-five

Angelica's awakening had been a miracle, but Becca didn't learn whether the miracle would extend to clearing her of the accusation against her until she reached the inquiry room later that day.

Sam had called her with the news shortly after David did, and Helen Walters had followed an hour after that.

"They're probably going to question Angelica in a few minutes," the head nurse had informed her. "Right now, Webster Bartlett, Arnold Hardinger, and Jose Vargas are in the PICU with her, and your attorney has just gone in to join them. He told me to call and tell you that he's sending someone from his office to get you. He'll meet you in the inquiry room at ten."

The fledgling law clerk sent by Sam to get her was late showing up and did a poor job of deflecting the reporters and publicity hounds who had already gotten word of the change in Angelica's condition. By the time she got to the inquiry room, Becca was disheveled and irate. Before she reached Sam's side, she caught the crestfallen look on David's face and the smug expression on his father's. It did nothing to reassure her.

"What's happening?" she whispered fiercely to Sam as she seated herself beside him. He started to tell her, then shook his head as Webster Bartlett rose to speak.

"Ladies and gentlemen," the chief of medicine said, glancing at Jose and Maria Vargas, "we have a lot to be grateful for today. Angelica Vargas has recovered from her coma. She seems to have suffered no residual damage. However, her memory has been affected, we hope only for the moment. When we questioned Angelica at nine this morning, she could not recall anything about the events of last Sunday night or its aftermath. We will, of course, continue to question her, but under the circumstances this inquiry will go forward as scheduled."

Becca had never been given to crying, but at that moment she was as close to tears as she'd ever been in her life. Sam Stedman leaned toward her. For an instant she had a sense that he wanted to offer comfort. It dissipated abruptly when he said. "Don't go to pieces on me, will you? I haven't got the time for it."

Unfeeling bastard, she thought resentfully, then realized his words had been purposeful. Anger shot through her. How dare he try to manipulate her this way! She met his eyes and saw the concern in them. She forgave him. "Sam," she said in a low voice, "you were there when they questioned her. Do you think Angelica was bluffing when she said she couldn't remember?"

He thought a moment. "It's hard to tell. Aggie was there also, and she wasn't sure."

His attention was diverted as Wasserstein rose to petition the panel. "I ask that Dr. Norman Gladstone take the stand."

Sam leaned toward her as the chief neurologist walked to the dais. "Gladstone is another Hardinger devotee, so don't get nervous when you hear his testimony. They're allowing me to put Sweeney Kessler on the stand right after him. He's on his way here now."

"Kessler?"

"Yes. The foremost expert on Guillain-Barré in the country. Do you know him?"

"I'm not sure. I know his name from somewhere."

Gladstone's testimony was impressive. Especially when it was pointed out that he was the neurologist who had treated Angelica from the onset and was therefore in a better position than anyone else to determine the extent of her paralysis. According to him it was too massive for Angelica to have dislodged the respirator herself. Sam kept glancing at the door all through it, his expression darkening by degrees. By the time Gladstone's testimony came to a close, he was glowering. "Damn!" he muttered. "Kessler must have been tied up in traffic."

"Where was he coming from?" Becca whispered.

"Eighty-fourth just off Park. He has a town house there

a few houses away from the one Vargas owns."

Something prodded at her brain but refused to come clear.

"No further questions," Wasserstein concluded. "Thank you, doctor. Your witness, Mr. Stedman."

"No questions," Sam said. "You may step down, Dr. Gladstone." He rose to address the panel, then paused as the inquiry room door burst open. A smile lit his face. "I call Dr. Sweeney Kessler to the stand."

Becca appraised Sweeney Kessler keenly as he made his way toward the dais. The doctor was a heavyset man in his fifties, balding, with a fringe of curly gray hair at his temples and the back of his head. His face was lean compared to his body, and to make up for the loss of hair, he sported a carefully trimmed goatee of a darker hued gray that covered his chin and came to a point two inches below it.

The doctor moved gracefully for all of his bulk and spoke in a deep resonant voice when Sam questioned him on the stand. Despite the familiarity of his name, Becca couldn't remember ever having seen or heard him before.

Kessler's words carried conviction as he informed the panel that after having gone over Angelica's records, he concurred with Dr. Gladstone about the paralysis of Angelica's extremities at the time the respirator was dislodged. However, after conferring with the nurses in the PICU, he had come to the conclusion that Angelica still had the use of her neck and shoulder muscles. She was able to turn her head from side to side and in his opinion would have been fully capable of dislodging that respirator without the use of her hands.

A sense of hope buoyed Becca as a murmur swept the inquiry room. She may have had no recollection of Dr. Sweeney Kessler before this, but she would have a hard time forgetting him now.

After dismissing the witness, Sam returned to their table with a glint in his eyes. "I think Dr. Kessler just lost a neighbor," he whispered to Becca. "Vargas looks as if he could kill." His eyes narrowed at her expression. "What's the matter with you?"

She clutched at his arm. "Sam, I have to talk to you." Her voice was urgent. "I just remembered where I heard Kessler's name before. It had to do with the cook."

"What cook?"

"The former Vargas cook. Margaret Quinlan told me that when the woman was fired she went to work for the Kesslers a few doors away."

"Christ!" he muttered. "Someone should have told me to wear shock absorbers when I tangled with you. Why didn't you tell me this before?"

She reddened. "I'm sorry. I forgot."

"About this and what else?"

"Would you rather I kept it from you?" she retorted.

His answer was cut short by Webster Bartlett's announcement of a recess.

At seven o'clock that evening Becca waited across the street from the Kessler town house for Sam Stedman to show. Sweeney Kessler had been kind enough to arrange an interview for them with his cook, Luz Garcia. An admitted gourmet, Kessler's only instructions had been that they take every precaution not to upset the lady. He didn't want to lose her because "she could make a paella like nothing he'd ever tasted."

Becca glanced at her watch. Sam was late, but she schooled herself to patience. She didn't want another flareup between them.

Dusk shadowed the tree-lined street as she waited. The streetlamps flickered to life, and a cool breeze prompted her to slip on the jacket of her mauve linen suit.

From where she was standing she could clearly see the Vargas town house. Four stories high and wider than its neighbors', it had been refaced in white limestone and had decorative gray grillwork to guard its tall windows and shiny black doors. In contrast, the Kessler house four doors away looked drab with its stained brick facing, beige shutters, and weathered oak door.

When Sam showed up ten minutes later, he was out of breath and taking a last puff of his cigarette.

"Sorry," he said. "My taxi broke down and I had to walk the last twelve blocks." He ground the cigarette beneath his heel, glanced across the street, then clutched her under the arm.

"Come on," he said.

Weaving in and out of traffic, they dodged between the cars until they reached the other side.

Dr. Sweeney Kessler greeted them at the front door and led them to a huge kitchen at the rear of the house. The walnut cabinets, brass fittings, and well-scoured pans hanging from the ceiling were vintage Americana as was the rest of the house, but in keeping with his penchant for food, the oversized stainless appliances in it were as up-to-date as today's news.

Luz Garcia was a small woman with birdlike features and a sharp tongue. "How do you do?" she said as the doctor introduced them, then left. Her accent was similar to that of Maria Vargas's, but without the refinement of careful tutoring. "Please come," she urged. "I have a few moments before I must see to the serving of the dinner."

She guided them into a windowed dinette where the help ate their meals. She took the initiative as soon as they were seated. "Señor Kessler has told me you wish to ask me some questions. Yes?" At Sam's nod, she suddenly grew reticent. "I know there is a trial. These questions, they will not cause me trouble?"

"No," Sam assured her. "Everything you say here will be held in confidence. I promise."

She folded her thin hands primly across her white-aproned lap. "Very well. What is it you wish to know?"

Becca leaned forward eagerly. "We wish to know about the Vargases. We wish to know what happened on the day Celmira Vargas died. We wish to know . . ." Her voice trailed off at Sam's reproving glance.

Luz Garcia wasn't aware of it. At mention of the Vargas name, her coffee-colored face had turned vindictive. "I will tell you of the Vargases," she said in her guttural accent. "Of Señor Vargas who rules that house like a king. And of his mother," her lip curled in scorn, "that *loco* who worships at his feet and talks only of a child to carry on the name. Of the Señora Vargas, God rest her soul. And of her sister who took her place." Her mouth twisted. "Twenty years I worked for those people, then the day after the Señora dies I am fired. With no reason, no warning." She muttered an imprecation in Spanish and twisted her hands in her lap.

"But you have a good job now," Becca appeased.

She shrugged. "Señor Kessler is a kind man, but not nearly so generous as the Señor Vargas."

"Tell us about Celmira Vargas," Sam said. "Was she a good mistress to you?"

"At the very beginning, yes. After that she was ill so much of the time. It was the old woman who ran that house and took care of the little Angelica. That is until that *puta* came to live with us."

"That *puta?*" Sam questioned.

"Maria Vargas!" She exaggerated the name in a way that made it a sneer. "The Señora's younger sister. From the very beginning it is clear that she wishes to take the Señora's place. The way she dresses and the way she looks at him. Did you know that he built a pool for her in the basement because she likes to swim? *Madre de Dios!* A small fortune he pays because she likes to swim. But he does not care. At night we can hear him laughing with her down there while the poor Señora she lays upstairs with her heart so weak it beats like a pigeon's. She has no shame, that *puta!* She who never believed in God goes all the time now to St. Andrews, crossing herself and making pious noises. *Que chiste!* What a joke!"

"Are you saying Maria Vargas became religious only after her sister died?" Sam asked.

She made a scoffing sound in her throat. "That one never saw the inside of a church unless the Señora shamed her into it. But after the Señora dies it is different. Afterward the *puta* goes to seek absolution. But God will not allow her to wash the blood from her hands."

Becca caught her breath at the implication. She met Sam's eyes across the table, and he signaled her not to interrupt.

"And he has punished them both," the cook went on. "They are not happy. There are sharp words between them all the time now. The maid in the Vargas house is my friend, and she tells me that they do not even share the same bedroom anymore."

That explained the impression of discord between them she'd gotten on the night of the party, Becca thought. She remembered Vargas's caustic remarks to his young wife and the look of unhappiness on her face.

"Miss Garcia, how do you think Celmira Vargas died?" Sam asked bluntly.

"I think the Señora was murdered."

"By whom?"

"By both of them. But it is only a suspicion I have no proof. And if you tell this to anyone, I will deny it."

"Could you tell us what took place the morning she died?" Becca asked.

She nodded. "I remember it well because Señor Vargas had returned to New York from Buenos Aires at six o'clock that morning. He woke me when he came in and demanded that his breakfast be made immediately and sent up to his wife's room."

"Was that unusual?" Sam asked.

"Only the early hour was unusual. When he wasn't travelling, Señor Vargas tried to have breakfast with the Señora every morning. We had to have red roses ready all the time for him to bring to her. It was a duty for him like brushing his teeth or shaving his face. And the Señor was a great one for duty. The servants would laugh at this hypocrisy behind his back."

"Where were the others?" Sam asked.

"They were all in the house when the Señora died. The Señor and the *puta* were downstairs in the pool swimming. The old woman was with me in the kitchen. She had just finished explaining to me that my arroz con pollo did not taste as good as the one she made because I used saffron instead of brown rice." She tapped her left temple. "I told you. *Loco!*"

"And Angelica? Where was Angelica?" Becca asked.

"I believe she was in her mother's room playing with her doll. I saw her there earlier when I brought up the tea for the Señora and the relief nurse who was there that day."

Becca looked at Sam in triumph. For the first time someone had corroborated that Angelica was in her mother's room at the time of her death.

She felt a sudden warmth for this little brown woman that bordered on affection. "Could you describe the Señora's bedroom to me?" she asked.

Her bony shoulders lifted in a shrug. "What is there to tell? It was a large bedroom with no color in it. It was kept very warm because the Señora's blood was so thin she shivered all the time."

"What do you mean, 'with no color in it'?"

"Well, the Señora liked everything . . ." She wrinkled her nose. *"Como se dice?* How you say . . . Tan, that is it."

"Sand color," Becca said, unable to keep the excitement from her voice.

"Yes."

There's sand on the floor. And it's hot, Angelica had said.

"Was there something like a ladder in the room? Something very high?"

Her forehead furrowed in thought. "The only tall thing in the room was a chest of drawers that sat between two windows.

The water is on top of the ladder and Gabriella is trying to reach it for me.

"Was there something kept on top of the chest?"

"Yes. An arrangement of dried flowers."

"Nothing else?"

"No." She put out a hand as Becca's face fell. "Wait! There was something else. Because Angelica liked to play in the room so much, the nurse has to keep the Señora's medicines on top of that chest." She cocked her birdlike head. "This is significant?"

Becca smiled. "This is *very* significant."

It was only when she leaned back in the maple captain's chair that she realized Sam was glowering at her.

"What was *that* all about?" he asked evenly.

She sighed, knowing what was to come. The dream was something else she hadn't gone into detail about.

Twenty-six

"I call Margaret Quinlan to the stand," Wasserstein announced the next morning. The room was steaming again, and he was jacketless in a white shirt with wide shirred armbands worn high up to keep the sleeves from sliding down.

To Becca it was a ridiculous affectation, but she had to admit that contrary to Sam's description of him as "a shark even the sharks were leery of," the picture he presented to the panel was a disarming one.

When they'd been in the taxi going home from the Kessler town house, Sam had told her that Quinlan would be testifying the next day. But only after she'd made her peace with him.

"Don't you see?" she'd pleaded. "I didn't tell you about the dreams because they didn't mean much without proof that Angelica was in that bedroom with her mother. But now it's different. Now we know—"

"We don't *know* anything," he'd countered sharply. "What we've heard is a sour-grapes rendition of what happened from a servant who paints an ugly picture, hints at foul play, and can't back up any of it."

Damn him and his lawyer's mind Becca chafed. If it wasn't black-and-white and nailed down, it didn't count. "But you will admit there's a good chance that Angelica was in the room with her mother when she died."

He nodded grudgingly. "There's a chance of that, yes."

"And that if there was a murder and Angelica witnessed it, the ensuing trauma could be a believable basis for a suicide attempt."

"I see where you're heading, but we're still talking in supposition. I need more to go with than that. I'm hoping Margaret Quinlan will supply it when she testifies tomorrow. Since Aggie witnessed it, Quinlan can't deny that Angelica was hoarding those pills. It isn't proof of anything, but it will at least make the panel admit to the possibility of suicide."

Becca watched now as the private nurse crossed the inquiry room in her starched whites, her broad bottom jiggling, her back rigid, her expression that of a zealot on a crusade. She threw Becca a disdainful look as she passed her, then took the stand and focused her attention fully on Wasserstein.

"Miss Quinlan, you are by profession a private nurse. Is that correct?"

"Yes, it is. I was trained here and in Buenos Aires, and I've been workin' in both places."

"Mostly for the Vargases, isn't that so?"

"Yes. I was takin' care of Señor Vargas's first wife for a lot of years before she died. And I was takin' care of Angelica afterward."

"Then you must know the child pretty well?"

"Objection," Sam called out. "Calls for a conclusion."

Wasserstein nodded. "Let me put it another way, Miss Quinlan. In all the years you spent with Angelica Vargas, was there anything about her behavior that would make you believe the child was suicidal?"

"Objection! The witness isn't capable of making that judgment."

Bartlett flicked a glance at Hardinger who was seated several rows behind Sam and Becca. Hardinger gave an imperceptible signal. "I'll allow it," he said.

"Ass licker," Sam muttered.

"Again, Miss Quinlan, did you see anything in Angelica Vargas's behavior that would make you believe she was suicidal?"

"I did not! Now, mind I'm not sayin' Angelica was a happy little girl, what with her mother so sick and all. But there's nothing unnatural about that, is there?"

"No. I would think not." Her quaint speech prompted Wasserstein to dart an amused glance at the panel. Anton Farlay, the dean of the Medical School smiled back at him.

"Besides," the nurse said, "the Vargas family is Catholic like I am. Angelica knows that takin' her own life would be a mortal sin. She would never be goin' against the Scriptures."

Wasserstein waited for her last words to sink in before proceeding. "Miss Quinlan, at the request of Mr. Vargas you came to Manhattan General a few weeks ago as a private nurse to Angelica Vargas, did you not?"

"Yes, I did. Angelica was diagnosed as having Guillain-Barré Syndrome, and Señor Vargas wanted her to have more personal care than the hospital nurses would be givin'."

"Was it something you were looking forward to?"

"Yes. I've always liked workin' for the Vargas family, and they've always been pleased with me."

"Yet you quit your job less than two weeks afterward. Why is that?"

The nurse's face flushed and her full bosom heaved. She pointed dramatically at Becca who sat less than a dozen feet from her. "It was because of her. Because of Dr. Landau! Nothin' I did for Angelica pleased her. But then nothin' anybody did was good enough. She wanted that little girl watched every second of the day, and it seemed like she was poppin' into the room to check on her every time I turned around. If Angelica was lookin' good, she took the credit, and if Angelica was lookin' bad, she blamed it on me. I couldn't win nohow. It was like she had to be provin' she was the only one who could help that little girl. She even called in a psychiatrist without consultin' the attendin', Dr. Gottlieb. And that's somethin' that's *never* done!"

Wasserstein nodded. "And did this behavior have an effect on Angelica?" She squinted at him in confusion. "Did you feel that Dr. Landau's protectiveness caused Angelica to be dependent on her?" he clarified.

"It certainly did. It was 'Dr. Becca this' and 'Dr. Becca that.' Why, that baby wouldn't even go down for tests without insistin' that her 'Dr. Becca' go along. There was somethin' unnatural about the whole thing. I tell you it didn't surprise me none when I heard that Dr. Landau had pulled that respirator."

Sam Stedman catapulted to his feet. "Objection!" he thundered.

"Sustained," Bartlett said.

Wasserstein's smile was smug. "No further questions. Your witness, Mr. Stedman."

Sam Stedman's anger was apparent in the way he stalked toward the dais. Becca could only pray that he would keep his temper in check.

"Miss Quinlan," he said with exaggerated politeness. "You have testified that you know Angelica Vargas well. Certainly you seem to be sure of her religious convictions. Isn't that so?"

"I believe I know them, yes."

"Tell me, Miss Quinlan, do you know Father Joseph Tortelli, the Catholic priest attached to Manhattan General Hospital?"

"I've heard of him," she said cautiously, "but I've never met him."

"That's a pity. Because if you had, he could have told you that he visited with Angelica a week before you came on duty. At least he tried to. Angelica refused to spend even a minute with him. She made it plain that whatever religious affiliation she had felt for the Church died when her mother died four years ago. I wonder since you know Angelica so well, why you didn't know that."

"Objection," Wasserstein called out. "Hearsay."

"Sustained," Bartlett sanctioned.

Becca relaxed. Sam's anger had made him keener than ever. Admiration filled her. Whatever her personal feelings about him, he was one hell of a lawyer.

He unbuttoned the collar of his white shirt and pushed his tie down a notch. "Miss Quinlan, you have testified that there was nothing in Angelica Vargas's behavior that would make you believe she was suicidal. Isn't that so?"

"Yes, it is."

"Miss Quinlan, what medication was Angelica on?"

"Prednisone, twenty milligrams."

"In pill form?"

"Yes."

Sam's lanky frame seemed to hover over her as he bent forward. "Miss Quinlan, isn't it true that on the afternoon of June fourteenth, Dr. Landau confronted you with six Prednisone pills that she found in the skirt pocket of Angelica's doll?"

"Yes, but—" Red veined her cheeks as he cut across her words.

"Six pills it was your job to see that Angelica swallowed. Six pills that Angelica was hoarding for the express purpose of taking her own life. And you say there was nothing suicidal in her behavior." His tone was scathing.

She half-rose in her seat. "Those pills couldn't have killed her!"

"But she didn't know that, did she? Angelica Vargas is only eight years old. She wouldn't know which pills would kill and which wouldn't. Isn't that so, Miss Quinlan?"

When she didn't answer, he stepped away from the stand. "No further questions." He caught Wasserstein's signal. "Your witness, Mr. Wasserstein."

Becca knew by the startled reaction of the panel that her side had scored heavily. She suddenly felt like sharing her triumph with David. There was no way after this that he could believe her contention of suicide was a myth.

She turned and caught him staring at her. She forgot her reason for seeking him out. The look of yearning on his face tore at her. It found an answering response. She was so tired of being alone, of putting on a brave front. She wanted his arms about her. She wanted him to make love to her. She wanted to rest her head on his chest after they spiraled downward and pour out all the fears that were riddling her sleep with nightmares. Anger shot through her. How could he keep denying her that and still say he loved her?

The question was too hurtful to contemplate. She pulled her gaze from his and concentrated on Jose Vargas instead. The man looked shrunken into himself, his eyes downcast, his white head grooved into his chest. Had the hoarding of the pills come as a shock to him? she wondered. Had it finally alerted him to the seriousness of Angelica's intentions? Beside him, wielding a lacy fan in one hand and fingering her jade crucifix in the other, Maria Vargas's lips moved in silent prayer.

But God will not allow her to wash the blood from her hands . . .

Becca stared at the svelte blond beauty in her sleeveless linen dress. She looked cool and elegant . . . and very young. Could she really have killed her sister?

Becca glanced up to see Sam standing beside her. She drew up her knees as he wedged past her. "You were great!" she whispered when he was seated.

"Don't count your chickens," he cautioned. His eyes were on Wasserstein.

The opposing attorney approached the stand slowly. Once there, he steepled his hands at chest level and rocked back on his heels. He regarded the nurse with calculated calm. "Miss Quinlan, after it was pointed out to you by Dr. Landau that Angelica had been hoarding the Prednisone pills, did you ask the child about it?"

"Yes."

"And did she offer any explanation?"

"She did. She told me that her doll Gabriella was after bein' sick and that she was savin' up the pills to give to her when she got worse."

"Then those pills were never intended for Angelica."

"Not accordin' to her." She shot a spiteful glance at Sam. "I would have told that to the other lawyer if he'd of given me half a chance. Like I said before, that child would never go against the Scriptures."

"Thank you, Miss Quinlan. You may step down."

"That last bit didn't detract one iota from the impact," Carolyn said, wielding a chicken leg aloft.

The chair creaked as Sam leaned back, balancing it on two legs. "You're wrong. It put a doubt in the minds of the panel. You could see it in their faces."

Becca dug into the bucket of *Kentucky Fried Chicken*. "But at least they're taking the possibility of suicide seriously."

"Wishful thinking." He straightened, crumpled his napkin, then threw it on the table and rose. He walked to the window and gestured in frustration. "Dammit! We need proof. The investigator I put on hasn't found out anything we don't already know. Has Helen Walters come up with a line on that relief nurse yet?"

Becca shook her head. "She checked with the State Nurses' Association, and she called the Licensing Bureau. She's come up with zilch. Fiona Andrews seems to have disappeared from this earth."

"Couldn't you try to establish that Angelica was in the room when her mother died?," Carolyn asked. "It wouldn't be necessary to prove foul play. At four years old the trauma of seeing her mother die, coupled with the guilt of not being able to help her is a believable enough basis for attempted suicide."

He turned on her so swiftly he almost crashed into the pine hutch in Becca's small dining area. "And who's going to confirm that she was in that bedroom?" he demanded. "Luz Garcia who'll turn deaf and dumb on me at the first hint of exposure? Jose or Maria Vargas who've got a barrelful to hide between them? Or maybe the semisenile grandmother who's dependent on her son for every breath she takes?"

Becca was stung by his sarcasm. He'd been a downer all evening, and she couldn't figure out why.

Carolyn didn't seem at all fazed. "Maybe Angelica herself could confirm it. It's possible that the shock of what she's been through has jogged her memory. Anyway, it might be worth a try. Becca tells me she's progressing at a remarkable rate."

His eyes narrowed. "That's something I haven't heard about." He turned to Becca. "How do you know that? You haven't tried to see Angelica, have you?"

"No, I haven't."

"Then how do you know?"

For a moment she considered saying she'd learned it from Aggie. The nurse hadn't arrived yet, so the lie would hold for now. Then her head snapped up. It wasn't in her to be furtive. "David told it to me." Her voice was defiant.

"And when did you see David?"

"It was at the hospital about an hour after the inquiry ended. I . . . I passed him in the hallway." She felt her cheeks grow warm. It was only partially true.

She had just left the pathology lab and was on her way to pick up a blood sample from Hematology, when she was grabbed from behind and hauled into the supply room. Her first reaction was fear. There were so many crazies after her hide since the trial began. Then she inhaled the antiseptic smell of the operating room on his crumpled greens and knew it was David even before he slid his cheek against hers. The stubble of his beard roughed her skin as he bit at the lobe of her ear.

"Becca . . ." he whispered.

"David, are you out of your—"

"Shush!" He turned her in his arms and kissed her. "Don't say anything. Please. Just let me hold you." He used his foot to swing the door closed, then pulled her into an aisle hidden by metal shelves stacked with linens and test tubes and petri dishes. His mouth came down on hers, and his tongue probed for entry. "Oh God!" he groaned. "If you only knew . . ." He kissed her frantically, his hands roving over her breasts, her back, her buttocks. He pulled her tight against him and ground himself into her.

"David, no!" Even as she wedged her hands between them she was trying to understand herself. A few hours ago she was hoping for this and now that it had happened . . . Was it because it was clandestine? Shabby? "Someone might come in," she murmured.

He made a hissing sound through his teeth, but he loosened his hold. "You never used to worry about that in Boston." He bent to nuzzle her neck. "I had to see you," he murmured. "I took a chance and came down here. I lucked out when you came out of the lab." He stroked her hair, pushed it back from her forehead. "Becca, I've been living in a void. I need to be with you, to hold you . . ."

She felt herself softening. "I've never stopped you from coming to me."

"I know."

"But not this way." She looked around her in distaste.

"I don't like it any more than you do." He cradled her cheek in his hand. "I'm sorry, darling. I know what you've been through. Just a little more patience. I think we're going to get a break. I've been to see Angelica . . ."

Sam's voice cut into her thoughts.

"What about Angelica?"

She blinked. He was standing above her, his foot tapping impatiently on the parquet floor. She realized he had asked the question twice.

He stared down at her as if he knew where her thoughts had been. "Are you having trouble hearing?"

She threw him a resentful glance. "David told me that they took the trach tube and the respirator out today. According to Gladstone the Guillain-Barré is receding, and if she progresses at this rate, they'll move her back into her room tomorrow."

"And you're figuring that if they do, I'll be able to get to her and pump her for information which up to now she's been either unwilling or unable to give. You're grasping at straws — both of you. Even if Angelica did remember and was willing to talk about it, do you think Vargas would allow anyone near that girl now?"

He glared at Becca. "And while you're doing all this clever strategizing, don't take it into your head to try to see Angelica yourself. You're under the gun for attempted murder, and if you show up anywhere near that girl you could do yourself and me irreparable harm. Or don't you give a damn about that?"

Becca sprang from her chair and took a step toward him. "You're being impossible!" It galled her that she only came up to his shoulder.

"Sam, don't you think you should be getting back to the office?" Carolyn suggested in a bid for diplomacy.

"Good idea." He stalked toward the front door, then stopped abruptly. He turned to Becca, a frown on his face. "Do you know a Wanda Alpert?"

"Yes. She's a med student I didn't like very much. She was on my team at the hospital a few weeks ago. Why do you ask?"

"Because I've been informed that she's going to testify tomorrow, and I have no idea what she's going to say."

Neither do I, Becca thought.

Twenty-seven

"Miss Alpert, you are a medical student, are you not?" Wasserstein began.

"Yes. I'm in my third year of med school, and I'm currently doing four-week rotations at the hospital in the different specialties."

Becca marveled at the changes that had been wrought in Wanda. Except for a trace of lip gloss, her face had been wiped clean of makeup. Her unruly blond hair was pinned back in a French twist, and a loose lab coat covered the tight clothes beneath. Molded by Wasserstein's fine hand, the former debating team captain presented a picture of sedate femininity.

"Miss Alpert, when Angelica Vargas was admitted to the hospital you were on a team with Dr. Landau, isn't that right?"

"With Dr. Landau and Dr. Flanders," Wanda corrected. "It was in the last week of my rotation in Pediatrics."

He nodded. "During that four-week rotation how many cardiac arrests were you present at?"

"Two."

"And who was the doctor in charge of those arrests?"

"Dr. Landau was the senior staff member at both." She crossed her legs. Her black skirt hiked up to reveal her shapely thighs. At Wasserstein's frown, she uncrossed them.

"Miss Alpert, did the staff on the pediatric floor have a nickname for Dr. Landau?"

"Yes. They called her 'The Miracle Worker.' "

"How flattering."

"It wasn't meant to be flattering."

His shaggy brows shot upward. "Oh. How so?"

"It was said in sarcasm. None of the staff wanted to be anywhere near Dr. Landau when she was in charge of an arrest."

Is that how they had really felt? Becca wondered. So many of them had congratulated her after the last success. Had it been with tongue in cheek? A lie? A sop to her ego?

She kept her face expressionless as Sam turned toward her. Not for anything would she allow him to see her hurt. The words they'd exchanged last night still rankled and had put a distance between the two of them that gave Becca the feeling of being a ship without a rudder. She hadn't realized how much she'd come to depend on him.

"And why didn't they want to be near Dr. Landau when she was in charge of an arrest?" Wasserstein asked.

"Because she would never let go. I mean, we all understand dedication and we all want to save a life. That's what we're there for. When that monitor shows flatline we're down, and when we hear that first blip that tells us maybe the patient's going to make it, we want to stand up and cheer. But with Dr. Landau it was different. It was like she had a personal thing going. She *had* to save that patient. She *had* to show everyone that she was better than they were, that only *she* could pull off the miracle, be the . . . the . . ."

"Savior," Wasserstein supplied.

"Objection!" Sam called.

"Withdrawn. Tell me, Miss Alpert, of the two arrests you were present at, did both patients survive?"

"No. The first one died. The second made it."

"Thank you. No further questions. Your witness, Mr. Stedman."

Sam dawdled in getting to the stand, and Becca suspected that he was using every second to come up with some kind of strategy. Wanda's testimony had been very damaging, and unless he could turn it around, it would score heavily against her.

"Miss Alpert," Sam said when he reached the stand, "you've just told us that at the second arrest, the child survived."

"Yes, he did."

"Do you remember how long you worked over him?"

"I remember it very well because I missed a lunch appointment. Counting the emergency team it was almost a full hour."

"Is that unusual?"

"Yes. Most times it's no more than thirty minutes, forty-five at the outset."

"Then why did you continue trying to save him?"

"Because Dr. Landau insisted."

"Then what you're saying is that because of Dr. Landau's persistence—a trait you downgrade as being a 'personal thing with her'—a life was saved. Think of it, Miss Alpert. A child's life was saved. But that's not a very big deal to you is it, Miss Alpert?"

Wasserstein opened his mouth to protest, but Wanda Alpert was already answering.

"You're wrong, Mr. Stedman. Normally, it is a big deal. But this patient we're talking about is a six-year-old who'd had leukemia for seven months and had been through excruciating pain. He'd had two short remissions and two arrests, and there wasn't enough left of him to make a dent in the bed. Euthanasia is a dirty word at the hospital, but when a little boy like that arrests for close to an hour, we feel like God is trying to tell us something."

"And was he?"

"I think so. That little boy died three days later. He was in terrible pain."

"No further questions, Miss Alpert. You may step down."

Despite his 'stiff upper lip' policy, there was a defeated slump to Sam Stedman's shoulders. He reached Becca's side just as a candy striper tapped her on the shoulder. "Message for you," she whispered. She pressed a folded piece of paper into Becca's hand, then scooted for the exit. Becca opened it and read: "There's news of the relief nurse." It was signed "Helen."

The paper shook in her hand. She was afraid to hope.

"We'll handle it at recess," Sam murmured over her shoulder.

"I can handle it myself."

"No way."

He was a bully, she thought. But she preferred him overbearing rather than distant. It reassured her that he was still in her corner.

Wanda's testimony was a downer that carried over into the recess Webster Bartlett called half an hour later. Sam and she both knew that the inquiry was going badly for her. The only ray of hope was the note the head nurse had sent. If Fiona Andrews had been found and could corroborate murder, the whole picture would change.

When they got to the fourth floor, they found Helen Walters in her cubicle of an office. At sight of them she came around her desk and offered them raisins from a small pack on the filing cabinet.

"I'm going cold turkey on chocolates," she said. She glanced at their strained faces. "How did it go today?"

"Not so good," Sam said tiredly.

"Well, maybe this will help. I couldn't find Fiona Andrews because she went inactive for the last few years. Her husband is a soldier who was stationed in the Mideast, and they didn't return here until his stint was up a month ago. She just registered for her license again, and the gal who took the information remembered that I'd been asking about her and called me." She handed Becca a piece of paper. "Here's Andrews's home number."

"That's great. Thanks." She slipped it into her pocket. "Helen, how's Angelica? I miss her so much." She glanced up the hallway toward the PICU. The longing in her face was evident. "If I had the guts I'd slip in to see her right now."

Sam paused in his examination of a five-year-old's artwork. "Over my dead body you would."

Helen nodded. "He's right, you know. Even if he didn't stop you, I would. Hardinger was up here to give us a pep talk. Right now there are more empty beds on this floor then filled ones. The publicity on this thing has scared people off, and the hospital is hurting bad. Hardinger told us that the inquiry is almost over and that you're yesterday's news. He finished up by giving strict orders not to let you anywhere near that kid."

"How is she, Helen?"

"Physically she's unbelievable. She's hungry. She's beginning to get movement in her arms and legs, and she'll probably be returned to 401 East later today or tomorrow morning."

"And emotionally?"

"Awful. She just lies there staring into space like a zombie. It gives me the creeps to be with her."

"Does she . . . does she ask about me?"

"When she talks, which isn't often, that's all she does ask about. She misses you, Becca. We all do. Kip and me and the whole gang." She cast an oblique glance at Sam. "When are you going to untangle her from this mess so she can come back to us? The fourth floor isn't the same without her."

Sam smiled at the stocky woman with the pushed-in features. "I'm working on it, believe me."

By the afternoon the media was having a field day with Wanda Alpert's testimony. "Dr. Becca: Miracle Worker or Monster?" the headlines read. It made Sam's attempt to coerce Fiona Andrews into granting them an interview almost impossible. She and her husband, an artillery gunner in the marines, had just returned from Kuwait, and the soldier wanted "no trouble." It was only after three calls and Sam's promise to sign a document stating that everything Fiona said would be held in confidence that the husband consented, but only if he could be there with her.

The Andrewses had rented the lower floor of a garden apartment on Mystic Lane in Yonkers. It boasted clumps of multi-colored impatiens under a plum tree that shed purple leaves onto the minuscule lawn. "We've just moved in," Fiona Andrews said as she and her husband ushered them into the living room. The explanation was unnecessary. Unopened cartons of every shape and size surrounded a battered gray couch and two flowered chairs on a bare oak floor. A rolled rug lay tied beneath the picture window.

Bud Andrews placed a protective arm about his wife. He was a hulking thirty-year-old in Marine fatigues with spikey blond hair cropped to within an inch of his head. "We moved our stuff all the way from the Mideast," he said proudly, "but there's no sense putting anything down until we finish painting the place." He indicated the fresh coat of white paint on one wall.

"No sense at all," Fiona echoed. She was younger than her husband and half his size, but from her jutting chin and the firm set of her lips, Becca got the feeling that it was she who made the decisions for the family.

The feeling was borne out when they were all seated and Fiona made her position clear. "Bud and I have been reading the newspapers and listening to the TV. We know all about the inquiry." Her glance darted toward Becca, then away. "We don't know who's guilty of what and we don't want to know. But after you called, I thought about it. The day, Señora Vargas died I saw a lot in that

Vargas house that bears examining, and I feel it's my Christian duty to tell it to someone."

"Amen," Sam murmured. "Mrs. Andrews, you were the relief nurse for Celmira Vargas on that day, weren't you?"

"Yes. I filled in for Margaret Quinlan every Thursday. That was her day off."

"Where was everybody at the time it happened?"

"Well, Jose Vargas and Maria — she was his wife's sister — were in the pool downstairs swimming. Angelica was playing on the floor in her mother's bedroom upstairs, and I don't know where the grandmother was."

"Luz Garcia said she was in the kitchen showing her how to make arroz con pollo," Becca said.

"That doesn't surprise me. The old lady was always on that cook's back."

Sam worked his fingers slowly across the worn arm of the couch. "According to Miss Garcia, Celmira Vargas's medicines were kept on a highboy out of Angelica's reach. What medicines was she referring to?"

"Inderal, Cardizem, and nitro in case of a heart attack." She shook her head ruefully. "If not for that nitro, I might be telling you a different story today. You see, when I came into the bedroom that morning, there was a note on the night table from Margaret Quinlan. There were only two nitroglycerin pills left in the bottle and she wanted me to have them refilled." She sighed. "I suppose I could have called it in, but it was such a beautiful day and I had such an urge to stretch my legs . . ." She gave her husband an appealing glance, and he tightened his hand on hers.

"What time was this?" Becca asked.

"About ten. When I got downstairs, I met Señor Vargas and Maria. They were just coming up from the pool. Their hair was wet and they had on white terrycloth robes . . . you know. I told them that I would be at the drugstore for a few minutes and asked them to keep an eye on things until I came back. Señor Vargas said, *'No problema.'* I remember it clear as can be. *'No problema.'*"

Her husband slid an arm about her shoulders. "Don't upset yourself, honey." He turned to them with a fatuous smile on his broad face. "We're going to have a baby."

"Congratulations," Becca said.

239

"Same here," Sam murmured. "Mrs. Andrews, how long were you gone from the house?"

"No more than twenty minutes."

"And what did you find when you came back?"

"Bedlam. The house was in an uproar. The servants were screaming and crying that their mistress had suffered a heart attack. I ran upstairs and found Celmira Vargas in her bed. Señor Vargas was on the phone trying to reach Dr. Gottlieb. I checked for a pulse. I wasn't surprised when I couldn't find one. I knew by the look of her that she was dead."

"Where was her sister Maria?" Becca asked.

"In the same room. She was sitting in a chair, still in that terry robe, her hands covering her face. Angelica's grandmother was rocking back and forth on the loveseat. Angelica was in her arms in a state of shock. According to the servants, she was with her mother when she died." She shrugged. "There isn't much more to tell. The next day Señor Vargas fired me along with all the other servants who had been in the house when it happened."

Sam made a sympathetic noise in his throat. "Why do you think he did that?"

"I think he did it because he was trying to hide something about his wife's death." She paused for effect, then went on. When I spoke to the Señora's personal maid, she told me that just before Celmira Vargas died, she had passed by the Señora's bedroom door. It was closed, but she could hear voices. Señora Vargas's, Angelica's, and that of a third person. She was sure there was someone else in Señora Vargas's room when she died."

Sam hunched forward. "Are you suggesting . . ."

Bud Andrews held up a warning hand. "Now hold on. Fiona isn't suggesting anything. She's just telling it like it was. Isn't that right, honey?"

Bud's hand was the size of a bear's paw. Sam settled back. "Where were the nitro tablets?" Sam asked her.

"There were two of them still in that bottle on top of the chest of drawers. They hadn't been touched."

Sam spoke as if he were voicing his thoughts aloud. "Celmira Vargas was too sick to get them and Angelica was too small to reach them. But if there was someone else in that room who could have administered those pills and didn't . . ."

His glance met Becca's.

And then a shadow creeps up on the sand, Angelica had said. *And I'm so glad. I know I'll be saved now. Help me, I tell the shadow. But the shadow only laughs.*

"Where is that maid now?" Becca asked.

Fiona shrugged. "My guess, Venezuela. That's where she came from. Her name was Nita or Lita or something like that. But it wouldn't do you any good even if you found her, because she couldn't identify the voice she heard. Not even if it was a man or a woman. The only thing she was certain about was that there was a third person in that room."

In Becca's apartment that evening, Carolyn Stedman tried to lift their spirits every which way. When all else failed, she went on the attack. "Come on, Sam," she said, directing a withering glance at him. "Wasn't it you who always said, 'The song isn't over 'til the last note dies away?' Why all the doom and gloom?"

"Because we're back to square one," Becca answered for him. She poked at her salad in the plastic container. She had barely taken two bites.

Carolyn shook her head. "I don't agree. I think we've made progress. We're sure now that Angelica was in the room when her mother died, and we have every indication that a murder was committed."

Sam's laugh held no mirth. "Ever the optimist, aren't you, sis?"

"Don't patronize me!"

"Then don't try my patience. Bud Andrews threatened to break me in two when I suggested that his wife give me a deposition attesting to what she said. Without it what do I do for proof? Resurrect the victim?"

The sound of the buzzer saved Carolyn from having to answer. Becca disappeared into the hallway, then came back a second later. "Aggie's on her way up." She glanced at her watch. "She wasn't supposed to be here for another hour."

Aggie joined them in the living room a few minutes later. Becca handed her the salad she had taken from the refrigerator. "How come so early?"

"I've been taken off the Vargas case, that's how come. Angelica went back to 401 East this afternoon and Vargas has put Margaret Quinlan back on. She'll be on double shifts for the time she'll be there, which from the looks of things won't be very long."

"What do you mean?" Becca asked.

"I mean Jose Vargas wants Angelica out of the hospital and back home. Gar — Dr. Gottlieb had all to do to convince him to keep her at Manhattan General for another day or two. But I don't think she'll be there past that."

"Oh God!" Becca whispered. "Does he know what he's doing?"

Aggie's face was bleak. "I doubt it. That little girl's face turned white when she heard she might be going home. I warned Quinlan to watch her carefully from now on, but she told me 'to be mindin' my business about what don't concern me.' " Her mimicry of the nurse's accent would have brought a laugh under other circumstances.

Sam walked toward the bedroom muttering something unintelligible. "I have to call my office," he said.

"I can alert Helen and the other nurses," Carolyn said when he was gone. "They can keep coming into Angelica's room on one excuse or another. It's not great, but it will give some extra protection while she's in the hospital."

"And what about afterward?" Becca asked. "What about when she goes home and nobody really understands how desperate she is? What then?"

The ensuing silence created a void that was broken by the sound of Sam's returning steps. "Wasserstein's office called mine," he said. "They left word that Gottlieb is due to testify tomorrow. That should nail the coffin shut for sure."

Aggie concentrated hard on a roughened cuticle. "You never know. He might surprise you."

His skeptical look caused her to color. "You wanna bet?" he asked.

Twenty-eight

The scene could have been taken from a Grade B movie, Becca thought. On the stand, Gottlieb was so nattily turned out that he could have made the Ten Best Dressed list. And Wasserstein postured around him as if about to elicit the eleventh commandment from God. Next to her, Sam was engrossed in a brief he had removed from his attaché case. He had sent his bumbling law clerk to get her, and beyond a "hello" he hadn't lifted his head or said a word to her since she'd entered the inquiry room. She suspected it had to do with the conversation they'd had when she'd walked him to the door of her apartment last night.

"Look, Becca," he'd said, bent on easing the strain between them, "I know you think I'm trying to run your life, but it isn't like that. After the trial you can run naked in the streets with Davey for all I care, but right now do me a favor and don't see him."

"Why not?"

"Because he's a loose cannon. Nobody knows which way he's going to swing, and you can't afford that. You might say something or give something away."

"That David would use against me. That's what you're trying to tell me, isn't it?"

"Yes, dammit, that's what I'm trying to tell you."

She had opened the door wide. "Thanks for the warning," she had said curtly. "I'll see you at the inquiry tomorrow."

Wasserstein's voice brought her back to the present.

"Dr. Gottlieb, you are Board Certified in both pediatrics and internal medicine?"

"That is correct."

"And you are attending physician to Angelica Vargas at Manhattan General Hospital?"

"Yes, I am."

"Doctor, is it true that at the time Angelica Vargas was admitted to the hospital, you specifically requested Dr. Landau as resident?"

"Yes. I considered her to be an excellent pediatrician."

"Do you still feel the same way?"

He hesitated. "I would have reservations now."

His gaze strayed to where Aggie sat in the back row of the room. His whole body tightened. He had hoped she wouldn't be here this morning. She had refused to see him alone since the inquiry began and his testimony today would only compound her distrust of him.

Wasserstein's cherub face was all innocence. "Oh? And why is that, Dr. Gottlieb?"

"Because Dr. Landau tends to break the rules. And that is a serious flaw in any young resident."

"Would you give us an example of that behavior, please?"

"Yes. Dr. Landau came to me about a week after Angelica was admitted with the misplaced idea that the child needed a psychiatrist. I told her that Angelica's father was strongly against such interference and that in my opinion there was no necessity for one."

"And what did Dr. Landau do?"

"She obtained the services of a psychiatrist for the child without my knowledge. Because of it, she was dismissed from the Vargas case with the admonition that she was not to try to see Angelica Vargas again. Both Angelica's father and I felt it would be harmful to Angelica for her to do so."

Across the distance he met Aggie's implacable stare and averted his eyes. Damn her and that unyielding integrity of hers.

"And why is that?" Wasserstein asked.

"Well, often because of the nature of the relationship, the bond between patient and doctor can become a strong one.

Where the patient is very young, it can become a reliance on the child's part that is difficult to break. In the case of Angelica and Dr. Landau, it had become so tight that it was almost . . ." He groped for words.

"Unnatural?" Wasserstein supplied.

"Objection!" Sam Stedman called.

"Withdrawn. Dr. Gottlieb, did Dr. Landau try to see Angelica after she was dismissed from the case?"

"Not for the first few days. At least not to my knowledge."

"But then on the night of June 21, knowing she had no right to do so, Dr. Landau broke another rule, didn't she, doctor?"

"Yes, she did."

"That night Dr. Becca Landau went looking for Angelica Vargas where she lay helpless in that PICU and needing to prove her indispensability to the child, she deliberately pulled that respirator—"

"Objection!" Sam shouted.

"Sustained!"

Wasserstein waited for the inquiry room to settle down. "Dr. Gottlieb, you have been the family physician to Angelica and the Vargas household for a good number of years. In fact, you have treated Angelica almost from birth. Isn't that so?"

"Yes, it is."

"Tell me, doctor, in all that time, have you ever seen anything in Angelica's behavior that would lead you to believe she was contemplating suicide?"

"No, I haven't."

"Thank you, doctor. No further questions. Your witness, Mr. Stedman."

In the moment it took Sam Stedman to reach him, Gottlieb searched the back row for Aggie. But the slight figure in white was no longer there.

Sam approached the stand with lanky nonchalance. "Dr. Gottlieb, you have stated that you were the family physician for the Vargases for many years."

"When the family was in New York I was, yes."

"Tell me, doctor, how did Angelica's mother die?"

Becca's knee jerked so hard it hit the skirt of the wood table she sat at. What was Sam up to? She turned and saw that she wasn't the only one affected. Jose Vargas had become as colorless as the white linen suit he wore. Beside him his wife was whispering frantically in his ear.

"Objection!" Wasserstein called out. "Irrelevant."

"Sustained," Bartlett said.

Sam nodded. His complacency told Becca that he had expected the reproof. "Dr. Gottlieb, how old was Angelica Vargas when her mother died?"

"I believe she was four."

"And you were her physician at the time."

"Yes, I was."

"Doctor, did you notice a drastic change in Angelica's personality after the death of her mother?"

"I don't think I'd call it drastic, but there was a change, yes."

"Would you describe this change for us?"

"Well, she seemed quieter, more withdrawn."

"Often into a world of her own?"

"Yes."

"And the screaming tantrums and nightmares reported by the nurses, were they part of the behavior pattern, too?"

He looked uncomfortable. "At times."

"Dr. Gottlieb, you have just described a child who was morose, lived in fantasyland, had recurrent nightmares, and suffered bouts of hysteria. And you still say Angelica Vargas had no need of psychiatric help?" His palms-up gesture to the panel conveyed his puzzlement. "No further questions. Your witness, Mr. Wasserstein."

Wasserstein waddled up to the dais. "Dr. Gottlieb, you have stated that you were aware of the changes that took place in Angelica Vargas after her mother died."

"Yes, I was."

"What did you attribute them to?"

"Grief, counselor. Pure and simple grief. Angelica Vargas withdrew from a world that had done a hurtful thing to her, just as we all do when someone close to us dies. And she had nightmares because she was blocking her mother's death from her consciousness and it had no other way to surface. But grief is a natural thing, a healthy thing. Angelica's father and I talked about it, and we both felt that given time, she would lay it to rest."

"So that in your opinion, Dr. Landau's overriding your instructions and calling in a psychiatrist to attend Angelica had no real purpose."

"None whatsoever."

"Unless it was to once again convince herself and those around her of the extraordinary lengths to which she was willing to go to benefit her patient."

Becca kept her face expressionless beneath his glance of contempt. His stress on "benefit" had been obvious to all.

"Objection!" Sam called. "Move to strike!"

"I withdraw the statement," Wasserstein said smoothly. "Thank you, doctor. No further questions. You may step down."

Back in Pathology Becca tried to concentrate, but her sense of defeat was so overwhelming that the slides under her microscope blurred before her eyes. She was going to lose. And she couldn't face up to it.

Neither could Sam. Before they left the inquiry room he had told her that the opposition had run through their string of witnesses. It was up to him now to defend. The first one he would put on the stand tomorrow was Carolyn. She would be followed by Kip Flanders and Helen Walters as character witnesses.

She had looked at him dubiously. "Carolyn only worked with Angelica for a week and a half. Will her testimony be credible?"

"It's up to me to make it credible, isn't it?"

It had been said to hearten her, but she knew him by now. He didn't believe Carolyn's testimony would hold up anymore than she did.

"The handwriting's on the wall, isn't it Sam?"

He had avoided eye contact by busying himself with the papers in his attaché case. "I never read what's scribbled on walls. You shouldn't either."

Gripping her microscope now, she forced herself to get through another batch of slides, but by four o'clock she was making so many mistakes, it became pointless to continue. She shrugged off her lab coat and was just pulling her purse from the cabinet drawer when Esther Pemberton entered the room.

Her gray hair was crimped into tight curls, her mouth a thin line above her pointed chin. "Dr. Landau, Mr. Hardinger would like to meet with you."

The purse almost dropped from her hands. "When?"

"Now. He'll be in the third-floor conference room. It's next to Cardiology."

For a moment, she thought to call Sam. She didn't know if it was wise to see Hardinger alone under the circumstances. Then she remembered that Sam had told her he'd be driving out to Kings Point to meet with a client and wouldn't be back at her place until seven that evening.

Becca nodded. "Tell him I'll be there in ten minutes."

She took her time freshening her face, then, needing the exercise, walked the stairs to the third floor. It was obvious that Hardinger didn't want anyone to know of this meeting. The third-floor conference room had become obsolete when the building had been enlarged in 1968. It was used for extra storage now, and the only reason she knew of it was because of her repeated trips to the lab when she'd done a rotation in Cardiology.

She passed the cardiology lab now and knocked on the oak door with the faded lettering on it.

"Come in!"

When she opened the door Arnold Hardinger was sitting at the head of an oval table with only a few chairs around it. The musty conference room had been stripped of all the amenities — paintings, sideboard, drapes, even the carpet that had graced the floor. In their place, piled against the wall, were cartons marked "tongue depressors," "gauze bandages" and "disposable thermometers."

Hardinger's face worked at a semblance of friendliness. "Sit down, Dr. Landau," he said in an even voice.

Becca sat down a few feet away from him. She was sorry now that she hadn't waited for Sam. She had dealt better with Hardinger's fury at their confrontation in his office than she was dealing with this thin veneer of civility he wore. The man was watching her as he would an animal who had turned on him.

She suddenly wanted to end this quickly. "Mr. Hardinger, why have you asked me here?"

"To do you a favor." He gestured toward a tray that held a silver carafe along with china cups and saucers—compliments of Esther Pemberton, no doubt. "Help yourself."

She shook her head, then waited while he poured himself a cup and swished a sugar cube about.

He took a sip of the coffee. "You know I have to admire you, doctor. You've sat through grueling hours of testimony, taken a terrible beating in that inquiry room, and been slammed over and over by the media. There aren't many people who could have taken that, but you've held up very well. It makes me understand what David sees in you."

Her back went rigid. "If you don't mind, I'd rather not talk of David."

"I didn't intend to." He put the cup down. "I was only pointing out that you were a survivor, just as I am. And a survivor is gifted with a basic set of instincts that tell him when to advance, when to hold position, and when to retreat."

"I don't understand what you're trying to say."

She pulled a tissue from her purse and wiped the perspiration from her upper lip. The windows were wide open, but the light and air that filtered through them were deflected by the overhang of the fourth-floor parapet above them. In another moment there were going to be visible splotches of sweat seeping through her silk blouse, she thought.

"I'm about to make it very plain, Dr. Landau. You're going to lose this case. You're going to be charged with attempted murder and you're going to have your license revoked. But the hospital is going to lose, too. Because the adverse publicity is taking its toll. Now, make no mistake. We can afford to hold out. But what's the point? Why drag this on?" He slid the familiar black cigarette holder into his mouth and clenched it in his teeth. His blue eyes fixed on hers intently. "Doctor, for your sake and ours, I'm prepared to make you a deal."

"What kind of deal?"

"In exchange for your consent to end this inquiry now, I'll see that the panel comes up with an inconclusive verdict casting no blame. When the publicity dies down you'll leave the hospital, of course, but your medical license will remain intact."

Becca licked her lips. She was wet everywhere else, but her mouth had suddenly gone dry. "Mr. Hardinger, I'm not prepared to—"

He waved his hand magnanimously. His fingertips were buffed to a shine. "No, of course not. I didn't expect an answer right now. You'll want to think on it; talk to your lawyer about it. Though in the end the decision will have to be yours. You're the one who has the most to lose if you turn it down. You understand that, don't you?"

She nodded. She felt completely numb.

"The only thing I ask is that whatever your answer, this conversation stays strictly between the two of us. It won't do anybody any good if the media gets hold of it." He paused. "I meant the four of us," he corrected himself. "I'm including your attorney. And David, of course."

Her voice was scarcely audible. "Does David know about this?"

"Not yet. But I'm going to tell him. I think he'll want to talk to you about it."

When she reached home, Becca took a warm bath. She wasn't given to baths, but she wanted to immerse herself until the tension drained from her along with the film of dried perspiration. She stretched out her legs and pushed against the back of the oversized tub. She had plenty of time. Aggie had gone on some errand and wouldn't be there until later. And Carolyn was up in Boston for the day on some "mission of mercy" she was being mysterious about.

She knew she should be thinking of what Hardinger had said, but her thought processes seemed to have come to a halt. She was in a no-win situation. Whether she accepted Hardinger's offer or rejected it, she came up a loser. She needed input. She needed Sam. She had phoned his office and left word for him to call as soon as he contacted them, but so far she hadn't heard from him.

She had wrapped herself in a yellow towel and was drying her hair when the buzzer rang. She wasn't surprised to hear it was

David. He must have come straight from the O.R., she thought when she opened the door. He had thrown a lab coat over his greens. The mark on his forehead where the headgear had cut in was still visible. He carried a plastic bag with him which he propped against the living-room buffet.

She stiffened when he took her in his arms and kissed her. "Mmm," he murmured. "You smell good." He buried his face in her still-damp hair.

She tried to move from him, but he wouldn't let her. It galled her that after all this time of excuses, he suddenly felt free to come to her. She saw his gaze go to her breasts. She tightened the knot of the towel around her. "I thought Wasserstein didn't want you to come here. What happened? Did he let you off the leash or did you break free?"

He looked at her in disbelief. His arms dropped to his sides. "You're getting mean in your old age."

Remorse filled her. He was right. He had finally come to her, and she was acting like a shrew. She didn't understand herself. "I'm sorry. What's in the package?"

His face split in a wide smile. He reached into the bag and pulled out a bottle of Pinot Grigio and two plastic goblets. "It's the best I could do on short notice."

"What are we celebrating?" It was an inane question. She knew what they were celebrating. Like his father, he was sure she was going to accept the offer.

He reached into the middle drawer of the buffet and pulled out a corkscrew. "Come on, darling. Don't be coy with me. It's over. You're free." He popped the cork, poured the wine into the goblets, and offered her one.

She shook her head. "It's premature. I haven't decided yet."

A frown creased his face. "What is there to decide?" He placed the goblets on top of the buffet. "Don't you see, love, we can be together again. We can go on with all the plans we had before. Nothing's changed. There'll be no charges and you'll still have your license."

"To practice where? In some second-rate hospital or clinic where I'll pray every day that nobody's ever heard of me, the way I have for the past two years at Manhattan General? Can't you see David, if I go that route, it's a repeat of what happened at Boston Memorial?"

"But you won't be accused of anything."

"I wasn't accused of anything in Boston either. But the stigma still stuck. I was guilty because I hadn't been proven innocent. I was confused then. I didn't know which way to turn. I listened to my father. I listened to you. And instead of staying and fighting as I should have, I ran to Manhattan General to make a new beginning. What a crock!"

"It was the best move you could have made."

"In your eyes. Not in mine. But I'm not confused anymore."

"No. You're not confused. You're masochistic. For the sake of a principle," he made it sound like a dirty word, "you're willing to be charged with attempted murder. And make no mistake. My father will make it stick. Don't cross him on this, Becca. If you do, he'll go down, but he'll take you with him. Because this is his last chance to get that twenty million."

"I don't understand."

"I know you don't. You see, it wasn't my father's idea to offer you this deal. It came from Vargas. He found out that you and your lawyer have been asking questions about his first wife's death, and he's running nervous. Vargas hates publicity. He wants this inquiry stopped. And he wants the questions stopped. He's counting on my father to put an end to both. Now. Otherwise he reneges on his offer."

Becca gripped his arm. She couldn't hide her elation. "David, don't you see? If Vargas is reacting, then we're on the right track. Given a little time—"

"You have no more time!" he shouted. He shook her as if she were a rag doll. The towel loosened, but he didn't notice. "For God's sake, come to your senses, Becca. You don't have a prayer. The odds are so high against you, it's pitiful. Your lawyer doesn't have a single witness that's going to make a difference, and unless you come up with a miracle . . ." He took a deep breath and strove for calm. "Becca, I love you. You've been offered a reprieve. Take it. And let's get on with our lives."

She stared at him. Something peculiar was happening to her. She couldn't feel anything toward him. Not even closeness. It was as if he were a stranger she had loved a long time ago. The memory of it was still there between them. But it had been at another time, and she had been a different person.

She opened her mouth to speak, then shut it when the buzzer rang. She clicked through to the intercom in the downstairs hall, then felt a vast relief when she heard the deep voice on the other end.

"It's my lawyer," she said to David.

"Damn!"

"I don't want him to find you here."

He nodded and strode toward the foyer. "I'll take the stairs down." At the door he took her in his arms and kissed her. She didn't resist. "I'll call you later. Don't decide anything until I do."

But she already had, Becca realized as she closed the door behind him. She went into the bedroom and slipped into a checked shirt and a pair of jeans. She hadn't needed anyone's input after all, she thought. Not David's. Not Sam's. Only her own. While David was giving her all the reasons to accept his father's offer, a gut feeling was telling her to reject it. And that's all it was. A gut feeling. She admitted that David was right. Her decision wasn't a practical one. And she might rue it when the axe finally fell. But she couldn't live with herself if she walked away from this the way she had from the other.

She crossed the foyer to the door again. Tired, but comfortable with herself, she leaned her head against the frame and waited for Sam to come.

Twenty-nine

In his apartment at the Claymore Hotel, G. N. Gottlieb sprawled on the couch in a lightweight sweatsuit, a shotglass of bourbon held loosely between his fingers. He was drunk. But not as drunk as he wanted to be. He was vaguely aware that the TV was on too loud, but he didn't have a remote, and the idea of getting up to lower the volume was too much to contemplate.

He was watching Connie Chung host a special called "Hospital in the Hot Seat." At least he was trying to watch. The fifth of Wild Turkey he'd bought that afternoon was on the cocktail table marring his line of vision, but he wasn't about to move it.

He squinted at the screen trying to solidify the double image it gave off. He had been listening to Judge Ellen Ryker expound on the terrible public apathy she'd encountered in her fight for hospital reform. And Anthony Whitcomb, Manhattan General's medical director was agreeing with her about the need for it and promising that his hospital would be the first to institute changes. In fact, he concluded coyly, there was a major shakeup already in the works. But it was something he couldn't talk about.

Gottlieb snorted. It was pure bullshit. Something he was an expert on after the testimony he gave this afternoon. It was amazing how people were taken in by bullshit. "You could fool some of the people all of the time, and all of the people some of the time . . ." But not Aggie, he thought. Aggie hadn't been fooled. He had seen that on her face when he looked at her.

He stumbled to his feet, turned off the TV, and poured himself another drink. His lips quivered. He'd lost her. He'd almost had her back, and he'd lost her. The bourbon shook in his hand and slopped onto the pristine white carpeting. But he deserved to lose her, he thought. He deserved everything he got.

The telephone rang. He frowned. He wanted to answer it, but he couldn't remember where it was. It rang twice more before he found it on the wall leading into the kitchen.

"Hello?"

"It's the front desk, sir. There's a Miss Agatha Bates here to see you."

Gottlieb shook his head at the mouthpiece. "Can't be. I've lost her."

"I beg pardon, sir. Would you like me to send her up?"

Gottlieb slid the phone back into its cradle. It was cruel of people to play jokes like that. He went back to the couch and fell across it.

When the knock sounded a few minutes later, it roused him from a semistupor.

He dragged himself to the door. "Who is it?" He tried to maneuver the peephole but couldn't manage it. Frustrated, he flung the door open. He squinted at what had to be an apparition. "Aggie?"

"You're damned right it's Aggie." She pushed past him. In a single glance she took in the bottle of bourbon, the yellowed stain on the carpeting, and Gottlieb's wobbly stance.

Hands on hips, her gray eyes rebuked him. "You're drunk!"

"And you're beautiful." It was a lie. Her flowered red dress overpowered her slender figure and did terrible things to her skintone. But it didn't matter to him. The only important thing was that she was here. He tried to take her in his arms and almost fell on his face.

Aggie made a sound of disgust. "Show me where you keep your coffee."

Six cups of coffee later, Gottlieb sat at the kitchen table

with his head pillowed in his hands. He groaned aloud as Aggie made a move to refill his cup. "For Gods sake, Aggie, no more. I've got enough in me to float a battleship."

"You're still not sober." She relented enough to put the coffeepot back on the trivet.

"I don't want to be sober." He regarded her from reddened eyes. His gut felt queasy and his head was pounding like a sledgehammer.

"That's because you can't stomach yourself." Her voice cut into him with razor-sharp effectiveness. "I never thought I'd be saying this, but you're a goddamned liar."

He staggered to his feet. "Hah!" It was meant to be a laugh. It came out like a cry of pain. "Look who's talking. Aggie Bates. Aggie never lies. No. She does a disappearing act instead." He covered his eyes, then released them and blinked. "Aggie Bates. Now you see her, now you don't!"

He gestured wildly and smashed his hand against the refrigerator. He would have toppled over if Aggie hadn't risen quickly to support him. His arms closed around her, then tightened at the familiar feel of her. His chest heaved in longing. "Aggie, why did you do it?" he whispered. "Ten years without a word. Was it something I did? Something I said? I went over it and over it in my mind until I was almost crazy with it. If there was some other guy—"

"There was no one else, Gar."

"Then what?"

Her voice was low, pleading. "It was my mother."

He held her at arms length and stared at her. "Your mother?"

She nodded. "I found out she had Alzheimer's."

He looked bewildered. "But if you had told me, I would have—"

"I know you would have. But I wouldn't have been able to stand myself if I let you. That's why I left. The doctors said it would be a long haul and she'd need constant care. They advised me to lock her up, but I couldn't do that."

Her expression filled with sorrow. "We never talked much about my mother, did we, Gar? Did you know she brought me up herself when my father deserted us? She wasn't trained for anything. She worked in the post office by day and when money got tight, she took in sewing at night. And never a word of complaint out of her. We were . . ." She cleared her throat. "We were close. If I had locked her up, it would have been like locking myself up."

"Where did you go?"

"California. There was some insurance money and she wanted to go where it was warm."

"But I had detectives . . ."

"I used an assumed name. And we kept moving. When her behavior got too bizarre and the neighbors began to complain . . ." She shrugged. "We covered five states in ten years. Finally landed up in Connecticut. She . . . she died there a little over a month ago."

"Aggie . . ." His features were contorted with the pain he felt for her. "I'm sorry for everything you've gone through. But I'm glad it's over."

Her face turned bleak. "I'm not sure it's over."

"What do you mean?"

"I'm showing signs of it, Gar. At least I think I am. I get irritable and I don't remember things . . ."

"Neither do I. Does that make me a candidate for Alzheimer's?" His voice was sharp with censure. "What the hell kind of nurse are you? Since when do you try to diagnose yourself? Where's the objectivity? The clinical measurement? This is the first time you've worked in a hospital for over ten years. Fear. Stress. Depression. Any number of things could be causing those symptoms."

A glimmer of hope began to surface. "Gar, do you really think—"

"Yes, I do. But it doesn't matter what it is. From now on we handle it together." His expression was fierce. "Understood?" She leaned into him and he kissed her, then held her pressed against his chest.

Her voice was muffled when she spoke. "Gar, you lied about Angelica on the stand today, didn't you?"

He was silent for a second. "Yes."

"Why?"

"Because Vargas supplies half my income."

She pulled away from him. "And your standard of living is more important to you than your integrity?" Her voice was laced with contempt.

He shook his head. "You don't understand. Vicky wants a million dollars to divorce me. Before I found you again, I didn't give a damn how long it took. I was living high off the hog, putting the money together slowly. But now it's different. Now I want my freedom. And fast. Another year or so with Vargas's input and I'll have it."

"And it's worth doing what you did today to get it?"

"Yes," he said fiercely. "I've gone too many years without you." His hands tightened on her convulsively. "Empty years with no meaning. I won't let that happen again. I want to marry you. Soon." His eyes pleaded with her. "Aggie, if I tell the truth I take a chance on losing you."

Her mouth twisted in grim determination. "If you don't, you lose me for sure." She pulled him toward the living room. "Come with me." She drew him onto the couch. "Now tell me what it was you held back at that inquiry today."

It took an hour for him to relate his story and supply the details she insisted on. It took another half for her to convince him that she was never going to leave him again. And still another to get him to promise he would reverse his testimony, no matter what the outcome. Then she called Becca at her apartment and asked to speak to Sam Stedman.

Thirty

Becca dressed carefully the next morning. A pink Armani suit, two-inch sandals, a large shoulder pin in the shape of a peacock, and silver hoop earrings. Clothes to triumph in. And she would relish that triumph as much as she was relishing the first decent breakfast she'd been able to stomach since the inquiry began.

The only thing marring her exhilaration was the news that Helen Walters had given her when Becca had called earlier to ask how Angelica was.

"Lousy," the head nurse had said. "She found out that her father's taking her home this afternoon, and she started climbing the walls. Quinlan had to ask for help to restrain her, so you can imagine. Becca, are you there?" she said into the silence that followed.

"Yes." She found it hard to speak. "Helen, I know I'm asking a lot, but could you smuggle me in to see her for a minute? I swear that's all I want. One minute. Just to let her know I'm still there for her."

"I'm going to make like I didn't hear that," Helen said. "For your sake as well as mine."

Becca was still brooding on it when Sam called to tell her that the inquiry was being postponed until twelve. The air conditioner in the room had broken down and they expected it would take until then to fix it.

"Think you can wait?" he teased, a feat so out of character for him that she didn't know how to respond.

"Sam, do we really have a chance of winning?"

"A very good chance. The element of surprise is on our side. And that's three-quarters of the battle."

"Did Carolyn get back from Boston yet?"

"Yes. She left a message on my machine saying she has some interesting stuff to tell me, but she's been tied up with a patient since early morning, and I haven't been able to talk to her. But she'll be there at the inquiry. I've slotted her to testify after I recall Gottlieb. Look, I'll pick you up at eleven-thirty, okay?"

"Don't bother. I'll put in some work at the lab this morning and meet you in the inquiry room at twelve."

A minute before Bartlett signaled for the inquiry to begin, Becca slid in beside Sam at the defense table. For an air conditioner that was supposed to have been fixed, this one was a joke, she thought. The room was a furnace and the makeshift fans were fluttering rapidly.

She wondered if the tension she sensed around her was real or merely a reflection of her own feelings. Her eyes roamed the room. Except for David, all the key players were there. They looked as wound up as she felt. Only Arnold Hardinger seemed relaxed. He sat directly behind Vargas, his arms outstretched across the tops of the chairs on either side of him, a smug expression on his florid face. If only he knew . . . Becca thought. The promise of victory was like a ripe fruit in her mouth. She savored the anticipation, tasted the sweetness of it.

Sam cursed under his breath and dabbed at his brow with a sweat-soiled handkerchief. "Old lawyers never die," he muttered. "They just melt away."

At Bartlett's nod, he rose to his feet. "I wish to recall Dr. Gottlieb to the stand."

Becca held her breath. Sam had told her that if the opposition sensed an upset, they might try to block Gottlieb from testifying.

There was no objection from Wasserstein.

"Dr. Gottlieb, if you please," Bartlett called.

Gottlieb made his way to the dais, then tripped on the step leading up to it. Sam stretched out a hand to steady him, but he shook his head. He straightened and mounted the step with exaggerated care. The Wild Turkey binge had left its mark. His eyes were puffy, and the skin beneath his fading tan was an unbecoming ash color. He sat down in the chair, stretched out his legs, and crossed them at the ankles.

Sam waited until he was settled before he began.

"Dr. Gottlieb, in your testimony yesterday you stated in essence that . . ." He held up a transcript of the proceedings and squinted behind his black-rimmed glasses. ". . . that in all the years you had known Angelica Vargas, you had seen nothing in her behavior that would lead you to believe she was contemplating suicide. Is that correct?"

"Yes, it is."

"Do you wish to stand by that statement?"

"No, I don't. I recalled something last night that I had forgotten. An incident that might cast a different light on Angelica's intentions."

Becca glanced at Arnold Hardinger anticipating the consternation she'd see on his face. A chill went through her. There was no surprise there, no change of expression. The same held true for Jose Vargas. What was going on here?

"When did this incident occur, doctor?"

"Three years ago. Angelica was five then. It was about a year after her mother had died."

"Would you tell us what happened, please?"

Gottlieb ran a hand across his cropped hair. "It was in the fall. Mid-September, I think it was. I was awakened and summoned to the Vargas house at two in the morning. When I got there I was taken up to Angelica's room where Mr. Vargas and his wife—uh, the present Mrs. Vargas—were in nightclothes, waiting for me. They were both very worried. Angelica was lying in bed in a semiconscious state. There were lacerations and shallow gouges across her body and arms. According to her father they had been inflicted by a puppy that he had recently bought for Angelica."

"Did you agree with that statement?"

"No, I did not. I had seen animal wounds before. They mostly take the form of bites and they are usually confined to one or two areas. The extent and type of the lacerations on Angelica's body suggested that they were made by something else."

"Like what?"

"Like a metal toy or some other pointed instrument."

"Did you tell this to Mr. Vargas?"

"Yes, I did. He became angry with me. He insisted that the wounds had been made by the dog. I asked to see the puppy then. I explained that if there was even a possibility that the dog was rabid, Angelica would have to undergo a series of rabies shots."

"And what were you told?"

"I was told that the puppy had run away."

"And what did you do then?"

He shrugged. "What could I do? I suggested that Angelica be taken to a hospital for treatment, but Mr. Vargas felt there was no need. I administered a light sedative and treated the wounds as best I could. I warned that if any of the gouges showed signs of redness, swelling, or any kind of drainage, that I was to be called immediately. Then I left."

Sam's lean frame arched forward. "Dr. Gottlieb, in your opinion how did the wounds on Angelica's body come about?"

"I believe they were self-inflicted."

The words were said a split second before Wasserstein's "Objection . . . calls for a conclusion!" resounded in the room.

"Sustained," Bartlett said.

Sam pressed his point home. "Dr. Gottlieb, in view of your current testimony, do you now believe that Angelica Vargas was and still is suicidal?

"Yes, I do."

"Objection!" Wasserstein repeated.

"Withdrawn." Sam straightened up. "Thank you, doctor. No further questions. Your witness, Mr. Wasserstein."

Wasserstein moved toward the stand with supreme confidence. He should have been devastated, Becca thought. Annihilated. Gottlieb had just knocked the pilings out from beneath his case against her. Instead he was smiling, his gaze keen, his manner that of a soldier kept from battle too long.

Sam wedged himself in beside her and folded his long legs beneath the chair. He fumbled in his jacket pocket for a cigarette, then remembered where he was. "Something's wrong," he said, echoing her thoughts. "I can smell it."

Wasserstein idly rubbed a thumb across a brass button on the witness chair. He tilted his head toward Gottlieb with the inquisitiveness of a child. "Doctor, how many years have you been practicing medicine?"

"Seventeen . . . eighteen."

"In all that time how many cases have you treated that involved animal attacks?"

"I wouldn't know."

"Oh, come now, doctor, give us a ball-park figure."

Gottlieb shrugged. "Possibly ten."

"All perpetrated by dogs?"

"No. Some by cats, one by a squirrel, one by a pet beaver, perhaps two or three by dogs."

"So that when it comes to the symptoms manifested by an attacking puppy, you'd hardly call yourself an expert."

Gottlieb looked annoyed. "I never said I was an expert."

"No, you didn't, did you?" Wasserstein paused long enough for the panel to absorb the thought. "Dr. Gottlieb, since you have stated that you believe Angelica's wounds were self-inflicted, then you must also believe that the puppy Mr. Vargas told you about never existed. That it was a figment of the imagination used to allay your suspicions."

"It had occurred to me, yes."

"And rightfully so. After all, you never saw the dog. Then or at any other time. Isn't that correct?"

"Yes, it is."

Wasserstein walked back to the prosecution table and drew a sheaf of papers from his brown alligator briefcase. He approached the panel. "Ladies and gentlemen, I have here a bill of sale and a deposition from Mr. Joseph Corelli, owner of

Corelli Kennels of Larchmont, New York, testifying to the fact that he sold a six-week-old beagle puppy to Mr. Jose Vargas on September 9th, 1988."

Becca sat as if stunned. Beside her she saw Sam grip the edge of the table. The opposition had been lying in wait for them. But how had they known?

A horrible suspicion began to gnaw at her.

"I also have a deposition here from Mr. Walter Heilbrun, tutor to Angelica Vargas," Wasserstein went on. "Mr. Heilbrun has testified that the beagle puppy bit and severely scratched him on the morning prior to the incident Dr. Gottlieb has described."

Wasserstein placed the two documents before the panel then held up a third and waved it in front of them. "I also have two other depositions here. One from Dr. Isaac Baldwin, the other from his nurse, both attesting to the fact that starting on the morning of September 20th, 1988, Dr. Baldwin administered to Angelica Vargas a full course of rabies shots. This was done at the Baldwin Medical Center, a small private hospital located on Madison Avenue and Seventy-Seventh Street in New York." The attorney's expression begged the panel's indulgence. "Now I ask you, ladies and gentlemen, would any father in his right mind subject his daughter to a series of rabies shots based on 'a figment of the imagination'?"

Wasserstein placed the documents in front of Webster Bartlett. "Any or all of these witnesses are at your disposal for questioning. Also, Dr. Baldwin, who has treated a great many patients who have been attacked by dogs of all ages, would be more than happy to personally confirm what he has stated in the deposition, that in his opinion the gouges and scratches that appeared on Angelica Vargas's body were made by a very young dog."

He turned to Sam with a small smile on his lips. He made a half bow, which despite his girth succeeded in appearing graceful. "Your witness, Mr. Stedman."

Sam shook his head. He looked as if all the wind had been knocked out of him.

Wasserstein shrugged, then turned to a gray-faced Gottlieb. "Thank you, doctor. You may step down."

Bartlett's gavel followed almost immediately. "I call a short recess."

Sam waited until he and Becca were alone in the vestibule before he exploded.

"They were ready for us," he grated, his hands flailing, his body in movement. "We walked in like rookie cops at a gang massacre. So sure of ourselves we never saw it coming." He slammed his fist on the counter. "I should have known better. The moment they came up with that crap about the air conditioner, I should have known. It was a ruse to buy time and I didn't spot it."

"Maybe those depositions won't check out?" It was scarcely audible, but he heard it.

His laugh was short. "Oh they'll check out all right. You'd be surprised at how money can buy consciences. I see it all the time." He jammed his hands into his pants pockets, almost ripping the seams. His lank brown hair fell across one eye. He flung it back with a sweep of his hand. "That sonofabitch Gottlieb. I should have known he couldn't be trusted. It was too good. Too fast. One day he's on their side. The next day he's on ours. Vargas must have offered him a bundle to play Judas."

"It wasn't Gottlieb." Her voice was toneless.

"Then who was it? They knew everything that Gottlieb had told us last night. Someone had to leak the information to them, and only four of us knew about it. I didn't even have a chance to tell it to Carolyn."

"It was me."

He halted as if pole-axed. He grabbed her arm and pulled her up from her chair. "What the hell are you saying?"

"You're hurting me." He loosened his grip. His expression was so fierce she couldn't meet his eyes. "David called me after you left last night. He was very angry when I told him I wasn't going to accept the offer his father made me. He said that I was a fool, that I was throwing away whatever chance we had to be together, that it was the last opportunity I would have to avoid being charged with attempted murder. I . . . I guess I wanted to defend myself. To prove to him that it wasn't completely hopeless . . ."

"So you told him what Gottlieb had said."

"Yes." She gripped the lapel of his suit. Her eyes pleaded with him. "Sam, I still can't believe he would do such a thing. Maybe there's another explanation. Maybe something else happened to give it away. Something we don't know about . . ."

He pried her fingers from his jacket. "Let's go back inside."

"But there's still time. We've only been here . . ."

"Let's go back inside." His face could have been carved in wood. He turned and walked to the door. He didn't look to see if she followed.

Thirty-one

The next ten minutes were horrendous. She sat at the defense table alone. Sam had left her to confer with Carolyn in the hallway. If only he'd shouted at her, told her what an ass she'd been! She could have taken that. Hell, she would have agreed with him. But he'd shut her out. As if she didn't exist. As if she were beneath his contempt. She told herself that he was only her attorney. A paid-for-hire employee. He had no right to come down on her like that. So she had made a mistake. Granted, a bad one. But she was the one who would pay for it, not him.

It was no use. For the moment, the loss of his respect was affecting her more than the penance that awaited her.

She was vaguely aware that aside from her revulsion at David's treachery, she hadn't given him a single thought. He had lost the ability to hurt her, she realized, because she didn't feel anything for him anymore.

The inquiry-room door opened and Arnold Hardinger entered with Jose Vargas. Hardinger was talking animatedly. He was relaxed, smiling . . . as if it were all over. With a sinking feeling, she conceded that it was. Carolyn's testimony wouldn't make a difference. The verdict was a foregone conclusion. She met Hardinger's eyes. There was no compassion in them. Only triumph. He was in Vargas's good graces, he had David back, and in a short while he would witness her total destruction. He had accomplished everything he had set out to do.

She severed eye contact a second before Sam seated himself beside her. He didn't say anything, and she didn't expect it.

"I call Dr. Carolyn Stedman to the stand," he said when Bartlett gave him the nod.

In a navy silk dress with her chestnut hair pinned atop her head, Carolyn seemed more composed than any of the other witnesses had been. Under the circumstances Becca suspected that it was a valiant effort, but that only made it more admirable.

Sam's initial questions stressed her schooling, her impressive degrees and honors, her fellowship at Boston Memorial, and the jump in opportunity and position that her transfer to Manhattan General had afforded her. Then he focused on more recent events.

"Dr. Stedman, about a month ago you were called in by Dr. Landau to treat one of her patients, isn't that so?"

"Yes. Dr. Landau felt that the child's behavior warranted my professional help, and after speaking with Angelica Vargas at length, I agreed."

"Doctor, in the course of your treatment of Angelica Vargas, what were your observations?"

"I observed that Angelica was in deep depression, suffered from severe guilt stemming from the death of her mother, and had recurrent thoughts of death. I also noted that she was apathetic and withdrawn, and had in recent months become overly generous with her possessions."

"And did those observations lead you to any conclusion?"

"Yes. I concluded that Angelica Vargas was suicidal."

"Thank you. No further questions, Dr. Stedman. Your witness, Mr. Wasserstein."

Becca glanced at the panel. It was obvious from their faces, especially that of Libby Gruber, the chief of Pediatrics, that Carolyn's demeanor, her impressive background, and her decisive comments had made a strong impression. But Becca knew it wouldn't last.

Wasserstein's manner was as respectful as his tone. "Dr. Stedman, from all I've just heard I would certainly say that you are an asset to Manhattan General. They're lucky to have you."

"Thank you."

"Doctor, forgive me for becoming personal, but you are my learned colleague's sister, are you not?"

"Objection!" Sam called. "Irrelevant!"

Bartlett glanced at Hardinger. "I'll allow it."

Wasserstein picked his words carefully. "I am not suggesting prejudice, doctor, but naturally there would be a tendency on your part to . . ." His voice trailed off. His embarrassed shrug to the panel made it plain that the matter was a delicate one.

Carolyn's face grew cold. "I resent your implication, Mr. Wasserstein."

Wasserstein's hands came up in apology. "As you should, doctor. As you should. I'm sure you are too much of a professional to let family ties influence your judgment." He wrinkled his brow in puzzlement. "And yet . . . there are things having to do with that very professionalism that make me wonder. For instance, would you tell the panel what the sum total of the time you spent with Angelica Vargas was?" He tilted his head. "Three months? Six months? Longer perhaps?"

Becca had known that Wasserstein would take this tack, but it didn't make it any easier to hear. Again her admiration for the psychiatrist came to the fore. Carolyn knew that her credibility was about to evaporate, but her composure remained unruffled.

"Two weeks," she replied evenly.

He pursed his lips in wonder. "Two weeks. Hardly enough time to get on a first-name basis, wouldn't you say, doctor?"

"Objection!" Sam called.

"Withdrawn," Wasserstein conceded. "Doctor, in your *professional* judgment, do you really think that any conclusion arrived at in two weeks should be taken seriously. Or should it rather be regarded for what it is — a valiant attempt to bolster a brother's effort to—"

"Objection!" Sam was on his feet, his hands balled into fists at his side.

The moment was so tense that when the disruption came, it took a second for it to register. The noise was coming from just outside the inquiry-room door. Becca swiveled in her seat in time to see Esther Pemberton burst through it. She elbowed her way to Arnold Hardinger with little regard for the people between them. Her cheeks were veined with red, and her tight gray curls were frizzed out into a halo. She clutched at the string tie of her blouse as if it were a lifeline.

An incredulous expression crossed Hardinger's face at her whispered words. He leaned down quickly and spoke with Jose and Maria Vargas. The tycoon's hoarse cry rent the air. With a visible effort he pulled himself together. He signaled imperiously to Gottlieb. Within seconds, the four of them left the room.

Lips pinched into a thin line, Esther Pemberton approached the panel.

A moment later a shaken Webster Bartlett rose from his chair. He spoke with an effort. "Ladies and gentlemen, this hearing will be postponed until further notice."

On her feet, Becca clutched at Sam's shoulder. "Sam, what's happening?"

"I don't know, but I'm damn well going to find out!"

Along with Wasserstein he cornered Bartlett before the chief of medicine could leave the room. When he returned to Becca, he saw that she had been joined by Carolyn and Aggie. His face was grave.

"It's Angelica, isn't it?" Becca said. "Something's happened to her!"

He nodded. "I don't know all the details, but Angelica is outside on the parapet of the fourth floor. She somehow managed to climb out of her wheelchair and wedge herself in one of the spaces between that cement column railing that surrounds it. She's threatening to jump if anyone comes near her."

"My God!" Aggie said. "Has Security been alerted?"

"Yes. They're with her now, but they're keeping their distance." He looked at Becca sharply. "Are you all right?"

"Sam, I've got to go to her."

Carolyn shook her head. "They'll never let you near her."

"I've got to try."

Sam grabbed her hand. "Come on. I'll go with you."

The tension on the fourth floor was so heavy, it weighted the air. Ten feet past the elevator they ran into a distraught Kip Flanders.

"Becca, thank God you're here! Have you heard?"

"I've heard. What's happening?"

"Vargas went out there a minute ago. He's talking to her. But I don't think he'll get anywhere. You know how scared she is of him. Maybe you could—"

"She'll try," Sam cut in. He tugged at her arm. "Let's go."

They raced down the corridor. The glass double doors that led to the parapet were between the nurse's station and Room 401 East. Along the way, they dodged doctors, nurses, aides, and visitors clustered together in pockets pointing at the parapet and talking in hushed whispers.

Within twenty feet of the glass doors two uniformed guards barred their way.

"I'm sorry," the shorter guard said. "Nobody's allowed past this point."

"Please," Becca said. "I'm Dr. Landau. The girl is a patient of mine."

The taller one regarded her knowingly. "You mean *was* a patient of yours, don't you? Everyone in the hospital's been following this case, *doctor.*" He made the title sound like an epithet.

Sam's face contorted with anger. He poked a finger into the guard's chest. "You keep a civil tongue in your head, you hear?"

"Sam, don't!" Her fear wasn't for the security guard. It was for Sam. The man was almost double his weight.

She glanced past the guard. Arnold Hardinger stood with Gottlieb and Maria Vargas in the hallway outside the glass doors, watching the scene on the parapet unfold. From their expressions it wasn't going well.

"Mr. Hardinger," she called.

Startled, he glanced up. A vein pulsed in his temple as he stared at her in disbelief. He mouthed a silent curse, then turned back to Maria Vargas and put a comforting arm around her.

"Mr. Hardinger, please . . ."

He murmured something to the woman beside him, then strode the twenty feet to where she stood. He ignored Sam. "What are *you* doing here?"

Her gaze beseeched him. "Mr. Hardinger, hear me out. I know we have our differences, but they're not important now. I can help. Angelica trusts me."

"How noble! Dr. Becca to the rescue! Right?" His laugh was savage. "You're never satisfied are you, doctor? By what that little girl just did, she saved you from disgrace, maybe even a prison term. But that's not enough for you, is it? No. You have to make a grandstand play and come out a heroine on top of it. Well, you'll never get the chance to do it. You hear me? Never!"

"Please . . ." She lifted a hand to him.

Sam caught it in midair. "Dammit, don't beg."

Hardinger turned from them abruptly. "These people don't belong up here," he said to the guards. "See that they leave immediately." He strode back to where Maria Vargas stood.

"I can't let it go at that," Becca said as they doubled back to the elevators.

"I don't see that you've got much choice." He cupped her elbow and guided her forward. "But that bastard's right about one thing. This suicide attempt proves your case for you. You're off the hook, Becca."

"I can't think about that now. All I can focus on is Angelica out on that terrace getting ready to jump. I've got to stop her, Sam. I've got to!"

Head down, she wasn't aware of his compassionate glance. Only of his silence.

They had just passed the nurse's station when she heard her name called. Helen Walters was rounding a corner, puffing like a racer in a marathon. "This whole floor's gone crazy," she said. "Every patient suddenly has an emergency. It's amazing how they can sense a crisis."

She exhaled sharply, the hand beneath her breast pressed against her flabby middle. She glanced up the hall toward the glass double doors. "Did they let you talk to her?"

"No."

"Assholes!" She regarded Becca with concern. "Where are you going now?"

"I don't know." A tightness constricted her chest. "I have to stay up here, Helen. At least I'll be near her that way."

She saw Sam start to say something, then decide against it.

The nurse was silent. "All right," she said finally. "It will probably mean my head. But there are a couple of rooms vacant." She thought a moment. "The one you want is 423. You can wait there. But only you. He," she jerked her thumb at Sam, "has to go."

He scowled at the nurse. "Becca's in no shape to be alone."

"I can handle myself," Becca said in exasperation.

Helen looked amused. "I'll take care of Becca. You get."

"I'll be at my office," he said. "Call if you need me. And Becca . . ." He hesitated.

"Yes?"

"Don't do anything foolish."

"Goodbye, Sam."

The moment Becca walked into 423 West she knew why

Helen had chosen it. Going from east to west, the building angled, and the window in the small drab room gave her a clear though slanted view of the parapet. Paved in gray stone, the makeshift terrace held a few scattered tables and chairs.

The cement pillars that formed a railing for the thirty-foot parapet stood three feet high. Eight inches in diameter at their widest point, they were shaped like an hour glass and connected at the top by a green marble ledge that revealed streaks and gashes under the piercing sunlight. The spaces between the pillars had been pointed out only last year as a danger, but like so much in the hospital that needed shoring up, it had been put on the "things to do" list.

By flattening her cheek against the windowpane, Becca could see Angelica. Her small body was wedged in the space between two pillars. It was curved in an impossible arc. Her pink silk nightgown had shredded in her desperate attempt to squeeze into the opening. Caught in the sudden breeze that swept the parapet, it flew about her like a pitiful banner. Her face was obscured from Becca, but about ten feet from Angelica, holding to the abandoned wheelchair like a crutch, she could see Jose Vargas. His hand was outstretched, and he was pleading with his daughter.

"How's he doing?" Helen called when she entered the room five minutes later. She carried a tray holding two cups of coffee and an iced chocolate donut.

"Not too good."

"Well, it won't be in his hands much longer. The cops are on the way. That should make for pure tumult up here." She set the tray on the nightstand and handed the coffee to Becca. She eyed the donut like a convict his freedom. "That donut is for you. I'm abstaining."

"Thanks." She sipped the coffee gratefully. "Helen, how did Angelica get out there?"

"I can tell it to you in one word: Quinlan! The idiot wheeled her out there to distract her from carrying on about going home. When Angelica demanded that her doll be brought to her, instead of asking someone to get it, Quinlan left her alone for a minute. Angelica didn't need more than that."

"I tried to warn Quinlan," Becca murmured.

She shrugged. "You can't make a silk purse . . ." She put her coffee cup down. "I've got to get back out there."

Becca took her post at the window after she left. Within minutes she saw Jose Vargas's head swing toward the glass doors. What appeared to be a heated argument followed, then Vargas retreated and two police officers came forward. One a man, the other a woman, her dark hair cut in a severe bob. It was the policewoman who spoke with Angelica. Her partner, a strapping six footer in his mid-forties with a gunbelt worn low on his hip, stayed within earshot but didn't interfere.

Fifteen minutes later, a strained look on her perspiring face, her hands in motion along with her mouth, the woman was still filibustering, but her partner had disappeared.

Becca caught her breath as the policewoman suddenly threw out her hands, her face petrified with alarm. *Please no!* Becca prayed as she saw Angelica's body tilt outward from the base of the pillar. It hung there for a second, then drew back. The policewoman sagged with relief. Becca exhaled slowly. Angelica was still in this world—but for how long?

So intent was she on the scene being played out on that terrace that she didn't hear the footsteps crossing the threshold.

"Dr. Landau?"

Becca turned. The policeman she'd seen on the parapet stood a few feet from her with Helen Walters coming up fast behind him. He had taken off his jacket with all the stripes on it and wore a short-sleeved blue shirt that showed dark stains beneath the armpits. The gunbelt with a club hanging from it was still strapped to his hip.

"Doctor, I'm Sergeant Kincaid." He was stocky with a broad pockmarked face and a stubborn jaw. He took off his cap and wiped at the inside rim with a handkerchief. It had left a red ring on his wet forehead.

"How's Angelica?"

"Well, that's why I'm here. His voice was ragged with frustration. "For the last ten minutes, I've been fightin' with the head of this place about callin' you in to help get that little girl down." He yanked his thumb toward his chest and shoved out his jaw. "But I'm the one runnin' this show, not him. And it's you that little girl is askin' for. Will you come with me?"

"Gladly."

Behind him Helen Walters gave her the thumbs-up sign. She was smiling broadly.

Thirty-two

The sun on the parapet had baked the slate to the temperature of hot coals. Becca could feel the heat rise through the thin soles of her sandals as she made her way toward Angelica. The sergeant had posted himself on the outside, a good ten feet away from the glass doors. Despite his insistence that Jose Vargas join the others inside, Angelica's father waited there beside him.

The tycoon put a hand on Becca's arm as she passed him. "Save her and you can have anything you want," he said. His black eyes were glistening unashamedly. He had aged ten years since she last saw him.

A conscience offering, she thought. Where was he all those years when Angelica needed him?

"I'll do what I can," she said.

She moved on. Four feet from Angelica she stopped.

"Dr. Becca?" The child's voice wavered.

Tears stood in the sunken hazel eyes. Her skin was reddened, her baby-fine hair wet and plastered to her scalp. One cheek had been scraped raw in her effort to mold herself round the pillar it now rested on. The scrape was turning an ugly purple-brown. Her torn nightgown had worked its way down to her waist. She wore a pink slipper on her left foot. The other was nowhere to be seen.

"Yes. It's Dr. Becca." She covertly gauged the distance between them. Another step or two and she'd be able to—

"Don't come any closer."

Becca halted. Angelica's distrust of her cut deeply. So

277

much ground lost, she thought. Could she make it up in time?

"How do you feel, Angelica?"

"Fine."

"Are we back to 'fine' again?"

She didn't answer.

"You must be awfully cramped in that position."

"Don't matter. Won't be here long." Her underlip quivered. She fixed Becca with a hurt stare. "You said you were my friend."

"I am. Believe me, I am."

"Then why didn't you come? I wrote you." Her voice grew faint, and she blinked to keep her eyes open. "Aggie had to help me."

There wasn't much strength left in her, Becca thought. If she didn't jump she'd surely fall. "There were people who wouldn't let me come," she said.

"Bad people?"

"Yes. Bad people. And when I finally did find a way to see you, you were too sick to know I was there. But I thought about you all the time. And I missed you very much."

There was no response. Angelica's head lolled against the upper curve of the stone pillar. She tightened her arms around its middle and shifted position slightly. Becca saw that the pillar was porous. Pitted gashes, some of them long and insidious eroded its century-old surface. Pressured by Angelica's weight, a piece of cement chipped away from the base and fell to the gray slab of the terrace.

"Dr. Becca?"

"Yes?"

"Would you . . . would you do something for me?"

"Of course. What would you like me to do?"

"It's Gabriella. She's going to die soon. Would you bury her for me?"

278

Becca froze. She had to reach this child before it was too late. But how?

"Put Gabriella with my mama." Angelica continued. "Papa will show you where. That way Mama won't be so lonely."

There was a weariness in her voice that said she would leave this world with no regret. But first she had to tidy up behind her.

"And tell Papa to put some extra roses on the grave," she whispered.

If only Carolyn were here, Becca agonized. She'd figure something out. She was trained for this, though she often made light of the mechanics of it.

There's no great magic in what I do. People hurt. I just reach in and show them where. It doesn't stop the hurt completely, but it eases it enough for them to go on.

Becca stared at the child. She suddenly knew what she was going to do. It might not work, but it was worth a try.

She kept her voice even, conversational. "Did your mama like roses?"

"Yes. Papa . . . he brought her new ones every morning."

"Red ones to brighten up the sand colors in her room."

Something flickered behind the hollowed-out eyes. "How do you know about her room?"

"You told me about it. In your nightmare. 'There's sand on the floor,' you said. Only it wasn't sand. It was the carpeting in your mama's bedroom. Isn't that right, Angelica?"

She pushed her cheek against the stone, wincing as it rubbed against the abrasion. "Don't want to talk about it."

For a moment Becca was stymied. Then she spotted the doll lying face down on the wrought-iron chair, the bandage askew, the satin skirts bedraggled and dirty. "You may not want to talk about it, but Gabriella does."

Angelica stilled as if mulling over the possibility in her mind.

Becca gave her no time to think it through. "You told me all about what was in that room, remember? You said, 'The water is on top of the ladder in a bottle and Gabriella is trying to reach it for me.' Isn't that right? But the ladder was really a chest of drawers, and there wasn't water in that bottle; there were pills. Isn't that so, Angelica?"

"Go 'way!"

"And it wasn't Gabriella trying to reach those pills. It was you, wasn't it, Angelica?"

From her peripheral vision she saw that Jose Vargas had edged forward and was straining to hear. She signaled for him to stop and saw the sergeant restrain him.

"And then a shadow creeps up on the sand," Becca went on inexorably. "That's what you said, 'a shadow.'"

"No," she whispered. Terror crossed her face. She shifted outward so that her leg and shoulder hung over the edge.

With an effort Becca kept herself from reacting. Not so Jose Vargas. Kincaid was having an awful time holding him back. Dear God, Becca thought. What if I'm wrong? I'll have to live with her death for the rest of my life. She had a terrible urge to grab Angelica, yank her back to safety. But she wasn't close enough yet. And she knew the minute she made a move, Angelica would jump.

"Someone came into that room," she went on. "Someone you thought would get those pills for your mother. But they didn't, did they, Angelica?"

Angelica's mouth worked. Tears trickled down the sides of her cheeks. She looked down at the ground, four floors below. There were police there now, trying to unfurl a net to catch her.

Hurry! Becca silently urged them. *Hurry.* She took a step forward. The child shifted outward yet another inch.

Becca halted. "Who was that someone?" she demanded. "Who killed your mother, Angelica?"

A hoarse cry escaped her. "I did! I killed her!"

"No! You didn't kill anybody!"

"The pills . . . I couldn't reach them!"

"No, you couldn't. But you were a very little girl then. You weren't expected to reach those pills." Becca took another step forward. "But someone else could. Someone who was in that room with you. Who denied your mother those pills, Angelica?"

"No! No!" Her eyes were rolling in her head, her breath coming in choppy gasps.

"Was it your stepmother?" Becca persisted.

"*No!*" she screamed. "*No mi tia!*" The small body shook with sobs. "*No mi tia,*" she whispered brokenly. "*Mi abuela.*"

She swayed outward just as Becca took the final step and lunged. Heedless that the backs of her hands were being torn up by the cement pillar, she clutched Angelica around the waist. She held tight to the small writhing body as Angelica's words penetrated her consciousness. *Not my aunt. My grandmother.* In her blind devotion to her son, that semisenile peasant had sacrificed one sister so that he could have the other and breed the heir she so desperately wanted.

The enormity of it hit her. The grandmother! The woman who had brought Angelica up. The person Angelica had trusted above all others. What a horror that little girl had lived with all these years. No wonder she had buried it deep within the layers of her subconscious, letting it fester and eat away at her, its only outlet the nightmare form it took.

Angelica had stopped struggling. She didn't resist when Becca knelt and, disregarding her bruised hands, carefully eased her from the curved stone niche. In a gesture of trust, the child put her arms around Becca's neck and laid her head in the crook of it.

"Hold on tight, lovey," Becca whispered. "It's going to be okay from now on. I promise you."

She picked her up and carried her across the steamy parapet. "Get me Nurse Agatha Bates," she called to Sergeant Kincaid in passing.

Thirty-Three

They sprawled in Becca's living room weary but triumphant—Sam on the couch with his red-stockinged feet resting on the antique trunk next to the fifth of Dom Perignon, Becca in a full jungle print skirt that hid the hassock beneath her, and Carolyn reclining crosswise in the chintz wing chair with her legs dangling over its arm. Aggie had bowed out with an excuse that was acceptable to all. She was with Gottlieb.

Becca spoke with careful sobriety. She was on her third glass of champagne. "I have come to the conclusion that I am a vindictive person. I would like to say to Arnold Hardinger, 'Okay. Let bygones be bygones.' But I don't really feel that way. The truth is, I would like to see him get his."

"I doubt he's got any love for you either," Carolyn said dryly.

Sam pinged the rim of his goblet with his thumb and forefinger. He was more relaxed than Becca had ever seen him. The fact that it was all over was only now becoming a reality to her. She felt relief. And with it an odd feeling of loss. Certainly not for the stress. But she would miss the camaraderie between them that the inquiry had brought. Which didn't make sense, because she would be seeing all of them again.

Except for Sam, of course.

"No question about it," he said. "The man's a sonofabitch. But his days are numbered. I've got enough on him to crucify him." He pursed his lips thoughtfully. "Though I may not have to lift a finger to do it. If Vargas doesn't come through with that twenty million, Hardinger is finished anyhow."

"But Vargas will come through with it," Becca stated.

"How do you know that?"

"Because he came to me before I left the hospital and said he would."

He sighed in exasperation. "You never told me that."

"Didn't I?"

She probably hadn't, Becca thought. She had spoken to Sam from the hospital, but she had been in such a daze that she hardly remembered what she had told him.

But she recalled Vargas's talk with her very clearly.

He had come to her in the Medicine Room where Helen Walters had just used a gauze pad to saturate her scraped hands with peroxide. "I'd like to see Dr. Landau alone," he'd said.

Helen had nodded respectfully. "No problem. I'm finished anyhow."

Left alone with Becca, he'd inclined his head in a short bow. "I have a great deal to thank you for." His olive-skinned face was lined with strain.

"I don't want your thanks."

"Nevertheless, you have it. You have not only saved my daughter's life, you have made my family whole again."

"I don't understand."

"Let me explain. You see, I had long suspected that my first wife was murdered and that Angelica had witnessed it. But I thought that it was Maria who had done it. I knew that Angelica had retained no recollection of what she saw, but I was afraid that one day it would surface. In order to protect Maria, I shut Angelica away from everybody. And I closed myself off to her needs. I did a terrible thing to my daughter. And, as I have just learned, to my young wife also. You see, Maria distrusted me as well. Not at first. But several months after she married me she began to believe that it was I who had killed her sister and that she had been the cause. Since she couldn't bring herself to leave me, she turned to the Church to expiate her guilt."

He took Becca's bruised hands in his as if they were a talisman of her bravery. "You have given me the wherewithal to make up for my transgressions. I am deeply indebted to you. And I wish to repay in some way. Tell me how I can do that."

Becca had thought a moment. She wanted nothing from this man. But neither did she want the interplay of her refusing and his persisting.

"I would like two things," she had said. "First, the right to see Angelica whenever I choose."

"Granted."

"Second, I would like you to go through with your offer to Manhattan General. The hospital is badly in need."

He had smiled. "I never intended to do anything else. My threats to the contrary were a matter of gaining control." His dark eyes held an amused gleam. "I will tell you a secret, Dr. Becca. It isn't necessary to use a club to get what you want. Only to wield one."

If that cat and mouse game was the key to power, Becca thought, as she brought her attention back to Sam, then she wanted no part of it.

She balanced her goblet on her knee. "What did you mean when you said, 'I've got enough on Hardinger to crucify him'?"

He smiled and pulled his black-rimmed glasses down low on his nose. "I was betting that hadn't slipped by you. I was referring to Carolyn's trip up to Boston yesterday. She went to Boston Memorial on a hunch, and it paid off. She found out a few things you'll be happy to hear about."

Becca turned to her. "Like what?"

"Like the answer to why you couldn't get through to David on the night that little girl died." Carolyn pulled her long hair from her neck and twisted it into a coil. "Lila Brodin," she said in response to Becca's unspoken question. "The little nurse who warmed his bed after you left. She was with him that night."

Becca frowned, trying to recollect. "David and I had an argument that evening before he left the hospital . . ."

Carolyn nodded. "And little Lila was on hand to comfort him. But she wanted to make the most of the only chance she'd get to make her pitch, so she pulled out the phone jack in his bedroom and buried his beeper under a pillow. When she was ready to leave, she put everything back in place again."

"And that's when the head nurse called David."

"And got through immediately. Which made you look like an awful liar."

An invisible weight lifted from Becca. She had carried it with her for two long years. It didn't matter if what she'd just heard was never found out. It was enough that she knew it.

"Did David know about this?" she asked.

Sam laughed. "He certainly knew Lila was there."

Carolyn's glance censured him. "I doubt if he knew what Lila had done. David's weak, not devious. At least he wasn't then," she corrected herself. "But his father knew. Hardinger figured it out somehow. According to Lila, he gave her a hefty sum to keep her mouth shut. That way David was off the hook and the onus of that little girl's death remained with you. As long as David was up there with her, Lila kept to her bargain. But she's angry now that David has left her to be with you at Manhattan General. With a little pressure, she became very talkative."

Sam trickled the last of the champagne into his mouth. "And I'm going to see that everything she said reaches the proper ears. Especially the part about Hardinger bribing her. I believe that goes under the heading of obstructing justice." He set his goblet on the trunk carefully. With an effort he pulled his long length from the couch. "I have to clean up some stuff at the office." He glanced at Becca. "Walk me to the door, will you?"

She nodded. For some reason when they reached it she felt self-conscious. Perhaps it was the way he was looking at her. She cloaked it under a formality that brought a stiffness to her words. "Sam, I'd like to take this opportunity to thank you for—"

He brushed her words aside with a flick of his fingers. "Is that all Vargas said when he spoke to you? That he was going to come through with the twenty million?"

The unexpectedness of it threw her. "Well, no. There was more. I mean, he said that he suspected early on that his first wife was murdered . . ."

He threw up his hands in disbelief. "And you held out on me with that? Christ, Becca, I've been as involved in this case as you were. The least you could have done—"

"I'm sorry. Okay?"

He scowled at her, obviously not mollified.

Her voice rose. She didn't want to part from him in anger. "I apologized, Sam. What more can I do?"

"You can meet with me tomorrow night and fill me in on what he said. I can't lay this case to rest until I have all the details. That's the way my mind works." He flung the door open, then looked thoughtful. "You know, I've just remembered a restaurant in Chinatown that has the best leechee nuts I've ever tasted. What say I pick you up at your apartment at seven? We can talk on the way there."

The man was irrational, she thought. Absolutely irrational.

"Why don't we make it seven-thirty," she said.

HAUTALA'S HORROR— HOLD ON
TO YOUR HEAD!

MOONDEATH (1844-4, $3.95/$4.95)
Cooper Falls is a small, quiet New Hampshire town, the kind you'd miss if you blinked an eye. But when darkness falls and the full moon rises, an uneasy feeling filters through the air; an unnerving foreboding that causes the skin to prickle and the body to tense.

NIGHT STONE (3030-4, $4.50/$5.50)
Their new house was a place of darkness and shadows, but with her secret doll, Beth was no longer afraid. For as she stared into the eyes of the wooden doll, she heard it call to her and felt the force of its evil power. And she knew it would tell her what she had to do.

MOON WALKER (2598-X, $4.50/$5.50)
No one in Dyer, Maine ever questioned the strange disappearances that plagued their town. And they never discussed the eerie figures seen harvesting the potato fields by day . . . the slow, lumbering hulks with expressionless features and a blood-chilling deadness behind their eyes.

LITTLE BROTHERS (2276-X, $3.95/$4.95)
It has been five years since Kip saw his mother horribly murdered by a blur of "little brown things." But the "little brothers" are about to emerge once again from their underground lair. Only this time there will be no escape for the young boy who witnessed their last feast!

Available wherever paperbacks are sold, or order direct from the Publisher. Send cover price plus 50¢ per copy for mailing and handling to Zebra Books, Dept. 3857, 475 Park Avenue South, New York, N.Y. 10016. Residents of New York and Tennessee must include sales tax. DO NOT SEND CASH. For a free Zebra/Pinnacle catalog please write to the above address.